THE ROYAL GAME AND OTHER STORIES

Stefan Zweig was born in 1881 in Vienna to a wealthy Austrian-Jewish family. He was first known as a poet and translator and then as a biographer, fitting into the great vogue for the 'vie romancée', and producing studies of a variety of characters notably Erasmus, Joseph Fouché and Marie Antoinette. His well-known collection of stories, *Kaleidoscope*, appeared in 1934 and his one, truly remarkable, novel, *Beware of Pity* (to be published by Penguin in 1985), appeared in 1939.

Zweig travelled widely, and, living in Salzburg between the wars, he made friends with such great figures as Romain Rolland, Bruno Walter, Thomas Mann and Toscanini. By 1914 he had achieved recognition as a writer, particularly amongst the group of European artists and intellectuals who, after the First World War, were committed to building a new international order. During the 1920s his output for that cause was considerable, and, at this time, his literary reputation also soared. In 1934, as the Nazis became entrenched across the border, Zweig left Austria for England, acquiring British citizenship in 1940. Two years later he took his own life in Petropolis, Brazil.

THE ROYAL GAME
& OTHER STORIES

STEFAN ZWEIG

with an introduction by
John Fowles

translated from the German by
Jill Sutcliffe

PENGUIN BOOKS

Penguin Books Ltd, Harmondsworth, Middlesex, England
Penguin Books, 40 West 23rd Street, New York, New York 10010, U.S.A.
Penguin Books Australia Ltd, Ringwood, Victoria, Australia
Penguin Books Canada Ltd, 2801 John Street, Markham, Ontario, Canada L3R 1B4
Penguin Books (N.Z.) Ltd, 182–190 Wairau Road, Auckland 10, New Zealand

This translation first published in Great Britain by Jonathan Cape Ltd 1981
Published in Penguin Books 1984

Printed in Great Britain by
Richard Clay (The Chaucer Press) Ltd,
Bungay, Suffolk

Contents

INTRODUCTION

STEFAN ZWEIG has suffered, since his death in 1942, a
darker eclipse than any other famous writer of this century. Even 'famous writer' understates the prodigious
reputation he enjoyed in the last decade or so of his life, when
he was arguably the most widely read and translated serious
author in the world. Yet I suspect very few English-speaking
readers who have grown up since the Second World War know
anything of him at all, except the name. No one has been
deeper drowned in the shade of his great German and Austrian
contemporaries: Thomas Mann, Hesse, Rilke, Schnitzler,
Hofmannsthal and the rest. Virtually all his books are long out
of print in English. Even in Germany, where he is still read,
there has been a marked lack of academic interest in his work.
Why should this remarkably fertile and gifted writer be so
neglected? Before that can be answered, I must try to tell his
life briefly.

Zweig was born in Vienna on 28 November 1881, of a
cosmopolitan and cultured Jewish family, then typical of
many others in that easy-going city. The silver spoon that met
him when he entered the world was later to become something
of a crucifix; but few writers can have had an easier first thirty
years of existence. After 1914 the memory of them, of a lost
world, was permanently to haunt him. A younger son, he met
no obstacles, either private or public, in his early literary
career. His millionaire father did not force him into the family

textile business. Such men were only too happy for their children to show that the racial genius extended far beyond a mere talent for business. Much later, Zweig was to blame his parents for the 'lax' religious atmosphere in which he was brought up. The family's Jewishness was very lightly worn; much more a matter of international connections, of urbane tolerance, of belief in the Semitic yeast among nations, than of any orthodoxy. The household was virtually trilingual. French (there were relatives in Paris) and English were spoken, as well as German.

All this was to mark Zweig very young, and is why he became the greatest German francophile of his age, the most fervent internationalist, with a lifelong hatred of passports and frontiers. It is difficult today to read the story of early twentieth-century pan-Europeanism without cynicism, so flagrantly did history jackboot it into oblivion, so petty and mercenary has been its attempted re-establishment in recent years. Even in the early days (perhaps the movement was already wise in deciding that Britain and Russia could never be part of Europe) idealism and fine words were a good deal more in evidence than practical action – a perennial fault, it must be said, in Zweig himself. Yet however much we may sneer now at the notion of a 'world-Switzerland', of a continent of *sans-patries*, the creed of one Europe was a vital influence among many French and German writers and intellectuals between 1900 and 1930.

Zweig had become, by 1914, a brilliant and much-travelled young star in this movement, already successful both as an interpreter of French writing to the German world and as an author in his own right. His 'guru' was the internationalist poet, Emile Verhaeren, whom he had first gone to Belgium to meet in 1902. To Zweig's distress Verhaeren lost his faith after the German atrocities of 1914; but by then he had already met a more enduring master and influence, Romain Rolland. Though he never agreed with Rolland's Marxist side, he was to venerate him for the rest of his life.

During the war Zweig worked for a time in Vienna, in uniform, as a propaganda clerk; but in 1917, increasingly disillusioned by the futility of what was happening, he got himself into Switzerland. His first brief enthusiasm for the conflict (seen as a kind of necessary purge) was long over; now a better Europe had to be built from the ashes of defeat. There was then a collection of pacifists and humanists from all over Europe in Switzerland, including Rolland, Hesse and James Joyce; and for the next fifteen years Zweig was committed to this general movement – artists and intellectuals as harbingers of a new and nobler international order.

His output for the cause during the 1920s, both in terms of published work and private correspondence, to say nothing of endless journeys, articles, translations, lecture-tours, almost defies belief. The same decade saw his sales and world-wide reputation soar. The European public adored him – an admiration unusually shared, apart from one or two exceptions like Hofmannsthal, by most of his fellow-writers. In a way he became, with Rolland, the best-known representative of the humanist, war-hating side of the European conscience. His literary success, in the theatre, in fiction, in his famous biographical studies, was far from merely popular. Freud, Einstein, Schweizer, Toscanini, Thomas Mann, even Goering, were among his devoted readers. 'Friendship is his religion,' wrote Rolland. Most of the friends were very famous people. On 13 May 1924 Zweig gave a lunch in Vienna for Richard Strauss and Schnitzler to meet Rolland; the next day they all went off to visit Freud. Such Olympian gatherings were commonplace in his life. He was a great linker, a cultural diplomat – some said, knowing his restless nature, a little bit of a *poseur*.

For this was the public face. The private one was much more complex and shadowed. By true temperament he was a shy and reserved man (the least personal biography he ever wrote was his own); and nothing if not modest about his own gifts. One side of him hated the adulation he met wherever he went, the endless letters he received. Another could never turn down an invitation, a literary project, a foreign tour, a call for help from a less successful writer. He kept talking of his need for peace and solitude; whenever he found it, he grew rapidly depressed and bored. In his unhappy last years of exile he spoke of himself as a wandering Jew; but for most of his life 'wandering' abroad (the idea of *die vielfache Heimat*, the 'manifold homeland') was a way of life he chose and loved. There was often a deep divorce between what he wrote publicly and what he felt privately. The black despair that was finally to kill him is already in evidence behind the scenes during this period. As early as 1921 he had smelt the rise of Fascism during a visit to Italy.

The immediate post-war spirit of Vienna disgusted Zweig, and in 1919 he installed himself in a house in Salzburg—ominously, had he but known it, in sight of Berchtesgaden. Since before the war the woman in his life had been Friderika von Winternitz. She was unhappily married, with two daughters, and because of the difficulty of divorce then, they were not able to regularise their liaison until 1919. It was to be a modern marriage, in theory; in practice it was the husband who took all the freedoms, and patient Friderika all the domestic troubles and responsibilities. In spite of his marked psychological understanding of women in general, Zweig often showed painfully little for her feelings, and none at all when the marriage finally broke down in the 1930s. He knew it, for if on the one hand he was hopelessly addicted to his own personal liberty, on the other he was very seldom dishonest about his own failings. The most celebrated story here, *Letter from an Unknown Woman*, must be read in the context of his first marriage. There can be little doubt that close behind 'the novelist R.' sits an aspect of the author himself.

A further shadow lies over his attitude to the rise of Nazism. Normally so prescient, he was strangely slow to react to the clear danger signal of the 1930 Reichstag election. Like so many others, he seems even to have seen National Socialism as a potentially rejuvenating factor in German politics. The signals of 1933 — the Reichstag fire, the burning of the books, Thomas Mann's exile — could not be misread, and in October Zweig went on what was effectively a reconnaissance to England, to see if he could face living in a country he knew better through its literature (which he admired) than its reality. In fact he fell for the calm and peace of London after Vienna and Salzburg, though he never came to love England as he did France. On a further visit in 1934 he hired the German refugee secretary, Charlotte Altmann, who was to become his second wife.

That was not the only unwise (or widely misunderstood) decision he took that year. In 1932 Richard Strauss, who had not got over the loss of his great librettist Hugo von Hofmannsthal, had read a Zweig version of Ben Jonson's *The Silent Woman*. Zweig's libretto from it delighted the composer. At last he had a worthy collaborator again. By 1934 the music was nearly ready. The Nazi Party did not want to alienate the great man; but Strauss insisted that this new partner 'of undesirable race' should be given due credit. With his usual shrewd nose for propaganda values, Goebbels argued for expediency against his more blindly anti-Semitic colleagues; and it was Hitler himself who finally sanctioned production and public announcement of the partnership. All this distressed many in the growing émigré community, who felt that if anyone could afford – and ought – to take a stand it was the rich, world-famous Zweig. In the end, in 1935, *Die Schweigsame Frau* was banned after two performances. But the damage was done.

In hindsight we may perhaps judge Zweig's attitude, then and later, more kindly than many of his contemporaries did. At least it was principled, for he had a quintessential hatred of all racism, and for condemning any nation *en bloc*. He also believed that too outspoken action could only aggravate Nazi intransigence and make life worse for the Jewish writers and intellectuals still in Germany and Austria. Of course history was to prove him wrong, but at least – at that time – he was obeying deeply held beliefs over the proper function of the writer and the role of intelligent persuasion in human affairs. He can certainly not be faulted for the considerable work he did behind the scenes (and the money he gave) on behalf of refugees less fortunate than himself.

For the growing estrangement with Friderika he must be entirely blamed. He insisted she remained behind in Austria to sell the Salzburg house (also to look after his ailing mother in Vienna); and then proceeded to blame her for not doing it, in appallingly difficult circumstances, more quickly. All this came during the secret affair with Lotte, and must have added private to public guilt. As so often in his life, he took refuge in work, making it at least partly an excuse for sins elsewhere.

The year 1938 was particularly grim for him. After the Anschluss he lost his last remaining publisher in the German-speaking world, and from then on felt cut off from his mother-tongue. He lost his real mother also, since she died in Vienna;

and at the end of the year he lost Friderika, in divorce. By 1939 he declared himself totally exhausted, and without hope: nothing could stop Hitler, Europe was done for. He must have felt a bitter irony when, in Paris that year, Jules Romains hailed him as the 'Great European'. More and more his reluctance to declare himself (he still maintained that Jewish meddling in politics was a chief cause of anti-Semitism) shocked his more active and positive friends; more and more they smelt an 'inner cowardice' in his *Abseitsstehen*, or staying aloof. Again he knew it, and agonised.

In 1939 he and Lotte Altmann moved to Bath. They married there on 6 September, a week after the invasion of Poland. Still the old internationalist, he hated the suspicion of German-speaking émigrés then rife in England, and the insensitive bureaucracy installed to deal with them. Red tape nearly stopped him from going to London for Freud's funeral on 26 September. At times his anger over such matters seemed dangerously irrational. He was furious one day when another train taking him to London was delayed and made him miss an appointment. The delay was caused by the mobilisation emergency – against those who did make trains run on time.

On 12 March 1940 he and Lotte became naturalised Britons. But the fall of France in June upset him deeply, and he saw no chance of his new homeland holding out against Germany. In July the Zweigs sailed for the United States, and two months later went on from there for a lecture-tour of South America. Treated as the great artist-ambassador from suffering Europe, he was given an overwhelming welcome. But by now his sense of irreversible world catastrophe, the defeat of all he believed in, was making him lose touch with reality. There was a return to New York early in 1941, and a meeting with Friderika and his two stepdaughters, who had managed to escape from France. He and Friderika had never stopped writing to one another; and fate had punished him over his second marriage. He seems to have married Lotte in the hope of regaining a second youth. But she turned out to have poor health, and to need his help quite as much as he needed hers. The plunge back into the New York émigré world also distressed him. Once again he tried to bury despair under work.

In August he returned to Brazil with Lotte, and they rented a house at Petropolis, not far from Rio de Janeiro. There, among other things, he wrote perhaps his finest story, *The Royal Game*. But by this time the first terrible rumours about the concentration camps were reaching the outside. Zweig entered a state of pathological depression. Only just 60, he wrote to friends as if his life was over and all his old powers gone (the latter in the face of abundant evidence to the contrary). As in the past, though Petropolis gave him the peace he claimed to crave, he hated the lack of letters, of intellectual friends, of the old peripatetic literary life.

On 16 February 1942 the Zweigs drove down with neighbours to Rio to see the famous carnival. On the 17th they heard that Singapore had fallen. Stefan insisted that he and Lotte return at once, alone, to Petropolis. Five days later, with an almost Stoic calm – they had spent the intervening time in scrupulously arranging their affairs and writing farewell letters – they both took massive doses of veronal. The news of the joint death shocked a world already in a quite sufficient state of anxiety and doubt. When André Maurois wrote of 'the shame of a civilization that can create a world in which a Stefan Zweig cannot live' he spoke for more than we may easily imagine today. If the 'Great European' himself had given up hope, what else was left?

I have in this very cursory account of Zweig's crowded life – Donald Prater's excellent biography *European of Yesterday* (Oxford, 1972) will amply satisfy the more curious – deliberately stressed the private defects rather than the public qualities. A blame still attaches to his name for not declaring himself more openly in the 1930s; as also for being too prolific, too successful, too famous and too known by the famous, and thus implicitly guilty of a kind of élitism, the belief that the world can be changed by art and international colloquia, benign conspiracies of the celebrated. If in one way Zweig was the last of the nineteenth-century *poètes maudits*, in another he was (a little like Somerset Maugham) a victim of his own immense living reputation. And then, perhaps, he has an even worse fault in the eyes of our own age.

One of his less gifted biographers has written of him, with an infelicity bordering on the sublime, that 'No one has ever accused Zweig of a sense of humour'. He was not in fact without a dry humour in his letters, but it is true that he took life far too seriously, or anxiously, for his own eventual good. It is probably why he never really fathomed the British during his exile; and, one might hazard a guess, why he did not spend more time on the fiction for which, with his striking narrative powers and psychological insight, he had such an obvious natural bent. He wrote only one full-length novel. It was his seriousness, his sense of social and intellectual responsibility, that too often led him to disperse his tremendous energy in minor fields – in translations, tributes, commemorative essays, the pan-European gospel.

It is easy to dismiss all this side of his life, to say that it was often absurdly idealistic, that it was blown away like thistledown before the reality of the storm-troopers, that Zweig ought to have seen there was only one option after 1933 – total public opposition to Nazism. But to dismiss an idealist just because his ideal failed and finally went unheard seems to me distinctly unjust. As I have tried to suggest, the inner Zweig was very far from being temperamentally suited to the public role of 'Great European', and his suicide proves the bitterness of the battle between the two sides of his personality.

It was also, of course, a battle between cultural reality and a cultural dream. Today we might think more of Zweig in terms of the former, as a representative – or victim – of those extraordinary last decades of Imperial, and Jewish, Vienna, the mother-city of Auden's Age of Anxiety. Certainly the psychological sign of the zodiac that dominated his life was *Angst*. It explains all the paradoxes about him – his yearning for a motherland, a 'home', his obsessive need to travel; his internationalism, his despair in exile; his constant grumbling about the pressure of work, his constant taking refuge in it; his curiosity about the secrets of other lives, his acute shyness about revealing his own; his eternal self-doubt, his need to cultivate his own success; his extraordinary generosity to other writers (he was deeply hurt when he discovered how much Hofmannsthal disliked him, yet refused to change his high literary opinion of the poet), his final lack of it for his own work; his selfless conscientiousness over countless public things, his sometimes alarming insensitivity at home, as a husband and stepfather.

Zweig's literary reputation must rest on two aspects of his work: the *Novellen*, and the historical and literary biographies. He and his readers took the latter very seriously, and a great deal of his living reputation came from them. They were all essentially designed to illustrate various facets of the European spirit, and sometimes (as with *Erasmus* in 1934) may be seen as self-justification for Zweig's own philosophy of life. The best of them are still very readable. *Fouché* remains one of the finest studies of a time-serving politician ever written. No less a historian than J. E. Neale praised *Maria Stuart* highly – and suggested that a literary 'amateur' like Zweig might have more penetrating insight into character and psychology than a trained professional. Even Freud, usually sharp as a lynx on those who misrepresented his work, was (after one or two light criticisms over theory) patently pleased with the essay devoted to him. The huge success of this side of Zweig's work was not gained by 'amateur' gifts alone; he did massive (in the case of *Marie Antoinette*, much original) research as well.

Rather the same is true of the *Novellen*. Zweig explained his method with them in a little piece ('I seek in shadow') he wrote for the Readers Union during his stay in England.

If I had to confess which quality has been predominant to make me a writer, I believe that I would have to name one which generally is not very much appreciated in private life – a great and insatiable curiosity . . . A psychological problem is as attractive for me in a living man as in an historical person; so my novels and biographies come out of the same source and are complementary to each other . . . In my endeavour to explain a character or a problem to myself I write at first for my own pleasure. Then I begin to shorten, to leave out everything which is not strictly necessary, and books which have in my own manuscript more than a hundred thousand words appear when printed with only thirty or forty thousand. This constant and repeated work of concentration is what I like most and I believe that a part of the success of my books is due to the fact that I have tried to eliminate much that is superfluous. Many of my stories (as *Amok*, *Letter from an Unknown Woman*) are in fact concentrated full-size novels . . .

The two earliest stories in the present selection, *The Burning Secret* (*Brennendes Geheimnis*) and *Fear*, were both written before 1914. In them we may already detect the unease, *Angst* indeed, behind the green and gold façade of Imperial Austria. It is in the very language, the recurrence of emotional key-words: German equivalents of passion, frenzy, shame, excite-ment, fear, stammering, blushing, nervousness, guilt. As in the disturbing undertones of the outwardly posed and carefully calculated art of the Secession, we sense a culture already in trouble, already predicating the later century, and far beyond Austria.

Though Zweig resented the common assumption that the *Novellen* were autobiographical, it is hard not to see personal echoes in *The Burning Secret*. His relationship with his mother, something of a frivolous socialite, was never too happy. A picture of him exists when he was four. Even then there is something frighteningly precocious and knowing in the little boy's eyes: an unnatural inquisitiveness, an incipient re-bellion. Edgar in the story is clearly foreshadowed, and it is surely significant that Zweig ends the story with Edgar safely returned to his family. This is well beyond where a Maupas-sant or a Schnitzler would have laid down the pen. They would have ended with the flight, not the reconciliation. Not for the last time, and despite Zweig's great gifts as a classic story-teller, an inner need was allowed to prevail – the therapeutic content, not an orthodox neatness of form.

The 1922 collection to which *Amok* (*Der Amokläufer*) and *Letter from an Unknown Woman* (*Brief einer Unbekannten*) belong (the over-all title was *Amok: Tales of Violent Feeling*) was Zweig's first great commercial success. Intended to por-tray adult passions (as opposed to the stories of childhood like *The Burning Secret*), the book was translated all over the world. One result was the enormous response from readers who saw him less as a writer than as a spare-time psychiatrist, a role Zweig found increasingly wearisome. Stories like *Amok*, with Conrad's literal typhoons carried over into the domain of the sexual, seemed both daring and decadent, and immensely revealing, to their first audiences.

Letter from an Unknown Woman, later to be filmed by Max Ophuls, is Zweig's most famous story. Its lasting power is a little mysterious, since in one way it is clearly a period piece. It comes not only from a past society – and a set of conventions about the relationship between the sexes – but deals with an almost vanished mode of feeling. An intelligent modern woman may well find the heroine's endless self-denial hideously improbable. Even the basic situation must seem implausible now, to any but the most resolute contemporary Casanovas – though perhaps less so in terms of *fin de siècle* city society, tacitly as permissive as our own, at least on the matter of prostitution and the middle-class male. In my view the hidden secret of the self-denial is precisely its endlessness. One has heard of mistresses who sob as they take lethal revenge; of lovers who foster the very crime a word from them might have avoided. There are countless other strange ambiguities in this memorable *conte*. As I have already mentioned, there is plenty of evidence that the author's own relationships with women were less than perfect in his always self-examining eyes. The masochism is not all on the female side; and what the 'unknown woman' and 'R.' stand for in Freudian terms is, I think, sufficiently obvious.

The Royal Game (*Schachnovelle*, or 'chess-nouvelle') was written in the last four months of his life. This fine story of a man who outwits the Gestapo and manages, though scarred, to find the courage to go on living – in other words a man who has neither run away nor given free course to despair – must be seen partly as an attempt to exorcize guilt and unhappiness through wish-fulfilment, a very common phenomenon in novelists. Never was there a clearer literary case of 'Doctor, cure thyself'.

We may also see a parallel between the mad, but saving, sanctuary the hero finds in 'imaginary' chess and Zweig's own habitual retreat into the imagination (or literary work) when domestic or political reality threatened him too closely. The mystery is how he failed to see that this last fiction, surely one of the most powerful ever based on the imagery of a game, proved the very contrary of what he persisted in believing: that his daimon was gone, he was 'written out'. It shows how tyrannical – one might almost say totalitarian – his pessimism had become at the end. Zweig in Petropolis is like a classical tragedy. A divine malevolence broods over all; and a cruel irony. Alamein, where the war at last turned against the Axis, lay only a few months ahead.

But now I must let Zweig's troubled, but always humane, spirit speak for itself. It has wandered much too far out of the English-speaking world's memory. It is time, on this centenary of his birth, that we read him again.

1981   JOHN FOWLES

THE ROYAL GAME

THE usual eleventh-hour bustle and commotion reigned on the big liner that was due to sail from New York to Buenos Aires at midnight. Visitors who were not sailing forced their way through the crowds to see their friends off, telegraph boys with caps worn at an angle called out names as they darted through the public saloons, cabin trunks and flowers were being delivered, children ran, full of curiosity, up and down the companionways, while the orchestra played imperturbably on deck. I was standing somewhat apart from this turmoil, talking to a friend on the promenade deck, when two or three flashbulbs went off near by. Apparently some important person was being quickly interviewed and photographed by the press just before we sailed.

My friend looked over and laughed. 'There's a rare bird you have on board. That's Czentovic.' And as I reacted to this information with a rather obviously blank expression, he went on to explain: 'Mirko Czentovic, the world chess champion. He has traipsed around the whole of America from the east coast to the west, playing tournaments, and now he's off to Argentina for fresh triumphs.'

In fact I did now recall this young world champion and even a few details connected with his meteoric career. My friend, a more observant reader of the newspapers than I, was able to supplement these with a whole string of anecdotes. At a stroke Czentovic had established himself about a year earlier alongside such reputable past-masters of the chess world as Alekhine, Capablanca, Tartakower, Lasker and Bogoljuboff. Not since the appearance of the ten-year-old prodigy Reshevsky at the New York chess tournament in 1922 had the breakthrough of a completely unknown person into the magic circle caused quite such a sensation. For Czentovic's intellectual attributes didn't appear in any way to predict at the outset that he would have such a dazzling career. The secret soon leaked out that this champion was, in his private life, incapable of writing any sentence in any language without making spelling mistakes and, as one of his exasperated colleagues angrily jeered, 'his lack of education is almost universal in all departments'. He was the son of a poverty-stricken southern Yugoslav who worked as a boatman on the Danube, and whose small craft was run down one night by a barge carrying grain. After his father's death the twelve-year-old boy was taken in out of pity by the priest of his remote village. The good man strove honestly, by coaching him at home, to make up for what the taciturn, unresponsive boy with the broad forehead seemed unable to learn at the village school.

But his efforts continued to be fruitless. Mirko went on staring at the letters, which had been explained to him a hundred times, as though he had never seen them before. His slow-functioning brain also lacked any retentive capacity for the simplest lessons in any subject. He had to use his fingers for counting even at the age of fourteen; and to read a book or newspaper required even more effort for this lad already halfway to adulthood. No one, however, could call Mirko unwilling or difficult. Obediently he did as he was told, fetched water, chopped wood, worked in the field, cleaned the kitchen, and always punctiliously completed every task he was given, even if he did it with infuriating slowness. But what upset the good priest most about the strange boy was his total apathy. He did nothing unless someone particularly asked him to; he never put a question, didn't play with other lads, and never looked for any occupation beyond what had been specifically organised by someone else. As soon as Mirko had finished doing his household chores he would sit dourly looking round the room, with the empty expression of the sheep in the meadow, utterly ignoring any activity going on around

2

him. In the evenings, when the priest smoked his long, countryman's pipe and played his usual three games of chess with the village police sergeant, the fair-haired lad squatted dumbly beside them and stared from under his heavy lids, apparently half-asleep and with indifference, at the board with the black and white squares. One winter evening, while the two men were deep in their daily game, they heard out on the village street the bells of a fast-approaching sleigh. A farmer, his cap covered in snow, stepped quickly into the house. His old mother lay dying, and he wanted the priest to hurry to be in time to give her Extreme Unction. The priest went with him immediately. The policeman, who hadn't finished his beer, lit up his pipe again. When he was just putting on his heavy knee-boots ready to leave he noticed how Mirko's gaze was fixed unwaveringly on the chessboard with the unfinished game.

'Well now, would you like to finish the game?' he said jokingly, completely convinced that the sleepy youngster had no idea how to move a single piece on the board. The boy looked up shyly, then nodded, and sat down in the priest's chair. After fourteen moves the police sergeant was beaten and had to admit his defeat was not the result of a careless move on his part. The second game produced the same result.

'Balaam's ass!' the priest exclaimed in astonishment when he returned, explaining to the policeman – who was not so well versed in the Bible – that more than two thousand years ago a similar phenomenon had occurred, when someone who was dumb had suddenly discovered the gift of wise speech. Despite the late hour the priest couldn't resist challenging his semi-literate stand-in to a match. Mirko beat him easily, too. He played toughly, slowly, imperturbably, without once lifting his broad forehead from the board. But he played with undeniable certainty. Neither the policeman nor the priest was able to win one game against him over the next few days. The priest, who was better equipped than almost anyone else to assess the otherwise total backwardness of his protégé, was now eagerly curious to know how far this single, special gift would stand up to a more serious examination. After he had taken Mirko to the village barber to have his unkempt, straw-coloured hair cut, to make him more or less presentable, he took him in his sleigh to the small town near by. He knew some really keen chess players gathered in a corner of the café in the main square, and that they were more experienced players than himself. There was no small stir among them when the priest pushed the fair-haired, red-cheeked lad of fifteen, with his inside-out sheepskin and heavy knee-boots, forward into the café. The youngster stood apart, shyly, in a corner, his eyes cast down, until he was summoned to one of the chess tables. Mirko was beaten in the first game because he had not seen the so-called Sicilian opening played at the good priest's table. In the second game he drew with the best player there. From the third and fourth games on he beat all his opponents without exception.

Now, exciting things rarely happen in a small provincial town in southern Yugoslavia; so for the assembled worthies the début of the peasant champion was an instant sensation. It was agreed unanimously that, whatever happened, the boy wonder must stay in the town until next day, so that the other members of the chess club could be called together; and above all, so that a message could be sent to the castle to tell the elderly Count Simczic, who was a chess-fanatic. The priest, who looked on his ward with quite new pride, but who did not wish to neglect his duties at the Sunday service merely on account of the pleasure of his discovery, agreed to leave Mirko behind for a further test. The chess group paid for young Czentovic to be put up at a hotel and that evening he saw a water-closet for the first time. The chess-room was full to capacity the following Sunday afternoon. Mirko sat for four hours continuously at the chessboard and, without saying a word or even looking up, defeated one player after another. Finally a simultaneous game was suggested. It took some time for the uninstructed boy to grasp that in a simultaneous game he had to play alone against a number of the other players at the same time. But once Mirko had grasped this procedure, he quickly got the hang of it, and walked in his heavy, creaking boots, slowly from table to table. In the end he won seven of the eight games.

Great consultations now began. Although strictly speaking this new champion didn't belong to the town, native and national pride was keenly aroused. Hardly anyone would have noticed the existence of this little town on the map. But perhaps at last, for the first time, it would gain the honour of sending a famous man out into the world. An agent named Koller, who until now had dealt only in soubrettes and singers for the garrison cabaret, declared himself willing, if someone would guarantee his expenses for a year, to have the youngster taught all about chess professionally in Vienna, by an excellent local champion he knew. Count Simczic, who had not met such a notable opponent in sixty years of playing chess daily, guaranteed the sum immediately. That Sunday the astonishing career of the boatman's son began.

After six months Mirko had completely mastered the secrets of chess technique, but with one strange limitation, which was to be much noticed and made fun of later in chess circles. He never managed, even for one single game, to play from memory — or as the experts say — to play blindfold. He completely lacked the ability to visualise the board in the unrestricted space of the imagination. He always had to have the black and white board with the sixty-four squares and the thirty-two pieces physically in front of him. Even when he was world famous he carried a folding pocket chess set with him, so that if he wanted to reconstruct a championship game or solve a problem, he could have the positions displayed visually. This defect, trivial in itself, betrayed a flaw in imaginative power, and it was often discussed within the small world of chess in the same way that musicians do if an outstanding virtuoso or conductor proves unable to play or conduct without a written score.

But this odd peculiarity in no way slowed down Mirko's stupendous progress. By the time he was seventeen he had already won a dozen chess prizes. At eighteen he had won the Hungarian championship and at twenty the world championship. The most audacious champions, each one vastly superior to him in intellectual ability, imagination and daring, were nevertheless beaten by his tough, cold logic, as Napoleon was by the ponderous Kutusov, or Hannibal by Fabius Cunctator. The latter, according to Livy, had similarly shown in childhood conspicuous signs of impassivity and stupidity. So it came about that a complete outsider, a ponderous, taciturn, country lad, from whom even the most cunning reporters were unable to extract even one usefully publishable word, fought his way into the illustrious gallery of chess champions, in whose ranks were assembled men of the most varied types of intellectual superiority – philosophers, mathematicians, calculating, imaginative and often creative temperaments. To be sure, what Czentovic denied the papers in the way of polished speech he soon more than adequately made up for in anecdotes about himself. Inescapably, the moment he left the chessboard, where he was undisputed master, Czentovic became a grotesque and almost comic figure; despite his formal black suit, his splendid cravat with the somewhat ostentatious pearl tie-pin, and his painstakingly manicured nails, he remained in behaviour and manners the same limited country bumpkin who had cleaned out the priest's room in the village. In a blatantly crude and clumsy way he set about extracting from his gift and his fame whatever money there was to be had. He did this, to the amusement and vexation of his professional colleagues, in a petty way, often showing what amounted to sheer vulgar greed. He travelled from town to town, always staying in the cheapest hotels. He played in the most awful clubs provided they paid his fee. He allowed himself to appear on advertisements for soap, and even lent his name – ignoring the jokes of his rivals, who knew well enough that he couldn't put three sentences together correctly – to a *Philosophy of Chess*, which was really written for its commercially-aware publisher by an insignificant student from Galicia. As with every truly stubborn person, he lacked a sense of the ridiculous. From the moment he won the world championship he thought he was the most important man in the world; and the knowledge that he had beaten all those clever, intellectual, brilliant speakers and writers in their own field, and above all, the plain fact that he had earned more than they had, turned his initial insecurity into a cold and tactless display of pride.

'But how could such an early rise to fame fail to turn such an empty head?' my friend concluded, having just given me a classic demonstration of Czentovic's childish propensities. 'How can a twenty-one-year-old peasant from the Banat fail to succumb to an attack of vanity if, suddenly, by moving a few pieces around on a wooden board, he can earn more in a week than his entire village back home in a whole year of wood-cutting and bitter hard work? Besides, isn't it confoundedly easy to think you're a great man if you aren't burdened with the slightest idea that Rembrandt, Beethoven, Dante or Napoleon ever even lived? This lad knows only one thing in that walled-in brain of his: that for months now he hasn't lost a game of chess. And as he's really no idea that anything else in the world apart from chess and money has any value, he's every reason to be pleased with himself.'

The information given me by my friend couldn't fail to arouse my particular curiosity. All my life I have been attracted by every kind of monomania, by people obsessed with one single idea. For the more a man limits himself, the nearer he is on the other hand to what is limitless; it is precisely those who are apparently aloof from the world who build for themselves a remarkable and thoroughly individual world in miniature, using their own special equipment, termite-like. So I made no secret of my intention of examining this particular specimen of intellectual one-track-mindedness closely under the microscope during the twelve-day journey to Rio.

'You won't have much luck there,' my friend warned me. 'As far as I know no one's been able to extract the slightest bit of psychological material from Czentovic. Behind his abysmal stupidity the wily peasant conceals the ultimate in cleverness. He leaves no chinks in his armour, thanks to a simple technique. He talks only to fellow Yugoslavs from his own background. He looks for them in small bars. If he gets a whiff of education in a man he retreats into his shell. Then no one can boast of having heard him say anything stupid. And no one can claim he has sounded the allegedly boundless depths of his lack of culture.'

My friend was right, in fact. During the first day of the voyage it proved absolutely impossible to approach Czentovic without being boorishly importunate, which definitely isn't my way. Sometimes, to be sure, he would walk on the promenade deck, but always with his hands clasped behind his back and with a proud self-absorbed bearing, as in those well-known pictures of Napoleon. Besides, he took his walk round the deck with such speed and thrustfulness that you would have had to follow him at a trot to be able to speak to him. Again, he never appeared in the public rooms, in the bar, in the smoking-room. As I was told by the steward of whom I inquired discreetly, he spent most of the day in his cabin practising or going over games of chess on a large board.

After three days it began really to annoy me that his skilful defence technique was stronger than my determination to approach him. I had never yet in my life had the opportunity of actually meeting a chess champion, and the more concerned I became about fitting a label to this specific type of man, so the thought processes involved seemed to me the more incredible – that a man could spend his whole life revolving exclusively round a space consisting of sixty-four black and white squares. I knew well enough from my own experience the mysterious attraction of 'the royal game', that game among games devised by man, which rises majestically above every tyranny of chance, which grants its victor's laurels only to a great intellect, or rather, to a particular form of mental ability.

But are we not already guilty of an insulting limitation in calling chess a game? Isn't it also a science, an art, hovering between these two categories as Muhammad's coffin hovered between heaven and earth? Isn't it a unique bond between every pair of opponents, ancient and yet eternally new; mechanical in its framework and yet only functioning through use of the imagination; confined in geometrically fixed space and at the same time released from confinement by its permutations; continuously evolving yet sterile; thought that leads nowhere, mathematics that add up to nothing, art without an end product, architecture without substance, and nevertheless demonstrably more durable in its true nature and existence than any books or creative works? Isn't it the only game that belongs to all peoples and all times? And who knows whether God put it on earth to kill boredom, to sharpen the wits or to lift the spirits? Where is its beginning and where its end?

Every child can learn its basic rules, every bungler can try it; and yet it requires, within those unchanging small squares, the production of a special species of master, not comparable to any other kind, men who have a singular gift for chess, geniuses of a particular kind, in whom vision, patience and technique function in just as precise divisions as they do in mathematicians, poets and musicians, only on different levels and in different conjunctions.

8

At an earlier stage of the great interest in research into physiognomy, someone like Gall would have dissected the brains of chess champions to establish if such geniuses had a unique coil in their grey matter, a kind of chess muscle or chess bump which was more intensively inscribed there than in other skulls. And how a case like Czentovic's would have excited such a physiognomist, where this precise type of genius appears to be deposited in intellectually totally inert matter, like a single vein of gold in a hundredweight of dead rock!

In principle I understood the time-honoured fact that such a unique, such an ingenious game must produce its own special matadors. But how difficult it is, how impossible even, to visualise the life of an alert, intelligent man who reduces the world to the narrow linear traffic between black and white, who looks for his life's apogee in the mere toing and froing, back and forth, of thirty-two pieces. How hard it is to understand a man who, through using a new opening, moving the Knight instead of the pawn, achieves a feat, and his tiny little scrap of immortality tucked away in a chess book reference – a man, an intelligent man, who without losing his reason, for ten, twenty, thirty, forty years, concentrates all his mental energy over and over again on the ludicrous exercise of manoeuvring into a corner a wooden king on a wooden board!

And now one such phenomenon, one such genius or incomprehensible fool, was physically near me for the first time, six cabins away on the same ship. And there was I, feeling wretched, because my curiosity about how the mind works has always been a kind of passion with me, and I was not in a position to approach him. I began to think up the most absurd stratagems: perhaps to flatter his vanity by pretending to interview him for an important paper, or to arouse his greed by offering him a lucrative tournament in Scotland. But eventually I remembered that the hunter's most successful technique for enticing the blackcock is to imitate its mating call; what could really be more effective in attracting the attention of a chess champion than to play chess oneself?

Now I have never in my life been a serious exponent of the art of chess, the reason being simply, in fact, that I have always entered into a game light-heartedly and entirely for pleasure. If I sit down at a chessboard for an hour, I am not going to exert myself in any way. Quite the opposite: I shall be seeking relaxation from intellectual tension. I 'play' chess in the truest sense of the word while others, the real chess players, work at it. For chess, then, as for love, a partner is essential, and at that time I didn't know if there were any other chess enthusiasts on board. To lure them out of their hiding places I set up a rudimentary trap in the smoking-room. Although my wife is an even weaker player than I, she and I sat there at a chessboard like bird-catchers. In fact we hadn't completed six moves before someone passing by stopped, and a second asked permission to watch us. Eventually the partner I was hoping for arrived to challenge me to a game.

His name was McConnor and he was a Scots mining engineer. As I heard it, he had made a large fortune out of oil wells in California. He was stocky in appearance, with strong, firm, almost square, jaws, strong teeth, and a rich ruddy complexion for which, it would appear, a copious intake of whisky was at least in part responsible. His shoulders were strikingly broad and almost athletically mobile. Unfortunately and characteristically they drew one's attention as he played, for this Mr McConnor was one of that breed of successful self-made men for whom a defeat, even in the most unimportant game, diminishes their self-esteem. Accustomed in life to getting his own way ruthlessly, and spoiled by material success, this massive self-made man was so unshakeably convinced of his own superiority that any opposition provoked him as being unwarrantable, almost an affront. When he lost the first game he became bad tempered and began to explain dictatorially and at length that it could only have been because his attention must have wandered for a moment. In the third game he blamed the noise in the next room for his failure. He was never prepared to lose without at once seeking a return game. At first this driving determination amused me. In the end I accepted it only as an unavoidable accompaniment to the achievement of my own objective: to lure the world champion to our table.

On the third day it worked, but only by half. It could have been that Czentovic noticed us at our chessboard through the window from the promenade deck, or it could have been by pure chance that he honoured the smoking-room with his presence – anyway, as soon as he saw us amateurs practising his art, he instinctively took a step over in our direction and from a measured distance cast a searching glance at our board. It was McConnor's move. And this one move was quite sufficient to tell Czentovic how little worthy of his expert interest a closer study of our unskilled efforts would be. With the same obvious gesture that one uses to put down a bad detective novel one has been offered in a bookshop, without even leafing through it, he walked away from our table and left the smoking-room. 'Weighed in the balance and found wanting,' I thought to myself, slightly put out by that cool, contemptuous look. To relieve my feelings a little, I said to McConnor, 'The champion didn't seem to be very enthusiastic about your move.'

'Which champion?'

I explained that the person who had just walked past and given our game a disapproving glance was Czentovic, the chess champion. However, I continued, the two of us would survive and come to terms with his illustrious contempt without breaking our hearts; beggars can't be choosers. But to my surprise my off-hand remarks had quite an unexpected effect on McConnor. He immediately became so excited he forgot our game, and you could almost hear his ambition building up steam. He had no idea Czentovic was on board. Czentovic simply must play him. He had only once in his life played against a world champion, and that was in a simultaneous match with forty others; even that had been frightfully exciting, and he had very nearly won. Did I know the champion personally? I said I didn't. Would I speak to him and ask him over? I declined, on the grounds that I knew Czentovic was not very responsive to new acquaintances. Besides, what sort of attraction would there be for a world champion in playing with third-rate players like us?

Well, I ought not to have spoken of third-rate players to a man of McConnor's overweening nature. He leaned back angrily and declared bluntly that, for his part, he couldn't believe Czentovic would decline the polite challenge of a gentleman; and he would soon see about that. At his request I gave him a brief description of the world champion. With uncontrolled impatience he soon rushed off after Czentovic on the promenade deck, unconcernedly leaving our game abandoned. Once again I felt the owner of the broad shoulders was not to be restrained once he was determined to have something.

I waited quite anxiously. After ten minutes McConnor returned, not looking very pleased, it seemed to me.

'Well?' I asked him.

'You were right,' he replied, somewhat annoyed. 'He's not a very pleasant gentleman. I introduced myself, told him who I am. He didn't shake hands. I tried to explain how proud and honoured we would all be on board if he would play a simultaneous match against us. But he was damnably stiff-necked about it. Said he was sorry, but he had contractual obligations to his agent which expressly forbade him to play on the whole trip without payment of a fee. His minimum is 250 dollars a match.'

I laughed. 'It would never have occurred to me that pushing pieces about from black to white could be such a profitable business. Well, I hope you said goodbye just as politely.'

But McConnor remained utterly serious. 'The match has been arranged for tomorrow afternoon at three o'clock. Here in the smoking-room. I hope we won't let him make mincemeat of us too easily.'

'What? You've agreed to pay him 250 dollars?' I exclaimed in astonishment.

'Why not? It's his trade. If I had toothache and there happened to be a dentist on board I wouldn't ask him to extract the tooth for nothing. The man's right to ask a fat price. In every field the real experts are also the best businessmen. And as far as I'm concerned, the more straightforward the deal the better. I'd rather pay cash than have to be obliged to our Mr Czentovic and thank him afterwards. Besides, I've often lost more than 250 dollars in an evening at our club and still not played with a world champion. It's no disgrace for a "third-rate" player to be beaten by a Czentovic.'

I was amazed to note how deeply I had dented McConnor's self-esteem with that unforgivable phrase, 'third-rate player'. But as he was disposed to pay for this expensive amusement I had no objection against his misplaced vanity, which was after all to be the means of my meeting the object of my curiosity.

Quickly the four or five gentlemen who had already declared themselves chess players were told of the impending event. So that we wouldn't be disturbed too much by passengers walking by, we reserved in advance of the match not only our own table but also the neighbouring ones.

The next day our little group mustered in full strength at the appointed hour. The centre seat opposite the champion was naturally allotted to McConnor, who relieved his nerves by lighting up one strong cigar after another and frequently looking anxiously at his watch. But – as I suspected he would, after what my friend had told me – the champion kept us waiting a good ten minutes, so that the effect of his coolly superior entry was heightened. He walked quietly and calmly over to the table. Without introducing himself – 'You know who I am, and I am not interested in knowing who you are,' seemed to be the inference to draw from this rudeness – he began to give the necessary instructions in a dry, professional manner. As it was impossible to play a proper simultaneous match here on the ship owing to a lack of chessboards, he proposed that we should all combine together to play him. So as not to disturb our deliberations, after each move he would go to another table at the far end of the room. As soon as we had made our next move we should tap on a glass with a spoon, as there was unfortunately no small table-bell handy. He suggested ten minutes should be the maximum time for each move, unless we wanted some other arrangement. Of course we accepted every suggestion, like timid schoolchildren. The draw gave Czentovic Black. Without sitting down he made his first move in reply to ours and went immediately to his appointed table, where he sat back idly and leafed through an illustrated magazine.

There is little point in going into the details of the game. It ended, as of course it had to, with our total defeat, and after only twenty-four moves at that. Well, it wasn't surprising that a world champion had defeated half-a-dozen average or below average players, using his left hand. What really did leave a bad impression on us all was the arrogant, unpleasant way Czentovic made us all feel very clearly that he was indeed beating us with his left hand. Each time, he appeared to give the board the most casual glance, and looked right through us as though we were wooden chessmen ourselves. This rudeness unconsciously reminded me of how one throws a morsel to a mangy dog without looking at him. In my opinion he might have had the tact to point out our mistakes or to encourage us with a friendly word. But even after the match was over this inhuman chess automaton never uttered a syllable, once he had said 'Mate', but waited stolidly at the table to see if we wanted a second game. Being helpless, as one always is in the face of thick-skinned, boorish behaviour, I had already decided to indicate by a gesture that now this dollar transaction had been completed, the pleasure of our acquaintance was at an end, at least as far as I was concerned. To my annoyance McConnor, sitting next to me, said huskily, 'Return game!'

I was taken aback by his challenging tone; in fact at that moment McConnor gave more the impression of being a boxer about to cut loose than a well-mannered gentleman. Was it Czentovic's unpleasant behaviour towards us or just his own pathologically sensitive ego? Whichever it was McConnor's personality had completely changed. His face flushed right up into the roots of his hair, his nostrils flared stiffly with inner tension; he was visibly perspiring, and there was a sharp crease between his tight-set lips and his belligerently thrust-out chin. Uneasily I recognised in his eyes that flickering of uncontrolled passion that you sometimes see gripping people at the roulette table when, after they have doubled their stakes six or seven times, the right colour doesn't come up. I knew, then, that this was driving ambition, and if it were to cost him his entire fortune McConnor would go on playing Czentovic over and over again, for single stakes or double, until he had won at least one game. If Czentovic kept at it he would find a goldmine in McConnor. He should be able to extract several thousand dollars from him before we reached Buenos Aires.

Czentovic remained impassive. 'As you wish,' he answered politely. 'You gentlemen will take Black this time.'

The second game went the same way, the only difference being that our circle was not only enlarged by interested bystanders but through them it became more lively. McConnor stared fixedly at the board as though he wanted to magnetize the pieces and will them to win. I sensed he would gladly have sacrificed a thousand dollars for the satisfaction of shouting 'Mate' at our cold, insensitive opponent. Strange to say, some of the determination in his excitement seemed to rub off unwittingly on to us. Every single move was discussed with considerably more heat than hitherto; repeatedly we would hold one another back until the last moment, before giving Czentovic the signal to return to the table. Eventually we came to the seventeenth move. To our own astonishment a position on the board had been reached which appeared amazingly advantageous to us because it was possible to move one of our pawns from the third file (QB6) to the last square but one, at QB7. We had only to push it forward to QB8 to change it into a second Queen. We weren't, of course, altogether comfortable about this all too obvious chance. To a man, we suspected that Czentovic, who assessed the situation over a much wider range of moves than we did, must have deliberately put this apparent advantage in our way as a bait. But despite the closest study and discussion we couldn't between us discover the hidden trick. Eventually, already nearing the agreed time limit, we decided to chance the move. McConnor already had his hand on the pawn to move it to the last square when he felt someone grab his arm quickly. In an urgent undertone a voice whispered: 'For God's sake! Don't!'

Involuntarily we all turned round. In the last few minutes a man of about forty-five, whose thin, sharp features I recognised – for I had noticed him on the promenade deck on account of his pale, almost chalky, complexion – must have come over to us while we were concentrating on our problem. Aware that we were looking at him, he went on rapidly.

'If you make a Queen now he will take her immediately by moving his Bishop to QB8. You will take that with your Knight. But meanwhile he will move his pawn to Q7, threatening your Rook. And even if you check the King with your Knight you will lose in nine or ten moves. It is almost the same combination Alekhine used against Bogoljuboff at the tournament at Pistyan in 1922.'

Astonished, McConnor took his hand off the pawn and stared in no less wonderment than the rest of us at this man, whom we took to be an unexpected guardian angel from heaven. Anyone who could see check-mate nine moves ahead must be a first-class player, possibly in the running for the championship, travelling to the same tournament. His sudden arrival and intervention at precisely such a critical moment had something of the supernatural about it. McConnor was the first to react.

'What would you advise?' he whispered excitedly.

'Don't advance straight away. For the moment act defensively! First withdraw your King out of the line of fire from KKt1 to KR2. He'll probably then move his line of attack over to the other flank. But you parry that with Rook QB1–QB5; that will cost him two moves, a pawn, and consequently his advantage. Then it will be pawn against pawn, and if your defence is sound you'll make a draw of it. That's the best you can hope for.'

Once more we were astonished. The precision, no less than the speed, of his calculation was quite bewildering. It was as though he had been reading the moves from a book. Anyway, the unexpected chance for us to force a draw in a game with a world champion, thanks to this man's intervention, worked wonders. By common consent we stood back to give him a clearer view of the board. McConnor asked again:

'So it's King from KKt1 to KR2?'

'That's right. Play safe!'

McConnor obeyed, and we tapped on the glass. Czentovic came over to our table at his customary even pace and at a glance assessed the counter-move. Then he moved his pawn on the King's side, KR2–KR4, exactly as our unknown helper had forecast. And immediately our man whispered excitedly:

'Advance your Rook, the Rook QB8 to QB4. Then he'll have to cover his pawn. But that won't help him! Don't bother about his other pawn. Attack with your Knight QB6–Q4, and you'll be back on even terms again. Press the attack instead of defending!'

We didn't understand what he meant. It was double-Dutch as far as we were concerned. But once under his spell McConnor did as he was told, without stopping to think about it. We tapped on the glass again to re-call Czentovic. For the first time he didn't decide on his move quickly but looked intently at the board. Then he made his move exactly as the stranger had told us he would, and turned to go. Before he went, though, something new and unexpected happened. Czentovic raised his eyes and looked at us all. Clearly he wanted to find out who was offering him such energetic opposition for once.

From this instant our excitement grew immeasurably. Until now we had played without real hope, but now the thought that we might break Czentovic's cold pride made all our pulses race. Our new friend had soon directed our next move, however, and we could call Czentovic over – my fingers were trembling as I tapped the glass with the spoon. And now we had our first triumph. Until this moment Czentovic had played standing up, but now he hesitated, went on hesitating, and finally sat down. He sat down slowly and heavily, but this action was enough to neutralise – purely physically – the 'high and mighty' distance between us. We had forced him, at least spatially, to put himself on the same level as ourselves. He reflected for a long time, his eyes fixed unwaveringly on the board, so that you could scarcely see the pupils under the heavy lids. The effort of concentration gradually made his mouth fall open, which gave his round face a slightly silly expression. Czentovic considered for a few minutes, then he made his move and stood up. And soon there was our friend whispering.

'A delaying tactic! Good thinking! But don't go along with it! Force an exchange, make him exchange, then we'll have a draw and even the gods can't help him.'

McConnor did as he was told. In the next few moves between the two – the rest of us had long since been reduced to being inactive extras – there began what was to us meaningless interplay. About seven moves later Czentovic, after a long pause for thought, looked up and said, 'Draw.'

For a moment everything was very still. You could suddenly hear the sound of the waves, and the jazz on the radio in the saloon, you were aware of people walking on the promenade deck and of the light, gentle sighing of the wind as it came in through the open windows. No one breathed: it happened too suddenly and we were all frankly startled by the improbability of what had occurred – that this unknown man should have imposed his will on the world champion in a game that was already half lost. McConnor leaned back all at once, releasing his pent-up breath from his lips in an audible, happy 'Ah!' I looked again at Czentovic. I had already thought he seemed to grow paler while the final moves were being made. But he knew how to conduct himself. He maintained his apparently imperturbable equanimity and merely inquired in an off-hand way, while he removed the pieces from the board, 'Do you gentlemen want a third game?'

He asked the question in a purely matter-of-fact way, purely businesslike. But what was noteworthy was that he didn't look at McConnor as he spoke, but directed his eyes searchingly and straight at our rescuer. As a horse recognises a new and better rider from the firmness of his seat, Czentovic must have recognised from the last few moves who his real — his only — opponent was. Instinctively we followed his gaze and looked anxiously at the stranger. Before he could think about it, however, or had a chance to answer, McConnor, in his boundless excitement had already called out to him triumphantly.

'Of course! But now you must play him on your own! Just you against Czentovic!'

Now, however, something unforeseen happened. The stranger, who oddly enough was still staring intently at the now empty chessboard, took fright when he saw everyone was looking at him and how enthusiastically he was being appealed to. He seemed embarrassed.

'Oh no, gentlemen,' he stumbled, visibly disconcerted. 'That's quite out of the question ... count me out ... it's twenty years, no, twenty-five, since I sat down at a chessboard ... and I have just realised how rude it was of me to meddle in your game without being asked. Please, excuse me for being so presumptuous. I really won't disturb you further.' And before we could recover from our surprise he had withdrawn from the group and left the room.

'But that's really quite impossible!' McConnor boomed out boisterously, gesticulating with his fist. 'It's not credible that that man hasn't played chess for twenty-five years! He calculated every move, every counter-move, five or six moves ahead. No one can do that right off the cuff. It's totally impossible — isn't it?' McConnor had without thinking turned to Czentovic with his last question. But the world champion remained completely impassive.

'It isn't for me to give an opinion on that. However, the gentleman did play a quite surprising and interesting game;

that's why I deliberately left him a chance.' As he spoke, he stood up languidly, and continued in his matter-of-fact way. 'If he, or you, should wish to play another game tomorrow I shall be at your disposal from three o'clock.'

We couldn't suppress a mild chuckle. We all knew Czentovic hadn't left our unknown helper a chance out of generosity at all, and that his remark was nothing but a naive excuse to cover up his own failure. It only intensified our desire to see such an unshakeably arrogant man humiliated. All at once a wild, overpowering wish to do battle came over us peaceful, relaxed sea voyagers; for we were fascinated in a challenging way by the thought that right here on our ship, in the middle of the ocean, the victory wreath could be taken from the champion — a record that would then be flashed around the whole world by the telegraph offices. Moreover, there was the fascination of the mystery of the unexpected intervention of our rescuer at precisely the critical moment, and the contrast of his almost timid diffidence and the unshakeable self-confidence of the professional. Who was this unknown man? Had a hitherto undiscovered chess genius been brought to light here by chance? Or was a famous champion keeping his name from us for reasons of his own? We debated all these possibilities in a state of great excitement. Even the most far-fetched hypotheses were not outrageous enough for us to reconcile the stranger's puzzling shyness and astonishing avowal with his undeniable ability at the game. In one respect, however, we remained united: whatever happened we were not going to turn down the spectacle of another contest. We resolved to try every way of inducing our helper to play Czentovic the next day. McConnor undertook to put up the stake. As, meanwhile, inquiries of the steward had established that our man was an Austrian, it fell to me, as his compatriot, to put our request to him.

It didn't take me long to find our swiftly disappearing fugitive on the promenade deck. He was sitting in a deckchair, reading. Before I went up to him I took the opportunity to have a good look at him. His sharply chiselled head was resting on the cushion as though he was a little tired. Once again I was struck by the noticeable pallor of his relatively young face, and by how the hair framing his temples was absolutely white. I had a feeling, I don't know why, that this man must have aged suddenly. I had scarcely approached him before he stood up politely and introduced himself. I recognised the name immediately as belonging to an old and well-respected Austrian family. I recalled that a bearer of that name had been one of Schubert's closest friends, and that one of the physicians of the old Emperor came from the same family. When I put our request to Dr B., that he should take up Czentovic's challenge, he was visibly taken aback. It turned out he had had no idea that in that game of ours he had stood up magnificently to a world champion and, indeed, the most succeessful player of the day. For some reason this information seemed to make a particular impression on him, because he kept on asking me if I was sure his opponent was really an acknowledged grand master. I soon realised this made my task easier, but I thought it advisable none the less, in order to spare his sensibilities, not to tell him that McConnor would be taking the financial risk if he were defeated. After hesitating a long time Dr B. eventually declared he was prepared to play, but not without expressly asking me to warn the others not in any way to set too much store by his ability.

'Because', he went on with a pensive laugh, 'I honestly don't know if I'm capable of playing a match according to all the rules. Please believe me, it wasn't false modesty at all when I said I haven't touched a chess-piece since my schooldays, that's to say more than twenty years ago. And even then I wasn't considered a player of any special merit.'

He said this so naturally that I couldn't entertain the slightest doubt about his sincerity. Yet I couldn't refrain from expressing my surprise that he had been able to remember every detail of combinations by a variety of champions; at least he must have made a serious study of chess theory. Dr B. laughed again in his curiously dreamy way.

'A serious study! – God knows, that's true. I have studied chess a great deal. But that happened in quite special circumstances; indeed they were absolutely unique. It's quite a complicated story and one that could be taken, possibly, as a little contribution to the delightful, splendid times we live in. If you have the patience to listen for half-an-hour …?'

He motioned me towards the deckchair next to his. I

accepted his invitation gladly. We had no neighbours. Dr B. took off his reading glasses, put them away and began.

'You were good enough to say you remembered my family name, being Viennese yourself. But I don't suppose you will have heard of the firm of solicitors I ran with my father, and later alone, because we didn't take any cases that would get into the papers and we avoided new clients on principle. Strictly speaking we didn't actually have what you could call a proper legal practice. Instead we restricted ourselves exclusively to advising the great monasteries, and above all to administering their estates. My father had connections with them, having been earlier a Member of Parliament representing the Catholic Party. In addition – now that the Empire is part of history one can talk about these things – we were entrusted with the management of the finances of several members of the Imperial family. Our connection with Court and Church went back two generations – my uncle was physician to the Emperor, another was an abbot in Seitenstellen. We had only to supervise their investments, and it was an unobtrusive, I might say, silent function which was allotted to us through this inherited trust. Really it called for no more than the utmost discretion and trustworthiness, two qualities my late father possessed in the highest degree. He managed, in fact, substantially to maintain the value of his clients' fortunes through the years of inflation and at the time of the fall of the Empire. Then when Hitler took the helm in Germany and began his raids on the property of the Church and the monasteries, many negotiations and transactions to save at least the movable assets from confiscation passed through our hands from across the frontier. The two of us knew more about certain secret political matters concerning the Curia and the Imperial family than the general public would ever imagine. But it was precisely the inconspicuousness of our office – we didn't even have a name-plate on the door – as well as the precaution we both took of pointedly avoiding all monarchist circles, that gave us the surest protection from over-zealous investigation. It was a fact that in all those years no official in Austria ever suspected that the secret couriers of the Imperial household collected or delivered their most important mail in our insignificant fourth-floor office.

'But the Nazis had begun, long before they re-armed their military forces against the world, to organise another army – just as dangerous and well-trained – in all neighbouring countries: the legion of the underprivileged, the down-trodden, the maladjusted. In every office, in every business, they established their so-called 'cells'; in every government department, right up to the private offices of Dollfuss and Schuschnigg themselves, they had their eavesdroppers and spies. They even had their man in our insignificant office, as unfortunately I only found out too late. It's true he was only a wretched, run-of-the-mill clerk, whom I had taken on on the recommendation of a priest, just to give our office the outward appearance of a bona fide business. All we used him for really was running innocent errands, answering the telephone and filing papers, unimportant and harmless papers, that is. He wasn't allowed to open the post. I typed all the important letters myself, without taking copies for the files. I took every important document home with me, and confidential conversations were held exclusively in the priory-house of the monastery or in my uncle's consulting room. Thanks to these precautions our eavesdropper obtained no information about what was really going on. But by some unlucky accident this place-seeking and self-important young man must have become aware that he wasn't being trusted and that whatever was of interest was happening behind his back. Perhaps in my absence one of the couriers had carelessly spoken of 'His Majesty' instead of the agreed 'Baron Bern', or disobeying instructions, the scoundrel must have opened letters. Anyway, before it occurred to me to suspect him, he had instructions from Munich or Berlin to watch us. It wasn't until much later, long after my arrest, that I remembered how his initial idleness at work had suddenly changed over the previous few months into enthusiasm, and how more than once he practically insisted I let him post my letters. I am not free from blame myself, therefore, for a certain amount of negligence; but weren't the most important diplomats and generals craftily outmanoeuvred in the end by Hitler?

'How closely and with what loving care the Gestapo had been keeping me under surveillance for so long became very tangibly evident from the fact that I was arrested by the SS on the very evening that Schuschnigg announced his resignation, and one day before Hitler took possession of Vienna. Luckily I was able to burn the most important documents the moment I heard Schuschnigg's resignation speech. The rest of the papers, along with the essential certificates for the securities held abroad on behalf of the monasteries and two archdukes, I sent – literally at the last minute, just before those fellows smashed my door in – to my uncle, hiding them in a laundry basket carried by my elderly and reliable housekeeper.'

Dr B. broke off to light a cigar. I saw in the flickering light a nervous tic at the right-hand corner of his mouth. I had noticed it before, and observed that it happened every minute or two. It was only a slight movement, not much stronger than a breath, but it made his whole face look remarkably restless.

'I expect you are thinking I'm going to tell you now about the concentration camp where everyone who was loyal to our old Austria was sent, and about the degradations, suffering and torture I endured there. But nothing of the kind happened. I was in a different category. I wasn't one of those unfortunates on whom they vented their long accumulated resentment by inflicting physical and spiritual degradation. I belonged to that other quite small group from whom the Nazis hoped to extract money or important information. In my own right I was, of course, too insignificant to be of interest to the Gestapo. They must have discovered, though, that we were the front-men, the administrators and confidants of their bitterest opponents. What they hoped to extract from me was incriminating evidence: evidence against the monasteries to prove financial malpractices, evidence against the royal family and everyone who devotedly supported the monarchy. They suspected – and, in fact, rightly so – that of the money which had passed through our hands substantial amounts were still hidden and out of reach of their rapacious designs. That's why they sent for me on the first day, to force those secrets out of me by their tried and tested methods. People like me, from whom important information or money might be extracted were, therefore, not bundled into concentration camps, but were reserved for special treatment. You may perhaps recall that our Chancellor and also Baron Rothschild, from whose relatives they hoped to extort millions, weren't put behind barbed wire in a prison

23

camp at all, but were taken, apparently as a favour, to a hotel, the Hotel Metropole – which was at the same time Gestapo headquarters – where each had his own room. This consideration was also extended to my unimportant person.

'A single room in a hotel – that sounds extremely liberal, doesn't it? But, believe me, what they had in mind for us wasn't at all liberal. It was merely using a refined method when they didn't cram us "big-wigs" twenty to a freezing army hut, but lodged us in tolerably warm, separate hotel rooms. The pressure they were going to put on us to obtain the required information was to be more subtle than crude beating or physical torture. It was to be through the most complete isolation you could conceive. They did nothing to us – they just placed us in a complete vacuum, for as everyone knows, nothing on earth puts more pressure on the human spirit than a vacuum. Locking each of us up alone in a complete void, in a room hermetically sealed from the outside world, was to produce the pressure from within ourselves that would finally make us speak, without resort to beatings and freezing conditions.

'At first sight the room I was allotted didn't seem at all unpleasant. It had a door, a bed, a chair, a wash-basin, a barred window. But the door stayed shut day and night. There was no book, newspaper, sheet of paper or pencil on the table. The window looked out on to a blank wall. A total void surrounded me physically and spiritually. They had taken away every possession: my watch, so I couldn't tell the time; my pencil, so I couldn't write anything; my pocket knife, so I couldn't slash my wrists; even the smallest narcotic, like a cigarette, was denied me. I saw no human face except for the warder, who wasn't allowed to speak or answer any questions. I heard no human voice. Eyes, ears, none of one's senses received the slightest stimulus from morning to night, from night to morning. I was alone with myself and the four or five silent objects, table, bed, window, wash-basin, inescapably alone. I lived like a diver in his bell in the black ocean of that silence; and, at that, a diver who suspects his cable to the outside world has snapped and he will never be hauled back out of the soundless deep. There was nothing to do, nothing to hear, nothing to see. All around, and unbroken, was a void, a complete vacuum in time and space. I walked up and down, up and down, endlessly. But even thoughts, however trivial, need an anchorage, otherwise they begin to spin and chase themselves in mad circles. And they can't bear a vacuum either. You waited for something to happen, from morning to night, but nothing did. You were waiting, waiting, waiting and thinking, thinking, thinking until your head ached. Nothing happened. You were alone. Alone. Alone.

'I lived out of time and out of the world for a whole fortnight. Had war broken out I wouldn't have known. My world consisted only of table, door, bed, wash-basin, chair, window and wall, and I stared continuously at the same wallpaper on the same wall. Every line of its crenellated pattern registered as though engraved with steel on the innermost folds of my brain, I stared at it so often. Then at last the interrogation began. They summoned you suddenly, without your really knowing if it was day or night. They sent for you and you were taken along a corridor or two. You didn't know where you were going. You waited somewhere, and you didn't know where you were. Then abruptly you were standing in front of a table with a few people in uniform sitting at it. On the table was a pile of papers: documents whose contents you knew nothing about. Then the questions started, genuine and fake, straightforward and crafty, superficial questions and catch questions. And while you answered, the hands of strangers with evil intent leafed through the papers whose contents you didn't know, malicious hands wrote things in a record of the proceedings and you didn't know what they were writing. But what I found most frightening about this interrogation was that I couldn't guess or work out what the Gestapo already knew about the workings of my office, and what they wanted to get out of me. As I've told you already, at the last moment I had sent my housekeeper to my uncle with the really incriminating documents. But had he received them? Had he not? And how much had that clerk betrayed? How many letters had they intercepted? How much had they meanwhile wormed out of some naive cleric in one of the German monasteries with whom we dealt? And they went on with question after question. What securities had I bought for this monastery, what banks did I deal with, did I know Mr So-and-so, did I receive letters from Switzerland or Timbuctoo? And as I couldn't tell how much they knew already every answer was a terrible responsibility. If I gave something away that they didn't know I might perhaps be needlessly sending someone to his execution. If I told too many lies I might be putting myself at risk.

'But the interrogation was not the worst part. The worst was being returned afterwards to my vacuum, to the same room with the same table, the same bed, the same wash-basin, the same wallpaper. Scarcely was I alone again than I tried to recapitulate, to think what I ought to have said if I had been clever, and what I must say next time, to divert any suspicion that a careless remark of mine might perhaps have aroused. I reflected on, pondered over, examined and checked every word of my own testimony, everything I had told the chief interrogator. I repeated every question they had asked me, every answer I had given. I tried to assess what they had been able to put in their report, and yet I knew I couldn't ever possibly do that. But these thoughts, once conjured up in the empty room, wouldn't stop going round in my head, always in new or different combinations, and they seeped into my sleep. After every interrogation by the Gestapo my own thoughts took over, just as relentlessly, the torment of questioning and searching and harassment. Perhaps it was even more horrible in that every interrogation did end after an hour but this recapitulation never ended, thanks to the insidious torture of my isolation. And still I had only the table, the wash-basin, the bed, the wallpaper, the window. No diversion, no book, no newspaper, no other face, no pencil to write with, no matchstick to play with, nothing, nothing, nothing.

'It was then that I first became aware of how devilishly clever, how psychologically murderous the concept of this system of using hotel rooms was. In a concentration camp you might have had to cart stones, perhaps, until your hands bled and your feet froze in your shoes. You might have been crammed together with two dozen others, stinking and shivering. But you would have seen faces, had a field, a square, a tree, a star, something, anything, to look at; instead of here, where everything was never changing, always the same, always unbearably the same. There was nothing here that could release me from my thoughts, from my obsession with them, from my pathological reiteration of them. And that was exactly what they intended. I was to choke and choke on my thoughts until they asphyxiated me, and until I couldn't do other than spit them out, in the end to confess, to tell all, everything they wanted, to hand over, finally, information and men. Gradually I could feel how my nerves were beginning to break up under the terrible pressure of the vacuum; and recognising the danger, I braced myself to my nerve-ends, to try to find or invent some kind of diversion. To occupy myself I tried to recite and reconstruct everything I had ever learnt by heart: the national anthem, nursery rhymes, schoolboy jokes, clauses of the Code of Civil Law. Then I tried arithmetic, adding and dividing random figures, but I had no power of concentration in that void. The same thought kept on flickering in and out. What do they know? What did I say yesterday? What must I say next time?

'This really indescribable state of affairs lasted four months. Well – four months, that's easy to write: just one figure, one word! Easy to say, too: four months – two syllables. The lips can articulate a sound like that in no time at all: four months! But no one can describe, can measure, can visualise for someone else, for himself even, how long such a time seems within an infinity of time and space. You can't explain to anyone how this vacuum, this void, this nothingness around you corrodes and destroys; how you go mad having nothing but table, and bed, and wash-basin and wallpaper, and always the silence, always the same warder pushing the food into the room without looking at you, always the same thoughts going round in circles in the void. I became uneasily aware from small signs that my mind was falling into disarray. At first I had been quite clear in my own mind at the interrogations. I had answered calmly and with deliberation; the process of thinking of both sides – what I should say and what I should not – still functioned. Now I could only haltingly articulate the simplest sentences, for while I answered, I would be staring hypnotically at the recording pen as it ran across the paper, as though I wanted my own words to run after it. I sensed that my strength was failing. I sensed the moment was drawing ever nearer when, to save myself, I would tell them everything I knew and perhaps even more; when, to escape the asphyxiation of this vacuum, I would betray twelve men and their secrets without gaining anything for myself beyond a breathing space. One evening it had really gone that far. When the warder by chance brought me my food at that moment of asphyxiation, I suddenly screamed after him. "Take me for questioning! I'll tell them everything! I'll confess it all! I'll tell them where the papers are, where the money is! I'll tell them everything, everything!" Luckily he was too far away to hear me. Perhaps he didn't want to hear me.

'In my extreme moment of need, however, something unexpected happened. It held out salvation, at least salvation for a certain time. It was the end of July, a dark, gloomy, rainy day. I remember those details quite clearly because the rain was beating on the windows in the corridor along which I was taken for interrogation. I had to wait in the ante-room belonging to the chief interrogator. You always had to wait before every session. Making you wait was also part of the technique. First your nerves would be ripped apart by the summons, by suddenly being fetched from your cell in the middle of the night. Then when you'd adjusted to the idea of being questioned, had tensed your mind and will to resist, they made you wait, pointlessly, pointlessly waiting, one hour, two hours, three, before the interrogation, to exhaust your body and break down your spirit. And they made me wait particularly long that Thursday, 27th July. Two solid hours I stood waiting in the ante-room. I remember the exact date, too, for a particular reason, because in the ante-room, where – of course I wasn't allowed to sit down – for two hours my legs had to hold my body up, there was a calendar. I don't have to tell you how I stared at those figures, that word on the wall, "27 July", in my hunger for the printed or written word. My brain devoured them. And then I went on waiting and waiting and staring at the door to see when it would eventually be opened. I pondered, too, over what my interrogators would ask me this time. I knew even then that they would ask me something quite different from what I expected.

'But despite everything the ordeal of waiting and standing was nevertheless a blessing, a pleasure, because this room was after all different from my own. It was slightly bigger, had two windows instead of one, and had no bed or wash-basin, and didn't have the same crack in the window sill that I had looked at a million times. The door was painted a different colour, there was a different chair against the wall, and on the left a filing cabinet with documents, as well as a coat-stand with hangers, on which hung three or four wet uniform overcoats, my torturers' coats. So I had something new, something different to look at, at last something else for my staring eyes, and they pounced eagerly on every detail. I noticed every fold of those coats. I noticed, for example, a raindrop hanging on the wet collar of one of them, and however ridiculous it may sound to you, I waited with absurd excitement to see if that droplet would eventually run down the collar or would defy gravity and just stay there. Yes, I stared at that droplet and went on staring for several minutes, with bated breath, as though my life depended on it. Then, when it had eventually rolled down, I counted the buttons on the coats: eight on the first one, eight on the second, ten on the third; then I compared the insignia of rank. My hungry eyes took in, played with and seized on, all those silly, unimportant details with an avidity I can't describe.

'Suddenly my gaze was riveted on something. I had discovered that the side pocket of one of the coats was bulging slightly. I stepped nearer and believed I recognised the rectangular shape of the protrusion: what was in the swollen pocket — a book! My knees began to tremble: a BOOK! For four months I hadn't held a book in my hand, and already the mere idea of a book, in which you could see words following one another, lines, pages, a book in which you could read different, new, strange, entertaining thoughts, follow them up, absorb them into your brain, was both intoxicating and stupefying at the same time. My eyes were hypnotized by that little bump in the pocket made by the book. They bored into that insignificant spot as though they wanted to burn a hole in the coat. In the end I couldn't control my greed; instinctively I drew nearer. Already the thought of at least feeling a book through the material made my fingers tingle to their tips. Almost without realising it I was going closer and closer. Luckily the warder ignored my odd behaviour. Perhaps it seemed natural to him that after two hours standing up a man wanted to lean on the wall. At last I was standing right up against the coat and I deliberately put my hands behind my back so that I could touch the coat unobtrusively. I fingered the material and there, right enough, through it was something rectangular, something flexible, that rustled slightly—a book! A book! A thought struck me like a shot: steal the book! Perhaps you can do it, and you can hide it in your cell and then read, and read, and read, read again at last!

'Scarcely had the thought entered my head than it began to work like a strong poison; all at once there was a singing in my ears and my heart began to pound, my hands were ice-cold and unresponsive. But after the first moment of paralysis I moved slowly and slyly ever nearer the coat. All the time keeping an eye on the warder, and with my hands behind my back, I lifted the book from the bottom of the pocket higher and higher. And then, gripping it, I gave a slight and cautious tug and suddenly I had the small, slender volume in my hand. Now for the first time I was frightened by what I had done. But there was no going back. Still, where could I put it? Behind my back I pushed the volume inside my trousers, where the belt would hold it, and then gradually moved it round to my hip so that when I walked I could hold it there by keeping my hand military-fashion straight down the seam of my trouser leg. Now came the first test. I moved away from the coat-stand, one step, two steps, three. It worked. It was possible to keep the book in position while I walked, if I pressed my arm against my belt.

'Then came the interrogation. It required more attention from me than ever, for really while I was answering I was concentrating all my effort, not on what I was saying, but above all on holding on to the book without arousing suspicion. Luckily the hearing was a short one, and I carried the book safely to my room—I won't waste your time with all the details, but once the book slid dangerously down my trouser leg in the middle of a corridor, and I had to pretend to have a bad bout of coughing to be able to bend down and push it safely back up under my belt. But what a moment that was when I went back into my hell-hole, alone at last, yet not alone any more!

'I expect you think I seized upon the book straightaway, examined it and read it! Oh no! First I wanted to enjoy to the full the pleasure of anticipation, of having a book. I wanted the artificially protracted pleasure – which stimulated my senses wonderfully – of day-dreaming about what kind of book I most hoped this stolen one would be. Very closely printed, above all, containing many, many letters, many, many thin pages, so that there would be more in it to read. And then I wanted it to be a work that stretched me intellectually, not shallow, light reading; something I could learn, memorise, poetry, and best of all – what a bold dream – Goethe or Homer. But at last I couldn't contain my eagerness and curiosity any longer. Stretched out on the bed so that the warder couldn't catch me by surprise if he opened the door, I pulled the book out from under my belt, trembling.

'The first glance brought disappointment and indeed a kind of bitter anger. This book, captured at such awful risk, anticipated with such glowing expectation, was nothing more than a chess handbook, a collection of 150 championship games. If I hadn't been barred and bolted into the room I would have hurled the book through an open window in my initial rage. For what should I do, what could I begin to do, with this nonsense? As a schoolboy I had tried playing chess from time to time, like most other boys, out of boredom. But what was I to make of this theoretical stuff? You can't very well play chess without an opponent and certainly not without chessmen and a board. I thumbed through the pages sullenly, hoping even now to find something readable, an introduction, some instructions; but I found nothing except the bare squared-off diagrams of the individual championship games and beneath them what were to me the almost unintelligible symbols QR2-QR3, KKt1-KB3 and so on. It all seemed a kind of algebra to me, to which I could find no key. Only gradually did I puzzle out that the numbers stood for the ranks and the letters for the files, so that you could establish the position of each piece. That way the purely graphic diagram had a language of its own.

'I wondered if perhaps I could make some sort of chessboard in my cell and then try to play these games through. It seemed like a sign from heaven that my bed-cover happened by chance to have a coarse check weave. If I folded it correctly I could make sixty-four squares out of it. Next I tore the first page out and put the book under the mattress. Then I saved some of my bread and began to model little chessmen, King, Queen, and so on, out of it – of course they were comically inadequate. After endless attempts I was finally able to reconstruct the positions shown in the book on the chequered bed-cover. But when I tried to play the whole game through, my comical bread men, half of whom I had differentiated by darkening them with dust, failed completely. I repeatedly got into a muddle for the first few days. I had to begin this one game from the beginning five, ten, twenty times. But who on earth had so much spare and useless time as I, the slave of the void? Who could command as much boundless eagerness and patience? After six days I could play this game right through without a mistake. A week later and I didn't even need the bread men on the bed-cover to be able to visualise the positions in the book. And another week after that the bed-cover was unnecessary. The signs, which had at first been mere abstractions in the book – QR1, QR2, QB7, QB8 – were transformed automatically in my head into real objects, actual positions. The transition was indefatigably achieved: I had projected the chessboard and its pieces into my mind and, thanks to the basic rules, could survey the current position in the same way that a musician can hear all the instruments and their harmony just by looking at the full score. In another fortnight I could play every game in the book from memory without effort, or as the terminology has it, blindfold.

'I began for the first time to understand the immense benefit of my daring theft. For I had all at once an occupation – pointless, useless, if you like – but nevertheless an occupation, which negated the vacuum around me. With these 150 tournament games I possessed a wonderful weapon against the crushing monotony of space and time. To preserve intact the attractiveness of this new occupation, I divided my day exactly from now on: two games in the morning, two in the afternoon, and a quick recapitulation in the evening. In that way my day, hitherto as formless as unset jelly, took shape. I was occupied without exhausting myself, because chess possesses a wonderful quality: it concentrates one's mental energy on one narrow area, so that the brain isn't worn out by the most strenuous effort of thought. Its agility and vigour are actually improved.

'I played these championship games quite mechanically at first, but gradually they awoke in me artistic and pleasurable understanding. I learned to appreciate the finer points, the tricks and stratagems in attack and defence. I grasped the technique of thinking ahead, of combinations and counter-attacks, and soon came to recognise the personal mark of each chess champion in his individual play as unerringly as one recognises a poet from just a few of his lines. What began merely as a way of filling in time became a pleasure, and the great chess strategists such as Alekhine, Lasker, Bogoljuboff and Tartakower joined me in my isolation like valued friends.

'My silent cell was blessed every day with continuous variety; and, indeed, the regularity of the exercises restored the soundness of my thought processes, which had been disturbed earlier. I was aware that my brain felt refreshed and even newly sharpened by the regular discipline of thinking. It was noticeable at the interrogations that I was thinking more clearly and to the point. Without realising it the chessboard had improved my defence against false threats and concealed tricks. From that time on I gave them no openings through contradictory statements and even fancied that the Gestapo was beginning gradually to view me with a certain respect. Perhaps when they saw everyone else breaking down they asked themselves privately what the secret source of strength was that enabled me alone to put up such unshakeable resistance.

'This happy time during which I played the 150 games in that book systematically day by day, lasted about two-and-a-half to three months. Then unexpectedly I came to a standstill. Suddenly the void opened up again in front of me, because once I had played every single game twenty or thirty times the pleasure of novelty and surprise was lost, and their power, which had been so exciting and so stimulating until then, was spent. What point was there in playing games over and over again when I long since knew every move off by heart? No sooner had I made the opening move than the completion of the game sewed itself up quite automatically in my head. There was no longer any surprise, any tension, any problem. I needed a different book with different games in it to occupy me and produce essential exertion and diversion. As this was completely impossible there was only one way out of this peculiar maze: instead of the old games I had to invent new ones. I had to try to partner myself or, rather, to play against myself.

'Now I don't know how much thought you have given to the intellectual character of this royal game. But even the most superficial reflection should be enough to make it clear that, chess being a game of purely mental processes with no element of chance, it is absurd, logically speaking, to want to play against yourself. The attraction of chess lies, therefore, only in the fact that its strategy evolves in two different brains, that in this battle of the mind Black doesn't know what White's next move will be, and he is constantly trying to guess and to thwart it. While for his part White, countering him, strives to outdo Black and oppose his concealed intentions. Imagine Black and White being one and the same person, then, and you have the contradiction that the same brain knows something, and yet isn't supposed to know it, simultaneously; that when it is functioning as White's partner it can completely forget on command what a minute earlier it wanted to do and what it intended when it was Black's partner. Such two-way thinking really presupposes a complete split in one's consciousness, an arbitrary ability of the mind to switch on and off as though it were a mechanical machine. Wanting to play chess against oneself involves a real paradox, like jumping over one's own shadow.

'Well, to be brief, I was so desperate that I explored this absurd impossibility for months. But I had no choice apart from this nonsense, if I wasn't to go quite mad or lapse into a total mental decline. The frightful situation I was in forced me at least to try to split myself into this White ego and Black ego, if I was not to be overwhelmed by that awful void.'

Dr B. leaned back in his deckchair and closed his eyes for a minute. It was as though he was trying forcibly to suppress a disturbing recollection. Once again I noticed the nervous tic that he couldn't control at the corner of his mouth. Then he pulled himself up a little in his chair.

'So – I hope up to now I have explained everything to you reasonably clearly. But I don't know, unfortunately, if I can be as clear about what happened next, because this new occupation required such absolute harnessing of the brain that it made it impossible to exercise self-control at the same time. I have already told you that I think it is absurd to want to play chess against yourself; but even this absurdity might possibly have a minimal chance if you had a real chessboard in front of you. For the board, being real, allows after all a certain distance, a physical separation of territory. Faced with a real board and real pieces you can introduce pauses for reflection, you can actually stand first at one side of the table and then at the other and see the position from Black's viewpoint and from White's. But to conduct this battle, as I had to, against myself or, if you prefer, with myself, projecting it in space in my imagination, I had to hold firmly in my mind's eye the current positions on the sixty-four squares; and not just the existing configuration. I also had to calculate the possible further moves of both players, and that meant – I know how absurd it all sounds – imagining double or treble, no, six, eight, twelve-fold for both my selves, for Black and White, always four or five moves ahead.

'I apologise for expecting you to follow this madness. In this game in the abstract space of fantasy I had to calculate four or five moves ahead for White and the same for Black. So I had to work out with two brains – a White and a Black – all the combinations for deploying the pieces in given situations. But even this division of myself was not the most dangerous element of my abstruse experiment; instead, through having to invent my own independent games, there was the risk that I would no longer be standing on firm ground, but would fall into an abyss. Playing through championship games mechanically, as I had done in the earlier weeks, was after all nothing but an achievement of recall, a pure recapitulation of given material, and as such not more demanding than when I had learnt poetry by heart or had memorised sections of the Civil Code. It was a limited, disciplined activity and therefore an excellent mental exercise. The two games I played in the morning and the two in the afternoon represented a definite task I could complete without getting worked up about it. They took the place of normal employment, and furthermore, I had the book to fall back on if I went wrong in a game or forgot the next move. This task was healing and calming for my shattered nerves because I could be objective in re-playing someone else's game. It didn't matter to me who won, Black or White. It was either Alekhine or Bogoljuboff fighting for the champion's laurels and I personally — my mind, my heart — was involved only as an onlooker, as a connoisseur of the crises and highlights of each game. However, from the moment I began to play against myself I began involuntarily to compete. Each of my egos, my Black self and my White, had to vie with the other and strive ambitiously and impatiently to gain the upper hand and win. After every move as Black I was in a fever to know what my White ego would do. One side of me triumphed as the other made a mistake; and each was equally downcast over its own incompetence.

'All that sounds senseless; and indeed it was a form of artificial schizophrenia, of split personality in fact, which contributed to a dangerous state of inner turmoil inconceivable in a normal person in normal circumstances. But don't forget that I'd been dragged violently away from all normality. I was a prisoner, locked up although I was innocent, and for months suffering intense loneliness. I was a human being who wanted to vent my accumulated rage on something. And as I had nothing but this senseless game against myself, this is what my rage, my lust for revenge focussed on single-mindedly. Something within me wanted to win, but I had only this other ego to fight, so an almost manic state of agitation grew in me while I played.

'At first my thoughts had been calm and deliberate. There had been a pause between one game and the next, so I could recover from the effort involved. But gradually my over-wrought nerves wouldn't allow me to wait. My White ego had scarcely made a move before my Black ego feverishly pushed itself forward. Scarcely was one game finished before I was challenging myself to the next, because every time one of my chess egos was, of course, beaten by the other, it wanted a return game. I couldn't ever tell you, even approximately, how many games I played against myself in my cell as a result of this insatiable madness — a thousand, perhaps, possibly more. It was an obsession I couldn't resist. From morning to night I thought of nothing else except Bishops and pawns, Rooks and Kings, ranks and files, and Castling and Mate. My entire being and senses were concentrated on the chequered board. Playing for fun turned into enthusiasm, which became a compulsion, a mania, a frenetic madness that gradually invaded not only my waking hours but my sleep, too. I could think only in terms of chess, chess moves, chess problems. Sometimes I woke with sweat on my forehead and realised I must have been playing a game of chess in my sleep without knowing it. If I dreamed of people they immediately seemed to move like a Bishop, or a Rook, or jump back or forward like a Knight. Even when I was called for interrogation I couldn't concentrate on my responsibility any more. I had the feeling I must have expressed myself in a rather confused way at the last few hearings because my questioners sometimes looked at each other in surprise. But while they were asking questions and deliberating I was really waiting, just wretchedly eager to be returned to my cell, to go on with my game, my mad game: a new one, and then another and another.

'Every interruption disturbed me, even the quarter of an hour when the warder cleaned the cell; and the two minutes it took him to bring my food tortured my burning impatience. Sometimes the bowl with my supper in it was left untouched: I had forgotten to eat because of playing a game. The only physical thing I noticed was a frightful thirst. It must have been the fever of this continuous mental effort and playing. I drank the water jug dry in two goes and pestered the warder for more; and yet my tongue still felt dry in my mouth a moment later. Eventually my frenzy mounted during the game itself – and I did nothing else from morning to night – to such a pitch that I couldn't sit still any more. I walked up and down ceaselessly while I thought out the moves, going faster and faster, up and down, up and down; and the nearer I came to the winning move the more rapidly I walked. The driving desire to win, to dominate, to defeat myself, gradually became a kind of madness.

'I trembled with impatience, because the one chess ego in me was always too slow for the other. The one urged the other on. It will seem laughable to you, I'm sure, but I began to berate myself. "Faster, faster," I would shout, or "Move! Do get on with it!" if one of my egos didn't respond quickly enough to the other. I understand perfectly today, of course, that my behaviour was nothing less than a thoroughly pathological form of mental overstrain. The only name I can find for it isn't in the medical textbooks: chess-poisoning. In the end this monomaniac obsession began to attack my body as well as my mind. I lost weight, my sleep was disturbed and restless. When I woke up I had to make a special effort every time to force my leaden eyelids open. Sometimes I felt so weak and my hands were shaking so much I had difficulty in raising a tumbler to my lips. But as soon as I had begun a game I was in the grip of an overwhelming force. I rushed up and down with clenched fists, and sometimes I heard my own voice shouting hoarsely and angrily at myself through a red fog, or so it seemed, "Check!" or "Mate!"

'How this horrible, unspeakable situation came to a head I can't tell you myself. All I know about it is that I woke up one morning and the process was different from usual. It was as though I was outside my body. I was lying there comfortably relaxed. A warm, pleasant drowsiness of a kind I hadn't experienced for months caressed my eyelids, so warm and comforting that I couldn't bring myself, at first, to open my eyes. I lay awake for several minutes and savoured this languid torpor; just lying there with my senses agreeably numbed. Then I thought I heard voices behind me, living, human voices, using words — and you can't imagine my delight, for it was months, almost a year, since I had heard any speech except the hard, sharp and evil questions of the panel of interrogators. "You're dreaming," I told myself. "You're dreaming! Whatever you do, don't open your eyes! Let it go on, this dream. Otherwise you'll see that accursed cell again, the chair and the wash-basin and the wallpaper with that same eternal pattern. You're dreaming—go on dreaming!"

'But curiosity got the upper hand. I opened my eyes slowly and cautiously. It was a miracle! I was in a different room, wider, more spacious than my hotel cell. An unbarred window let light in freely and gave a view of trees, green trees stirring in the wind, instead of my blank wall. The walls of the room shone white and smooth, the ceiling was white and high above me—surely, I was lying in a new, different bed, and indeed, it wasn't a dream, there really were soft human voices whispering behind me. Without realising it I must have moved noticeably, I was so surprised, for at once I heard an approaching step behind me. A woman came softly over. A woman with a white cap on her head, a nurse, a nun. I felt a thrill of delight: I hadn't seen a woman for a year. I stared at this charming apparition, and it must have been a wild, ecstatic look, because she said soothingly but firmly, "Quiet! Keep still!" But I hung only on her voice—was this really a human being who spoke to me? Was there really still someone on earth who didn't question and torment me? And wasn't it—inconceivable miracle—the gentle, warm, almost tender voice of a woman? Greedily I stared at her mouth, for this year of hell had made it seem unlikely that one person could speak to another in a kindly way. She was smiling at me—yes, smiling. There were still people who could smile sympathetically. Then she put her finger to her lips as a warning, and went gently away. But I couldn't obey her order. I hadn't seen enough yet of this miracle. I struggled to sit up in bed to gaze after this apparition of a human being who was kind. But as I went to support myself on the edge of the bed I couldn't do it. Where my right hand had formerly been, with fingers and wrist, I discovered something strange: a thick, large, white lump, apparently an all-embracing bandage. I stared at this white, thick, strange object at first without understanding it. Then slowly it began to dawn on me where I was, and I started to consider what could have happened to me. They must have injured me, or I must have damaged my hand myself. I was in hospital.

'The doctor, a friendly, elderly man, came at midday. He knew my family and made such a deferential reference to my uncle, the physician to the Imperial household, that I felt at once he was on my side. In the course of conversation he asked me all sorts of questions, but there was one which particularly astonished me: was I a mathematician or a chemist? I said no, I wasn't. "Odd," he murmured. "In your fever you kept crying out such strange formulae—QB3, QB4. We didn't know what to make of it." I asked him what had happened to me. He smiled wrily. "Nothing serious. An acute nervous upset."

'After he had looked round cautiously, he went on in a low voice, "Quite understandable, too. It started on March 13th, didn't it?"

'I nodded.

"It's no wonder with that way of doing things," he murmured. "You aren't the first. But don't worry."

'I knew from the soothing way he whispered this to me and from his reassuring expression that I was safe with him.

'Two days later the kindly doctor explained to me quite frankly what had happened. The warder had heard me shouting out in my cell and thought at first someone was in there with me and I was fighting him. He had scarcely appeared at the door before I had set on him and screamed wildly at him, such things as, "Will you ever move then, you scoundrel, you coward!" I had tried to grab him by the throat and had attacked him so furiously he had to call for help. As they were dragging me out to be medically examined, I had suddenly broken loose in my mad frenzy, thrown myself at the corridor window, broken the glass and cut my hand. You can still see the deep scar here. The first night in hospital I had had a kind of brain fever, but now the doctor found my mental faculties quite healthy. "Of course," he said in an undertone, "I had better not report that to the authorities, otherwise they'll take you back there in the end. Leave it to me. I'll do my best."

'I don't know what that helpful doctor told my torturers about me. Anyway he achieved his aim: my release. It's possible he declared me insane; or perhaps in the interval I had ceased to be important to the Gestapo, for Hitler had by then occupied Bohemia and that settled the outcome in Austria as far as he was concerned. So I had only to sign an undertaking to leave our homeland within a fortnight; and those two weeks were taken up to such an extent with all the hundred and one formalities the would-be citizen of the world needs today for a journey abroad – military papers, police, tax, passport, visa, health certificate – that I had no time to dwell on the past. Apparently there is some mysterious regulating capacity in the brain which automatically cuts out anything that can be disturbing or dangerous to the mind. Whenever I wanted to think back about my imprisonment it was as though a light switched off in my brain. Only now, here on this ship weeks later, have I found the courage to reflect on what happened to me.

'So now you will understand my impertinent and apparently puzzling behaviour with your friends. It was quite by chance that I was strolling through the smoking-room and saw your friends at the chessboard. Instinctively my feet felt rooted to the spot, I was so surprised and frightened. I had completely forgotten that you can play chess with a real board and real chessmen; that for this game two quite different men sit physically opposite each other. It took me a couple of minutes to remember that what those players were doing was basically the same as I had tried to do, playing against myself while I was helpless all those months. The code I had used in my ferocious exercises had been nothing more than a substitute and a symbol for these solid figures. I was astonished that the movement of figures on the board was the same as the imaginary moves I had made in my head. It must be similar to how an astronomer feels when he has used some complicated method to calculate on paper the position of a new planet and then really sees it in the sky as a white, distinct, substantial object. I stared at the board as though held there by a magnet. I saw my diagrams there – Knight, Rook, King, Queen, and pawns, as tangible figures carved out of wood. To grasp the state of play I had first instinctively to change my abstract world of symbols into the moving pieces. Gradually I was overcome with curiosity to watch a real game like this one between two opponents. It was then that I so embarrassingly forgot all good manners and interfered in your game. But that bad move your friend was going to make cut me to the quick. It was pure instinct, an impulsive movement that made me hold him back, as you grab a child who is leaning over a parapet. It was only later I realised just how rude my impetuous intervention had been.'

I hastened to assure Dr B. how very pleased we all were to have made his acquaintance through this occurrence and that I would be doubly interested, after everything he had told me, in seeing him at our improvised tournament next day. Dr B. shifted uneasily.

'No, really, don't expect too much. It will just be a test for me ... a test to see if ... if I can really play an ordinary game of chess, on a real board with actual chessmen and a live opponent ... for I'm now more doubtful than ever whether those hundreds or possibly thousands of games I played were in fact played by the rules and weren't just a form of dream-chess, fever-chess ... a hallucinatory game in which, as always in dreams, intermediate steps were left out. I hope you don't seriously expect me to presume I can stand up to a grand master, and the best in the world at that. What interests and motivates me is purely retrospective curiosity, to establish whether it was really chess I played in my cell or if it was madness – if I was right on the brink of the slippery slope or had already gone down it – that's all, there's no other reason.'

At that moment the gong sounded, calling us to dinner. We must have been talking for two hours or so, for Dr B. had told me everything in much greater detail than I have put down here. I thanked him warmly and said goodbye. But I hadn't gone the length of the deck before he came after me and said nervously and somewhat haltingly:

'One more thing. Would you please tell your friends in advance, so that I don't appear to be uncivil later on, that I'll play one game only … it has to be the closing line beneath an old account – a final settlement, not a new beginning. I mustn't fall into that passionate obsession with the game a second time. It fills me with horror to recall it. And besides – besides, the doctor warned me, expressly: the victim of any mania is always in danger. With chess-poisoning – even if you are cured – it's better not to go near a chessboard. So, you understand – just this one trial game for my own sake – and no more.'

The next day we gathered in the smoking-room punctually at the agreed time of three o'clock. Our circle had increased by two more lovers of the royal game, two ship's officers who had sought leave from their duties to watch the match. Even Czentovic didn't keep us waiting as he had done the day before. After the necessary choice of colours the memorable game between this *homo obscurissimus* and the famous world champion began. I regret it was played before such thoroughly incompetent spectators as we were, and that its course is as lost to the annals of chess as Beethoven's piano impromptus are to music. True, we tried the next afternoon between us to reconstruct the game from memory, but without success. Quite possibly we had all concentrated too much on the two players during the game instead of taking note of its progress. For in the course of the game the intellectual contrast between the two opponents became more and more physically apparent in their manner. Czentovic, the man of routine, remained as immovably solid as a rock the whole time, his eyes fixed unwaveringly on the board. Thinking seemed almost to cause him actual physical effort, as though he had to engage all his senses with the utmost concentration. Dr B., on the other hand, was completely relaxed and unconstrained. Like the true dilettante in the best sense of the word, who plays for the pure joy — the *diletto* — of playing, he was physically relaxed and chatted to us during the early pauses, explaining the moves. He lit a cigarette with a steady hand and when it was his move looked at the board only for a minute. Each time it seemed as though he had expected the move his opponent made.

The routine opening moves were made quite quickly. It was only at about the seventh or eighth move that a definite plan seemed to emerge. Czentovic was taking longer over his pauses for thought; from that we sensed the real battle for domination had begun. But to tell you the truth the gradual unfolding of the positional play was something of a disappointment for us non-specialists — as in every true tournament game. For the more the pieces wove in and out in a strange design the more impenetrable the actual position seemed to us. We couldn't perceive what either opponent had in mind or which of the two really had the upper hand. We noticed only that individual pieces were being moved like levers to breach the enemy front, but we were unable to grasp the strategic objective behind these manoeuvres. For with these two experienced players every move was combined in advance with other projected moves.

We were gradually overtaken by mild fatigue, principally because of Czentovic's interminable pauses for reflection. These began visibly to annoy our friend as well. I noticed uneasily how the longer the game went on the more restlessly he began to fidget about on his chair. Soon he was so tense he began to light one cigarette after another. Then he grabbed a pencil to make a note of something. Then he ordered mineral water, which he gulped down quickly, one glass after another. It was obvious that he could plan his moves a hundred times faster than Czentovic. Every time the latter, after endless reflection, decided to move a piece forward with his heavy hand, our friend smiled like someone who had seen something he had long expected, and made his counter-move immediately. With his agile mind he must have worked out in advance all the possibilities open to his opponent. The longer Czentovic delayed his decision the more Dr B.'s impatience grew, and as he waited his lips were pressed together in an angry and almost hostile line. But Czentovic didn't allow himself to be hurried. He studied the board stubbornly and silently and his pauses became longer the more the field was emptied of chessmen. By the forty-second move, after two and three-quarter hours had gone by, we were all sitting wearily round the tournament table, almost indifferent to it. One of the ship's officers had already gone, the other had taken out a book to read and looked up for a moment only when a move was made. But then suddenly the unexpected happened, following a move by Czentovic. As soon as Dr B. saw Czentovic touch his Knight to move it forward he gathered himself together like a cat about to pounce. His whole body began to tremble, and scarcely had Czentovic moved his Knight than Dr B. pushed his Queen forward with a flourish, and said loudly and triumphantly: 'There! That settles it!' He leaned back, folded his arms on his chest and looked challengingly at Czentovic. His eyes were suddenly aglow with a burning light.

Instinctively we bent over the board to try to understand this move that had been proclaimed so triumphantly. At first sight no direct threat was visible. Our friend's exclamation must therefore have referred to a development we, as amateurs who couldn't think far ahead, were unable to calculate as yet. Czentovic was the only one among us who hadn't stirred when the challenging statement was made. He sat quite unmoved as though he had completely missed the insulting 'That settles it!' Nothing happened. You could hear us all involuntarily draw in our breath and also the ticking of the clock that had been placed on the table to measure the time for each move. Three minutes, seven, eight passed — Czentovic didn't stir, but it seemed to me that his thick nostrils were flaring as a result of inner tension.

Our friend found this silent waiting just as unbearable as we did. He stood up suddenly in one movement, and began to pace up and down the smoking-room. At first he walked slowly, but then faster and faster. Everyone looked at him in surprise but none as uneasily as I did. For it struck me that in spite of the vigour of the way he paced up and down his steps covered only a precisely measured area: it was as though in the middle of this spacious room he ran up against an invisible cupboard which forced him to turn back every time. And I recognised with a shudder that without his being aware of it this reproduced the limits of the area of his former cell. He must have paced rapidly up and down like a caged animal in exactly this way during the months of his incarceration, with his hands clenched and his shoulders hunched. He must have rushed up and down exactly like this a thousand times, with the glowing light of madness in his staring expression.

His thought processes seemed completely unimpaired, however, for occasionally he would turn to the table impatiently to see if Czentovic had made a decision yet. But nine minutes, ten minutes went by. Then what no one had expected finally happened. Czentovic slowly lifted his heavy hand, which until then had rested motionless on the table. Intently we all hung on his decision. But Czentovic didn't move a piece; with a sweep of the back of his hand he pushed all the pieces slowly off the board. It took us a moment to grasp the situation: Czentovic had conceded the match. He had given in to avoid our seeing him being checkmated. The improbable had happened. The world champion, winner of countless tournaments had struck his colours in the face of an unknown player — and one who hadn't touched a chessboard for twenty or twenty-five years. Our friend — anonymous, unknown — had beaten the strongest chess player on earth in open battle!

Without thinking, one after another of us jumped up, we were so excited. We all felt we had to say or do something to release our pent-up joy. The only one who remained calmly unmoved was Czentovic. After a measured interval he raised his head and looked stonily at our friend.

'Another game?' he asked.

'Of course,' Dr B. answered with an eagerness that made me apprehensive. He sat down again before I could remind him of his intention of being satisfied with one game only, and began to set up the pieces with desperate haste. He assembled them with such passionate intensity that twice a pawn slipped to the floor through his shaking fingers. My earlier embarrassed unease in the face of his abnormal agitation grew to something approaching alarm. This hitherto calm, quiet man was now visibly over-excited. The nervous tic at the corner of his mouth was more frequent, and his body was quivering as though racked with fever.

'No!' I whispered to him softly. 'Not now! That's enough for one day! It's too much of a strain for you.'

'Strain! Ha!' He laughed loudly and with contempt. 'I could have played seventeen games in the time instead of dawdling like that. The only strain I have, playing at that speed, is to stop myself falling asleep! Well! Go on, begin!'

He addressed these last remarks to Czentovic in a vehement, almost churlish, tone. Czentovic looked at him calmly and evenly but his stony expression had something of the clenched fist in it. All at once a new element had sprung up between the two players: a dangerous tension, a violent hatred. They were no longer two opponents wanting to test each other's playing skill, but two enemies who had sworn to annihilate each other. Czentovic hesitated a long time before he made the first move, and I had a definite feeling his delay was deliberate. Clearly this trained tactician had already noted that he wearied and annoyed his opponent by playing slowly. So he sat for at least four minutes before he made the most normal and simplest of all openings, pushing the King's pawn the customary two squares forward. Our friend immediately followed by advancing his own King's pawn, but again Czentovic created an almost unbearably long pause. It was like seeing a fierce flash of lightning and waiting with bated breath for the thunder — and then the thunder not happening. Czentovic didn't move. He thought silently and slowly, and I was increasingly certain his slowness was malicious. However, he gave me ample time to observe Dr B., who had just gulped down a third glass of water. I recalled involuntarily how he had told me about the feverish thirst he had had in his cell. He was showing clearly all the symptoms of abnormal excitement. I saw the perspiration on his forehead, and the scar on his hand growing redder and standing out more distinctly than it had done before. But he was still self-controlled. It was not until the fourth move, when Czentovic again went on thinking interminably, that he could no longer restrain himself.

46

'For heaven's sake make a move, will you!'

Czentovic looked up coldly. 'As I recall, we agreed ten minutes per move. I don't play to a shorter limit on principle.'

Dr B. bit his lip. I noticed how he was moving his foot up and down under the table more and more restlessly and I became uncontrollably more nervous myself. I had an awful premonition that some kind of madness was working itself up inside him. In fact there was a further incident at the eighth move. Dr B. had been growing increasingly impatient while he waited and couldn't contain his tension any further. He shifted about on his chair and started involuntarily to drum on the table with his fingers. Once again Czentovic lifted his heavy, peasant's head.

'Would you mind not drumming, please? It disturbs me. I can't play if you do that.'

'Ha!' Dr B. gave a curt laugh. 'That's obvious.'

Czentovic went red in the face. 'What do you mean by that?' His question was sharp and angry.

Dr B. gave another tight and malicious laugh. 'Nothing. Only that you are obviously feeling the strain.'

Czentovic was silent and lowered his head again.

It was seven minutes before he made his next move, and the game dragged on at this funereal pace. Czentovic became more like a block of stone than ever, in the end always taking the maximum of agreed time for thought before deciding on a move. And from one interval to the next our friend's behaviour grew stranger. It seemed as though he was no longer interested in the game but was occupied with something quite different. He stopped walking up and down and remained motionless on his chair. He had a fixed and almost crazed expression as he stared into space, ceaselessly muttering unintelligible words to himself. Either he was lost in endless combinations or – as I suspected deep down – he was working through completely different games. For whenever Czentovic eventually moved Dr B. had to be brought back from his private reverie. Then he always needed a whole minute to find out exactly how the game stood. The suspicion was borne in on me more and more that he had long since quite forgotten Czentovic and the rest of us in this chilling form of madness, which could suddenly explode in violence of some kind. And indeed the crisis came at the nineteenth move. Czentovic had scarcely made his move before Dr B. suddenly, without looking at the board properly, pushed his Bishop forward three squares and shouted out so loudly that we all jumped.

'Check! The King's in check!'

We looked at the board at once in expectation of a particularly significant move. But after a minute what happened was not what any of us had anticipated. Czentovic raised his head very, very slowly towards our circle — something he hadn't done before — and looked from one man to the next. He seemed to be relishing something immensely, because slowly a satisfied and clearly sarcastic smile began to play about his lips. Only after he had savoured to the full the triumph that we still didn't understand, did he turn with pretended courtesy to our group.

'I'm sorry — but I see no check. Do any of you gentlemen see a check against my King, by any chance?'

We looked at the board and then uneasily at Dr B. The square Czentovic's King occupied was in fact — a child could see it — fully protected from the Bishop by a pawn, so the King couldn't possibly be in check. We were uneasy. Had our friend in his excitement mistakenly pushed a piece one square too far or too short? Roused by our silence Dr B. now gazed at the board and began to stammer and protest.

'But the King should be on KB7 … its position is wrong, quite wrong. You've moved incorrectly! Everything is quite wrong on this board … the pawn should be on KKt5, not on KKt4. That is a completely different game … That's …'

He stopped abruptly. I had grabbed him fiercely by the arm, or rather had gripped his arm so tightly that even in his fevered and confused state he must have felt my hold on him. He turned round and stared at me like a sleep-walker.

'What do you want?'

All I said was 'Remember!' and lightly drew my finger at the same time over the scar on his hand. Involuntarily he followed my movement, his eyes staring glassily at the inflamed line. Then he began to shiver suddenly and his whole body shook.

'For God's sake,' he whispered, his lips pale. 'Have I said or done anything untoward? Has it really happened again?'

'No,' I whispered gently. 'But you must stop playing at once.

It's high time you did. Remember what the doctor told you!'

Dr B. stood up quickly. 'Please excuse me for my stupid mistake,' he said in his earlier polite voice. He bowed to Czentovic. 'What I said was of course complete nonsense. Clearly, it's your game.' Then he turned to us. 'I must also ask you to forgive me. But I did warn you at the outset not to expect too much. Excuse me for making a fool of myself — that's the last time I shall try my hand at chess.' He bowed and left us, in the same modest and mysterious way as he had first appeared. I alone knew why this man would never again touch a chessboard. The others remained slightly bewildered. They had a vague feeling they had only just escaped something unpleasant and dangerous. 'Damned fool!' McConnor growled with disappointment. The last person to stand up was Czentovic. He glanced at the half-finished game.

'Pity,' he said generously. 'The attack was quite well conceived. That gentleman is really exceptionally able. For an amateur.'

AMOK

I N MARCH 1912, when a large ocean-going liner was unloading at Naples, a strange accident happened. It was
widely reported in the papers but in a very exaggerated and
highly coloured way. Although I was a passenger on the
Oceania I saw no more of the incident than the other passengers, because it occurred after dark while the ship was taking
on coal and discharging cargo, and we had all gone ashore to
escape the noise and pass the time in cafés or at the theatre.
Nevertheless, it is my personal conviction that several suspicions I had then but kept to myself were the true explanation of
the disturbing scene; and I think the passage of time permits
me now to make use of the confidential conversation which
directly preceded that strange episode.

When I tried to buy a ticket on the *Oceania* in the shipping
agent's office in Calcutta for the journey back to Europe, the
clerk shrugged his shoulders apologetically. He didn't know if
it would be possible to obtain a cabin for me. The ship was
already fully booked from Australia, just before the rainy
season started. He would have to wait for confirmation by
wire from Singapore. Next day he told me cheerfully that he
had a reservation for me, though of course it was not a particularly comfortable cabin, below deck and amidships. I was
already impatient to go home, so I didn't really hesitate and
made the booking.

The clerk was right. The ship was overcrowded and the cabin a bad one, a small, cramped, rectangular cubby-hole near the engine-room, lit only by the dim light of the circular porthole. The stale, fetid air reeked of oil and decay. Not for a moment could you do without the electric fan which circled over your forehead like a crazy, fluttering bat whirring round. From below the engines clattered and groaned like a coalman puffing and blowing his way interminably up the same flight of stairs. From above came the incessant shuffling back and forward of feet on the promenade deck. So as soon as I had stowed my luggage in that musty grey-ribbed hole I fled back on deck, and coming out of the depths of the ship, drank in the soft, southerly wind that wafted the gum-tree scents of land over the waves.

But the promenade deck, too, was overcrowded and full of commotion. People flitted and flapped about, full of the pent-up energy that enforced idleness causes, talking as they walked up and down. The twittering skittishness of the women, the non-stop wandering in circles round the restricted deck area, where the garrulous and seething mass negotiated its way past the deckchairs only unfailingly to bunch up again, somehow offended me. I had seen a new world, absorbed a kaleidoscope of pictures in a flash. Now I wanted to reflect, to separate these confused first impressions and put them in order, reproducing them and marshalling them. But here on this overcrowded boulevard there was not a minute's peace and quiet. If I read a book the lines merged under the moving shadows of this passing crowd of conversationalists. It was impossible to be alone on this unshaded, undulating, ship's thoroughfare.

For three whole days I tried my best; I resigned myself to watching the passengers and looking at the sea. But the sea was always the same, blue and empty; only at sunset was it suddenly splashed violently with colours. As for the people, after seventy-two hours I knew them inside out. Every face was familiar to the point of boredom. The shrill laughter of the women no longer annoyed me, neither did the blustering arguments of two neighbouring Dutch officers. Flight was the only option: but the cabin was hot and steamy, and in the saloon some English girls played jerky waltzes interminably and very badly on the piano. In the end I decided to reverse the order of time and dived into my cabin in the late afternoon, after I had doped myself with a few beers, determined to sleep through dinner and the evening dance.

When I awoke it was quite dark and stuffy in the little coffin of a cabin. I had switched off the electric fan, so the sticky, wet air clung to my perspiring forehead. I felt disorientated; it took several minutes for me to realise where I was and what time it was. It must at all events have been after midnight, because I couldn't hear any music or any footsteps overhead. Only the engines, the breathing core of the leviathan, wheezily pushed the creaking body of the ship through the darkness.

I fumbled my way up to the deck. It was empty. And as I lifted my gaze over the steaming solid block of the funnel and the ghostly, gleaming spars, a magical light met my eyes. The heavens were shining. The sky was dark against the stars which were embroidered in white all over it; and yet the sky itself shone. It was as though a velvet curtain of overwhelming light was hanging there, as though the sparkling stars were mere holes and chinks through which that indescribable light shone forth. Never had I seen the sky as it was on that night, so shining, so steel-blue hard, yet scintillating, shimmering, glittering, coruscating with light, which emanated from the waxing moon and the stars and which nevertheless seemed to blaze out from a secret inner source. White paintwork, the whole outline of the ship, glistened in the moonlight in sharp contrast to the velvet-dark sea; the cables, the spars, all the ledges, all the contours were dissolved in this flood of light. The lights on the masts shone as though they hung in empty space, and above them the round lamp of the look-out seemed to hang like an earthly yellow star between the shining rays of the heavens.

Directly overhead was the Southern Cross, that magic constellation, with shimmering diamond nails hammered into the darkness, apparently suspended in the air while only the ship produced movement, the gently repeated up and down motion of a giant swimmer breasting the water as he takes in breath and forges through the dark waves. I stood and looked upwards. It was as though I was in a bath into which warm water poured from above, except that this was light which, white and tepid, washed over my hands, poured mildly over my head and shoulders, and seemed somehow to penetrate right inside me, for all my inner gloom was suddenly cleansed away. I breathed freely, clean, and suddenly happy. I felt the air on my lips as though it were a pure liquid; this soft, fermented, slightly tipsy-making air in which there was the fragrance of fruit, the aroma of distant islands. Now for the very first time since I walked these decks I was seized with an intense longing to dream, and with another, voluptuous feeling, wanting to yield myself physically like a woman to this soft embrace. I wanted to lie down and gaze up at the white hieroglyphics. But the sun-beds and deckchairs had been stacked away and there was nowhere on this empty promenade deck where you could drift comfortably off into dreams.

So I stumbled my way slowly towards the ship's fore-deck, quite dazzled by the light, which seemed to press ever more strongly round me. Soon this chalk-white, glaring and searing starlight seemed almost to hurt, whereas I had wanted to bury myself somewhere in the shadows, stretched out on some matting, feeling the light not directly on me so much as flowing over me, dappling over objects, as one sees a landscape from a darkened room. Blundering over ropes and past the iron cap-stans I came at last to the bows, where I looked down and watched how the bow bit into the blackness and the foaming, molten moonlight sprayed away on either side of the cutting edge. With a regular movement the plough rose and fell in the black-turning furrow, and I felt all the pain of the vanquished element, all the joy of the earthly power in this sparkling combat. And in observing all this I lost track of time. Did I stand there for an hour, or only for a few minutes? The ship was an enormous cradle that rocked me up and down and beyond time. I felt only the blissful sensation of sleepiness overtaking me. I wanted to sleep, to dream, but not away from this magic, not back in my enclosed box. I found that without realising it, I was standing on a coil of rope. I sat down on it. My eyes were closed and yet they did not fully bring me darkness, because the silver light still streamed across them and over me. I felt the water gently rustling below me; above me, the inaudible white torrent of this world. And gradually these noises overwhelmed me. I was not myself. I no longer knew if the breathing I heard was my own or was the noise of the ship's distantly beating heart. I was caught up completely in the restless sounds of the midnight world.

A light, dry cough near by startled me. I came sharply out of my almost intoxicated reverie. My eyes, blinded by the white light on the long-closed lids, were dazzled. Directly opposite me in the shadow of the ship's side something glinted. It seemed to be the reflection of a pair of spectacles, and now I could see the deeper, rounder glow of a pipe. When I had sat down, looking only down at the foaming bow and up at the Southern Cross, I had evidently not noticed this neighbour, who must have been sitting here quite still the whole time. Instinctively, still not fully having my wits about me, I said in German, 'I beg your pardon!' 'Oh, think nothing of it,' the voice answered in the same language out of the darkness.

I can't explain how strange and eerie it was to be sitting silently in the dark, really close to someone you couldn't see. Instinctively I had the feeling that this man was staring at me, exactly as I was staring at him. But the light above us was so strong, as it flowed over us shimmering white, that neither of us could see more than the outline in the shadows. But I thought I could hear his breathing and the sucking noise of his pipe.

The silence was unbearable. I would really have liked to have got up and gone, but that seemed too brusque, too precipitate. Out of embarrassment I took out a cigarette. The match flared up; for a second, light flickered over a limited area. Behind the spectacles I saw an unfamiliar face that I had not seen before on board, not at any meal or on any deck; and it seemed as though the sudden flame hurt one's eyes, or was it an hallucination? His face seemed horribly distorted, morose and hobgoblin-like. But before I had taken in the details clearly, darkness returned to swallow up the fleetingly illuminated features, and I could see only the outline of a form, merging darkly into the blackness, and occasionally the circular red glow of the pipe in empty space. Neither of us spoke and the silence was oppressive, heavy like the tropical air. At last I could bear it no longer. I stood up and said politely, 'Good night.'

'Good night,' a husky, austere, rasping voice answered out

of the darkness. I stumbled laboriously forward through the ship's tackle and past the mast. I heard a step behind me, hurried and uncertain. It was my erstwhile neighbour. Instinctively I stopped. He didn't come right up to me. Through the darkness I could feel there was a hint of anxiety and hesitation in his step.

'Excuse me,' he then said quickly, 'if I ask you a favour. I ... I ... ' he stuttered and was too embarrassed to go on immediately. 'I ... I have private – quite private reasons for keeping to myself out here ... a bereavement ... I am avoiding company on board. I don't mean to ... no, no ... I would only like to ask ... I would be much obliged if you wouldn't tell anyone on board that you have seen me here. There are ... that is to say, private reasons which prevent me from mixing with people at this time ... yes ... well ... it would distress me if you were to mention that someone was here at night ... but I ...' He was lost for words again. I quickly reassured him by promising most fervently to do as he wanted. We shook hands. Then I returned to my cabin and fell into a torpor of remarkably disturbed sleep, full of muddled images.

I kept my promise and told no one on board of my strange encounter, although I was sorely tempted. For on a sea voyage the most trifling incident, a sail on the horizon, a dolphin leaping out of the water, a newly discovered flirtation, was a momentary pleasure. Because of that I was plagued with curiosity to know more about this unusual passenger. I searched through the passenger list for a name which might fit him; I studied people to see if they could be related to him; all day long I was gripped with tense impatience, and to be truthful I was waiting only for the evening – would I meet him again? Psychological mysteries have a downright unsettling power over me. It stirs my blood to ferret out inter-relating facts, and unusual people can, through their mere presence, kindle in me a passion for detective work which is not much short of the desire a man feels to possess a woman. The day seemed long and crumbled emptily between my fingers. I went to bed early: I knew I would wake up about midnight, that this puzzle would wake me.

And so it was. I awoke at about the same time as on the

previous night. The two hands on the luminous dial of my watch were together in a shining line. Hurriedly I left the sultry cabin for the even more sultry night.

The stars shone as they had done the night before and cast a diffused light over the quivering ship; the Southern Cross blazed high overhead. Everything was the same as it had been yesterday – in the tropics days and nights are more closely akin than in our parts of the world – only within myself the gentle, flowing, dreamy sense of being cradled was not as it had been yesterday. Something else drew me, threw me into disarray, and I knew where I was being drawn: to the black coil on the fore-deck, to see if he was sitting there again, motionless, the man of mystery. Above, the ship's bell sounded. This jerked me forward. Step by step, against my will and yet attracted, I yielded. I was not quite at the ship's stem when, suddenly, something glowed like a red eye – the pipe. So he was there.

Instinctively I shrank back and stood still. Another moment and I would have gone. Something stirred down there in the darkness, it stood up, took two steps, and then I heard his voice right beside me, polite and depressed.

'Excuse me,' he said. 'You obviously want your place back, and I had the feeling you turned away when you saw me. Please do sit down. I'm just going.'

I hastened to tell him, for my part, that he should stay, that I had stepped back only so as not to disturb him.

'You aren't disturbing me,' he said with a degree of bitterness. 'On the contrary, I am pleased not to be alone for once. I haven't spoken a word to anyone for ten days ... really not for years ... and it is so difficult, perhaps precisely because one is already choked by it, to keep everything to oneself. I can't sit in my cabin any more, in that ... that coffin ... not any more, I can't ... and I can't bear people any more, because they laugh all day ... I can't stand laughter now. I can hear it even in my cabin and I have to cover my ears. Of course, they really don't know that ... well, they really just don't know, and after all, what do strangers care ...'

He hesitated again. And then said quite suddenly and hurriedly: 'But I don't want to bother you – forgive me for being so talkative.'

He bowed and would have left. But I quickly contradicted

him. 'You aren't bothering me in the least. I, too, would be glad of a quiet chat. Would you like a cigarette?'

He took one. I lit a match. Once again his face was snatched flickeringly out of the dark side of the ship, but now it was fully turned towards me. His eyes behind his glasses searched my face avidly and with a deranged intensity. A shudder went through me. I sensed that this man wanted to speak, had to speak. And I knew that I had to keep silent if I was to help him.

We sat down again. He had a second deckchair there, which he offered me. Our cigarettes glowed, and I could see by the way the burning end of his quivered in the darkness that his hand was shaking. But I remained silent and so did he. Then in a soft voice he asked suddenly: 'Are you very tired?'

'No, not in the least.'

The voice out of the darkness wavered again. 'I would very much like to ask you something ... that is, I would like to tell you something. I know, I know very well, how absurd it is, to turn to the first person I meet, but ... I'm ... I'm at the end of my tether ... I'm at a point where I absolutely must talk to someone ... otherwise I shall go under. You will certainly understand if I ... yes, if I just tell you about it ... I know you won't be able to help me ... but I am somehow ill from keeping silent ... and other people always find a sick person's behaviour ridiculous ...'

I interrupted him and begged him not to distress himself in this way. He had only to tell me ... naturally I couldn't promise him anything, but one had a duty to show one was willing to help. If a man saw another in distress, then naturally it was his duty to help ...

'Duty ... to show one is willing ... duty to try ... You think, you too, that one has a duty ... a duty to show one is willing.'

He repeated the phrase three times. I quailed before this blunt, morose way of going over things. Was this man mad? Was he drunk?

But as though I had spoken the conjecture out loud, he suddenly said in a completely different tone: 'You will think I am mad or drunk, perhaps. No, I'm not — not yet. Only the words you spoke struck me as so remarkable ... so remarkable, because that is precisely what is troubling me, that is to say, whether one has a duty ... a duty ... '

57

He began to stutter again. Then he broke off abruptly and all at once started afresh.

'I am, in fact, a doctor. And we often have such cases, such fateful ... indeed, let's call them borderline cases, where you don't know if you have a duty ... that is to say, there isn't just only one duty, one against all the rest, but a duty to yourself, and to the State and to science. You ought to help, naturally, that's why you are there ... but such principles are always only theoretical. How far should you go to help, then? There you are, a stranger, and I am a stranger to you, and I ask you not to tell anyone you have seen me ... good, you keep quiet, you fulfil this duty ... I ask you to talk to me because staying silent is killing me. You are willing to listen ... good. But that is easy, of course ... But if I were to ask you to grab hold of me and throw me overboard ... at that point you would cease to be obliging and willing to help. It ends somewhere then ... where one's own life, one's own accountability begins ... it must stop somewhere ... this duty must cease. Or perhaps it should never be allowed to cease in the particular case of a doctor? Must he be a healer, a helper to all the world, merely because he has a diploma in Latin? Must he really throw his life away and turn blood into water, when someone ... anyone, comes and asks him to be noble, helpful and good? Yes, somewhere duty ends ... where you can't do any more, there precisely ... '

He paused, and launched himself afresh.

'Forgive me. I am talking so wildly ... but I'm not drunk ... not yet. That wish, too, comes over me often, I admit to you frankly, in this hellish loneliness. Just think, I have lived for nearly seven years with only natives and animals ... that way you forget how to speak calmly. Then when you do start to talk, it comes in a torrent. But wait ... yes, I remember ... I wanted to ask you, to put such a case before you, whether one has a duty to help ... so absolutely pure and angel-bright a duty to help, whether one ... however, I am afraid it may take a long time. Are you sure you aren't tired?'

'No, absolutely not.'

'I ... thank you. Will you have a drink?'

He fumbled in the dark behind him. Something clinked against something else; two, three, possibly more bottles, which he put down beside him. He offered me a glass of whisky, which I sipped casually while he downed his in one go. For a moment there was silence between us. Then the bell sounded: twelve-thirty.

'Well ... I want to tell you about a case. Let us assume there was a doctor in a ... a small town ... or to be precise in the country. A doctor who ... a doctor who ... ' He hesitated again. Then suddenly he dragged his chair round close to mine.

'That won't do. I must tell you everything straight, from the beginning, otherwise you won't understand. It can't be explained in the abstract, by a hypothesis. I must tell you about my own case. That way there is no shame, no concealment. People stand naked before me and show me their scabs, their urine and their faeces ... if they want me to help them they don't have to be evasive and conceal things. So, I won't tell you about the case of a mythical doctor. I will bare myself to you and say: I ... I have forgotten what shame is in my foul loneliness, in that accursed country which devours a man's soul and sucks the marrow from his bones.'

I must have moved somehow, for he broke off.

'Ah, you protest ... I understand. You are delighted with India, the temples and the palm trees, with all the romance of a two-month journey. Yes, the tropics are indeed magical, if you are touring by train or car or in a rickshaw: I felt exactly the same way when I first came out East seven years ago. What dreams I had then. I wanted to learn the languages and read the holy books in the original, study tropical diseases, do scientific work, probe into the native psyche – as we Europeans call it – I wanted to be a missionary of humanity, of civilisation. Everyone who comes out East dreams the same dream. But imperceptibly one's energy is sapped in that hothouse. Fever – it gets you eventually however much quinine you swallow – it gets right into your bones, you become slack and lazy, soft, a jellyfish. Somehow a European who leaves the big cities for a God-forsaken posting in a swamp like the one I was in is cut off from his true roots. Sooner or later he goes off the rails. Some take to drink, others smoke opium, some start brawling and become animals – everyone has his own road to madness. You pine for Europe, dream of it, of one day being able to walk on a proper street, to sit among white people in a solidly built room. Year after year you dream of it, and then, when the day comes for you to go on leave, you are too idle to go. You know that back home you have been forgotten, you are a stranger, a pebble on the beach that everyone walks over. So you stay where you are and go to the dogs, and decay in the steamy damp of those rain forests. It was an accursed day when I sold myself to serve in that stinking hole ...

'Besides, I wasn't there quite so voluntarily. I had studied in Germany and qualified as a doctor. I was a good physician in fact, with a post at the Leipzig Clinic: somewhere in a back number of the *Medical Bulletin* you will find they made quite a fuss about a new injection I pioneered. Then I had an affair with a woman I had met in the hospital. She had driven her lover so crazy that he wounded her with a shot from a revolver, and soon I was as crazy as he was. She had a way of being proud and cold which sent me wild – haughty and pushing women could always wind me round their little finger, but this one reduced me to a complete jelly. I did what she wanted, I – well, why shouldn't I tell you, it was eight years ago – I put my hand in the hospital's till, and when I was found out there was the devil to pay. An uncle of mine made good the loss, but my career was finished. Just then I heard that the Dutch government was recruiting doctors for the colonies and was offering a cash inducement. Well, I thought there must be a catch in it, if they were offering cash in hand; I knew gravestones grew in those fever plantations three times as quickly as they do at home, but when you are young you believe fever and death happen only to other people. Of course, I didn't have much choice. I went to Rotterdam, signed up for ten years and was given a bundle of banknotes. I sent half of them back to my uncle and blued the rest on a girl down by the harbour – she had the lot off me just because she was so like that other damned cat. Without money, without a watch, without illusions, I sailed away from Europe and didn't feel particularly unhappy as we cleared the harbour. And then I sat on deck as you have done, as everyone did, and looked at the Southern Cross and the palm trees, my spirits rising – oh I dreamed of the jungle, of solitude, peace! Well – I had soon had enough of solitude. I wasn't sent to Batavia or Surabaya, to a town where there were people and clubs and golf and books and newspapers, but to — well, the name isn't important — it was one of the District Stations, a day's journey from the nearest town. All I had for company were a few boring, desiccated officials, a few half-castes, otherwise as far as the eye could see there were rain forests, plantations, thickets and swamps.

'At first it was quite bearable. I embarked on all sorts of studies. Once, the Vice-Resident had a car accident on one of his tours of inspection, and smashed his leg up. I operated on him single-handed and word got around about that. I collected native poisons and weapons, I occupied myself with a hundred different things to keep myself alert. But all that lasted only as long as my store of European energy; after that I dried up. The few Europeans bored me stiff. I gave up being sociable, took to drinking, and turned in on myself. I had only two more years to go, then I would be free, with a pension, and could return to Europe to begin a new life. In fact all I did was to wait, do nothing, and go on waiting. And I would still have been sitting there today if she hadn't ... if it hadn't happened.'

The voice in the darkness stopped. His pipe had gone out, too. It was so quiet I could hear the water again as it broke and foamed along the bow, and the distant dull heartbeat of the engine. I would have liked to light a cigarette but I was afraid of suddenly striking a match and startling him. He remained silent a long time. I didn't know if he had finished, if he had just dozed off or was fast asleep, his silence was so complete.

Then the ship's bell sounded sonorously again: one o'clock. He stirred; I heard his glass clink. Obviously he was looking for the whisky. I heard him take a gulp — then suddenly the voice began again, but this time it was tenser, more impassioned.

'Yes, well ... just a minute ... yes, well, that is how it was. There I am, sitting in my accursed trap, like a spider motionless in its web, for months on end. It was just after the rainy season. For weeks rain had poured down the roof, no one had come near me, no European. Day after day I sat there in the house with my sallow-skinned women and my good whisky. Sometimes I was quite "down", sick with longing for Europe; if I read a novel about bright streets and white women my fingers began to twitch. I can't quite describe to you how I felt; it's a kind of tropical disease, a rabid, feverish, and yet impotent nostalgia that sometimes grips you. There I sat then, on this occasion, with an atlas in front of me, and dreamed I was on a journey. Someone knocked urgently on my door. The houseboy was standing there and one of the women, their eyes wide with astonishment. They were very excited: a lady was here, a real lady, a white woman.

'I jumped up. I hadn't heard any carriage, any car arrive. A white woman here in this wilderness?

'I want to rush down the stairs but pull myself back. A look in the mirror; hastily tidy myself up a bit. I am tense, uneasy, somewhat disturbed by an unwelcome presentiment, for I know that no one in the whole world would be coming to see me out of friendship. Eventually I go downstairs.

'The lady is waiting in the hall and comes towards me quickly. Her face is hidden by a thick veil she has used on the car journey. I want to greet her but she gets her word in first. "Good day, Doctor," she says smoothly in English (almost too smoothly and as though she has rehearsed it). "Forgive me for calling on you unexpectedly. But we were just up at the Station, our car stopped there – and the thought came into my head all of a sudden, why don't I go on as far as your house – for I remembered you live here. I've heard so much about you already, you worked a miracle on the Vice-Resident, his leg is perfectly all right again, he plays golf as well as he did before. Oh yes, it's still the talk of the town down where we are, and we would all give away our grumpy surgeon and the two other doctors if we could have you. Really, why don't we see you in town, you live just like a Yogi?"

'And so she babbles on, faster and faster, without letting me get a word in. There is something tense and unstable about this inconsequential torrent, and it makes me uneasy too. Why is she talking so much, I ask myself, why doesn't she introduce herself, why doesn't she remove her veil? Has she a fever? Is she ill? Is she mad? I become more and more tense, because I am conscious of how ridiculous it is for me to stand there saying nothing, with her prattling rigmarole pouring over me. Eventually she eases off a bit, and I am able to ask her to come up into the living-room. She gives a sign to the boy to stay behind, and goes ahead of me up the stairs.

"It's pleasant here," she says, looking round my room. "Oh, your beautiful books! I'd love to read them all!" She goes over to the bookshelf and inspects the titles. For the first time since we met she is silent for a minute.

"May I offer you some tea?" I ask.

'She doesn't turn round and goes on looking at the books. "No, thank you, Doctor. We must move on again soon. I haven't much time. It's only a short outing ... ah, I see you have Flaubert's books here, I love them very much ... wonderful, quite wonderful, his *Education Sentimentale*. I see you read French too. How clever you are! Yes, you Germans, you learn it all at school ... really marvellous to know so many languages! The Vice-Resident swears by you. He says you are the only one he would allow to operate on him ... our precious surgeon down there is only fit for playing bridge. However, you know (she still didn't turn round) it came into my head today that I should consult you for once ... and as we were driving in this direction, I thought ... but you are busy now ... I will come back another time."

"Put your cards on the table," I thought to myself at once. But I didn't show what I was thinking, I just reassured her that I would deem it an honour to be of service now and whenever she wanted.

"It's nothing serious," she said, half turning round and at the same time leafing through a book she had taken from the bookcase. "Nothing serious ... little things ... women's complaints ... dizziness, fainting. Early this morning, as the car was taking a bend, I suddenly passed right out, quite unconscious. The boy had to sit me up again in the car and fetch me some water. Well, perhaps the driver was going too fast ... do you think that is what it was, Doctor?"

"I can't really say. Do you often faint like that?"

"No, that is, yes ... recently ... just recently ... yes. I've fainted a lot and had such nausea." She turns again to the bookcase, puts the book back, takes another out and leafs through it. It's odd. Why does she go on leafing through the books so — so tensely? Why doesn't she remove her veil? Deliberately I say nothing. I take pleasure in making her wait.

Eventually she begins again in her nonchalant, babbling way.

"That's right, Doctor, isn't it, it's nothing serious? It isn't some tropical disease ... nothing dangerous?"

"I must see first if you have any fever. May I take your pulse?" I go over to her. She turns lightly aside.

"No, no, I haven't any fever ... absolutely, certainly not. I've taken my temperature myself every day, since ... since I had these fainting fits. There's no fever, it's always precisely 98·4. My digestion is all right, too."

'I hesitate a moment. I have been growing increasingly suspicious. I sense that this woman wants something from me. One doesn't come into the jungle to talk about Flaubert. I keep her waiting one, maybe two minutes. "Excuse me," I then say straight out, "may I ask you some rather direct questions?"

"Of course, Doctor! After all you are a doctor," she replies, but she has already turned her back on me again and is toying with the books.

"Have you any children?"

"Yes, a son."

"And have you ... did you have ... I mean that time ... did you have similar symptoms?"

"Yes."

'Her voice has changed completely now. It is quite clear, quite firm; she's not babbling on at all, not tense any more. "And is it at all possible that you ... forgive the question ... that you are in the same condition?"

"Yes."

'The word comes out sharp and cutting like a knife. There is no movement of her head, which is still turned away from me.

"Perhaps it would be best if I were to examine you ... may I ask you ... would you come into the other room?"

'Then she suddenly turns round. I feel her giving me a cold, determined look through the veil.

"No, that isn't necessary. I know what my condition is perfectly well."

The voice hesitated a moment. The full glass glinted in the darkness.

'So, you see ... but first try to picture it for a minute. A man

64

who is being consumed by his loneliness has a woman burst in on him, the first white woman to set foot in his room for years ... and suddenly I sense there is something evil in the room, something dangerous. Somehow it came over me: I flinched before the steely determination of this woman who had come in chattering sociably and then in one move had produced her demand, like drawing a knife. Because I knew what she wanted of me, oh yes I knew, immediately — it wasn't the first time that women had made such demands, but they were different. They came ashamed of themselves or entreating me, fearful and supplicant. But here was a ... yes, a steely, masculine determination ... I sensed from the first second I saw her that this woman was stronger than I was ... that she could bend me to her will if she wanted to. But ... but ... I had evil in me too ... a man putting up resistance, some sort of resentment, because ... well, I've told you already ... from the first second, yes, from the very moment I saw her, I saw this woman as my enemy.

'For the moment I said nothing. My silence was stubborn and resentful. I could feel her looking at me from under her veil — direct and demanding — she wanted to compel me to speak. But I wasn't giving in so easily. I began to speak, but ... in a non-committal way ... unconsciously I copied her babbling, inconsequential way of speaking. I behaved as though I hadn't understood what she wanted, because — I don't know if she could feel it — I wanted to force her to speak plainly. I wanted not to do the asking, but to be asked ... precisely because of her bearing, because she had come so masterfully ... and because I knew that I had no real defences against women of this kind of arrogant, cold disposition.

'So I talked round the subject, saying that her symptoms were of no consequence, it was quite customary to faint in the course of pregnancy, that on the contrary it was usually a sign that everything was going well. I cited cases from the medical journals. I talked on and on, being offhand and casual, treating the matter like an everyday occurrence and ... I went on waiting for her to stop me. Because I knew she wouldn't put up with it.

'Then she interrupted me sharply, brushing my whole reassuring discourse aside with a wave of her hand.

"That isn't what I am worried about, Doctor. Last time, when I had my baby, I was in better health ... but now I am not so well ... I have a heart condition."

"Ah, a heart condition," I repeated, apparently concerned. "I will look into that at once." And I moved as though I was going to fetch my stethoscope.

'But she intervened again. Her voice was now quite strong and decisive – as though she were on a parade ground.

"I *do* have heart trouble, Doctor, and I must ask you to believe what I say. I haven't time to spend on examinations – I think you might trust me rather more. After all, I have provided enough proof of my trust in *you*."

'Now war was declared: an open challenge. And I took it up.

"With trust goes frankness, total frankness. Tell me about it straight out. I am a doctor. And before all else do take off your veil, sit down, forget the books and the subterfuges. You don't come to a doctor wearing a veil."

'She looked at me, upright and proud. She hesitated for a moment. Then she sat down and lifted the veil. I saw a face exactly as I had feared it would be – inscrutable, hard, superior, of beauty untouched by age, a face with grey, English eyes in which was the appearance of total composure and yet behind which you could imagine every passion. These small, compressed lips gave away no secret if they didn't want to. For a whole minute we looked at each other – she commanding me and asking me and at the same time showing such cold, steely ferocity that I couldn't withstand it and involuntarily looked away.

'Her knuckles tapped lightly on the table. So she was nervous too. Then she burst out: "Do you, or do you not know, Doctor, what I want you to do?"

"I think I can guess. But I would rather we were absolutely clear about it. You want to terminate your pregnancy ... you want me to release you from fainting fits, your morning sickness, by ... by removing the cause of them. Is that it?"

"Yes."

'The word fell like a guillotine.

"You know, don't you, that such an attempt is dangerous ... for both parties?"

"Yes."

"That I am forbidden by law to do it?"

"There are circumstances in which it isn't forbidden, but is advisable."

"But these require medical grounds."

"So you will find these grounds. You are a doctor."

'Clear, wide open, without blinking, her eyes looked straight at me. It was an order and, weakling that I was, I trembled in admiration before the demonic arrogance of her will. But I wasn't going to give in yet. I didn't want her to see that she had already broken me. "Now, not so fast! Make difficulties! Force her to beg me to do it." Some desire of this sort sparked up in me.

"That isn't always in the doctor's control. But I am willing to consult a colleague at the hospital ... "

"I don't want your colleague ... I have come to you."

"May I ask why you chose me?"

'She looked at me coldly.

"I don't mind telling you that. Because you live up-country, because you don't know me — because you are a good doctor, and because you ..." — she hesitated for the first time — "you won't be staying here much longer, especially if you ... if you can take home a large sum of money."

'I felt a cold chill run through me. This brazen, this mercantile, this dealer-like clarity of calculation stupefied me. So far no plea had left her lips — but she had calculated everything long ago, first she would stalk me, and then trap me. I sensed how the devilish element in her will was penetrating me, but I fought back full of resentment. I forced myself yet again to be objective — indeed to be almost ironic.

"And this large sum, you would ... you would give me if I resigned from my position here?"

"For your help and your immediate departure."

"Do you realise I would lose my pension if I did that?"

"I will compensate you for that."

"You speak very plainly ... but I would like further clarification. What sum do you have in mind?"

"Twelve thousand guilders, payable by draft in Amsterdam."

'I ... trembled ... with fury and ... yes, with amazement. She had calculated everything, the amount and the method of payment, by which I would have to leave the country to get the money. She had weighed me up and bought me. Without knowing me, she had counted on my compliance with her will in advance. I wanted to slap her face ... but as I stood there trembling – she had stood up again too – and I was eye to eye with her, I was suddenly overcome by the sight of those sealed lips which wouldn't plead, of that haughty head that wouldn't be bowed ... I was overcome by a ... a ... kind of violent overwhelming physical desire. She must have sensed it, for she raised her eyebrows, as one does when one wants to dismiss someone who is being importunate. The hatred between us was suddenly out in the open. I knew she hated me because she needed me, and I hated her because ... because she wouldn't plead with me. In this one second of silence we were speaking to each other openly for the first time. Then a thought flooded like snake venom into my head and I said to her ... I said ...

'But just a minute, you will misunderstand what I did ... what I said. I must first explain how ... how such a crazy thought came to me ... '

His glass clinked again lightly in the dark. And his voice became agitated.

'Not that I want to make excuses, justify myself, seek absolution ... but you won't understand if I don't explain ... I don't know that I can say I was ever a good man but ... I believe I was always ready to help ... in that foul life down there that was the only satisfaction one had, to be able to keep someone's life going with the handful of knowledge one had filled one's brain with ... one had a sort of god-like omnipotence. Truly, my happiest moments were if a native fellow came, pale with terror, his foot swollen with a snake bite, and already wailing that he didn't want his leg cut off, and I caught it in time to save him. I have driven for hours when some woman lay in a fever – and I have helped women in the Clinic back in Europe in the way this woman wanted me to. But there at least you felt these people had a *need*, that you had saved them from death or despair – and you needed to know that. In order to help, you yourself had to have this feeling the patient needed you.

'But this woman — I don't know if I can explain it to you — she upset me, she aroused opposition in me from the moment she came walking in; through her pride, she stirred up in me — how shall I put it — everything I had suppressed, hidden, all the evil in me to pit against her. It maddened me that she was playing the lady, unapproachably cool and businesslike about this matter of life and death. And then ... after all a woman doesn't get pregnant playing golf. I knew ... that is, this shocking thought suddenly came clearly into my mind, that this cool, haughty, cold woman, who raised her eyebrows at me over her steely eyes ... yes, looked almost dismissive, that two or three months earlier she had tumbled hotly into bed with some man, naked as an animal and perhaps moaning with desire, their bodies clamped tightly together like two lips ... That, that was the burning thought that overcame me when she looked at me so imperiously, so unapproachably cool, like an English officer ... and then it all overwhelmed me. I was obsessed with the idea of humiliating her ... in this instant I saw her naked body through the clothes ... in this instant I had only one thought, to possess her, to force a moan of ecstasy from her hard-set lips, to enjoy the sensual pleasure of this cold, proud woman as that other man, whom I didn't know, had done. That's ... what I wanted to explain ... I have never, however low I have been, tried to exploit my position as a doctor. But this time it really wasn't lust, or passion, nothing sensual, truly it wasn't ... I would swear an oath it wasn't ... only the inordinate desire to act like a dominant male ... to be masterfully masculine. I have told you already, I believe, that arrogant, apparently cool women have always had power over me ... but this time there was this extra dimension; I had been living here for seven years, without having had a white woman. I hadn't known resistance ... for the local native girls, those delicate twittering little creatures, who quiver with awe if a white man, a "master" takes them ... they submit humbly. They are always straightforward, always willing, with their light clucking laughter ... but their submissiveness, acting like a slave, is repulsive after a while. You will understand then, won't you, the shattering effect it had on me when here suddenly was this woman, full of pride and disdain, totally unapproachable, yet full of mystery and bearing the fruit of earlier passion. If a woman like that walks boldly into the cage of a man like me, a desperately lonely, sex-hungry, frustrated caveman ... that ... I wanted to explain, so that you understand what happened next. Well ... full of wicked desire, poisoned by the thought of her, naked, sensual, giving herself, I took a grip on myself, so to speak, and simulated indifference. I said coolly: "Twelve thousand guilders? No, I won't do it for that."

'She looked at me, going pale. She obviously sensed that greed for money wasn't the obstacle. So she said, "What do you want then?"

'I dropped my cool tone. "Let's put our cards on the table. I am no businessman ... I'm not the poor chemist in *Romeo and Juliet* who sold his poison for 'corrupted gold' ... I am perhaps the opposite of a businessman ... you won't get what you want this way."

"You won't do it, then?"

"Not for money."

'There was silence between us for a moment. It was so silent I could hear her breathing.

"What else can you want, then?"

'I couldn't restrain myself any longer.

"First of all I want you to ... stop talking to me as though I were a shopkeeper and to treat me like a human being. I want you to come when you need help not – not with your infernal money – but asking me, begging me to help you, as one human being to another ... I am not just a doctor, I don't just have consulting hours. I have other hours ... perhaps you have arrived in one of those."

'She was silent for a moment. Then she twisted her lips slightly, shivered, and said quickly:

"So if I were to beg you ... then you would do it?"

"You still want to make a business deal out of it – you will only ask if I have first given my promise. You must ask me first – then I will give you my answer."

'She tossed her head like a mettlesome horse. She looked at me angrily.

"No – I won't plead with you. I would rather die!"

'I saw red. I was beside myself with fury.

"Then I will insist, if you won't ask me. I don't think I need

70

be too explicit—you know what I want from you. Then—afterwards I will help you."

'She gazed at me for a moment. Then—oh I can't tell you how awful it was—she seemed to unwind and ... then she suddenly laughed ... she laughed at me with unspeakable contempt on her face ... with such contempt that I was crushed ... and intoxicated at the same time. It was like an explosion, this disdainful laughter, it was so sudden, so spontaneous, released so powerfully by some monstrous inner force, that I ... yes, I could have sunk to the ground and kissed her feet. It lasted only a second ... it was like being struck by lightning, and my whole body was aflame ... and she turned at that moment and hurried to the door.

'Instinctively I wanted to follow her ... to apologise ... to implore her ... my spirit was quite broken ... and she turned round and said ... no, she *ordered* me:

"Don't you dare follow me or try to find out about me ... You'll regret it if you do."

'And then the door shut behind her.'

There was another pause. Another silence; again, there was only a rustling sound as though the moonlight were pouring down. And then at last there was his voice again.

'The door closed ... but I stood rooted to the spot. I was quite hypnotised by her order. I heard her go down the stairs, close the front door ... I heard all this, and my whole desire was to pursue her ... to ... I don't know what ... to call her back, or to strike her or strangle her ... but whatever else, to go after her ... follow her. And yet I couldn't. My limbs were paralysed as though I had suffered an electric shock. I was struck right through to the marrow by the imperious flash of her eyes ... I know I can't explain it, I can't tell you ... it must sound ridiculous, but I just stood there. It took several minutes, five perhaps, or ten, before I could lift my feet off the ground.

'But scarcely had I moved one foot than I was hot-blooded again and full of spirit. I was down the stairs in a trice ... she could only have taken the road back towards civilisation. I dashed to the shed to get my bicycle, saw that I had forgotten the key, forced open the door so that the bamboo split and cracked ... I flung myself on my cycle and tore off after her ... I must ... I must get to her before she reached her car ... I had to speak to her. The road threw up dirt all around me ... and I registered for the first time how long I must have been standing transfixed up there ... for there she was at the bend in the road in the jungle right by the Station, hurrying along and striding out firmly, accompanied by the boy. But she must have seen me too, for she says something to the boy, who stays behind while she goes on alone. What is she doing? Why does she go on alone? Does she want to speak to me alone, without the boy hearing? ... I pedal on in a blind fury. Suddenly something runs across the road in front of me ... the boy ... I am only just able to swerve round him and I fall off.

'I get up cursing ... instinctively I strike out with my fist to knock the fool down, but he jumps aside ... I pick up my cycle to remount it ... but the wretched fellow jumps out again, grabs the cycle and says in his stilted English, "You stop here."

'You haven't lived in the tropics ... you don't know what an unutterable impudence it is for a mere native to seize hold of the cycle of a white "master" and to tell him, a white man, to stay where he is. My only answer was to punch him in the face with my fist ... he staggered but he kept hold of the cycle ... his eyes, his slit-like yellow eyes were wide open in menial terror but he hung on to the handlebar like a limpet. "You stop here," he stammered again. It was lucky I didn't have my revolver with me. I would have shot him down if I had. "Out of my way, you dog!" I say to him. He stares at me sullenly but won't let go of the bike. I hit him again but he still hangs on. That makes me really angry ... I can see that she will soon be gone, perhaps has gone already ... so I strike him with a copy-book punch to the chin, like a boxer. He spins round and drops. Now I have my cycle back, but as I go to get on it the wheel sticks ... the spokes were bent out of shape when I fell. Feverishly I try to make the wheel turn ... but it won't ... so I throw the bike right off the road after the boy, who has just picked himself up, bleeding, and is retreating out of the way ... And then — no, you've no idea how ridiculous this looked to everyone, for a European — well, I didn't know what I was doing any more — I had only one thought: to follow her, to get to her ... and so I *ran*, ran like a madman along the road, past the huts where a crowd of natives pressed forward in astonishment at the sight of a white man, the doctor, *running*.

'I was dripping with perspiration when I reached the Station. My first question: where is the car? ... Just gone ... everyone looks at me in astonishment. I must have seemed mad to them, arriving with the sweat pouring off me, shouting out my question before I came to a stop ... I can see down the road the exhaust from the car ... she has succeeded ... as all her hard, inhuman calculations must succeed.

'But running away didn't help her. In the tropics there are no secrets among the Europeans ... one person knows another ... no event passes unnoticed ... not for nothing was her driver waiting an hour at the government bungalow. In a few minutes I have learnt everything. I know who she is ... that she lives in ... well, in the capital, eight hours away by train ... that she ... well, let us say, is the wife of a merchant, stinking rich, upper-class, English. I know that her husband has been to America for five months and is returning in the next day or two to take her to Europe.

'But she – and the thought burns in my veins like poison – she can be only two or three months pregnant.

'Up to this point I have been able to explain it all to you ... perhaps only because up to this point I understood myself. As a doctor I was able to diagnose my own position. But from here on it was as though I had a fever. I lost my self-control ... that is to say, I knew exactly what I was doing, how crazy it all was. But I had no influence over myself ... I didn't understand myself any more. I was totally consumed by my obsession with my objective. But wait a minute ... perhaps I can explain after all. Do you know what running amok is?'

'Amok? I seem to remember it's when the Malays get drunk.'

'It's more than getting drunk ... it's going on the rampage, a sort of human form of rabies ... a paroxysm of murderous, mindless monomania which isn't comparable to any alcoholic poisoning ... I studied several cases during my stay – one is always very clever and objective about other people – but I wasn't able to discover the terrible secret of its cause ... it seems to be something to do with the climate, with that sultry, oppressive atmosphere that plays on your nerves like a thunderstorm until they snap ... that's it, running amok ... yes, amok, that's it: take a Malay, any straightforward, good-hearted fellow, sitting there quietly drinking ... there he is, stolid, even-tempered, subdued ... just as I was sitting in my room – and suddenly he jumps up, takes his dagger, and runs out into the street ... he runs on and on ... without knowing where he is going. Whatever gets in his way, be it man or animal, he cuts it down with his *kris*, and the sight of blood makes him even more excited. As he runs he foams at the mouth, he howls like a madman ... but he runs and goes on running, looking neither to right nor left, making this piercing shriek, and wielding his blood-stained *kris* on his terrifying headlong run. The village folk know that nothing can deflect someone who is running amok ... so they shout out a warning that he is coming: "Amok! Amok!" and everyone takes flight ... but he goes on running, without hearing or seeing, cutting down what crosses his path ... until someone shoots him dead like a mad dog, or he himself collapses, foaming at the mouth ...

'I saw this once from my bungalow window ... it was awful ... but having seen it, I recognised what was happening to me that day ... because I was doing exactly the same, with this terrible expression on my face, not looking to left or right, I stormed out with this obsession on my mind ... after this woman ... I don't remember what I did in my mad rush, everything happened so quickly. Ten minutes, no, five, no two, after I had found out everything about this woman, her name, her address, about her husband's return, I galloped back home on a hastily borrowed bicycle, threw a suit into my case, grabbed some money and drove my car to the railway station. I went without reporting to the District Officer ... without calling in a locum, I left the house unlocked and just as it was ... the servants stood around me, the women wide-eyed and asking questions. I didn't reply, I didn't turn round ... I drove to the station and took the next train to town. An hour after this woman had entered my room I had thrown my whole existence overboard and was running amok into the void ...

'I ran head on into a brick wall. I arrived at 6 o'clock in the evening ... at ten-past six I was at her house. It was ... you will

74

understand ... the silliest, most stupid thing I could have done ... but when you run amok you run blindly, you don't see where you are going ... after a few minutes the servant returned to tell me ... politely and coolly ... that Madame was indisposed and could not receive me.

'I reeled back out of the doorway ... for an hour I hung around the house, obsessed with the crazy hope that perhaps she would come and look for me ... then I booked a room in the Strand Hotel and took two bottles of whisky up there ... those and a double dose of veronal helped me ... in the end I fell asleep ... and this heavy, unhealthy sleep was the only pause there was in this race between life and death.'

The ship's bell sounded for two o'clock: four solid, full strokes, which reverberated in the smooth pool of almost still air and then faded away in the light, ceaseless rushing noise that ran under the bow and constantly accompanied the passionate discourse. The man in the shadows must have been startled by the bell, for he broke off. Once again I heard him pick up a bottle, and again the light sound of his swallowing. Then he began again, apparently composed, in a firmer voice.

'I can scarcely tell you about what happened after that. I think now that I must have been in the grip of a fever, or at all events I was in a state of over-excitement bordering on madness — I had run amok, as I told you. But don't forget, it was Tuesday when I arrived, and on the Saturday — as I had found out meanwhile — her husband was arriving on the P & O liner from Yokohama. There were therefore three days, three days precisely, for a decision to be made and help to be given. Do understand: I knew I had to help her immediately and yet I couldn't speak to her. And it was also the need I had to apologise for my ridiculous, insane behaviour that agitated me all the more. I knew how precious every minute was, that for her it was a matter of life or death, and yet there was no way for me to approach her discreetly with some sign, because my tempestuous, boorish pursuit had terrified her. It was ... well, let me think ... as though when you run after someone to warn them about a murder threat, that person takes you for the murderer and so runs away to his destruction ... she saw in me only a man who had run amok, who was following her to humiliate her, but I ... that was the awful paradox ... I scarcely thought of that at all ... it had all been knocked out of me ... all I wanted was to help her, to be of use to her. I would have committed murder to help her, any crime. But she didn't understand that. When I woke next morning I went to her house again, but the boy was standing there, the same boy I had struck on the face, and when he saw me coming — he must have been expecting me — he scurried into the house. Perhaps he had gone in just to announce my arrival discreetly ... perhaps ... oh, this uncertainty, how it tormented me ... perhaps everything was already prepared for me to be received ... but then, when I saw the boy, I remembered my disgraceful behaviour and I became uncertain again, not daring to call at the house a second time ... my knees were knocking. I was practically on the doorstep when I turned round and went away. I went away, while she was perhaps waiting for me in similar torment.

'I didn't know what to do in this strange city, which burned like fire under my feet. Suddenly something occurred to me. I summoned a cab and drove to call on the Vice-Resident, the man I had helped at my Station. Something about my appearance must have been odd, because he looked at me somewhat askance, and his courteous reception seemed slightly strained ... perhaps he had already recognised I was running amok ... I told him straight out that I wanted a transfer to the city, that I couldn't carry on any longer where I was. I had to move immediately. He looked at me ... I can't tell you how he looked at me ... rather in the way a doctor looks at a patient. "A nervous breakdown, my dear Doctor," he said. "I understand only too well. You'll soon get over it. But wait ... shall we say four weeks ... I must first find a replacement for you."

"I can't wait, not even for one day," I replied. He gave me that look again. "You must carry on, Doctor," he said gravely. "We mustn't leave the Station without a doctor. But I promise I will put everything in hand this very day." I stood there biting my lips. I understood clearly for the first time that I was not a free agent, I was a paid slave. Everything was building up in me to have a row, but he, the smooth diplomat, forestalled me. "You've been lacking civilised company, Doctor, and in the end that will make you ill. We have all wondered why you never came to see us, never took a holiday. You should have had more company, more social life. At least come this evening, there's a government reception. The whole colony will be here and many people will want to meet you at last. They've often asked after you and wished you were here."

'His words struck me. Asked after me? Had she ... ? I was suddenly a different man. Straightaway I thanked him politely for the invitation and assured him I would arrive punctually. And I did, I arrived much too punctually. I have to tell you that I was so driven on by my impatience that I was the first to arrive in the large reception room at Government House. There I was, silently surrounded by the native servants, who glided quickly in and out in their bare feet and who – it seemed to me in my confused state of mind – laughed at me behind my back. For a quarter of an hour I was the only European in the midst of all the silent preparations, and I was so left to myself that I could hear my watch ticking in my waistcoat pocket. Then at last a few government officials arrived with their families, and eventually the Governor. He drew me into a long conversation in which I was endeavouring to answer him suitably, and I believe I was succeeding until ... until I was suddenly overcome by a mysterious tenseness, and I lost all my social grace and began to stutter. Even though I had my back to the door I sensed immediately that she had come in, that she was present. I can't tell you how much this sudden certainty disturbed me, but even while I was speaking to the Governor, with the sound of his words in my ears, I could sense her presence somewhere behind me. Fortunately the Governor soon ended our conversation – otherwise I think I might have turned brusquely away from him, so strongly did this mysterious compulsion play on my nerves, so burning was my eagerness. And truly, I had hardly turned round before I saw her standing in exactly the same pose as when she unknowingly sparked off my emotion. She was wearing a yellow ball-gown which reflected on to her delicate, neat shoulders, as though they were made of dull ivory, and she stood in the middle of a group, talking. She was laughing, but I thought I could detect signs of tension on her face. I approached – she didn't see me, or didn't want to – and I watched the laughter falling pleasantly and politely from her lips. And her laughter intoxicated me again, because it ... well, because I knew that it was a sham, an artifice or skill, a supreme disguise. It is Wednesday today, ran through my head, the ship is arriving on Saturday bringing her husband home ... how can she laugh like that ... with such composure, so carefree, and play idly with her fan instead of crushing it convulsively in her anxiety? I ... I, the outsider ... I have been trembling for two days about the hour of her husband's return ... I, the outsider, have been living her fear, her terror, with the utmost intensity of feeling ... and she goes to the ball and does nothing but laugh.

'From the back somewhere music struck up. The dance was beginning. An elderly officer had asked her to dance and she excused herself from the group where she had been talking. Her hand on his arm, she walked into the next room, passing right by me. When she saw me her face suddenly twisted violently – but it was only for a second, then she nodded to me in polite acknowledgment (before I had decided whether to greet her or not) as you would to a casual acquaintance: "Good evening, Doctor," and she had gone. No one could have suspected what was concealed in that grey-green glance, and even I did not know. Why had she greeted me? Why had she acknowledged me only with a brief word? Was it a gesture of rejection, was it conciliatory, was it only the confusion of being surprised? I can't describe to you how agitated I became again, everything was churned up again, compressed explosively inside me, and as I saw her, circulating easily on the arm of an officer, wearing the cool expression on her face of someone with no worries, while I knew, indeed, that she ... that she as well as I, was thinking only of *that* ... thinking of that ... that only the two of us shared a terrible secret ... and she was dancing ... in those seconds my fear, my desire and my admiration became more passionate than ever. I don't know if anyone had noticed me, but certainly I was much more indiscreet in my behaviour than she – I couldn't look in any other direction, I had to ... yes, I simply had to watch her, I drank her in, I strained from afar to see if the mask would fall for a second from her unrevealing face. And she must have found my blatant gaze disconcerting. When she returned on the arm of her dancing partner she shot me a quick, fierce look, a sharp order, as though telling me to go: once again that expression of imperious wrath that I had seen before spread angrily across her brow.

'But … but … as I have said already … I was running amok, I wasn't looking to left or right. I understood her immediately. This look meant: don't attract attention! Control yourself! I knew that she … how shall I put it? – that she wanted me to behave discreetly here in the public reception room. I understood that if I were to go home now, I could most certainly be sure she would receive me tomorrow … that it was only here and now that she wanted to avoid and be free of my conspicuous familiarity, that she – and how right she was – feared my clumsiness would cause a scene … you see. I knew all this, I understood that imperious, frosty look, but … but I was in too powerful a grip, I had to speak to her. And so I edged my way into her circle where she was standing chatting, and just out of inordinate longing to hear her speak, pushed myself – even though I knew only one or two of those present – right into the centre. And yet all the time I cringed like a whipped cur when I met her glance, when she looked coldly right through me as though I were part of the curtain I was brushing up against, or the air which slightly moved it. But I stood there, dying for any word she might say to me, for a sign of understanding. I just stood there stock still in the middle of the group, staring at her. Without doubt my behaviour must have been noticed, for no one spoke to me and my ridiculous presence must have embarrassed her.

'I don't know how long I stood there … it seemed an eternity. I just *couldn't* leave her spell-binding presence. My stubborn mania paralysed me. But she couldn't bear it any longer … suddenly she turned to the company with her magnificent inborn poise and said, "I am a little tired. I shall retire early tonight. Good night!" … and she walked firmly past me with a formal nod of the head to everyone. I saw again the disdainful furrow of her brow, and then only her back, that white, cool, bare back. It took me a second to grasp that she was leaving … that I wasn't going to be able to see her or speak to her again that evening – that last possible evening for saving her. So I stood there for a moment, still staring … until it had sunk in … then … then …

'But just a minute … hold on … otherwise you won't understand the folly, the stupidity of what I did ... first I must describe the whole room to you. It was the big reception room of Government House, brightly lit and nearly empty, this enormous room ... the couples had gone to dance, and some of the men to play cards. Only a few groups remained talking in the corners ... so the room was nearly empty and every movement in it was conspicuous and visible in the brilliant light ... and she was walking slowly and lightly across this great, wide room, with her shoulders back, with her indescribable composure, exchanging a greeting here and there ... with that imperious, ice-cold, haughty equanimity that so enchanted me. I ... I had stayed where I was, as I have told you, as though I were paralysed, before I grasped that she was leaving ... and then, as I grasped it, she was already at the other end of the room, right by the door. Then ... oh I am still ashamed even now when I think about it ... it suddenly seized me, and I *ran* – do you hear? I ran ... I didn't walk, I *ran*, with my heavy shoes that made the room echo, clean across the room to her ... I heard my footsteps, I saw all eyes turned on me with astonishment ... I could have died of shame ... even while I was running I recognised the folly of it ... but I couldn't ... I couldn't stop. I caught up with her by the door ... she turned round ... her eyes cut through me like a grey sword, her nostrils flaring with fury. I tried to begin stammering something ... and she ... she suddenly *laughed* out loud ... a clear, carefree, heavy laugh, and said loudly ... so loudly that everyone could hear. "Ah, Doctor, you've just remembered the prescription for my little boy then. Dear me, you men of science ..." A couple standing near by joined in the laughter good-humouredly. I caught on. I was amazed by the mastery with which she had saved the situation. I took out my notebook and tore off an empty sheet, which she took nonchalantly with another cold laugh of thanks before she went. It came to me at once. I saw that she had saved the situation through her mastery of it ... but I also knew immediately that everything was lost as far as I was concerned ... that this woman hated me for my hot-headed folly ... hated me more than she hated death ... that I could go a hundred times to her door after this and she would send me away like a dog.

'I stumbled across the room ... people were staring at me. I must have looked quite extraordinary. I went to the buffet, drank two, three, four cognacs in a row … that saved me from collapsing … my nerves had gone to pieces, shot through … then I slunk out through a side door and went home like a criminal. If you had offered me a fortune I couldn't have crossed that room again, where the laughter seemed to stick shrilly to the walls. I went … I really don't know where I went … into a couple of bars and got drunk … blind drunk … but … I couldn't shut it out from my senses … her laughter stuck with me, shrill and angry. I couldn't deaden that laugh, that accursed laugh … then I wandered round the harbour … I had left my revolver in my room, otherwise I would have shot myself. I thought of nothing else, and I took this thought home with me … this thought of the left-hand drawer of my wardrobe where my revolver was. I had only this one thought.

'That I didn't shoot myself, in fact … I swear to you it wasn't cowardice … it would have been a deliverance to have pulled the trigger which was ready and waiting … but how can I explain it to you? I still felt I had a duty, yes, that duty to help, that accursed duty. The thought of it drove me mad, that she might still need me, that she did need me … it was Thursday morning already when I returned to my room, and on Saturday … as I have told you … on Saturday the ship would arrive and I knew that *this* woman, this imperious, proud woman would not survive the scandal, could not face her husband and the world. Oh, how such thoughts have tortured me – the senselessly wasted precious time, my insane rashness that had frustrated the giving of timely help. Hour after hour, I swear to you, I walked up and down my room cudgelling my brain as to how I could approach her, how I could put everything right, how I could help her … for it was certain that she wouldn't let me into her house. I could hear her laughter still, and see her nostrils flaring with fury … for hours and hours I paced up and down the three yards length of my little room … daylight came. Then it was already mid-morning …

'And suddenly I flung myself down at the table … I grabbed a sheaf of writing paper and began to write her … everything … a cringing, whining cur of a letter, in which I begged her forgiveness, called myself a madman, a criminal. I swore she could trust me. I swore I would disappear within the hour, out of town, out of the colony, if she wished: out of the world ... if only she would forgive me and trust me, to let me help her at this eleventh hour ... I wrote twenty feverish pages ... it must have been a crazy, indescribable letter, written as though I were delirious, for when I stood up from the table I was soaked in perspiration ... the room was spinning, I had to drink a glass of water. Then I tried to read the letter through again, but I had the shudders after the first few words ... trembling, I folded it up and addressed an envelope ... then a thought struck me. For once I knew how to clinch matters. And I seized the pen again and wrote on the last page: "I shall wait here at the Strand Hotel for a word of forgiveness. If I hear nothing by seven o'clock I will shoot myself."

'Then I took the letter, rang for a boy, and told him to deliver it immediately. At last everything had been said — everything!'

Something jangled and rolled about near us. He had knocked over the whisky bottle with a sharp movement; I heard him groping about on the deck for it, and with a sudden motion of the arm he threw the empty bottle in a wide arc overboard. He was silent for several minutes, then he began raving on again, with more agitation and haste than ever.

'I don't believe in Christ any more ... for me there's no heaven or hell ... and if there is a hell, I'm not afraid of it, because it can't be worse than those hours I lived through from that morning until evening. Imagine a small room, hot in the sun, even stickier in the midday furnace ... a small room with only table, chair and bed ... and on this table nothing but a watch and a revolver and at the table a man ... a man who does nothing but stare at the seconds hand of the watch ... who doesn't eat or drink or smoke or move ... who only ... can you imagine? For three solid hours ... stares at the white dial and the hand that runs ticking round and round. That's ... that's ... how I spent the day, just waiting, waiting, waiting ... but waiting in the same way someone running amok behaves, mindless, with a mad dog's tenacity for running furiously in a straight line.

'Now ... I won't describe those hours to you. I can't describe them ... I don't understand myself, how anyone can experience what I did without losing his reason. So at twenty-two minutes past three ... I know it was that time exactly, as I was still staring at my watch ... someone knocked on the door ... I spring up ... spring like a tiger seizing its prey. In one bound I am across the room and fling the door open ... a frightened little Chinese boy is standing outside with a folded note in his hand, and while I eagerly grab it, he is gone in a flash and disappears.

'I tear the note open, I want to read it ... and I can't ... it swims in a blur before my eyes ... imagine my agony, here at last I have a word from her ... and it is shaking and dancing before my eyes. I put my head under the tap ... and now my head is clearing. I pick up the note again and I read: "Too late! But stay where you are. I may perhaps still send for you."

'There was no signature on the crumpled paper, which had been torn from some old leaflet ... the pencilled words were written hastily and unsteadily in what was otherwise a confident hand. I don't know why the note shook me so much. There was some horror, some mystery attached to it. It was as though the writer, running away, had written it at the ledge of a booking office window or in a moving vehicle ... some element of indescribable fear, haste, and horror in this homely note struck like ice into my soul ... and yet ... and yet, I was happy. She had written to me. I wasn't to die then, I might be permitted to help her ... perhaps ... I might be permitted ... oh, I had quite lost myself in senseless conjectures and hopes ... a hundred, a thousand times I read that little note, I kissed it ... scanned it for some forgotten or overlooked word ... my reverie became even deeper, ever more tangled, an unreal state of being asleep with your eyes open ... a kind of paralysis, something quite deadened and yet alive, between sleep and waking, that lasted perhaps a quarter of an hour, perhaps for hours ...

'Suddenly I was startled ... had someone knocked? I held my breath ... everything was absolutely silent for a minute, two minutes ... And there it was again, quite a gentle sound, like a mouse nibbling, a gentle but purposeful knock. I leapt up, still slightly bemused, flung the door open ... outside was the boy, the same one I had hit in the face with my fist ... his brown face had an ashen look, his worried expression told me something dreadful had happened. I immediately feared the worst. "What … What's happened?" was all I could stammer out. "Come quickly," he said … nothing else. Immediately I raced down the stairs, with him at my heels. A pony and trap was waiting and we got in. "What's happened?" I asked the boy … he trembled as he looked at me and bit his lips silently. I asked again, but he wouldn't say anything. I would dearly have liked to strike him in the face again with my fist, but … it was precisely his dog-like loyalty to his mistress that calmed me down … so I stopped asking. The little carriage was driven so urgently through the throng that people fell over themselves to get out of the way. We left the European quarter by the river and went down town and further still, into the screaming throng of China Town. Eventually we came to a narrow alley, lying quite off the beaten track. The driver stopped in front of a mean-looking house. It was dirty and seemed to be falling down. It had a small shop at the front with a tallow candle for a light … it was one of those dens where opium dealers or brothels are concealed, a thieves' kitchen or a fence's hide-out. The boy knocked urgently. A voice behind a crack in the door asked question after question … I couldn't stand it any longer. I jumped from my seat, leaned heavily on the slightly open door … an old Chinese woman fled with a little shriek … behind me came the boy, directing me down the passage, unlatched another door … another door into a dark room that reeked evilly of brandy and congealed blood. Something was groaning in there … I fumbled my way in … '

His voice stopped again. And then what he uttered was more like sobbing than speech.

'I … I fumbled my way in … and there … lying on a dirty mattress … twisting in pain … a groaning piece of humanity … was she …

'I couldn't see her face in the dark … my eyes weren't yet accustomed to it … so I only fumbled about … her hand … hot … burning with heat … fever, high fever … and I shuddered … I knew what had happened straightaway … she had fled here away from me … had allowed some dirty Chinese woman to mutilate her, only because she expected more discretion here … she had let herself be butchered by some devilish witch rather than entrust herself to me ... only because I had behaved like a lunatic ... because I hadn't respected her pride, hadn't helped her ... because she feared death less than she feared me ...

'I shouted for light. The boy jumped up. The disgusting old Chinese woman brought me, with shaking hands, a sooty kerosene lamp. I had to restrain myself from strangling the yellow bitch ... she put the lamp on the table ... the light fell golden and bright on the martyred body. And suddenly ... suddenly it all fell away from me, all depression, all anger, all that filthy cesspool of unrelieved passionate desire. I was the doctor once again, the helping, investigating, knowledgeable man. I had forgotten my own self. I was battling against this horrifying situation with alert, unclouded faculties. I examined the naked body, which I had lusted after in my dreams, now only as ... how shall I put it? As an object, an organism ... I was investigating not her but a life that was fighting against death, a human being who was twisted in murderous agony. Her blood, her hot, sacred blood flowed over my hands but I didn't think of it in any lustful way or in horror ... I was strictly a doctor. I saw only the illness ... and saw ...

'And I saw straightaway that all was lost, short of a miracle. She had been badly mauled and had half bled to death at the hands of this criminal bungler ... and I had nothing in this stinking den to staunch the flow of blood, not even clean water ... everything I touched was coated with dirt. "We must take her to the hospital at once," I said. But I had hardly spoken when the martyred body reared up in a spasm. "No ... no ... rather die ... no one must find out ... no one must find out ... home ... home ... "

'I understood ... she was fighting more for secrecy, for her honour ... not for her life. And—I listened to her. The boy brought a litter. We lay her down in it ... and so ... she was already like a corpse, weak and feverish ... we carried her through the night ... home ... fending off all the questioning, alarmed servants. We carried her like thieves into her room and locked the doors. And then ... then began the battle, the long battle against death ... '

Suddenly a hand gripped my arm, and I nearly cried out in

fright and pain. His face was so distortedly close in the dark that I saw his white teeth as he bared them in a sudden grimace, saw his spectacles, in the pale reflection of the moonlight, shining like two large cat's eyes. And now he was no longer speaking – he was shouting, shaking with raging anger:

'Do you know, then, you, a stranger to me, you who sit here idly in a deckchair, a wandering tourist, do you know what it's like when someone dies? Have you ever been there, ever witnessed it? How the body twists and tosses, the bloodless nails clawing the air, how the throat rattles, every limb struggles, every finger presses against the horror of it, and how the eyes bulge out in terror, for which there are no words? Have you ever experienced it, you loafer, you tourist, you who talk of helping being a duty? I have seen it often, being a doctor, I have seen it as ... a clinical event, a fact. I have, so to speak, studied it – but I have only *experienced* it once, shared the experience, shared the dying only once, that night ... that terrible night, when I sat and cudgelled my brain as to what to do, to find something, to stop the blood which ran and ran and ran, against the fever that burned before my eyes ... against death which came ever nearer and which I couldn't turn away from her bed. Do you understand what it means to be a doctor, to know all there is to know about every illness – to have a duty to help, as you so wisely put it – and yet to sit powerless beside a dying person, knowing but powerless ... knowing only this one terrible thing, that you can't help, even if you were to tear apart every artery in your body ... to see a beloved body wretchedly bleeding, martyred with pain, to feel a pulse racing and at the same time weakening ... to know that someone is slipping away under your fingers? To be a doctor and to know nothing, nothing, nothing ... only to sit there and stammer a few prayers like an old crone in church, and then to clench one's fists against a merciful God from whom one knows no mercy will come. Do you understand that? Do you? The ... the one thing I don't understand ... is ... how one contrives not to die, too, at such a moment. How one can get up next morning after a night's sleep and clean one's teeth and put on a tie. How one can go on living when one has experienced at first hand what I felt, how this living being, for whom I fought and wrestled, the first person I wanted to hold on to with all the power within me ... how she slipped away from under my hand ... wherever she was going, slipping ever more quickly, minute by minute, and I knew no way, in my fevered brain, of holding on to her ...

'And on top of that, to double my devilish torture ... on top of that, while I sat by her bed – I had given her morphine to alleviate the pain, and watched her lying there with flushed cheeks, feverish and weak – yes ... while I sat there I sensed behind me two eyes fixed on me with a fearful expression of tension. The boy sat there cowering on the floor and quietly murmured some sort of prayers. When our eyes met ... no, I can't describe it ... something so beseeching, so ... grateful came into his dog-like expression, and at the same time he put his hands out to me as though he wanted to implore me to save her ... do you understand? To me, he put out his hands as though to a god ... to me ... the powerless weakling who knew all was lost ... knew that I was as superfluous here as an ant that scurried over the floorboards. Oh that look, how it tortured me, that animal trust in my skill. I could have shouted at him and kicked him, he caused me so much distress ... and yet I sensed how we two were bound together in our love for her ... through the secret. He sat hunched up right behind me, like a watchful animal, in a numb heap ... if I wanted something he jumped up, his bare feet making no sound, and fetched it, trembling with expectation as though this would be the source of help and rescue. I know he would have cut his own arteries if it would have helped her. There was this woman, with such power over people ... and there was I ... who didn't have the power to save a drop of blood. Oh that night, that terrible night, that unending night between Life and Death!

'Towards morning she was conscious again ... she opened her eyes ... now they weren't haughty and cold ... fever glistened damply in them, as she looked round the room as though she didn't recognise it. Then she looked at me: she seemed to try to recollect, trying to remember my face ... and suddenly ... I saw it ... it came to her ... for some kind of terror, of resistance ... something ... something hostile, some sense of horror, crossed her face ... she tried to move her arms as though she wanted to escape ... far, far away from me. I saw that she was thinking of *that* ... of the earlier time. But then came reflection ... she looked at me more calmly, breathing heavily. I felt that she wanted to speak, to say something. Her hands began to brace themselves ... she wanted to sit up, but she was too weak. I tried to calm her, and bent down towards her ... then she gave a long, agonised look ... her lips moved slightly ... it was only a last fading whisper.

"Will anyone find out? Anyone?"

"No one," I said with utter conviction, "I promise you that."

'But her eyes were still uneasy. With her feverish lips she struggled with the words.

"Swear to me ... no one will ever know ... swear it."

'I raised my hand as though taking an oath. She looked at me ... with a ... an indescribable expression ... it was gentle, warm, grateful ... yes, truly, truly grateful. She wanted to say something else but it was too difficult for her. She lay there a long time, quite limp from the effort, with her eyes shut. Then began the awful ... the awful ... she fought on for another whole, difficult hour: only as morning came was it over ... '

He was silent for a long time. I hadn't noticed it until the bell sounded from the middle deck in the stillness, six strong strokes: three o'clock. The moonlight had become weaker, but some other yellow brightness already shimmered uncertainly in the air, and a breeze blew occasionally, light as a zephyr. Half an hour, an hour more, and it was day, and this horrific story I had heard was extinguished in the clear light. I saw his outline now more clearly, for the shadows were not as deep and black in our corner – he had taken off his cap, and beneath his bare head, his tortured face seemed even more frightened. But soon he turned his glinting spectacles towards me again, he pulled himself together, and his voice had a sarcastic, sharp tone.

'It was all over for her – but not for me. I was alone with the corpse – but alone in a strange house, alone in a strange city, which wouldn't allow any secret, and I ... I had to keep the secret. Yes, just think about it, the whole situation: a woman from the highest social circle in the colony, in perfect health, who had been dancing at the government reception only evenings earlier, lies suddenly dead in her bed ... a strange

88

doctor is in attendance, ostensibly called by her servant. No one in the house saw when he came and where he came from. She was brought in in the night on a litter and then the doors were closed ... and in the morning she is dead ... then for the first time have the servants been called, and suddenly the house resounds with clamour. In no time the neighbours know about it, the whole city ... and there is only one person who can explain it all. I, the stranger, the doctor from a distant Station. A delightful situation, isn't it?

'I knew what lay before me. Fortunately I had the boy with me, that sterling fellow who read my every wish – this gloomy yellow dog also understood that there was another battle still to be fought here. I said to him only: "Your mistress's wish was that no one should find out what has happened." He looked me straight in the eye with his dog-like, misty but determined look: "Yes, sir." That was all he said. But he washed the bloodstains from the floor, put everything back in proper order – and it was this very determination of his that gave me mine back.

'I know that never in my life have I had such concentrated energy, and I won't have it again. When you have lost everything, you fight to the last like a desperado – and the last in this case was her legacy, the secret. I received everyone very calmly, telling them all the same invented story, that the boy, whom she had sent to fetch the doctor, had met me by chance on the way. But while I was talking apparently calmly I was waiting ... waiting all the time for the crucial event ... the arrival of the coroner's doctor, who had to come first before we could close her up in her coffin and the secret with her. Don't forget, it was Thursday and her husband was returning on Saturday.

'It was nine o'clock when at last I heard the official doctor announced. I had had him sent for – he was my superior in rank and at the same time my rival, the same surgeon she had spoken about so scornfully and who obviously would have heard by now of my wish for a transfer. I sensed it at once from his first glance at me: he was against me. But that merely strengthened my resolve.

'In the ante-room his questions began: "When did Mrs ... – he named her – die?"

"At six o'clock this morning."

"When did she send for you?"

"At eleven o'clock the previous evening."

"Did you know I was her doctor?"

"Yes, but it was urgent ... and then ... the dead woman had asked specifically for me. She had forbidden any other doctor to be called."

'He stared at me: the colour heightened in his pallid, somewhat degenerate face; I sensed I had provoked him. But I needed precisely that to happen – all my energies were bent on getting a quick decision, for I could tell that my nerves wouldn't hold out much longer. He made as if to reply with some hostile remark but then he said easily: "If you mean you've been able to do without me so far, it is my official duty to verify the death and ... how it happened."

'I didn't reply and let him go in ahead of me. Then I went back, locked the door and put the key on the table. He raised his eyebrows in astonishment. "What is the meaning of this?"

'I faced him calmly.

"It isn't a matter in this case of determining the cause of death, but of finding another. This woman sent for me to attend her after ... after the consequences of an unfortunate intervention ... I couldn't save her but I promised I would save her honour, and that I will do. And I am asking you to help me!"

'His eyes had grown quite wide with astonishment. "You are not by any chance saying, are you," he stammered, "that I, the official doctor, should cover up a crime?"

"Yes, that's what I want, that's what I must insist on."

"For your crime I should ... "

"I have told you that I haven't touched this woman; if I had ... if I had I wouldn't be standing here before you, I would long since have committed suicide. She has atoned for her offence – if you want to call it that – the world doesn't need to know about it. And I won't permit this woman's honour to be besmirched unnecessarily now."

'My decisive tone roused him again. "You won't permit! So, now you think you are my senior – or at least you believe you soon will be – so you try to give me orders. I had already thought there was dirty work going on when you were sent for from your hole. A clean piece of work you've begun with, a clean trial run. But now I shall investigate, *I*, and you can depend on it that a report with my name at the foot of it will be correct. I won't sign any lies."

'I was quite calm.

"Yes — but this time that's exactly what you must do. You won't leave this room until you do."

'As I said that I reached into my pocket — I didn't actually have my revolver with me. But he shrank back. I took a step towards him and looked at him.

"Listen, I am going to tell you something ... so that it doesn't come to the worst. I don't value my life — or anyone else's — I am already up to my neck in this. All I am interested in is in keeping my promise that the cause of death remain a secret. Listen, I give you my word that if you sign the certificate to say that this woman died of ... an accident, I will leave this city and the Indies within the week. If you want, I will take my revolver and shoot myself, as soon as the coffin is in the earth and I can be certain that no one ... you understand: *no one* can look inside it again. That should be enough for you — that *must* be enough."

'There must have been something menacing, something dangerous in my voice because when I unintentionally stepped nearer to him, he retreated, as though in that scramble to escape as people fly before a man who has run amok, when he runs raving and swinging his *kris*. And all at once he changed ... almost cowed and paralysed ... his stiff-necked bearing left him. Noticeably softer in his opposition, he murmured, "It would be the first time in my life that I have signed a false certificate. Nevertheless, we can soon find a form of words. What happened is of course obvious. But I wouldn't be able to do it without further ... "

"Of course you wouldn't," I said helpfully, to strengthen his resolve — ("Quickly now! Quickly!" throbbed in my temples) — "but now, as you know that you would only be injuring a living man and doing a terrible thing to a dead person, you will surely not draw back?"

'He nodded. We went over to the table. In a few minutes the attestation was complete (the version that would be published in the papers and described the cause of death plausibly as heart failure). Then he stood up and looked at me.

"You will leave the country this week, won't you?"

"Word of honour."

'He looked at me again. I observed that he wanted to appear strong and businesslike. "I will order a coffin straightaway," he said, to cover his embarrassment. But what was it within me that made me appear so ... so frightening or so tormented? Suddenly he held his hand out and shook mine with hearty cordiality. "I hope you soon get over it," he said – I didn't know what he meant. Was I ill? Was I ... insane? I accompanied him to the door, opened it – but the last of my strength went in shutting it again after him. Then the throbbing in my temples returned, everything swam and went round: and I collapsed right by her bed ... as ... as the man running amok falls down unconscious at the end of his run, his nerves shattered.'

He was silent once more. For some reason I was shivering: was it the first spasm of the morning wind that was now just running lightly over the ship? But the tormented face – already half illuminated now by the reflected light of dawn – gathered itself together.

'How long I lay there on the matting, I don't know. Then I came to. I started up. The boy was standing there timidly, with his submissive bearing, and he looked at me anxiously.

"Someone wants to come in. Wants to see her ... "

"No one may come in."

"Yes ... but ... "

'His eyes were frightened. He wanted to say something but didn't dare to. The loyal creature was suffering an agony of mind.

"Who is it?"

'He looked at me, shaking with fright as though expecting me to strike him. And then he said – he named no name – how does it happen that such a lowly creature has so much understanding; how does it happen that quick as a flash this quite uneducated man can be inspired with such indescribable delicacy of feeling? For he said ... quite ... quite anxiously ... "*He's* here!"

'I started up, understanding immediately, and was straight away full of impatient curiosity about this unknown man. For you see how extraordinary it was that in the midst of all this torment, in this fever of demands being made on me, of fear and haste, I had completely forgotten *him* ... forgotten that another man was still involved ... the man whom this woman loved, to whom she had given herself in the passionate embrace which she had denied me. Twelve, twenty-four hours earlier I had hated this man, could have torn him to pieces. Now I can't ... I can't describe to you how much I wanted to see him ... to ... love him, because she had loved him.

'In a flash I was at the door. A young, quite young, fair-haired officer was standing there, very awkward, very slim, very pale. He looked a mere boy, so ... so movingly young ... and it upset me beyond words, too, how he was striving to be a man, to be composed ... to contain his emotion. I saw immediately that his hands were shaking as he took off his cap. I could have embraced him ... just because he was as he was, as I wanted the kind of man who had possessed this woman to be ... no seducer, no arrogant man ... no, he was an adolescent, an unspoilt, tender-hearted being, to whom she had given herself. The young man stood there quite embarrassed. My eager glance and sudden tempestuous appearance at the door confused him even more. The small moustache on his upper lip quivered traitorously. This young officer, this boy, was having to make an effort not to break down.

"Excuse me," he said at last. "I would have liked to have seen Mrs ... liked to have ... seen her ... again."

'Unconsciously, almost involuntarily, I put my hand on this stranger's shoulder and led him in, as one leads in a patient. He looked at me in some astonishment with an infinitely warm and thankful expression. There was in these brief moments some understanding between us of our fellowship. We went in to the dead woman. She lay there, white, in white linen – I sensed that my presence upset him ... so I stepped back to leave him alone with her. He went slowly up to her ... with such painful, dragging steps. I could see from his shoulders how emotion swelled up and tore him apart ... he went so ... like someone walking into a terrible storm. And suddenly he collapsed on his knees by the bed, much as I had done.

'I jumped quickly forward, lifted him up and led him to a chair. He let himself go now unashamedly and sobbed his torment aloud. I couldn't speak — I just unconsciously patted his fair, youthful head. He gripped my hand ... quite gently and yet anxiously ... and all at once I could feel his glance resting on me.

"Tell me the truth, Doctor," he stammered. "Did she commit suicide?"

"No," I said.

"And is ... I mean ... is any ... anyone to blame for her death?"

"No," I said again, although it welled up in my throat to cry out to him, "I, I, I ... and you! The two of us! And her pride, her confounded pride!" But I held myself back. I answered only again: "No. No one is to blame. It was a bolt from the blue."

"I can't believe it," he groaned, "I can't believe it. The day before yesterday she was at the ball, she was laughing, she acknowledged me. How is it possible, how can such a thing happen?"

'I told him a pack of lies. Even to him I wouldn't betray her secret. We talked together all day like brothers, equally warmed by the feeling that bound us together ... and by what we didn't confide in each other but which we sensed in each other, that our whole life depended on this woman. Sometimes it rose bubbling to my lips, but then I clenched my teeth — he never learned that she was carrying his child — that I ought to have killed this child, his child, and that she herself had dragged it over the precipice with her. And so we spoke only of her during the days which followed, while I hid myself in his quarters ... for — I had forgotten to tell you this — I was being looked for. Her husband had arrived after the coffin had been closed. He wouldn't believe the medical report. People were spreading all sorts of rumours ... and he was looking for me. But I couldn't bear to see him, him, with whom she had suffered unhappiness. I hid ... for four days I didn't go out, neither of us went out ... her lover had booked me a cabin on a ship, using a false name, so that I could escape. I slipped on board at night, like a thief, so that no one would recognise me. I left everything behind, all my possessions, my house with all my seven years' work, my goods and chattels, everything was left open for anyone to take what he wanted. The government officials must have struck me off by then because I had left my post without leave. But I couldn't live any longer in that house, in that town ... in that world, where everything reminded me of her. I fled, like a thief in the night ... just to escape from her ... just to forget. But ... as I came on board ... at night ... about midnight ... my friend was with me ... up there ... up there ... a crane was lifting something ... rectangular, black. Her coffin ... do you hear me? Her coffin. She had followed me here, as I had followed her ... and I had to stand by, as though I was a stranger, for he, her husband, was here too. He will accompany the coffin to England ... perhaps he will have an autopsy done there. He has snatched her back to himself. Now she belongs to him again ... not to us any more, to us ... to the two of us. But I am still here. I am going with her to the bitter end. He won't, he must never know what happened. I shall guard her secret against any attempt to know what happened ... against this blackguard on account of whom she went to her death. He won't find out anything, anything at all. Her secret belongs to me, to me alone.

'Now you understand ... now you understand why I can't meet people ... can't bear to hear their laughter ... when they flirt and pair off ... because down there ... down there in the hold, among the tea-chests and Brazil nuts, the coffin is stowed. I can't go down there, the hold is locked up ... but I know with every fibre in my being, I know it all the time ... even when people here are playing waltzes and tangos ... it is really stupid, the sea has millions of dead beneath it, and every step one takes on earth one is trampling on a body ... but even so, I can't bear it, I can't bear it when they give masked balls and laugh so lustfully. I can sense the presence of this dead woman, and I know what she wants of me. I know I still have a duty. I have not yet finished with this business. Her secret still isn't safe. She has not yet released me ... '

From amidships came the sound of shuffling steps and clattering noises: sailors were beginning to scrub the deck. He started up as though caught off guard: an anxious expression came over his already tense face. He stood up and murmured: 'I must go ... I must go.' It was painful to see him: his ravaged look, his puffy eyes, red from drink or tears. He brushed aside my sympathy. I sensed from his hunched-up bearing that he felt ashamed, deeply ashamed of having unburdened himself to me during the night. Instinctively, I said: 'May I come to your cabin in the afternoon, perhaps?'

He looked at me — a scornful, hard, cynical twist distorted his lips. Anger made him punch out and distort every word: 'Aha … your splendid duty, to help. Aha … you certainly loosened my tongue properly with that principle. But no sir, thank you. Don't think it's any easier for me since I've opened up my entrails for you to see, right down to the excrement. My wreck of a life can't be patched up any more. I have even served the esteemed Dutch government to no purpose. My pension is done for; I am coming back to Europe like a poor dog … a dog that whines in the wake of a coffin. A man doesn't run amok for long unpunished; in the end he is struck down, and I hope, I hope I am nearly at the end of my run. No, thank you sir, for your kind offer to visit me. I have my companions in my cabin already … a few good old bottles of whisky, they comfort me sometimes, and then my friend of that time, to whom unfortunately I haven't turned at the right time, my trusty Browning … that helps better in the end than any confession. Please, don't trouble yourself. The one single right of any man, the only one, remains: to die as he chooses … and to that end to remain unencumbered by help from a stranger.'

He looked at me once more scornfully, indeed defiantly, but I sensed it was only shame, boundless shame. Then he hunched his shoulders, turned round, without saying goodbye, and went remarkably unsteadily and shuffling across the already bright deck towards his cabin. I didn't see him again. I sought him in vain that night and the next in the usual place. He remained hidden, and I would have thought I had dreamt it all or he had been a figment of my imagination, if I hadn't meanwhile come across one of the passengers wearing a black crepe armband. He was an East Indies merchant who, I was told, had just lost his wife from a tropical disease. I saw him going up and down and keeping apart from other passengers, gloomy and grief-stricken; and the thought that I knew about his most personal sorrow filled me with secretive dread. I turned away if he came past me so that I wouldn't betray by my expression that I knew more about his fate than he did.

*   *   *

In the harbour at Naples, then, that remarkable accident happened, the clarification of which I believe I had discovered in the stranger's story. Most of the passengers had gone ashore for the evening; I myself had gone to the opera and then into one of the cheerful cafés on the Via Roma. As we returned to the ship by rowing boat I soon noticed that several boats were circling our ship, searching with torches and acetylene lamps, and up above on the darkened ship there was a mysterious coming and going of carabinieri and police. I asked a sailor what was going on. The way he evaded my question showed me immediately that instructions had been given to say nothing, and also on the next day, when calm had been restored to the ship and we were sailing on to Genoa without any sign of an untoward event having happened, I could find nothing out. Only in the Italian papers did I read, romantically embroidered, about that apparent accident in the harbour at Naples. That night, so the report ran, at a time when it was quiet, so as not to upset the passengers at the sight of it, the coffin of an upper-class lady from the Dutch colonies was being brought from the ship to a small boat. It was being taken down the rope ladder in the presence of her husband, when some heavy object crashed down from the upper deck and the coffin with its bearers and the husband, who were all helping it down, were thrown into the sea. One paper declared it was a lunatic who had thrown himself overboard and had hit the rope ladder. Another explained that the ladder gave way under the enormous weight. At any event, it appeared that the shipping line had done everything possible to conceal the precise circumstances. The bearers and the husband of the dead woman were rescued from the water, but not without some trouble. The leaden coffin, however, went straight down into the deep and couldn't be recovered. At the same time, a separate report briefly mentioned that the body of a man of about forty had been washed up in the harbour. As far as the general public was concerned this had no connection with the romantically reported accident. For me, though, hardly had I read the cursory lines than I could see suddenly staring at me once again from behind the sheet of newsprint, the moon-white countenance with the glinting spectacles, ghostlike, opposite me.

THE BURNING SECRET

THE PARTNER

THE engine gave a hoarse shriek: they had arrived at Semmering. The black coaches of the train waited a minute in the silvery light of the mountain, disgorging a miscellaneous collection of people and swallowing others. Sharp voices could be heard up and down the platform. Then the wheezy engine at the front squeaked again and drew the black chain rattling away into the cavernous tunnel. The broad sweep of country lay pure and peaceful once more, with its sharply etched backcloth scoured bright and clean by the damp wind.

One of the arrivals was young, pleasant, and from the look of his good clothes and the natural spring in his step, apparently worth some attention. He quickly took a cab to the hotel ahead of the others. The horses trotted unhurriedly up the steep road. Spring was in the air. The clouds floating white and restless in the sky were those you see only in May or June. They were innocent companions, still young and flighty, who ran playfully across the blue road to hide suddenly behind high mountains, linking arms and running away, sometimes crumpling up like handkerchiefs, sometimes unravelling into streamers, and eventually playing a practical joke by setting themselves down on the mountain like white caps. There was restlessness in the wind, too, as it boisterously shook the slender trees, still damp from the rain, so that their branches creaked slightly and a thousand droplets showered off them like sparks. Sometimes, too, there was a hint of snow in the cold air blowing across from the mountains. As you breathed you could sense something fresh and keen in the atmosphere. Everything overhead and on the ground showed signs of movement and fermenting impatience. Blowing lightly, the horses sped along the now descending road, their jingling harness announcing their presence far ahead.

Once at the hotel the young man made straight for the register of guests, which he skimmed through but soon found disappointing. 'Whatever am I doing here?' he began to ask himself uneasily. 'To be alone here in the mountains, without company, is worse than being in the office. Obviously I've come too early, or too late. I never have any luck with my holidays. There's not one single name I know among all these people. If only there were a few women. I could at least have a mild flirtation of some sort—if necessary it could be quite innocent—to make the week pass not too bleakly.'

The young man, a baron from a fairly obscure Austrian noble line, had a government post. He had not taken this short holiday for any pressing reason, but just because he and his colleagues had been allowed a spring break and he didn't want to make his employers a present of it. Although he did not lack inner resources, he had a thoroughly sociable disposition. Consequently he was popular and welcome in all circles, and was well known for his dislike of being alone. He had no taste for his own company and avoided such an encounter as much as possible, for the last thing he wanted was to make close acquaintance with himself. He knew he needed people to act as a tinderbox if all his talents and the warmth and high spirits of his heart were to blaze up. On his own he was as cold and useless as a match inside a matchbox.

He wandered about the empty lounge in a bad mood. Sometimes he browsed aimlessly through the newspapers, sometimes he tinkered with a waltz on the piano in the music room, but the rhythm wouldn't come to his fingers correctly. Eventually he sat down peevishly and watched dusk slowly falling and the mist swathing the fir trees in grey. He frittered away an hour in this way, inactive and tense. Then he took refuge in the dining-room.

Only a few tables were occupied and he cast his eye quickly over them. In vain! There was no one he knew, except over there — he feebly returned a greeting — a trainer he recognised from the racecourse, and over there a face he recalled from the Ringstrasse. Otherwise no one. Not a woman, nothing that promised a passing adventure. His ill-humour increased.

He was one of those young men blessed with a handsome face and as a result always in line for a new encounter and ready for a new experience; always eager to venture at full speed into the unknown. He was never taken by surprise, because he always calculated everything warily. He never missed a sexual trick, for his very first glance at any woman searched out her inner feelings, testing her. He made no distinction between the wife of a friend or the maid who opened the door for him.

When a man like that is called — with a certain amount of unthinking disdain — a woman hunter there would indeed appear to be, without the speaker being aware of it, some observable truth in the words. For in fact all the passionate instincts of the chase — stalking, excitement and mental cruelty — flare up in such men. They lie in wait constantly, always ready and determined to pursue the signs of an affair to the bitter end. They are always mad with passion; not the lover's noble passion but that of the gambler, cold, calculating and dangerous. Some of them persist, long after youth has gone, in a life-long expectation of never-ending adventure. For them each day dissolves into a hundred little sensual experiences — a passing glance, a fleeting smile, a knee brushed up against while sitting opposite someone at dinner — and the year in turn consists of hundreds of similar days. For them such sensual experience is the ever flowing, ever nourishing and ever stimulating source of life.

There was no partner for a game here: our searcher realised that immediately. And no annoyance is greater than that of a player sitting at the green-topped table with the cards in his hands and the knowledge of his own superiority, waiting in vain for a partner. The baron asked for a newspaper. Morosely he ran his eye over the lines but his mind was sluggish and he stumbled over the words as though he were drunk.

Then he heard a dress rustle behind him and a mildly impatient voice say in an affected French accent, 'Oh, do be quiet, Edgar!'

A silk dress rustled as it passed his table, a tall and well-built form threw a shadow across it. A pale lad in a black velvet suit, who glanced at him with curiosity, followed. The pair sat down opposite each other at their reserved table. The child was visibly trying to behave properly, but this seemed to be contradicted by the dark restlessness in his eyes. The lady — and the young baron was interested only in her — was very well groomed and dressed with obvious elegance. She was, moreover, a type he liked very much: one of those slightly voluptuous Jewesses, in age not quite past her prime, clearly still capable of passion, but on the other hand experienced enough to conceal her inclinations behind a refined air of melancholy. At first he was denied the chance of looking into her eyes and merely admired the beautiful line of her brow as it curved cleanly over her delicate nose. This revealed her race, it is true, but its noble form made her profile sharp and interesting. As with her other feminine attributes, her hair was noticeably voluptuous. Her considerable and striking beauty seemed to spring from secure self-confidence born of being much admired. She ordered in a very low voice, corrected the boy, who was making a noise playing with his fork — all this with apparent indifference in the face of the baron's cautiously sly look, which she appeared not to notice, though in reality it was precisely his lively attention that forced this subdued circumspection on her.

The cloud lifted from the baron's face at once. It was as though an underground spring bubbled through his nerves, smoothed away his frowns and tightened his muscles, so that his whole being felt invigorated and his eyes sparkled. He wasn't unlike women who need the presence of a man to bring out the best in them. Now a sensual stimulus fully engaged all his energy. The hunter in him scented a prey. Provocatively he tried to hold her eye with his, for sometimes she looked past him with a lively but uncertain glance that gave him no clear, unequivocal answer. He thought, too, he could occasionally detect the hint of a smile beginning to play around her lips. But he couldn't be certain, and the uncertainty itself excited him. The only thing that seemed promising was that she continued not to look at him directly, because this was opposition and embarrassment at the same time. And then there was the noticeably attentive way she talked to the child, which was obviously directed at an onlooker. Indeed the marked emphasis of the show she was putting on concealed, he felt, the beginnings of uneasiness.

He was aroused too: the game had begun. He lingered elegantly over his dinner. For half an hour he continued to gaze at this woman until he had traced every line of her face, and until, without appearing to, he had taken in every part of her curvaceous figure. Outside it was completely dark, the trees sighed as though they were children frightened by the big rain-clouds that stretched grey hands towards them. The shadows in the room grew ever darker and the people in it seemed more and more oppressed by the silence. Under the pressure of this silence the mother's conversation with her child became, he noticed, more forced, more artificial. It would have to stop soon, he thought. So he decided on a test. He was the first to stand up. He walked slowly to the door, looking fixedly through the window and not at her as he went by. Then he suddenly turned his head as though he had forgotten something. And he caught her: she was gazing after him with lively curiosity.

That delighted him. He waited in the foyer. She soon came out, holding the boy's hand, riffled through the newspapers in passing, and pointed out a couple of pictures to the child. But when the baron went over to the table, as though by chance, apparently looking for a paper but in reality to penetrate deeper into the sultry glitter of her eyes, perhaps even to open a conversation, she turned away, tapping her son lightly on the shoulder: 'Come along, Edgar! Bedtime!' And she rustled icily past him. The baron gazed after her, a little disappointed. For he had reckoned on an introduction this same evening, and her brusqueness was a disappointment. But after all, it was alluring to meet opposition, and indeed the uncertainty inflamed his desire. At least he had the partner he needed and the game could begin.

INSTANT FRIENDSHIP

When the baron entered the foyer the next morning he saw the child of the unknown beauty in eager conversation with the two lift-boys. He was showing them pictures in a book by Karl May. His mother wasn't there. She was obviously busy with her toilette. The baron now inspected the boy for the first time. He was a shy, immature, highly strung lad, about twelve years old. His movements were fidgety and his dark eyes took in everything around him. Like many children of his age he gave the impression of being unnecessarily startled, almost as though he had been torn from his sleep and suddenly placed in strange surroundings. His face didn't altogether lack good looks but its character was as yet unformed. The battle between manhood and childhood seemed scarcely to have begun. It was as though his features were being kneaded and had not yet taken shape. Nothing was stated in clear outlines; everything was still colourless and blended uneasily. Besides, he was at that awkward age when children's clothes don't look right, sleeves and trouser legs flap loosely round thin wrists and ankles, and vanity isn't yet an influence in making a boy want to look after his appearance.

He made a really pitiful impression, wandering around the hotel aimlessly. In fact he was in everyone's way. The hall-porter soon pushed him aside when the boy apparently bothered him with all sorts of questions. Now he was blocking the entrance. Obviously he was short of friendly company, and hence in his childish need to chatter he turned to the hotel staff. They answered him when they had time, but broke off the conversation when an adult appeared or they had something more important to do. The baron watched with indulgent interest as the wretched boy approached everything with curiosity and it all slipped away from him without response. Once he caught one of those inquiring glances himself, but as soon as the boy noticed he was being watched his dark eyes immediately turned anxiously away and hid behind lowered lids. That amused the baron. The lad really began to interest him. He asked himself if this child, whose shyness was evidently only timidity, might not serve as the quickest means of making an approach to his mother. At least he would try it.

Unobtrusively he followed the boy, who had just gone out of the revolving door again and in his childish need for affection was fondling the pink muzzle of a white horse. That was until – he really had no luck – he was sent packing quite roughly by the coachman. Upset and bored, he lounged about again, without purpose and looking a little sad. Then the baron spoke to him.

'Well, young man, how do you like it here, then?' he began unexpectedly, making an effort to sound as jovial as he could.

The child blushed fiery red and looked up nervously. He didn't know what to do with his hands and squirmed about in fear and embarrassment. As far as he knew it was the first time a strange man had tried to make conversation with him.

'Very much, thank you,' he managed to say. The last two words were more choked out than spoken.

'I'm surprised at that,' said the baron, smiling. 'It's really rather a boring place, especially for someone your age. What do you do all day, then?' The lad was still too embarrassed to answer quickly. Did this unknown, well-dressed gentleman really want to talk to him when no one else wanted to bother? The thought made him shy and proud at the same time. Gradually he pulled himself together.

'I read, and then we often go for walks. Sometimes Mama and I go for a drive. I have to get well again. I've been ill. The doctor said I was to sit in the sun a lot.'

He seemed to be more confident as he finished explaining. Children are always proud of being ill because they know danger makes them twice as important to their relatives.

'Yes, sunshine is always good for young fellows like you. You'll soon get a good tan. But you shouldn't sit still in it all day. A boy like you should be running about, in high spirits – even get up to a little mischief. I suspect you are too well-behaved. You look far too serious with that great, thick book under your arm. When I think what a dare-devil I was at your age – every evening I'd come home with my trousers torn. Don't be too serious!'

The child had to laugh despite himself, and he stopped being afraid. He would have liked to reply but it seemed too forward, too conceited in front of this charming gentleman who was so friendly. He had never been cheeky and was still slightly embarrassed. As a result he was now most dreadfully torn between feeling happy and feeling bashful. He wanted very much to say something, but he couldn't think of anything. Luckily just at that moment the hotel's big golden St Bernard padded up, sniffed at them both and willingly submitted to being stroked.

'Do you like dogs?' the baron asked.

'Oh, very much. My Grandmama has one at her house in Baden and when we stay there he's with me all day. But we only go there in the summer.'

'I think we have a couple of dozen dogs on our estate back home. If you are good I'll give you one as a present. A brown one with white ears, still a puppy. Would you like that?'

The child blushed with pleasure.

'Oh yes!'

He said it spontaneously and with enthusiasm. But then straight afterwards the thought struck him. He was shaken and said anxiously, 'But Mama will never allow it. She says she won't have a dog in the house. They are too much trouble.'

The baron laughed. At last the conversation had come round to the boy's mother.

'Is Mama so strict?'

The child reflected, looked at him for a second as though questioning whether he should trust this stranger or not. The answer was cautious.

'No, Mama isn't strict. She lets me have everything now, because I was ill. Perhaps she'll let me have a dog.'

'Shall I ask her?'

'Yes, please. You ask her,' the boy said excitedly. 'Then she'll be sure to agree. And what does he look like? He's got white ears, you said, didn't you? Can he retrieve?'

'Yes, he can do everything.' The baron had to smile at the eager light he had so quickly kindled in the boy's eyes.

All at once his initial reserve was broken down and his natural enthusiasm, which had been held back by fear, bubbled over. The child who earlier had been shy and cowed made a lightning transformation into a boisterous lad. If only the mother turns out the same way, the baron thought instinctively, hot-blooded behind her fear! But the boy was already bombarding him with a score of questions.

'What's the dog called?'

'Diamond.'

'Diamond!' the boy shouted with excitement. He had to laugh and shout over every word, he was so intoxicated by the unexpectedness of someone wanting to be his friend. The baron himself was astonished at the speed of his success and decided to strike while the iron was hot. He invited the boy to go for a walk and the poor child, who had been pining for company for weeks, was delighted at the suggestion. Without thinking, he told his new friend everything in response to the baron's apparently unimportant, coaxing questions.

Soon the baron knew all about the family and above all that Edgar was the only son of a Viennese lawyer, obviously from the well-to-do Jewish bourgeoisie. And by skilful questioning he soon discovered that the mother wasn't very pleased about having to stay in Semmering. She had complained about the lack of like-minded company. Indeed, he thought from the evasive way Edgar answered the question that perhaps the mother was quite pleased to be away from her husband and all was not well between them. He was almost ashamed of himself, it was so easy to elicit all the little family secrets from this innocent babe. For Edgar was really proud that anything he had to say was of interest to a grown-up and trusted his new friend absolutely. His youthful heart beat with pride – the baron had put his arm round the boy's shoulders as they walked along – to be seen publicly to be so friendly with an adult. Gradually he forgot he was still a child and chattered freely and spontaneously as though to someone his own age.

As his conversation showed, Edgar was very bright and somewhat precocious. Most sickly children are, because they spend more time with adults than with their schoolfellows. He had a marked tendency to like or to hate people to excess. There was nothing he seemed to have a calm relationship with: he spoke of every person or thing either with delight or with a hatred so fierce that he twisted his face unpleasantly and made himself look almost evil and repulsive. Somewhat wild and unsteady, possibly still affected by his recent illness, his conversation had a fanatical fire about it, and his awkwardness appeared to stem from a fear of his own passion that he suppressed only with difficulty.

The baron gained his confidence easily. In barely half an hour the boy's warm and sensitive heart was his. It is indeed so incredibly easy to deceive children; they are so innocent and their love is so seldom sought after. He had only to recall his own childhood to be able to make his conversation so natural and unforced that the boy accepted him completely as his equal and very quickly lost any sense of distance between them. He was blissfully happy at his good fortune in having suddenly found a friend here in this lonely place – and what a friend! He forgot everyone in Vienna – his young friends with their high-pitched voices and juvenile chatter; all thoughts of them were dissolved at this very instant! His entire, wholehearted enthusiasm belonged now to his new, his best friend. His heart swelled with pride when, before they parted, he was invited to go for another walk in the morning, and his new friend raised his hand in a farewell salute, like a brother. These moments were possibly the very best of his whole life. It is so easy to deceive children.

The baron smiled as the boy ran off. Well, he had secured his go-between. He knew the lad would pester his mother to the point of exhaustion recounting it all, every single word of it; and he was pleased when he remembered how dexterously he had introduced compliments on her appearance and how he had always spoken of Edgar's 'beautiful Mama'. He could be sure the communicative child wouldn't rest until its Mama and he had been brought together. He need not lift a finger to reduce the distance between himself and the unknown beauty. He could quietly dream and look at the scenery, for he knew a child's enthusiastic pair of hands was building him a bridge to her heart.

TRIO

It became evident some hours later how very well the plan had worked, down to the last detail. When the young baron entered the dining-room, deliberately a little late, Edgar jumped up from his chair, eagerly greeted him with a broad grin and waved to him. At the same time he tugged at his mother's sleeve, spoke to her quickly and excitedly, pointing out the baron with obvious gestures. Embarrassed and blushing, she rebuked him for his far too lively behaviour, but she couldn't avoid looking over to please the child. The baron immediately took this opportunity to bow respectfully. Acquaintance was made. She had to acknowledge him, but after that she bent her head deeper over her plate and took care through the rest of the meal not to look at him again. Not so Edgar: he gazed across the whole time and once tried to speak to the baron – an offence for which his mother immediately rebuked him. After dinner it was made clear to him that he was to go to bed, and an urgently whispered exchange took place between Edgar and his Mama, which resulted in his fervent plea being granted. He went over to the other table to say goodnight to his friend. The baron said a few cordial words to him which made the child's eyes light up again, and chatted for a few minutes. Then suddenly moving with practised grace, he turned towards the other table, stood up and congratulated his somewhat astonished neighbour on her clever, lively son. He spoke highly of the capital morning he had spent with him – Edgar stood there blushing with joy and pride – and finally he inquired after his health at such length and with such detailed questions that the mother was obliged to reply. In this way a long conversation developed, which pleased the boy and which he lapped up with a kind of awe. The baron introduced himself. He thought his noble name made some impression on the lady's vanity. At any event she was excessively polite towards him. She maintained her reserve, however, and soon moved to go, making the boy her excuse.

The boy protested vehemently. He wasn't tired and was quite ready to stay up all night. But his mother had already held out her hand to the baron, who kissed it respectfully.

Edgar slept badly that night. Rapture and childish desperation were in a jumble inside him. For that day something new had happened in his life. For the first time he had been involved in adult affairs. Already half asleep, he forgot he was a child and in one leap fancied he was grown up. Until now he had had few friends, being an only child and often ill. For all his emotional needs there had been no one except his parents, who scarcely bothered with him, and the servants. And the strength of a passion will always be wrongly measured if it is valued for its cause and not for the excitement that precedes it; and for that empty, dark space of disappointment and loneliness that is part of all great experiences of the heart. Over-abundant, untapped emotion had been lying dormant here, and it now leapt with outstretched arms at the first person who seemed to want to make use of it. Edgar lay in the dark, happy and in a turmoil: he wanted to laugh and yet he had to cry. For he loved this man as he had never loved any friend, or his parents—not even God. All the immature emotion of his young life clung to the image of this man whose name he hadn't known two hours earlier.

But he was intelligent enough, nevertheless, not to be carried away by the unexpectedness and singularity of this new friendship. What really bothered him was that he felt unworthy and insignificant. 'Do I deserve him? I, a small boy of twelve? I still have to go to school and be sent to bed at night before everyone else.' He agonised. 'What can I be to him? What can I offer him?' It was precisely this painful awareness of the impossibility of being able to demonstrate his feelings that made him unhappy. Usually if he had a friend he really liked, his first action was to share the few small treasures in his desk with him: stamps, stones, childish possessions. But all those things that had been of great significance and rare fascination to him yesterday seemed suddenly devalued, trifling and to be despised. For how could he offer such things to this new friend when he wouldn't even dare to speak really familiarly to him? What way, what possibility was there of revealing his feelings? Increasingly he felt the torment of being small, only half-grown, immature, a twelve-year-old child; and never before had he cursed being a child so violently. Never had he longed so much to wake up a different person, as he dreamed he was: big and strong, a man, a grown-up like the rest of them.

The first colourful dreams of this new adult world wove themselves quickly into his restless thoughts. Edgar fell asleep eventually with a smile, but even so the recollection of next morning's appointment disturbed his sleep. It was only seven o'clock when he woke with a start, fearful of being too late. He dressed quickly and went into his mother's room to say good morning. She was astonished, because usually she had difficulty making him get up. He rushed out again before she could ask him any questions. He wandered about impatiently until nine o'clock, forgetting his breakfast, his single preoccupation being not to keep his friend waiting a moment for their walk.

Eventually, at half-past nine the baron came sauntering in without a care. He had, of course, long since forgotten the appointment, but now, as the boy eagerly rushed up to him, he had to smile at so much enthusiasm and indicated he would keep his promise. He linked arms with the lad, who was radiant, and they strolled up and down – except that gently but deliberately he avoided actually setting off on their walk just yet. He seemed to be waiting for something. At least that was the implication of the tense way he kept looking at the door. Suddenly he straightened up. Edgar's Mama had arrived, and returning the baron's greeting in a friendly way, came over to the pair of them. She smiled in agreement when she learned of the proposed walk that Edgar had thought too precious to tell her about, and quickly accepted the baron's invitation to accompany them.

Edgar immediately became sulky and bit his lip. How annoying she had to arrive just exactly at that moment! This walk was supposed to be his property. When he had introduced his friend to Mama he had done it only out of kindness; but he certainly didn't want to share him. Already something like jealousy was stirring in him as he noticed how friendly the baron was being towards his mother.

So the three of them set off for their walk, and the feeling he was important and suddenly significant was further dangerously fostered in the child through the pointed interest they both took in him. Edgar was almost exclusively the subject of conversation. His mother spoke with somewhat exaggerated concern about his pallor and highly-strung state, while the baron rather laughingly dismissed this and emphasised the pleasant manners of his 'friend', as he called him, as they strolled along. Edgar was in his seventh heaven. He had privileges he had never been allowed in all his childhood. He was permitted to join in without being told at once to be quiet, and to express all kinds of quite cheeky wishes which would earlier have been taken amiss. And it wasn't surprising that the deceptive feeling grew mightily and ever more self-confidently within him, that he was an adult. His childhood already lay behind him in his bright dreams, like outgrown clothing he had thrown away.

At luncheon, following the invitation of Edgar's ever more friendly mother, the baron sat at their table. From being opposite one another they were now sitting next to each other; they had moved from acquaintance to friendship. The trio was in being, and the three voices of man, woman and child harmonised purely together.

ATTACK

The time seemed ripe now for the impatient hunter to creep up on his prey. The family element, the trio in this situation, displeased him. Of course it was quite pleasant for the three of them to talk together, but after all, conversation was not his objective. And he knew that being sociable, by disguising desire, always checked eroticism between man and woman. Ardour is removed from words and fire from the attack. She should never forget the true purpose of the conversation which —he was certain—she already clearly understood.

It seemed very likely that his attentions to this woman would not go unrewarded. She was at that critical age when a woman begins to regret having remained faithful to a husband she has never really loved, and when the twilight of already fading beauty calls for a final, urgent choice between behaving like a mother or like a woman. Life that has long since seemed settled is, at a moment like this, once again unsettled. The magnetic needle of the will quivers for the last time between the hope of a sexual experience and ultimate resignation. A woman has then to make a dangerous decision: to follow her own destiny or to live for her children, to be woman or mother. And the baron, who was observant in these matters, thought he noticed that dangerous indecision in her. She continually forgot to refer to her husband while they talked, and deep down she really knew little about her child's emotions. A shadow of boredom, disguised as melancholy, lay over her almond-shaped eyes and clouded their sensuality with uncertainty.

The baron decided to advance quickly but at the same time to avoid any appearance of haste. So, contrariwise, as the angler plays the fish enticingly, he wanted this new friendship to appear to be a matter of indifference on his side. He wanted her to make advances to him while in reality he was hunting her down. He decided to display a certain arrogance to underline sharply the difference in their social standing, and he was amused by the thought that he could win this luscious, ample and beautiful flesh just by emphasising his pride, by his appearance, his aristocratic-sounding name and aloof manners.

The hot pursuit was already beginning to excite him and he therefore became cautious. He spent the afternoon in his room in the pleasant knowledge that he would be sought after and missed. But his absence was not noticed so much by the lady at whom it was aimed as by the poor child, for whom it was a torment. Edgar felt utterly helpless and lost all the afternoon. The boy waited for his friend with the tenacious loyalty of youth, all through the long hours. He would have thought it a betrayal to have gone off and done something else on his own. Idly he wandered about the corridors and the later it became the more his heart ached with misery. In his uneasy mind he already imagined some accident or some unknown offence he had unwittingly given, and he was on the verge of tears with impatience and anxiety.

So when the baron came in to dinner he was warmly received. Edgar ran across to him, ignoring his mother's reproving call and the astonishment of other people, and threw his thin little arms fiercely round him. 'Where were you? Where have you been?' he cried quickly. 'We looked everywhere for you.'

His mother reddened at this unwelcome inclusion of herself, and said quite severely, 'Edgar, behave yourself. Come and sit down!' (She spoke French to the boy even though she wasn't at all fluent in it and was easily bogged down if she ventured on a complicated explanation.) Edgar obeyed but went on asking the baron questions.

'Now, just remember,' Edgar's mother said, 'the baron can do as he pleases. Perhaps he's tired of our company.' This time she included herself, and the baron felt pleased that this reproof to the boy was in effect a compliment to himself.

The hunter in him awoke. He was intoxicated and excited at having found the right track so quickly, at sensing his quarry almost within shooting range. His eyes shone, his blood coursed easily through his veins, and he himself did not know how the conversation flowed from his lips. Like many men endowed with strong sex appeal he was twice as attractive, twice the man, when he knew that women appreciated him. He was like many an actor who warms up only when he feels the audience, the breathing mass of people, under his spell. His friends considered him a good raconteur, gifted in conjuring up lively pictures, but today he excelled himself—having meanwhile drunk several glasses of the champagne he had ordered to celebrate their new friendship. He told stories about hunting in India, which he had done as the guest of a very aristocratic English friend. It was clever to choose that subject because it was neutral. He sensed, too, that this woman was intrigued by anything exotic and out of her reach.

The person he really bewitched, though, was Edgar, whose eyes were alight with enthusiasm. He forgot to eat or drink and hung on every word that fell from the story-teller's lips. It was beyond his expectations actually to meet a man who had experienced the tremendous things he had read about in books: tiger hunting, Hindus—those people with brown skins —and the juggernaut, the terrifying chariot that crushed a thousand people beneath it. Until now he had never believed such people existed, in the same way that he didn't believe fairy stories, and now a whole new part of the world sprang to life for the first time. He couldn't take his eyes off his friend. He gazed at the baron's hands, right in front of him, that had killed a tiger. He scarcely dared ask a question and when he did his voice sounded wildly excited. His vivid imagination conjured up continuously the scenes in the stories. He saw his friend high up on an elephant with a purple caparison on its back, brown-skinned men to right and left wearing expensive turbans, and then suddenly the tiger leaping out of the jungle with bared teeth and striking the elephant's trunk with its claws. Now the baron was telling them something even more interesting, how craftily elephants are caught, by using old, tamed beasts to lure the young, wild, high-spirited ones into the crates. The boy's eyes shone. Then—it felt like a knife thrust — his mother said suddenly, looking at the clock, 'It's nine o'clock! Bedtime, Edgar!'

The boy went pale with shock. Being told to go to bed is an awful order for all children. It is public humiliation in front of the grown-ups, the admission, the stigma, of being a child, being small, of needing more sleep. But how frightful was the disgrace coming at this interesting moment, just when he would miss hearing fantastic things.

'Just one more story, Mama, about the elephants, do let me hear one more.'

He wanted to start pleading, but quickly remembered his new dignity as an adult. He ventured one single attempt only. But his mother was being noticeably strict today. 'No, it's late now. Up you go! Be a good boy, Edgar. I'll tell you all the baron's stories later.'

Edgar hesitated. His mother usually took him up to bed. But he didn't want to plead with her in front of his friend. His youthful pride wanted him to save something at least from the painful departure by appearing to go of his own free will.

'Truly, Mama, you'll tell me everything, absolutely everything? About the elephants and all the other things?'

'Yes, darling.'

'And soon! Tonight?'

'Yes, yes, but now do run along. Off you go!'

Edgar wondered to himself how he managed to shake hands with the baron and his Mama without going red, for he had to choke back his tears. The baron ruffled Edgar's hair in a friendly way, which brought a smile back to his anxious face. But then he had to rush to the door or they would have seen the tears running down his cheeks.

THE ELEPHANTS

Edgar's mother stayed for some time in the dining-room with the baron, but they did not go on talking about elephants and hunting. Once the boy had gone their conversation became slightly uneasy and they felt mildly embarrassed. Eventually they went out into the foyer and sat in a corner. The baron was as dazzling as ever, himself exhilarated by the glasses of champagne he had drunk, so the conversation quickly took a dangerous turn.

The baron wasn't exactly handsome, only young. He looked very masculine with his close-cut hair, and he had a lively expression on his swarthy, boyish face. He delighted her with his fresh, uninhibited attitudes. She was pleased to look at him close to and was no longer afraid of his gaze. So gradually he became bolder in what he said, which flustered her mildly. It was as though he had touched her physically and taken his hand away again, somehow inconceivably filling her with desire, and making the blood rush to her cheeks. But then he would laugh again lightly, spontaneously, boyishly, and that gave all the little signs of desire the harmless appearance of a childish joke. Sometimes it seemed as though she felt she should rebuff him brusquely, but coquettish by nature, she was only tempted by those little innuendoes to expect more. And carried along by the daring game, she sought in the end to follow his lead. She threw him glances full of teasing little promises, encouraged him in word and gesture, and even let him move closer, hearing his voice at her ear and now and then feeling his breath warm and quivering at her shoulder. Like all flirts they forgot the time and were lost so completely in their absorbing conversation that they grew alarmed only when the foyer lights began to go out at midnight.

She jumped up quickly, responding to the initial shock, and realised at once just how far she had rashly ventured. She was, after all, no stranger to playing with fire, but now her awakened instinct told her how close this game had already come to the danger point. With a shiver she discovered she didn't feel at all sure of her self-control; something in her was beginning to give way and she was in a heightened state of excitement, seeing things as one does in a fever. Her mind was in a turmoil of anguish, the effect of wine and flirtatious talk. She was overcome by blind, senseless fear, of the kind she had experienced a few times before in her life at such dangerous moments, but never as overwhelmingly or as powerfully as now.

'Good night. I'll see you in the morning,' she said huskily, and made to hurry away. She was not running away from him so much as from the present danger and from a new, unaccountable, lack of firmness in herself. But the baron, with smooth assurance, held on to her proffered hand, kissed it, not just once, correctly, but four or five times, from her delicate finger tips right up to her wrist, moving his lips so that his moustache lightly tickled the back of her hand. A tingling sensation in her blood, warm and oppressive, coursed right through her. Insecurity welled up again, hammering menacingly at her temples. Her head felt as though it was on fire. Fear, blind fear, surged through her whole being, and she abruptly pulled her hand away from him.

'Stay a little longer,' he whispered. But she was already walking away with a hurried lack of poise which made her alarm and embarrassment obvious. She was pursued by the awful anxiety that the man behind her might follow and catch hold of her. But at the same time, as she made her escape, she felt regret that he did not do so. Something might have happened here tonight that she had subconsciously wanted for years—a romance, the merest hint of which she yearned for, though until now she had always intended to side-step it at the last-minute. It was a great, dangerous romance she longed for, not just a passing and unsettling flirtation. The baron was too proud, though, to rush precipitately after a favourable moment. He was too certain of his victory to behave like a pirate and take this woman at her weakest, when she was intoxicated with wine. On the contrary, he wanted to win fairly and her surrender to be a fully conscious one. She couldn't escape him. He had observed the torrid poison taking a grip on her.

Upstairs she stood with her hand pressed against her pounding heart. She must calm herself for a minute. Her nerves were in shreds. She let out a sigh, half in relief at having escaped danger, and half in regret. But everything was confused and all she felt now was a slight dizziness. She groped her way to her door, her eyes half-closed as though she were drunk, and breathed a sigh of relief when she grasped the cold handle. Now at last she felt safe!

She opened the door gently, and immediately stepped back in fright. Something in the darkened room had moved. Her taut nerves were jarred. She was on the point of crying out for help when a sleepy voice spoke from within the room.

'Is that you, Mama?'

'For heaven's sake, what are you doing here?' She rushed over to the sofa where Edgar lay huddled up and was just coming out of his sleep. Her first thought was that the child must be ill or in need of help.

But Edgar said drowsily and with mild reproach, 'I waited for you for such a long time and then I fell asleep.'

'Why did you wait?'

'Because of the elephants.'

'What elephants?'

Then it came back to her. She had indeed promised the child she would tell him all about the hunting and the adventures, this evening. And so the boy had slipped into her room. Her silly baby had waited for her, believing implicitly in her promise, and had fallen asleep there. She was outraged by his folly. Or rather she was furious with herself. She heard a low whisper of guilt and shame that she wanted to silence. 'Go to bed this minute, you naughty boy,' she shouted at him. Edgar stared at her. Why was she so angry? He hadn't done anything. But his astonishment roused his already overwrought mother even more. 'Go to your room at once.' As she vented her anger on him she knew she was being unfair.

Edgar went without a word. He was really very tired and perceived only dimly through the enveloping mists of sleep that his mother had broken a promise and that somehow he was in hot water. But he didn't rebel. He was heavy and apathetic with drowsiness. Besides, he was very angry with himself for going to sleep instead of staying awake while he waited. 'Just like a baby,' he reproached himself, before he went back to sleep again. After yesterday he hated being a child.

SKIRMISHING

The baron had slept badly. It is always risky trying to sleep after a flirtation has been interrupted. A restless night, full of uneasy dreams, had soon made him regret he hadn't struck while the iron was hot. When he came down to breakfast, still feeling thick with sleep and ill-humour, the boy leapt out at him from a hiding place, flung his arms round him boisterously and began to assail him with a thousand questions. He was delighted to have his big friend to himself again for a few minutes and not to have to share him with Mama. The baron was to tell him everything, not Mama, Edgar insisted vehemently. For despite her promise she hadn't told him those wonderful stories after all. The baron was scarcely able to conceal his bad mood in the face of this nasty shock, as Edgar pestered him in a hundred juvenile ways.

Moreover, the boy mixed the unrestrained display of his affection with these questions, showing how blissfully happy he was to be alone again with his long-sought-after friend, for whom he had been waiting since early morning.

The baron answered brusquely. He was beginning to be bored by constantly being waylaid by the boy and asked childish questions, and above all by his unwelcome show of affection. He was tired of going around day in, day out, with a twelve-year-old, swapping silly jokes with him. What he had in mind was to take the woman while he had the chance. But the boy's unwanted presence was a problem. He began to be oppressed by the first flicker of uncertainty in the face of the affection he had so carelessly aroused. For he could see no possibility, for the present, of being free of this all too devoted friend.

Nevertheless he must try. Until 10 o'clock, the time he had arranged with Edgar's mother to go for a walk, he let the boy's eager chatter wash over him without paying much attention. He put a word in now and again so as not to upset him, but browsed through the newspaper at the same time. Eventually, when the minute-hand of the clock was almost upright, he asked Edgar – as though he had just remembered – to run quickly across to the other hotel to ask if the baron's cousin, Count Grundheim, had arrived.

Happy to be able to do something for his friend at last, and proud of his position as a messenger, the unsuspecting boy jumped up immediately and rushed off so precipitately that people stared after him in surprise. But he wanted only to show how reliable he was when someone entrusted him with a message. At the hotel they told him the Count had not yet arrived. Indeed he wasn't expected for several hours. He raced back with this news. But the baron wasn't in the foyer. So he went and knocked on his bedroom door – in vain! Alarmed, he ran in and out of all the public rooms, the music room, and the café, and then stormed off to his Mama to ask if she knew where the baron was. She wasn't there either. He was nonplussed when the porter, to whom he finally turned in desperation, told him they had gone out together a few minutes ago!

Edgar waited patiently. In his innocence he suspected nothing. He was sure they wouldn't be long, because the baron was waiting for his answer. But the hours passed inexorably and he became anxious. After all, since the day this strange, seductive man had become involved in his simple young life the boy had been in a state of tension, over-excitement and confusion. In such a highly-strung child every emotion left its mark like an impression in wax. He began to blink rapidly again with nerves, and he went pale. He waited and waited, patiently at first, then in a state of disarray, and eventually near to tears. But he still wasn't suspicious. His blind faith in his wonderful friend made him think there had been a misunderstanding. He was tortured by an inner fear that perhaps he had made a mistake over his instructions.

How odd it was, though, that when they did return they stood there talking and showed no surprise at seeing him. It seemed as though they hadn't particularly missed him.

'We set off in your direction, Eddie, hoping to meet you on the way,' the baron said, without asking for the answer to his question about his cousin.

The child was quite upset to think they could have been looking for him in vain. He began to protest that he had only run straight back up the main street — which way had they gone? — when his mother cut him short.

'That's enough, Edgar. Children should be seen and not heard.'

Mortified, Edgar went red. That was the second time his Mama had made a mean attempt to humiliate him in front of his friend. Why did she do it? Why did she keep on treating him like a child, when he no longer thought he was one? She was obviously jealous of his friend and planned to win the baron over for herself. That was it; and it was certainly she who had deliberately led the baron off in the wrong direction. But he wouldn't let her treat him badly like that. He'd show her! He'd defy her! And Edgar decided he'd ignore her at table today and speak only to his friend.

That, however, was difficult. What happened was what he least expected: they didn't notice he was sulking. Indeed, they didn't seem to notice he was there at all – he, who only yesterday had been the centre of their attention! They spoke to each other across him. They joked and laughed as though he had slid under the table. The blood rushed to his cheeks and there was a suffocating lump in his throat. He realised with increasing bitterness how unbearably powerless he was. He had to sit there quietly and watch his mother take away his friend, the only person he loved. And was there nothing he could do about it other than stay silent? He wanted to stand up and bang suddenly on the table with both fists. Just so that they would notice him. But he controlled himself, lightly put down his knife and fork and left the rest of his food. For a long time they didn't even notice his stubborn self-denial. Only when they came to the last course did it attract his mother's attention. She asked if he wasn't feeling well.

'It's sickening,' he thought to himself. 'She only ever thinks of one thing, whether I'm ill or not. Otherwise she's not interested.'

He replied abruptly that he wasn't hungry, and that satisfied her. Nothing, but nothing, would draw their attention to him. The baron seemed to have forgotten him. He didn't once address a word to the boy. The hot tears were welling up into Edgar's eyes. He had to resort to the juvenile trick of covering his face with his table-napkin to prevent anyone seeing the accursed childish tears that ran down his cheeks until he could taste salt on his lips. He breathed a sigh of relief when the meal was over.

During lunch his mother had suggested they take a carriage to Maria-Schutz. Edgar bit his lip when he heard her. She wouldn't leave him alone with his friend for a minute. But he was really beside himself when, as they were leaving the table, she said to him, 'Edgar, you'll be forgetting all your school-work. You'd better stay here and do some revision.' Once again he clenched his fists. She was always belittling him in the eyes of his friend, always reminding him publicly he was a child, that he had to go to school and was only tolerated by adults. This time her motive was all too transparent. He didn't answer but turned abruptly away.

'Dear me, what a bad mood we are in.' She laughed and said to the baron, 'Would it really be so dreadful to make him do an hour's homework?'

And then—it struck a chill and deadly blow to Edgar's heart—the baron, whom he called his friend and who had mocked at him for being a stay-at-home, said, 'No, of course an hour or two wouldn't hurt.'

Was it a conspiracy? Had they both really joined forces against him? Edgar scowled.

'Papa said I wasn't to do any schoolwork here. Papa said I was to get strong again,' he flung at them with all the self-importance of the convalescent, clinging in despair to his father's word and authority.

His protest came out sounding like a threat. It was most remarkable: what he said did indeed seem to disconcert them both. His mother looked away and drummed her fingers nervously on the table. There was a painful gulf of silence between them.

'Just as you like, Eddie,' the baron said eventually, with a forced smile. 'I'm a bad example, it's true. I failed everything at school.'

But Edgar didn't laugh at the joke. He gave the baron a searching, wistful look, as though he wanted to penetrate right into his mind. What was going on? Their relationship wasn't the same, and the child didn't know why. Feeling uneasy, he looked away. His heart was hammering—doubt had crept in.

THE BURNING SECRET

'What has made her change like this?' the child pondered as he sat opposite them in the carriage. 'Why don't they treat me as they did earlier? Why does Mama avoid my eye when I look at her? Why is he always trying to make jokes at my expense and play the clown? Neither of them talks to me as they did yesterday and the day before. It's as though their faces have changed. Mama's lips are so red today, she must have painted them. I've never seen her do that before. And he is always frowning as though he's annoyed. But surely I haven't done anything to them, or said anything that could vex them? No, I can't be the reason, because they aren't behaving in the same way to each other either now. It's as though they've done something they can't trust themselves to talk about. They aren't lively like they were yesterday. They're not laughing. They look embarrassed. They're hiding something. They have a secret they don't want to share with me. I must find out what it is at all costs.

'I think I know what it is already. It must be the same one they have at home when they shut the doors on me. I've read about it in books and seen it at the opera. It's when the men and women are singing and they walk towards each other with outstretched arms. They embrace and push each other apart. It must be something like what happened when my French teacher got on so badly with Papa and was sent away. All these things are related, I'm sure of it. But I don't know how. Oh, if only I could find out and know this secret at last! If only I could put my hand on the key that opens all the doors. I wouldn't be a child any longer. People wouldn't conceal things from me, hold things back and lie to me! It's now or never. I'm going to snatch this terrible secret from them.'

A furrow appeared on his forehead, making the slender twelve-year-old look much older as he turned the question over seriously in his mind. He didn't even look at the scenery, spread out in bright colours all round, the mountains in the pure green of their pine forests, the valleys in the even softer shades of late spring. He looked at the pair opposite him at the back of the carriage, as though by fixing his intense gaze on them he could draw the secret out of the glittering depths of their eyes, like an angler fishing. Nothing sharpens the intelligence more than emotional suspicion. Nothing awakens the imagination more in an immature mind than to be following a trail in the dark. Sometimes there is only one single, flimsy door separating children from the real world, as we call it, and a chance puff of wind will blow it open.

Edgar felt all at once that what he didn't know, the great secret, was nearly in his grasp, as it had never been before. He sensed he was really close to it. True, it was still a mystery he hadn't yet unravelled, but he was close to it, very close. This stirred him and gave him suddenly an air of intense seriousness. For instinctively he had a presentiment that he had reached the last shores of his childhood.

The two sitting opposite him felt some kind of depressing resistance around them, without being aware that it emanated from the boy. They felt confined and restricted as a threesome in the carriage. The pair of eyes opposite glowed and flickered darkly and inhibited them. They scarcely dared to speak or look at each other. They were unable to re-establish their earlier light-hearted, sociable conversation. They were already too ensnared by the note of warm intimacy; their flattering words seemed dangerously suggestive of secret desire. Their talk went in fits and starts. They wanted to go on but came to a halt again in the face of the boy's obstinate silence.

His sullen refusal to talk was especially a burden for his mother. She watched him cautiously out of the corner of her eye and was frightened when she suddenly recognised for the first time how like her husband the boy was in the set of his mouth when he was angry or provoked. The thought made her uncomfortable. She didn't want to be reminded of her husband just now when she was engaged in a flirtation. The child seemed like a ghost and a guardian of her conscience, both unbearable here in the confines of the carriage, a foot away with his dark, inquiring eyes and suspicious mind behind his pale forehead. Edgar looked up at her suddenly for a moment. They both lowered their eyes. They felt for the first time in their lives they were spying on each other. Until then they had trusted each other implicitly, but now all of a sudden there was a barrier between mother and son; things had changed between them. For the first time they began to look at themselves, to turn their destinies away from each other, each one secretly hating the other. But it was still too new a sensation for them to dare admit it.

All three breathed a sigh of relief when the horses brought them back to the hotel. The outing had not been a success. They all felt it and no one dared say so. Edgar jumped down first. His mother excused herself, saying she had a headache, and went quickly to her room. She was tired and wanted to be alone. Edgar and the baron stayed behind. The baron paid the driver, looked at his watch and walked towards the foyer, ignoring the boy. He strode past him, this handsome, straight-backed man with his rhythmical, easy walk that so captivated the child that Edgar had yesterday secretly tried to copy it in front of his mirror. The baron strode clean past him. He had obviously forgotten the boy and left him standing by the driver and the horses as though he was nothing to do with him.

Something snapped in two inside Edgar when he saw the baron ignore him, the baron whom he still idolised despite everything. He was in despair that his friend should have walked off like that without patting his sleeve or saying a word. Edgar still couldn't think of anything he had done to annoy him. The composure he had maintained with difficulty, the burden of dignity he had artificially created slipped from his slender shoulders. He was a child again, small and humiliated, as he had been yesterday and before that. He forced himself forward against his will. His legs trembling, he followed the baron quickly and went up to him as he was about to go up the stairs. He said urgently, almost unable to hold back his tears, 'What have I done? Why don't you take any notice of me? Why aren't you friends any more? And Mama too? Why do you always want to send me away? Am I a nuisance or have I done something wrong?'

The baron was alarmed. Something in the child's voice disturbed and moved him. He was overcome with pity for the innocent boy. 'Eddie, what a silly fellow you are! I'm not in a very good mood today, that's all. You're such a good chap and I'm very fond of you.' He ruffled the boy's hair vigorously; but he half turned his head away to avoid having to look into those large imploring eyes, wet with tears. The game he was playing began to distress him. He felt thoroughly ashamed at having exploited the affection of this child. Edgar's tremulously tearful voice cut him to the quick.

'Run along now, Eddie. Tonight we'll make it up again. You'll see,' he said soothingly.

'But you won't let Mama send me up to bed early, will you?'

'No, no, Eddie, I won't let her do that,' laughed the baron. 'You'd better go upstairs now. I must dress for dinner.' Edgar went off, happy for the moment. But soon his heart started to hammer again. He had grown years older since yesterday. Mistrust, a stranger to him, had taken up residence in his youthful heart.

He waited. Now came the decisive test. They sat together at table. It was nine o'clock, but Mama didn't send him to bed. He became uneasy. Why was she letting him stay up so long today? She was so meticulous as a rule. Had the baron told her about his request after all, and betrayed their conversation? Suddenly he bitterly regretted having run after him in that emotional, trusting way. At ten o'clock his mother stood up and said goodnight to the baron. That was strange. The baron didn't seem surprised at this early leave-taking and made no effort, as he usually did, to detain her. The hammer in the child's heart pounded even harder.

Now came the crucial test. Edgar stood up too, as though he hadn't noticed anything unusual, and followed his mother to the door without a protest. Once there, however, he looked up quickly and intercepted a smile his mother was directing at the baron over the boy's head. It was a secretive smile, full of collusion. So, the baron really had betrayed him. That was why she had left the table early; he was to be lulled into a false sense of security so that he would keep out of their way in the morning.

'Rotter,' murmured Edgar.

'What did you say?' asked his mother.

'Nothing,' he muttered through clenched teeth.

Now he had his own secret. It was called hate, boundless hate against both of them.

SILENCE

Edgar was no longer uneasy. At last he had the benefit of one clear, simple feeling: hate, and open hostility. Now that he was certain he was in the way he took absolutely fiendish and perverse pleasure in being with them. He revelled in the thought of disturbing them, of opposing them with all the concentrated force of his enmity.

The baron was the first to suffer. When he came down in the morning and greeted the boy with a cheerful 'Hello, Eddie,' Edgar, without looking up or moving from his chair, growled back only a curt 'Morning.'

'Is your Mama down yet?'

Edgar went on reading the paper. 'I don't know.' The baron

was surprised. What was the matter? 'Sleep badly, did you, Eddie?' A joke should jolly him out of it. But Edgar responded only with a scornful 'No,' and buried himself deeper in the paper.

'Stupid boy,' the baron murmured under his breath, shrugged his shoulders and walked away. War was declared.

Edgar was also cool and formal with his mother. He quietly rejected a clumsy attempt to send him to the tennis court. His smile, which scarcely parted his lips and was mildly resentful, showed that he wasn't going to be taken in any more.

'I'd rather go for a walk with you, Mama,' he said with feigned friendliness, as he looked into her eyes.

The answer was clearly unwelcome. She hesitated and pretended to look for something. 'Wait here for me,' she ordered him, and went in to breakfast.

Edgar waited. But his suspicions were aroused. Now his troubled instinct put a gloss of secret, hostile intent on every word these two uttered. Now and then, distrust gave him a strange clearsightedness about their decisions. And instead of waiting in the foyer as instructed, he decided to go outside where he could watch not only the main entrance but all the exits. Something told him he was being deceived. But they wouldn't give him the slip again. He squeezed himself behind a stack of wood as he had learned to do from his books about Red Indians. He smiled with self-satisfaction as about half an hour later he saw his mother actually come out of the side-door, a posy of beautiful roses in her hand and followed by that traitor, the baron.

Both seemed in high spirits. Were they breathing a sigh of relief at having shaken him off so as to be alone to enjoy their secret? They laughed as they chatted and set off down to the woods.

Now was the moment. Edgar sauntered quietly from behind the stack of wood as though chance had brought him there. Keeping very calm and cool he went towards them, giving himself time, plenty of time, to gloat over their surprise. They were both dumbfounded and exchanged an astonished look. With a studied air of normality the child slowly approached, not taking his mocking eyes off them.

'Ah, there you are, Eddie, we were looking for you inside,' said his mother at last.

'What a brazen lie,' thought the child. But his lips remained firmly closed. They kept back the secret of his hatred.

All three stood irresolute, each one waiting for the other. 'Let's go, then,' said the exasperated woman in a resigned voice as she picked the head off one of the lovely roses. Edgar saw again how her nostrils moved slightly, betraying her anger. He stood there as though it was nothing to do with him. He looked around, waited for them to go and made to follow them. The baron tried another tack. 'There's a tennis tournament today. Have you ever seen one?' Edgar just looked at him scornfully. He scarcely bothered to answer him, and pursed his lips as though he was going to whistle. That was his response. His hatred was very evident.

His unwanted presence weighed heavily on both of them. They walked like convicts following a warder, secretly clenching their fists. The child wasn't really doing anything, and they found it even more unbearable now, with his watchful glances, moist with imminent tears, his sulks and irritability, the way he spurned all attempts at reconciliation.

'Do go on!' his mother suddenly exclaimed angrily, unsettled by his persistent eavesdropping. 'Don't keep getting under my feet. You are annoying me!' Edgar obeyed. But after every few paces he turned round and stood and waited for them if they had fallen behind. Like Mephistopheles' black dog he kept them encircled and trapped in his gaze, inescapably imprisoned in the fiery net of his hate.

His sullen silence blighted their good humour, his expression froze the conversation on their lips. The baron didn't try any more advances. He was furious as he sensed how this woman was slipping away from him, the passion he had worked so hard to arouse in her cooling now in her fear of this confounded, obnoxious child. They kept trying to talk to each other but every time they gave up. In the end all three were walking along in silence, listening to the trees rustling and to their own listless steps. The child had stifled their conversation.

Now all three were consumed with burning hostility. The betrayed boy felt with delight how defenceless they were against him, undervalued as he was. But he waited for their outburst against him with hate-filled impatience. From time to time he gazed mockingly at the baron's grim face. He observed that the baron was muttering imprecations under his breath and how he had to restrain himself from spitting them out at Edgar. At the same time he noted, too, with devilish glee, his mother's rising temper and how they were both longing for an excuse to attack him, to be rid of him, or to render him harmless. But he gave them no opportunity. His hatred had counted on having several hours of this satisfaction, and he gave them no opening.

'We'll go back now,' his mother said, all of a sudden. She felt she couldn't maintain her poise any longer. She had to take some action or this torture would make her scream.

'What a shame,' Edgar said calmly. 'It's such a lovely day.'

Both the adults knew the child was mocking them. But they didn't dare say so. This tyrant had learned remarkably well in two days how to behave. His face betrayed no sign of his cutting irony. Without a word they made their way back.

When Edgar and his mother were alone in her room once more, she was still in a state of tension. She threw her parasol and gloves down angrily. Edgar immediately knew her nerves were on edge and needed an outlet, but he wanted her to make a scene and he stayed in her room deliberately, just to annoy her. She walked up and down, sat down again, drummed her fingers on the table, jumped up again.

'How tousled you look! How dirty you are! You let me down in front of people. Aren't you ashamed to go around like that at your age?'

Without a word of protest the boy went and combed his hair. His silence, his cold, obstinate silence with a hint of a sneer on his lips, made her furious. She badly wanted to thrash him.

'Go to your room,' she shouted at him. She couldn't stand his presence any longer. Edgar smiled and went.

How those two trembled before him! How afraid they were, she and the baron, of his eyes' relentless, unwavering hold, every time they were together. The more uncomfortable they felt, the more happily contented his expression became and the more provoking his joy. Edgar tortured these defenceless souls now with almost animal-like ferocity. The baron was able to contain his fury because he still hoped he could trick the boy, and thought only of his goal. But Edgar's mother lost her temper again. It relieved her feelings to shout at him. 'Stop playing with your fork,' she told him at table. 'You are a badly behaved brat. You don't deserve to eat with grown-ups.'

Edgar just went on smiling and looking amiable, his head slightly on one side. He knew her shouting at him was caused by desperation, and he was proud to have made her give herself away like that. He looked quite unperturbed, like a doctor at a bedside. Earlier he would perhaps have been naughty to make her angry, but hate is a quick and thorough teacher. Now he was silent and maintained that silence, on and on, until they began to groan under the weight of it.

His mother couldn't bear it any longer. When she stood up to leave the table and Edgar as a matter of course dutifully went to follow her, she suddenly lost control. She forgot all discretion and spat out the truth. Annoyed by his brooding presence, she reared up like a horse plagued with flies. 'Why do you run after me like a three-year-old baby? I don't want you round me all the time. Children aren't supposed to be with grown-ups all day. Do you hear me? Do go and play on your own for a while. Read a book, or do what you like. Leave me alone! The way you sneak about, and your loathsome sulking, upset me.'

At last he had dragged an admission out of her! Edgar smiled, while the baron now seemed embarrassed. She turned away and wanted to leave, annoyed at herself that she had betrayed her feelings to the child. But Edgar merely said coolly, 'Papa doesn't want me to go around on my own here. Papa made me promise to be careful and to stay with you.'

He emphasised the word 'Papa', because he had noticed earlier that it had a certain inhibiting effect on them. His father must somehow be involved in this burning secret, too. Papa must exercise some secret power over them of which he was unaware, for the mere mention of his name seemed to make them fearful and uneasy. Besides, this time they didn't answer him. They gave up. His mother went out, accompanied by the baron. Edgar followed, not obsequiously like a servant, but as severe, firm, and relentless as a prison guard. Subconsciously he jingled the chain that held them and from which they could not escape. Hatred had reinforced his childish strength. He, who didn't know the secret, was stronger than the two of them whose hands were tied by it.

LIARS

Time was pressing. The baron had only a few more days and he wanted to make use of them. It was futile, he thought, to try to overcome the wretched child's stubbornness, so he snatched at the last and most ignominious solution of all: flight, if only to escape from his tyranny for an hour or two.

'Go and register these letters at the Post Office,' Edgar's mother told him. They were both standing in the foyer; the baron was outside talking to a cab-driver.

Edgar was suspicious as he took possession of the two letters. He had noticed that one of the staff had earlier given his mother a message. Were they both preparing to play some trick on him eventually?

He hesitated. 'Where will you wait for me?'

'Here.'

'Promise?'

'Yes.'

'You really won't go away? You'll wait for me here in the foyer until I come back?' He spoke with a feeling of dominating his mother, as though he were giving her an order. So much had changed since yesterday.

Then he went off with the two letters. He met the baron at the door, and spoke to him for the first time in two days.

'I'm only going to post these two letters. My Mama will wait until I return. Please don't go without me.'

The baron squeezed past him quietly. 'Yes, of course. We'll wait.'

Edgar raced to the Post Office. He had to wait. A man ahead of him was asking a dozen tedious questions. At last Edgar was able to fulfil his task and immediately ran back with the receipt. And he arrived just in time to see his mother and the baron driving off in the cab.

He was struck dumb with rage. He was almost tempted to pick up a stone and hurl it after them. They had escaped him after all, but with what a low-down, dirty lie! That his mother told lies he knew from the day before. But that she could be so brazen as to break an actual promise, that removed the last vestiges of trust. He didn't understand what life was about any more, for he had seen that words he supposed had reality behind them were only coloured bubbles which burst and disappeared into thin air. But what sort of terrible secret must it be that impelled the grown-ups to go so far as to lie to him, a child, and to steal away like criminals? In the books he had read men committed murder and cheated to gain money or power or a kingdom. But what was the cause this time? What did these two want? Why were they hiding from him? What were they trying to conceal with so many lies? He racked his brains. Dimly he perceived that this secret unlocked the door out of childhood. When you had discovered it, it meant you were an adult and finally, at last, a man. Oh, if only he could do it! But he couldn't think clearly any more. Rage that they had eluded him blazed up and the smoke prevented him from having a clear view.

He ran into the woods, where he could take refuge in the dark depths without anyone seeing him. There he burst into tears and cried his eyes out. 'Liars, dogs, cheats, scoundrels!' He had to shout these words aloud otherwise he would choke. The fury, frustration, anger, curiosity, helplessness and sense of betrayal of the last few days that he had struggled in his childish way to hold back, mistakenly thinking he was grown up, now welled up in him and were transformed into tears. It was the last emotional outburst of his childhood, the last time he would cry without restraint. He gave himself over just this once more to the womanly satisfaction of weeping. He cried now, beside himself with rage, rejecting everything—trust, love, faith, respect—his whole childhood.

The boy who returned to the hotel afterwards was a different person. He was calm and acted with deliberation. First he went to his room and carefully washed his face and bathed his eyes, to avoid giving his mother and the baron the triumph of seeing the traces of his tears. Then he prepared to settle his account with them. And he waited patiently without any qualms.

The foyer was very crowded when the cab containing the

fugitives drew up again outside. Two gentlemen were playing chess, others were reading their newspapers, ladies were chatting. The child, a little pale and with a timid expression, had sat down among them and was keeping very still. When his mother and the baron came through the door they were a little put out at seeing him there quite so quickly and tried to stammer out their prepared excuses. He, however, walked over to them, erect and unruffled, and said in a challenging voice, 'Sir, I would like a word with you.'

The baron felt uncomfortable. He was taken somewhat by surprise. 'Yes, all right. Later!'

But Edgar raised his voice and said clearly and distinctly so that everyone there could hear, 'I want to speak to you now. You have behaved like an absolute cad. You lied to me. You knew my Mama was going to wait for me and you ...'

'Edgar!' shouted his mother, who could see all eyes turned on her. She rushed towards him.

But the boy went on at the top of his voice, for it seemed she intended to shout him down. 'I'll repeat it in front of all these people. You have lied infamously, and that is mean and contemptible.'

The baron stood there, turning pale. People were staring. Some looked amused.

Edgar's mother seized the boy. He was trembling with excitement. 'Come up to your room at once or I'll spank you here in front of everyone,' she rasped out.

But Edgar was calm again. He regretted having been so emotional. He was annoyed with himself, because he had really wanted to be ice-cool when he challenged the baron. At the last minute, though, his anger had been stronger than his willpower. Quietly, without hurrying, he turned towards the stairs.

'Please excuse him for being rude,' his mother said to the baron. 'He's a highly-strung child, you know.' She was in disarray in the face of the other guests, who were staring at her as though they were mildly enjoying it.

She feared nothing in the world more than scandal, and she knew she must now maintain her dignity. Instead of rushing away she first went to the porter and asked if there were any letters for her and other trivial things, and then swept upstairs as though nothing had happened. Behind her, though, wafted up a gentle current of whispering and half-suppressed laughter.

On the way she slowed down. She always felt at a loss in serious situations and this confrontation made her really afraid. She couldn't deny she was at fault. Moreover, the boy's expression worried her. This new, strange, remarkable look of his paralysed her and made her feel unsure of herself. Afraid, she decided to tread softly with him. For she realised that if it came to a fight the boy, now he was roused, was the stronger.

She opened the door gently. Edgar was sitting there cool and collected. The eyes he raised to her contained no fear and betrayed not the slightest curiosity. He seemed very self possessed.

'Edgar,' she began in as motherly a voice as possible, 'What's come over you? I was ashamed of you. It's terribly rude for a child to speak to a grown-up like that! You'll apologise to the baron straightaway.'

Edgar looked out of the window. 'No,' he said, as though speaking to the trees outside.

She began to wonder at his assurance.

'Edgar, what's got into you? You're not the same boy. I scarcely recognise you as my own child any more. You've always been so clever and artistic. People could talk to you about anything. And all of a sudden you behave as though the devil's got into you. What's the baron done to you, then? You liked him so much. He was always so kind to you.'

'Yes, because he wanted to meet you.'

She felt uneasy. 'Nonsense! Whatever do you mean? How can you possibly think a thing like that?'

But the boy went on.

'He's a liar, he's dishonest. What he does is calculated and mean. He wanted to meet you, so he made friends with me and promised me a dog. I don't know what he's promised you and why he's being friendly to you, but he wants something out of you, too, Mama, I'm certain. Otherwise he wouldn't be so polite and friendly. He's a wicked man. He tells lies. Just have a good look at him, how insincere he always looks. Oh, I hate him, he's a beastly liar, a scoundrel ... '

'But Edgar, how can you say such things?' She was embarrassed and didn't know what to say. In her heart she felt the boy was right.

'Yes, he's a scoundrel. You won't persuade me otherwise. You must see that yourself. Why is he afraid of me, then? Why does he avoid me? Because he knows I've seen through him. I know what he is, he's a villain!'

'How can you say such things! How can you say such things!' Her mind had gone blank. Her pale lips just repeated the same words. She now began to feel suddenly afraid and she didn't quite know if she was frightened of the baron or of the child.

Edgar saw that his warning had made an impression. He was tempted to win her over to his side, to have a companion in hate, in enmity towards the baron. He went gently across to his mother, put his arms round her, and in his excitement his voice became coaxing.

'Mama,' he said, 'you must have noticed yourself that he's up to no good. He's quite changed you. You're the one who's changed, not I. He's turned you against me just so he can be alone with you. I'm sure he'll deceive you. I don't know what he's promised you. I only know he won't keep his word. You ought to be on your guard. Whoever tells lies to one person tells them to others. He's a wicked man and he's not to be trusted.'

This soft voice, near to tears, sounded as though it came from her own heart. She already had an uncomfortable feeling anyway, deep down, that told her the same thing, more and more insistently. But it was humiliating to admit her own child was right. She fell back, as many do in such an overwhelmingly emotional predicament, on taking an aggressive tone. She drew herself up.

'Children don't understand these things. You have no business meddling in such matters. You must behave properly. That's all there is to it.'

Edgar's face frosted over again. 'All right. I've warned you.'

'Well, then, won't you apologise?'

'No.'

They stood stiffly facing each other. She felt her authority was at stake.

'Then you'll eat here, upstairs. On your own. And you won't come and eat with us until you've said you are sorry. I'll see you learn some manners. You'll stay in here until I give you permission to leave. Do you understand?'

Edgar smiled. That wry smile seemed to be always distorting his lips. Privately he was angry with himself. How stupid of him to have opened up his heart again, wanting to warn her. She was a liar too.

His mother hurried out without so much as a glance. She was afraid of those piercing eyes. The child had become a source of anxiety since she felt he was seeing too much and had told her exactly what she didn't want to know and hear. It was terrifying, having shed her own conscience and scruples, to find them reappearing in the guise of her child, to have him turn round and warn her, to see herself mocked. Until now this child had been close to her, an adornment, a plaything, someone loving and trusting. Sometimes, perhaps, he had been a nuisance, but he had always reacted in the same way as she did, his life in harmony with hers. He had rebelled today and defied her for the first time. Something approaching hate was now involved whenever she thought about the boy.

All the same, as she walked down the stairs, feeling a little weary, in her heart she heard what the child had said. 'You ought to be on your guard against him.' She couldn't stop hearing the warning. On the way down she came upon a mirror, which she looked into in self-interrogation, going closer and closer until her lips parted in a slight smile and rounded themselves into what looked like a dangerous word. But still the inner voice would not be silenced. She threw her shoulders back, however, as though she was shaking off all those invisible thoughts, gave the mirror a bright look, gathered up her skirt and went down with the determined air of a gambler about to let his last gold coin roll and jingle over the table.

TRACKS IN THE MOONLIGHT

The waiter, who brought Edgar's dinner while he was under room arrest, closed the door. He turned the key behind him. The boy was furious. It was obviously on his mother's orders that he was being locked up like a wild animal. Dark thoughts ran round in his head.

'What's happening downstairs then while I'm shut away up here? What can they be talking about? Is the secret finally going to be revealed down there and I'm going to miss it? Oh, that great secret, I'm aware of it all the time, everywhere, when I'm with grown-ups, when they close doors against me at night, and lower their voices if I come in unexpectedly. I've nearly been on to it for days, almost had it within grasp, yet I can't quite catch hold of it. What haven't I done already, trying to discover it! Sometimes I've stolen books from Papa's desk and read them, and they were full of extraordinary things, only I didn't understand them. There must be a seal you have to break first before you can find out what the secret is, perhaps in me, perhaps in other people. I asked the housemaid, begged her to explain those passages in the books, but she laughed at me. It's dreadful being a child, full of curiosity and not being allowed to ask anyone, and having the grown-ups always laughing at you as though you were stupid and useless. But I'm going to find out. I feel I'm going to know what it is soon. I've got so far and I'm not going to give up until I know it all!'

He listened to see if anyone was about. A light breeze wafted through the trees and their branches broke the smooth mirror of moonlight into a hundred twinkling pieces.

'Those two can't have anything good in mind, or they wouldn't have tried to send me away by using such despicable lies. I'm sure they are laughing at me, the rotters. They think they have rid themselves of me at last. But I'll have the last laugh. How silly of me to let them imprison me here. I should have stuck to them and eavesdropped on their every move. I know adults are always careless and even those two will give themselves away. They always believe children are still very small and that we always sleep in the evening. They forget you can pretend to be asleep, too, and listen in, and that you can pretend to be stupid and really be clever. Recently when my aunt had a baby they knew about it a long time beforehand and they only pretended to be surprised in front of me. But I knew about it, too, because I'd heard them talking weeks before, one evening when they thought I was asleep. And so I shall surprise them this time, the miserable tricksters. Oh, if only I could see through the doors and watch them secretly while they think they are safe. Perhaps I should ring the bell. Then the chambermaid would come, unlock the door and ask what I wanted. Or I could throw things about, break some crockery. Then someone would unlock the door, and I could slip out and spy on those two. But no, I won't do that. No one must see how badly I'm being treated. I'm too proud for that. I'll pay them back tomorrow.'

Below a woman laughed. Edgar grew tense. That could be his mother's voice. She had reason to laugh, making game of him, small and defenceless as he was, having the man turn the key on him when he was a nuisance, and throwing him in a corner like a bundle of dirty washing. Cautiously he leaned out of the window. No, it wasn't his mother, just girls he didn't know being high-spirited and teasing a young man.

Then, at that moment, he noticed just how near the ground his window really was. And scarcely had he noticed this, than the thought came to him to jump out. Now, while they thought they were safe, he would spy on them. He became wildly, joyfully excited at his decision. He felt he already had the great, glittering secret of childhood in his hands. 'Jump, jump,' his inner voice quavered. It wasn't dangerous. No one was about, and he soon leapt out. There was a slight noise of crunching gravel but no one noticed.

In these last two days spying and lying in wait had become the passion of his life. Now he felt delight mixed with a slight shiver of fear as he tiptoed round the hotel, carefully avoiding the strong reflection of light coming from within. First he looked in the dining-room, his cheeks pressed cautiously against the window. Their usual table was empty. He reconnoitred farther, going from window to window. He dare not go into the hotel itself in case he ran into them unexpectedly in one of the corridors. He couldn't find them anywhere. He was on the point of despairing when he saw two shadows fall across the entrance and—he dodged back and hid in the shadows—his mother and her now inevitable companion came outside. He had come to exactly the right spot, then. What were they saying? He couldn't make it out. They were talking softly, and the wind was making too much disturbance in the trees. Now, however, a laugh drifted over distinctly

— his mother's voice. It wasn't the kind of laugh he had heard
from her before. It was a strangely shrill, over-excited, bewitched, enervated laugh that sounded odd and frightened him.
She was laughing. So it couldn't be anything dangerous, not
something absolutely enormous and powerful they were hiding from him. Edgar was a little disappointed.

But why were they leaving the hotel? Where were they going
now, alone at night? High overhead the wind must be speeding
on giant wings, for the sky which had been clear and moonlit a
few moments ago was now overcast. From time to time the
moon was enveloped in black coverlets thrown over it by
unseen hands, and the night was then so impenetrable you
could hardly see the path. Then it was suddenly light again
when the moon shook itself free. The countryside was coolly
bathed in silver. The interchange between light and shadow
was as mysterious and stirring as a naked woman playing with
a veil. At this moment the landscape was laid bare: on the path
opposite Edgar saw the strolling silhouettes, or rather only the
one, they were so close to one another, as though an inner fear
pressed them together. Where were they going, though, the
pair of them? The pine trees were moaning. There was an air of
sinister activity in the forest, as though Odin's horde was being
whipped up inside it.

'I'll follow them,' Edgar thought. 'They won't be able to
hear my footsteps in all this uproar of the wind and the trees.'
And while they walked below him along the wide, bright
road, he was up among the pines, leaping lightly from behind
one tree to another, from shadow to shadow. He followed
them tenaciously and relentlessly, blessing the wind for
deadening the sound of his feet, and cursing it because it kept
on taking their words down there away from him. If he could
only once have heard their conversation he was sure he would
have obtained the secret.

The two walked along, suspecting nothing. They felt blessedly alone in that wide, wild night and were lost in their
growing preoccupation with each other. Nothing warned
them that up in the shadows of the many branches someone
was following and two eyes peered down, concentrating all
their power of hate and curiosity on them.

They stopped suddenly. Edgar, too, drew back and flattened

himself against a tree. He was overcome with terrible fear. Supposing they turned round and arrived back at the hotel before he did, supposing he couldn't retreat safely to his room and his mother found it empty? Then all would be lost. Then she would know he'd been spying on her secretly and he'd lose all hope of snatching the secret from them. But the pair hesitated, obviously having a difference of opinion. Luckily the moon was visible and he could see everything clearly. The baron was indicating a dark, narrow path leading down the valley, where the moonlight didn't pour down in a broad full stream as it did here on the road, but only droplets and occasional shafts of light infiltrated.

'Why does he want to go down there?' Edgar wondered. His mother seemed to be saying 'No,' but the baron was urging her on. Edgar could see from the way he was gesturing how pressing he was being. The child became fearful. What did this man want from his mother? Why was he, the scoundrel, trying to drag her into the dark? Suddenly he remembered vividly from his books, which for him were the real world, moonlight and abduction and ominous crimes. The baron wanted to murder her – that was it. And that was why the baron had got him out of the way and had lured her here alone. Should he shout for help? Murder! The cry was almost out, but his lips were dry and no sound came. His nerves almost gave way, he was so agitated. He nearly fell over. Terrified out of his wits he grabbed for a hand-hold – a branch snapped off in his hands. Startled, they both turned round and peered into the darkness. Edgar stood stock-still, leaning against the tree, his arms pressed to his sides and his head drawn back deep into the shadow. Everything was deathly still. But even so, she seemed frightened. 'Let's go back,' he heard his mother say. She sounded anxious. The baron, obviously uneasy himself, agreed. They walked back slowly, clinging close to each other. Their private preoccupation was Edgar's good fortune. He crept on all fours, down in the undergrowth, tearing his hands and making them bleed, as far as the turning in the forest. From there he ran with all the speed he could muster to the hotel, and was upstairs in a few strides. Luckily the key that had been used to lock him in was in the door on the outside. He turned it, fled into his room and lay down on his bed. He must rest for a minute or two. His heart was pounding violently in his chest, like a clapper on the side of a pealing bell.

Then he made himself get up. Leaning on the window-sill, he waited for their return. They were a long time. They must have walked very slowly. He peered cautiously out of the darkened window. Now they were coming along slowly, moonlight reflecting on their clothes. They looked ghostly in the greenish light, and he was again overcome by dread as he wondered if the baron really was a murderer. But he felt satisfaction, too, as he speculated on what terrible event his presence had prevented. He could see their chalk-white faces clearly. His mother wore an expression of rapture which he'd never seen there before; the baron, on the contrary, looked hard and vexed. Obviously it was because his plan had miscarried.

They were quite close now. Just before they reached the hotel they began to walk with space between them. Would they look up? No, neither glanced his way. 'They've forgotten me,' the boy thought in utter fury and secret triumph, 'but I haven't forgotten them. They think I'm asleep or don't exist, but they'll discover their mistake. I'll watch their every step until I've taken the secret from that villain—the fearful secret that won't let me sleep. I'll soon break their alliance. I won't go to sleep.'

The pair walked slowly indoors. And as they went in, one behind the other, their silhouettes fell for a second like a single black stripe across the brightly lit entrance. Then the area outside the building lay bare once again like a large meadow full of snow.

SURPRISE ATTACK

Edgar drew in his breath as he stepped back from the window. He shivered at the horror of it all. Never in his life had he been so close to anything quite so mysterious. To him, the world of his books, that exciting world of thrilling adventure, murder and betrayal, was still valid, whereas fairy stories, following close on dreams, belonged to the category of the unreal and unattainable. Now, though, all at once he seemed to be in the midst of this frightening world, and his whole being was feverishly disturbed by the stirring contact. Who was this mysterious man who had suddenly entered their peaceful lives? Was he really a murderer who always sought out secluded places and wanted to drag his mother away where it was dark? Something awful seemed to be going to happen. He didn't know what to do. Tomorrow, without fail, he would write to his father or send him a telegram. But couldn't the evil, terrible, incomprehensible event take place this very evening? Indeed, his mother hadn't yet returned to her room. She was still with that detestable stranger.

Between the inner, solid door and the outer, easily-opened, flimsy one was a tiny passageway, no larger than the inside of a wardrobe. He squeezed into this pocket handkerchief of dark space so that he could hear his mother's steps in the corridor. He was determined not to leave her alone for a second. It was midnight, so the corridor was empty and dimly lit by one single light.

At last – he thought the minutes stretched out terribly – he heard cautious steps approaching. He strained to listen. They weren't the quick, passing steps of someone going straight to a room, but shuffling, hesitant, very slow steps, as though the person was climbing a long, difficult and steep path. In between he kept on hearing whispering followed by a silence. Edgar quivered with excitement. Was it still the two of them? Was he still with her? The whispering was too far away. But the steps, even though they were still hesitant, were coming nearer. And now all at once he heard the baron's detested voice, softly whispering something he didn't understand. And then straightaway he heard his mother quickly defending herself, 'No, not tonight! No.' Edgar shivered. They were coming nearer. He would be able to hear everything. Each approaching step, however gentle, stabbed at his heart. And that voice, how he loathed it, that covetously pleading, detestable voice of the man he hated!

'Don't be so cruel. You were so adorable this evening.'

And there was her voice again. 'No, I mustn't, I can't. Let me go.'

His mother sounded so frightened the child was terrified. What does he want her to do, then? Why is she afraid? They had walked nearer and must be right outside Edgar's door. He was standing there behind them, trembling and invisible, a hair's breadth away, hidden only by the thin material of which the outer door was made. The voices were now very close.

'Come on, Mathilde, come on!' Again Edgar heard his mother groan, weaker now, her opposition slackening. But what's happening? They've moved off again into the dark. His mother hasn't gone into her room but has gone on down the corridor! Where's he dragging her? Why doesn't she say something? Has he gagged her? Is he strangling her?

These thoughts drive him wild. He pushes the door open a crack, his hands trembling. Now he can see the pair of them in the dark corridor. The baron has his arm round his mother's waist and is propelling her lightly along. She has apparently given in. Now they have stopped outside his room. 'He's going to do away with her,' the child thinks, terrified. 'Now he's going to do the terrible deed.'

Wildly he throws the door open and rushes out towards them. His mother screams as now suddenly out of the darkness something pounces on her. She seems to faint and the baron has some difficulty in supporting her. At the same time he feels a small puny fist in his face, forcing his lips back hard against his teeth, and something scrabbling cat-like at his body. He lets go of Edgar's terrified mother, who quickly escapes, and hits out blindly with his fist before he even knows who his opponent is.

The child knows he is not as strong as the baron, but he won't give in. Now at last the long-awaited moment has arrived for all the betrayed affection and accumulated resentment to be passionately discharged. He pummels away blindly with his small fists, his lips set in feverish animosity. Now the baron has recognised him. But he, too, is full of hate against this furtive spy who has spoiled the last few days for him and ruined his game. He hits back strongly wherever he can make contact. Edgar gasps and grunts, but won't give in and doesn't call for help. They continue their midnight struggle doggedly for a while without speaking. Gradually it dawns on the baron how ridiculous it is to be fighting a half-grown boy. He grabs at him to push him away. But the child knows, as he feels his muscles tiring, that he'll have to admit defeat in a minute, thoroughly thrashed. In wild rage he bites the strong, firm hand which is trying to grab him round the neck. Instinctively the baron lets out a low cry and loosens his grip — the brief moment the child needs to escape to his room and bolt the door.

This midnight battle has lasted only a minute or two. No one in the neighbouring rooms has heard it. Everything is quiet; everyone seems to be fast asleep. The baron wipes the blood from his hand with his handkerchief, looking round uneasily in the dark. No one has seen anything. There is only one last guttering light above his head — he fancies it is mocking him.

THUNDERSTORM

'Did I dream it? Did I have an awful, frightful nightmare?' Edgar asked himself next morning when he awoke out of a confused state of anxiety. His hair was all tousled. His head was tormented by a dull thudding. His limbs felt stiff and wooden, and now, when he looked at himself, he realised with horror that he was still fully dressed. He leapt up, rushed to the mirror and staggered back when he saw his own pale, misshapen face. The top of his forehead was swollen with a red bruise. With difficulty he collected his thoughts. Now everything came back to him alarmingly: the fight last night in the corridor, rushing back to his room, and then how shivering with fever, fully dressed and ready for flight, he'd thrown himself down on his bed. He must have fallen asleep as he was. He must have gone into a deep, overwhelming sleep and dreamt all these events again in a jumbled way. Only they were different and even more frightful, with a clammy smell of freshly spilled, flowing blood.

Below footsteps were crunching over the gravel. Voices floated up like unseen birds, and the sun was climbing high in the sky. It must be quite late in the morning. But when he looked panic-stricken at his watch, it said it was midnight. In his overwrought state yesterday he'd forgotten to wind it up. The uncertainty, not knowing what time it was, disturbed him. Also he felt he didn't really know what was going to happen. He tidied himself up quickly and went downstairs, uneasy and feeling in his heart slightly guilty.

His mother was sitting alone at their usual table in the breakfast room. Edgar breathed again. His enemy wasn't there. He didn't have to see the face he hated and which the night before he had hit in anger with his fist. And yet, as he approached the table, he felt uncertain.

'Good morning,' he greeted his mother.

She didn't answer. She didn't even look at him, but observed the distant landscape with a noticeably fixed stare. She looked very pale, had dark shadows under her eyes, and her nostrils were flaring in that give-away fashion, showing how upset she was. Edgar bit his lip. This silence disturbed him. He wasn't really sure if he had badly hurt the baron and if she knew all about the fight they had had last night. And this uncertainty tortured him. But her expression remained so fixed he hardly dared even look at her. He was afraid those sunken eyes might suddenly jump out of their heavy lids and seize him. He was very quiet, not daring to make a noise. When he lifted his cup and put it down again he did so cautiously, and stole a glance at his mother's tensely bunched fingers, which seemed to betray her intense anger as she played nervously with her spoon. He sat there for a quarter of an hour with the suffocating feeling of waiting for something that never came. No word rescued him. And now, as his mother stood up, still apparently without noticing his presence, he didn't know what to do: to stay alone at the table or to follow her. Eventually he stood up, however, and meekly went after her. She deliberately ignored him and he felt how ridiculous he looked trailing along in her wake. He took shorter and shorter steps so as to fall well behind her, while she went into her room, paying him no attention. When Edgar eventually arrived he found the door firmly locked.

What had happened? He was at a loss. The self-confidence of yesterday had deserted him. Had he been wrong in the end yesterday in his surprise attack? Were they preparing some punishment for him or some fresh humiliation? Something had to happen, he felt. Something dreadful was going to happen soon. There was between him and his mother the sultry air of an imminent thunderstorm, the electric tension between two charged poles that must be released in the form of lightning. And he dragged this burden of foreboding round with him for four solitary hours, from public room to public room, until his slender, youthful bones gave way under the unseen weight. At midday, now feeling very humble, he came to table.

'Hello,' he said. He must break this terrible, menacing silence that hung over him like a black cloud.

Once again his mother didn't answer. Once again she looked straight through him. And with renewed alarm Edgar felt there was a calculated, intense anger opposite, the like of which he had never come across in his life before. Until now his mother's disputes with him had been only outbreaks of temper, caused more by nervous reaction than by emotion, and soon dispersed with a soothing smile. This time, though, he sensed he had aroused an uncontrollable feeling from the absolute depths of her being and he drew back in the face of this force he had conjured up so carelessly. He was scarcely able to eat. Something dry seemed to be sticking in his throat and threatened to choke him. His mother appeared to notice none of this. Only when they came to leave the table did she turn back to him, as though by chance, and say, 'Come upstairs now, Edgar. I have something to say to you.'

She didn't sound threatening, only so icily cold that Edgar shuddered at the words, as though someone had suddenly put a metal chain round his neck. His defiance was trodden underfoot. He followed her silently to her room, like a cringing dog.

She prolonged his torture by not speaking for some minutes. During that time he heard the clock strike and a child laugh outside, and his own heart hammering. But she must have been feeling very uncertain, too, because she didn't look at him while she spoke, but instead turned her back.

'I won't say any more about your behaviour yesterday. It was outrageous, and it fills me with shame just to think about it. You will have to take the consequences yourself. I'm telling you now, though, that that was the last time you will be permitted to mix with grown-ups. I've already written to your Papa that you must have a tutor or be sent to a boarding school to learn some manners. I'm not going to put up with you any more.'

Edgar stood there, head bowed. He sensed this was only the

preamble, a threat, and he waited, ill-at-ease, for what was to come.

'You'll apologise straightaway to the baron.'

Edgar started up, but she wouldn't let him interrupt her.

'The baron left this morning, and you will write him a letter which I shall dictate.'

Edgar went to protest again, but his mother was firm.

'I want no argument. There is the paper and ink. Sit down.'

Edgar looked up. Her eyes were hard and showed how fixed her purpose was. He'd never known his mother to be so stony and deliberate. He was overcome with fear. He sat down, took the pen and bent his head over the table.

'Put the date at the top. Have you done that? Leave a line space. Now. Dear Baron. Comma. Leave another line. I have just heard with regret — have you got that? — with regret that you have already left Semmering — two m's in Semmering — and so I must briefly do what I meant to do in person, that is — hurry up, it doesn't have to be copy-book writing — to ask you to forgive me for my behaviour yesterday. As my Mama will have told you, I am still recovering from a serious illness and am very excitable. I often exaggerate things and regret it the next minute ... '

The back that was hunched over the table straightened up quickly. Edgar turned round. His obstinacy was aroused again.

'I'm not writing that. It isn't true!'

'Edgar!' Her voice was threatening.

'It isn't true. I haven't done anything to be sorry about. I haven't done anything wrong that I need to apologise for. I only came to your rescue when you called out!'

Her lips went pale. Her nostrils flared.

'I called for help? You're mad!'

Edgar was angry. In one movement he was on his feet.

'Yes, you called for help, out there in the corridor last night when he took hold of you. You called out "Let me go." So loudly I heard it in my room.'

'Don't tell lies. I was never in the corridor here with the baron. He came with me only as far as the stairs ... '

Edgar's heart missed a beat at this brazen lie. Words failed him. He stared at her with a glazed look in his eyes.

'You ... weren't ... in the corridor? And he ... didn't take hold of you? Didn't seize you by force?'

She laughed. A cold, dry laugh.

'You must have been dreaming.'

That was too much for the boy. He knew already, of course, that grown-ups told lies, that they made silly excuses, told little white lies and used artful ambiguities. But this brazen, cold denial, face to face, drove him mad.

'And this bruise on my head, here. I dreamed that, too, did I?'

'Who knows with whom you've been fighting. But I'm not arguing with you. You'll do as you're told and that's the end of it. Sit down and write!'

She was very pale and it took all her strength to hold back the tension she felt.

But something in Edgar was snuffed out — some last flicker of faith. He couldn't accept that the truth could be crushed underfoot like a burning match. Ice entered his soul and everything he said became sarcastic, angry and unsure.

'So, I dreamed it? What happened in the corridor, and this bump on my head? And that you two went for a walk in the moonlight, and that he wanted to take you away from the main road, perhaps I dreamed that, too? Do you really think I let myself be shut up in my room like a little child! No, I'm not as stupid as you think. I know what I know.'

He looked her straight in the face, provocatively, and that broke her defences. To see her own child's face close up to hers and distorted with hate. She lost her temper completely.

'Get on with it. Write that letter immediately! Or else ... '

'Or else what ... ?' Edgar's challenging voice had lost all deference.

'Or I'll put you over my knee like a small child.'

Edgar took a step nearer, scornfully, and just laughed.

Her hand struck his face. Edgar cried out. And like a drowning man thrashing about him with his arms, a dull roaring in his ears and red flecks before his eyes, he struck out blindly with his fists. He felt his punches land on something soft, then on her face, and heard a scream ...

This cry brought him to his senses. Suddenly he saw what he had done and realised how awful it was: he had struck his mother. He was overcome instantly by shame and shock, and the impetuous urge to disappear, fall through the floor, escape, go away, out of her sight. He rushed to the door and down the stairs, through the building and out on to the road. Away! He must escape! It was as though a pack of rabid hounds was after him.

FIRST INSIGHT

He stopped eventually a long way down the forest path. He had to hold on to a tree, his limbs were shaking so much with fear and overwrought nerves, and his breath was rasping out from his overworked lungs. Running up behind him was the monstrosity of what he had done. Now it stuck in his throat and shook him as though he had a fever. What was he to do now? Where could he go? For here in the middle of the lower slopes of the forest, only fifteen minutes from the hotel, he felt quite forsaken. Everything seemed different, more hostile, more malicious, since he was alone and without help. The trees that had rustled about him yesterday and seemed brotherly, all at once gathered round him, ominous and threatening. But how much stranger and less familiar must everything be that lay before him? This isolation in the face of the great, unknown world made the boy dizzy. No, he couldn't endure it alone, he couldn't bear it. But to whom could he turn? He was frightened of his father, who was easily enraged and unapproachable, and who would send him straight back. He didn't want to go back, though. He'd rather set off into the dangers of the unknown. It seemed to him he would never be able to look at his mother again without thinking how he'd hit her with his fist.

Then he thought of his grandmother. She was an old lady, kind and friendly, who'd spoiled him when he was little. She'd always protected him when some punishment or injustice threatened him at home. He'd hide at her house in Baden until the initial anger had died down and then he'd write a letter to his parents from there and say he was sorry. He was so subdued by the events of the last quarter of an hour, just by the very thought of being alone in the world with his lack of experience of what to do, that he cursed his pride, that stupid pride, which a lying stranger had injected into his blood. He wanted nothing more than to be the child he'd been before, obedient and patient, without the presumptuousness he now felt had gone to ridiculous lengths.

How could he get to Baden, though? How could he cross the country to a place hours away? Hurriedly he rummaged in the little leather purse he always carried. Thank God, the new, gold twenty-crown piece he'd been given for his birthday still blinked up at him. He'd never been able to decide how to spend it. But almost every day he'd looked to make sure it was still there, had feasted his eyes on it, felt rich, and then always polished the coin with his handkerchief, lovingly, until it shone like a little sun. But—the sudden thought alarmed him— would it be enough? He'd often travelled by train but always without thinking it had to be paid for, or indeed, what it might cost, one crown or a hundred. For the first time he realised there were details about life he hadn't thought about, that all the many things around him had a value of some kind, a particular importance. He, who an hour before had imagined he knew everything, was, he now realised, carelessly ignorant of a thousand mysteries and questions, and he was ashamed that his limited wisdom was already tripping him up over the fundamentals of living. He became ever more despondent, and his uncertain steps ever more hesitant as he walked to the station. How often he'd dreamt of this flight, and thought about rushing out into real life, of becoming emperor or king, soldier or poet. Now he looked nervously towards a bright little house and only wondered if the twenty crowns would be enough to take him to his grandmother.

The railway lines glinted far out into the countryside. The station building was almost deserted. Diffidently Edgar crept up to the booking office window and in a whisper so that no one else could hear him, asked how much a ticket for Baden cost. A surprised-looking man peered out of the dark window and two bespectacled eyes smiled at the timid boy.

'Full fare—are you over ten?'

'Yes,' Edgar stammered, lacking confidence, only anxious in case it cost too much.

'Six crowns.'

'Yes, please.'

Relieved, Edgar pushed the polished, much-loved coin across, change jingled back, and all at once he felt immensely rich again. Now he had in his hand the brown piece of cardboard that guaranteed his freedom, and in his pocket he could hear the muffled music of silver coins.

He discovered from the timetable that the train was due in twenty minutes. Edgar tucked himself into a corner. There were a few people standing idly and unconcerned on the platform. But he was worried in case when they saw him they would all wonder why a child like him was making a train journey alone. He drew back even more into his corner, as though it looked obvious that his mind was indeed set on crime and flight. He sighed with relief when at last he heard the first sound of the train and then saw it roar in – the train that was to take him out into the world.

As he climbed aboard he noticed his ticket was third-class. He'd always travelled first-class before and again he felt that everything had changed. There were differences he'd never noticed before. His travelling companions were not like those he usually met. Some Italian workmen with hard hands and rough voices sat opposite, holding spades and shovels, and looked out with dull, bleak expressions. They had obviously been working hard, for some of them were tired and fell asleep in the rattling compartment, leaning against the hard and dirty woodwork, their mouths open. They had been working to earn money, Edgar thought, but he couldn't imagine how much it could be. Again he felt that money was something you didn't always have, but somehow it had to be acquired. He became aware for the first time that he was accustomed as a matter of course to an air of comfortable ease in his life, and that on either hand chasms he had never troubled to look into fell away sharply into darkness. For the first time he started to realise that people followed trades and professions, that rules and regulations existed, that all around his life mysteries were just under the surface, close at hand, yet he'd never noticed them.

Edgar learned much in the single hour he had been alone. He began to see many things from that narrow compartment with its windows to the outside world. And gradually something began to blossom out of his dark despair. It wasn't exactly happiness, but rather astonishment at the diversity of life. He had run away because he had been a frightened coward for those few moments, but after all, he had acted on his own initiative, experienced something of the real world that hitherto had passed him by. Perhaps he had become a mystery to his parents now too, as the world had been to him for a long time. He looked out of the window with new eyes. And it seemed to him that he saw everything in its proper light for the first time, as though a veil had been lifted from things, and he was being shown everything now, the inner purpose, the mysterious spring of life's action. Houses fled by as though snatched away by the wind, and this made him think about the people who lived in them. Were they rich or poor, happy or miserable? Did they long, as he did, to know everything? Were there children inside, perhaps, who had only played at life until now, as he had? The level-crossing keepers who stood by the track waving their flags now seemed for the first time not to be – as he had thought them before – frivolous puppets and lifeless toys, objects put there by random chance. Now he understood that that was their fate, their struggle in life. Now the wheels turned faster, taking the plump snake of a train down into the valley. The mountains became blurred in outline, ever more distant; and soon they had reached the plain. He looked back only once, where the mountains were blue now and indistinct, far-off and out of reach. And it seemed to him that there, where they slowly merged with the cloudy sky, he had left his childhood.

CONFUSING GLOOM

When the train stopped in Baden and Edgar was left on the platform, where the lamps had already been lit and the signals shone green and red in the distance, this colourful scene made him suddenly conscious of the approaching night. He had felt safe enough during the day, for there were people about. He could relax, sit on a bench or look in the shop windows. How would he manage, though, when people disappeared into their houses, where they all had beds, with conversation and a quiet night ahead, while he, with his sense of guilt, must wander about on his own in strange isolation? Oh, to have a roof over his head quickly now and not stay a minute longer out under the free but alien sky: that was his single clear feeling.

He hurried along the path he knew so well, without looking to right or left, until he reached his grandmother's villa at last. The house was beautifully situated on a wide avenue. It wasn't visible from the front because it stood behind ivy and other creepers in a well-screened garden, a moonbeam behind a green cloud, a white, patriarchal, friendly house. Edgar peeped through the railings like a stranger. Nothing moved inside. The windows were closed. Evidently they were all in the garden at the back with their guests. He already had his hand on the cool handle of the gate when something odd occurred. What had seemed so easy a couple of hours ago and such an obvious thing to do, was all of a sudden impossible. How could he walk in and greet them? How could he bear their questions and what answers could he give? How could he endure the initial expression on their faces when he had to tell them he'd run away from his mother without telling her where he was going? And how indeed could he explain the awfulness of what he had done when he no longer understood it himself? A door banged inside the house. All at once he was overcome by senseless fear. Someone might be coming out. And he ran off, without knowing where he was going.

He stopped in front of the Spa Gardens because they were in darkness and there was no one about. Perhaps he could sit there quietly, think long and hard, calm down and sort out his fate. Timidly he went in. Nearby, the light of a few lamps made the still tender leaves look a ghostly transparent green, as though they were reflecting water. Farther back, though, where he would have to descend the hill, everything lay in a unified, oppressive, black, fermenting mass in the confusing gloom of an early spring evening. Edgar slipped diffidently past the few people talking or reading in the pools of light shed by the lamps. He wanted to be alone. But even in the gloomy shadows of the unlit paths there was no peace. The air was filled with slightly furtive rustling and whispering, mixed many times over with the wind's breath among the stirring leaves, the shuffling of distant feet, voices speaking in restrained undertones, with some kind of sensual, sighing, anxious, groaning clamour that could have issued at one and the same time from man and beast and nature in her uneasy sleep. The turbulence was alarming. It was depressing, elusive, terrifying and incomprehensible. The air was alive here with some subterranean upheaval in the woods, associated only with the spring, but it had a strangely disturbing effect on the perplexed child.

Edgar huddled up as small as he could on a bench in the fathomless darkness and tried to consider what story he should tell up at the house. But his thoughts slipped clean away before he could grasp them. He could only go on listening against his will to the subdued noises, the mystical voices of the dark. How awful this darkness was, how bewildering and yet in some mysterious way beautiful! Was all this rustling and crackling, movement and murmuring woven together by animal or man, or only by the ghostly hand of the wind? He listened. It was the wind, prowling restlessly through the trees, but – now he saw it clearly – it was also people, couples entwined, walking up from the brightly lit town and animating the darkness with their puzzling presence. What did they want? He couldn't understand it. They didn't talk to each other for he heard no voices, only footsteps crunching restlessly on the ground, and here and there in the light he saw their shapes pass quickly by like shadows. But they were always blended into one, as he had seen once before when his mother was walking with the baron. So that secret, that great, glittering and fateful secret, was here, too. He heard steps approaching nearer and nearer, and now a muffled laugh. He was afraid: whoever was walking this way might find him. He tucked himself ever deeper into the darkness. But the couple didn't see him as they stumbled along the path through the impenetrable gloom. Inextricably entwined, they were going past him. Edgar breathed again, but then suddenly they stopped, right in front of his bench. They pressed their faces together. Edgar couldn't see anything clearly. He heard only a sigh fall from the woman's lips and the man stammering vehement, pressing words. Edgar's anxiety was swept through with some oppressive presentiment and yet also with a shiver of delight. They stayed there like that for a minute and then the gravel crunched again under their departing feet as they soon faded away into the darkness.

Edgar shivered. His blood stirred again and his pulse quickened. And all at once he felt unbearably alone in this disorientating gloom; he felt an overwhelming need to hear some friendly voice, to be hugged, for a brightly-lit room, for people he loved. It seemed to him that the whole bewildering darkness of that disordered night had sunk right into him and would burst him open.

He jumped up. Only home, home, anywhere to be in the warm, in a well-lit room in some contact with people. What could happen to him then? They could beat him and be angry with him; he wasn't afraid of that any more since he had experienced this darkness and the fear of loneliness.

He was propelled forward without realising it, and suddenly there he was again outside the villa, his hand once more on the cold handle of the gate. He noticed the lights in the windows glimmering through the greenery; he saw in his mind's eye the familiar room behind the bright panes, with his relations inside. Already being so close made him feel happy; it gave him that first calming sensation of being near people he knew loved him. And if he still hesitated now it was only to savour that pleasurable anticipation to the full.

Then a shrill, startled voice called out behind him. 'Edgar's here! He's arrived!'

His grandmother's maid had seen him. She rushed up and took him by the hand. The house-door was flung open, a dog jumped up at him, barking, someone brought lights out. He heard voices calling out with joy and surprise; there was a happy tumult of exclamations and footsteps approaching, and of figures he recognised now. His grandmother came first with outstretched arms and behind her — he thought he was dreaming — his mother. On the verge of tears, trembling and overcome, he stood even in the midst of this warm outburst of extravagant emotion, undecided what he should do, what he should say, and even unclear about what he felt: fear or happiness.

THE LAST DREAM

This is what happened: they had been looking for him and waiting for him at the house a long time. Despite her anger his mother had been alarmed at the furious way the overwrought boy had stormed out, and had instituted a search for him in Semmering. Soon everything was in the most terrible uproar and everyone was full of the most worrying conjectures. Then a man brought the news that he had seen the boy about three o'clock at the station booking office. There they quickly established that Edgar had bought a ticket for Baden, and his mother followed him without a moment's hesitation. Telegrams to Baden and to his father in Vienna sped ahead of her, spreading the agitation. Two hours ago everything had been set in motion after the runaway.

Now she held him fast but without exercising authority. He was led into the room in restrained triumph; but what seemed strange to him was that he didn't mind all her stern words of reproach because he saw joy and love in her eyes. And even this pretence, this sham annoyance lasted only a moment. Then his grandmother hugged him again tearfully, no one said another word about his offence, and he felt surrounded by wonderful loving care. The maid took his coat and brought him a warmer one. Then his grandmother asked if he was hungry or wanted anything. They pressed their tender care on him and enveloped him in it, until they saw how embarrassed he was, and they stopped their questions. He was delightfully aware of the feeling he had so despised earlier and yet had missed, that he was a child again. He was ashamed at his presumption over the last few days. He had exchanged all that privileged way of life for the illusory pleasure of being alone.

The telephone rang in the next room. He heard his mother's voice and the odd word or two, 'Edgar ... back ... coming here ... last train,' and wondered why she hadn't really shouted at him but had only given him such a remarkably restrained look. His remorse increased uncontrollably and he wanted to free himself from all his grandmother's and his aunt's attention and go to his mother. He wanted to ask her forgiveness and tell her in all humility, privately, that he wanted to be a child again and obey her. But when he stood up quietly, his grandmother said in mild alarm, 'Where are you going?'

He stood there abashed. They worried about him if he so much as moved. He had given them all such a fright, they were afraid now he wanted to run off again. How could they understand that no one regretted running away more than he did!

The table was set and he was brought a quickly prepared supper. His grandmother sat there and never took her eyes off him. She and his aunt and the maid enclosed him in a peaceful circle and he felt wonderfully calmed by this warmth of affection. Only the absence of his mother from the room made him unsettled. If she had any idea how mortified he felt she would surely have come in!

A carriage clattered up outside and stopped in front of the house. The others were so agitated that Edgar became uneasy too. His grandmother went out, loud voices called back and forth in the dark, and all at once he knew his father had arrived. Edgar observed nervously that he was once more alone in the room, and even this short moment of solitude upset him. His father was strict; he was the only person of whom Edgar was really afraid. Edgar listened to the voices outside. His father seemed excited. He was speaking loudly and sounded angry. In between he heard the soothing tones of his grandmother and his mother, obviously trying to calm his father down. But his voice remained firm, as firm as his step which was now approaching, nearer and nearer, now in the next room, now right outside the door, which burst open.

His father was very big. As he entered the room, tense and evidently furious, Edgar felt unspeakably small.

'What came over you, my boy, running away like that? How could you give your mother such a fright?'

His voice was angry and he was gesturing impetuously. His mother had now come in quietly behind him. Her face was overcast.

Edgar didn't answer. He felt he had to justify himself, but then how could he explain that someone had deceived him and they'd had a fight? Would his father understand?

'Well, lost your tongue? What was the matter? You can tell me about it! What was wrong? There has to be a reason before someone runs away! Did anyone hurt you?'

Edgar hesitated. The recollection made him so furious again, he was on the point of making his accusations. Then he saw – and it made his heart miss a beat – how his mother was making a special sign to him behind his father's back. He didn't understand what she meant at first. But now she was looking at him with earnest entreaty in her eyes. And quietly, very quietly, she raised her finger to her lips signalling him not to tell.

The child experienced a rush of warmth, of immense, boundless happiness, which spread through his body. He understood she had given him a secret to protect, that something fateful depended on what he said. And he nearly burst with pride that she trusted him. Swiftly he was seized by a spirit of sacrifice, a desire to exaggerate his own guilt, only to show how dependable and how very grown up he had become. He pulled himself together. 'No, no ... there wasn't a reason. Mama was very good to me, but I was naughty, I misbehaved ... and then ... then I ran away because I was afraid.'

His father looked at him, nonplussed. He had expected anything but this confession. His anger was disarmed.

'Well. If you're sorry, it's all right then. I won't say any more about it today. I trust you'll think more carefully another time! So nothing like this ever happens again.'

He stood there and looked at Edgar. His tone was gentler.

'How pale you look. But I think you've grown quite a bit. I hope you won't indulge in such childish pranks again. You really aren't a little boy any more and you ought to be able to behave sensibly now!'

Edgar was looking all this time at his mother. He thought there was a sparkle in her eyes. Or was it just the reflection of the light? No, they had a moist, bright gleam in them and a smile played round her lips that said 'thank you' to him.

They sent him to bed then, but he wasn't upset about it, for they all left him alone. He had so much to think over, such a kaleidoscope of impressions. All the distress of the last few days vanished in the powerful emotion of this first personal adventure, and he felt intoxicated with an unaccountable anticipation of future events.

Outside the trees were rustling in the darkness of the night, but he wasn't afraid any more. He had lost all impatience with life now he recognised how rich it was. It was as though he had seen reality laid bare before him for the first time, not wrapped up in the thousand deceits of childhood, but in its complete, incredible, dangerous beauty. He had never thought that days could be crammed so full of such a variety of interchange between pain and pleasure. He was happy to think that many more similar days were before him and a whole lifetime of discovery was waiting to unveil its surprises to him.

He had received a first intimation of the many-sidedness of the real world. He believed he understood for the first time the bare essentials about people. They needed each other, even if they seemed hostile, and it was marvellous to be loved by them. He was unable to hate anything or anyone; he regretted nothing; and he discovered a new feeling of gratitude even for the baron, that tempter, his bitterest enemy, because he had opened the door to this new world of novel emotions.

Thinking about everything now in the darkness made it seem very pleasant and promising. Gently everything became confused with pictures from dreams, and he was very close to sleep. Had the door opened suddenly? Had something come in? At first he thought he was mistaken; he was too much a prisoner of sleep to open his eyes. Then he detected breath from a face bent over him, soft, warm and gentle, rubbing up against his own, and he knew it was his mother, kissing him and smoothing his hair with her hand. He felt the kisses and her tears, responding softly to the caress. He took it only as reconciliation, as gratitude for his silence. Only later, many years later, did he recognise in those silent tears a pledge on the part of the woman, recognising she was no longer young, that from now on she wanted to belong only to him, to her child. It was a renunciation of adventures, a farewell to all her own desires. He didn't know she was grateful to him, too, for saving her from a futile affair, and with this embrace she was relinquishing to him the bitter-sweet burden of love as an inheritance for his future life. The child understood nothing of all that at the time, but he felt extremely happy to be loved so much, and through that love to be involved already in the world's great secret.

As she took her hand away her lips brushed his, and the gentle form hurried out leaving behind her something warm, a breath, on his lips. And a pleasurable longing came over him to feel soft lips like that often again, and to be embraced so tenderly. But this portentous intimation of the secret he had sought after so much was soon overcast by the shadows of sleep. Once again all the pictures of the last few hours went vividly by; once again the pages of the book of his childhood turned enticingly. Then the boy fell asleep and the deeper dream of his life began.

FEAR

As Irene walked down the stairs from her lover's flat she felt that senseless stab of fear again. A black top spun unexpectedly before her eyes, her knees stiffened alarmingly and she had to catch hold of the banister to avoid falling headlong. It wasn't the first time she had risked making the dangerous visit. This sudden spasm was in no way new to her. Despite putting up every inner defence she always experienced an unreasonable attack of absurd, ludicrous fear like this on her way home. Going to the rendezvous was undoubtedly easier. Then she stopped the taxi at the corner of the street and, without looking round, hurried the few steps to the door and flew up the stairs. She knew, of course, that he was waiting for her inside, behind the quickly opened door. And the anxiety of the moment, in which there was an element of impatience, disappeared in the warmth of their greeting embrace.

But then, when she wanted to go home, a different, mysterious, chill dread reared up. Now guilt mingled with it. She had the foolish illusion that every stranger who looked at her in the street might read her thoughts, know where she had been, and would respond to her embarrassment with an impudent grin. Even the last few minutes in his company were poisoned by the uneasy way this foreboding grew. In her wish to be gone her frantic hands shook with nerves, she caught only the odd word of what he was saying, and quickly brushed aside the parting expression of his passion. All she wanted now was to leave, to go away from his flat, his home, away from the affair, back to her calm, middle-class world.

She scarcely dared look in the mirror for fear of the misgivings in her own expression, and yet she had to check to make sure her clothes didn't betray the passion of the hour. Then came the final attempt at calming words — but she hardly heard, she was in such an agitated state — and that moment of listening behind the protective door in case anyone was coming up or down the stairs. Fear was waiting for her outside, though, impatient to seize her. It interfered so insistently with the beating of her heart that she was always out of breath going down the few steps, and felt the nervous energy she had gathered together was spent.

She stood for a minute with her eyes shut and eagerly breathed in the cool air of the dim hallway. From somewhere upstairs she heard a door close. She pulled herself together in alarm and hurried on down the steps, while her hands instinctively drew her thick veil closer round her. Now that last most awful moment was approaching: the terror of stepping out of someone else's front door into the street, the possibility of an importunate question from a passing acquaintance as to where she had been, and the embarrassment and danger of having to lie. She lowered her head like an athlete about to attempt a jump and sped with sudden decisiveness for the half-open door.

There she collided with a woman who was evidently on her way in. 'I'm so sorry,' Irene said self-consciously and tried to pass her quickly. But the woman blocked the doorway and stared at her with anger and also undisguised disdain. 'Now I've caught you!' she shouted in a powerful voice, with no concern for the noise. 'I might have known. A respectable lady, so-called! Not satisfied with a husband and plenty of money and everything, you have to entice a poor girl's lover away from her ...'

'For heaven's sake ... what do you ... you're mistaken ...' Irene stuttered, and made a clumsy attempt to squeeze past. But the woman placed her solid body right in the doorway and upbraided her stridently. 'No, I'm not mistaken ... I know you. You've come from Edward. My man. Now I've caught you at last. Now I know why he's had so little time for me recently. Because of you, is it ... you common ... !'

'For God's sake,' Irene interrupted in a weak voice, 'don't shout like that,' and instinctively stepped back into the building. The woman looked at her scornfully. Irene's trembling fear and visible helplessness seemed somehow to make her accuser feel better, for she inspected her victim with a self-confident, satisfied and derisive smile. Her voice became quieter and almost placid, she was so obviously pleased with herself.

'So that's what you look like then, my fine, fashionable, married lady, when you go stealing other people's men. Wearing a veil. Of course you would be, so you can go on playing the respectable wife afterwards.'

'What ... what do you want? I don't know you. I have to go.'

'Go ... yes, of course, back to your husband ... to your warm room, to play the society lady and have the servants help you off with your coat. But a fine lady like you doesn't care what happens to the likes of me. My sort can die of hunger. You'd steal the bread from the mouth of the likes of me, you would, respectable ladies like you.'

Irene pulled herself together, and obeying some vague prompting, delved into her purse, and brought out however many banknotes came to hand. 'There ... take these ... but leave me alone now. I won't come here again ... I swear I won't.'

The woman took the money and looked malicious. 'Hussy,' she murmured.

Irene winced at the word, but she saw the woman had moved away from the door for her. She rushed out, stupefied and breathless, as a suicide might throw herself from a tower. She was conscious of faces gliding by like distorted caricatures as she ran along the street. With an effort she struggled, only half-seeing, as far as a taxi standing at the corner. She threw herself, all of a heap, on to the upholstered seat. Then she went rigid and motionless. When the astonished driver finally asked his extraordinary customer where she wanted to go she stared at him blankly for a moment, until her numbed brain eventually took in what he had said. 'To the South Station,' she managed to say hastily. Then suddenly struck by the thought that the woman could have followed her, she added, 'Quickly, quickly, drive fast!'

On the way she began to realise how much this encounter had affected her. She felt how stiff and cold her hands were; they hung from her body as though they didn't belong to her. All at once she began to shiver and shake all over. There was a bitter taste in her throat, she felt sick and at the same time a senseless, muffled fury spread like a spasm within her breast. She wanted to scream or hit out with her fists, to free herself from the horror of that recollection – stuck fast in her mind like a fish-hook – from that coarse face with its baleful laugh; from the haze of vulgarity that arose from the bad breath of that loud-mouthed working-class woman who had spat her common words full of hate right in her face; and from that reddened, raised fist she had shaken at her. Her feeling of nausea and the bitterness in her throat increased as the fast-moving vehicle bounced and rolled. She was on the point of asking the driver to slow down when it struck her just in time that possibly she didn't have enough money on her to pay him, since she had given all her banknotes to the blackmailer. Hurriedly she signalled the driver to stop, and to his renewed surprise jumped out. Fortunately the money she had left was sufficient. But then she found she was in a neighbourhood she didn't know, in a crowd of busy people who upset her physically with every word or glance. Fright made her weak at the knees and her legs were unwilling to carry her forward. But she had to get home, and summoning all her energy, she stumbled with superhuman effort from one street to the next, as though she were knee-deep in snow or wading through a morass. Eventually she arrived home and began to scurry up the steps in anxious haste. But she immediately checked herself so that her agitation would not attract attention.

Only when the maid took her coat, and she heard her little boy playing with his younger sister near by, and cast a reassuring glance over all that was hers, her possessions and her security, did she regain an outward appearance of composure; while under the surface waves of excitement still rolled painfully through her tense body. She took off her veil, made a great effort of will to put a smooth, innocent expression on her face, and walked into the dining-room, where her husband was reading the paper. The table was set for dinner.

'You are late, my dear Irene, you are late,' he greeted her with a gentle reproach. He stood up and kissed her on the cheek, which awakened in her a painful sense of shame. They sat down to eat, and he asked her casually, hardly glancing up from his paper. 'Where have you been, to be so long?'

'I was ... at ... at Amelia's ... she had some shopping to do ... and I went with her.' She elaborated her excuse and was promptly annoyed with herself for being so unprepared and lying so badly. Usually she prepared in advance a carefully thought-out lie that would bear any possible examination, but today anxiety had made her forget and forced her into such an inept improvisation. Supposing, it went through her mind, her husband telephoned and made inquiries, as had happened in the play they had seen at the theatre recently ...

'What's the matter, then? You seem so tense – and why don't you take off your hat?' her husband asked. She was alarmed, as she felt caught out yet again in her embarrassment. She stood up quickly and went to her room to remove her hat, and she gazed at her troubled eyes in the mirror until she thought her expression seemed more settled and reliable. Then she returned to the dining-room.

The maid came in with the dinner, and it was an evening like all others, perhaps a little more silent than usual and less companionable, an evening of poor, jaded and often desultory conversation. Her thoughts kept wandering inexorably back and she was filled with fear and alarm whenever she reached that moment when she was in the terrifying presence of the blackmailer. Then she would look up each time to feel secure, to fix fondly on every item of her cherished surroundings, each object in the room standing there as a reminder and a souvenir, and a gentle calm would return. And the clock on the wall, breaking the silence in a leisurely way with its steely step, imperceptibly gave her heart back something of its evenly measured, carefree and certain beat.

On belated examination in the clear light of day, next morning when her husband had gone to his office, the children had gone for a walk and she was alone at last, the frightful encounter lost much of its horror. Irene reflected first of all that her veil was very thick and it was impossible for that creature to have seen through it to establish precisely the contours of her face and to be able to recognise her again. Calmly she now considered all precautions and safeguards. In no circumstances would she visit her lover again at his flat — and in that way the most likely possibility of another such encounter would be avoided. There remained only the danger of a chance meeting with that person, which was also unlikely, for she couldn't have been followed once she had fled in the taxi. The woman didn't know Irene's name or address, and there was no cause to fear a positive identification anywhere else from the vague outline of her face. But she was also prepared for this if it came to the worst. For, no longer in the clutches of fear, she now decided it would be easy to remain calm, deny everything, coolly to claim there was some mistake and, since proof of that visit was hardly likely to be forthcoming in any other way, if necessary to accuse the woman of blackmail. Not for nothing was Irene the wife of the best-known defence counsel at the law courts. She knew enough from conversations she had heard with other lawyers that blackmail could only be stopped by immediate action and a show of the greatest composure. Any delay, any appearance of agitation on the part of the victim, only increased the opponent's dominance.

The first counter-measure was a short letter to her lover to tell him she couldn't come tomorrow at the usual time, or for the next few days. As she read it through, the note — in which she had disguised her writing for the first time — seemed rather frosty in tone. She was on the point of substituting more loving words for the blunt ones when the recollection of yesterday's encounter caused her to feel resentment welling up within her. That was unconsciously responsible for the coldness of what she had written. Her pride was hurt by the painful discovery that she had inherited her lover's affections from such a low-born and unworthy predecessor; and examining the words resentfully, she derived spiteful pleasure now from the off-hand way in which she elevated her visits, as it were, to the sphere of a gracious whim.

She had met this young man at an informal evening gathering. He was a pianist by profession, admittedly known as yet only in a limited circle. Soon, without really wanting to and almost without realising it, she had become his mistress. Nothing in her blood had really made her desire him; nothing physical and hardly anything intellectual had bound them together. She had given herself to him without needing to be his or even greatly longing for him, rather out of a certain lack of opposition to his will, and a kind of restless curiosity. Nothing, neither her fully satisfied needs through a happy marriage nor that feeling women so often have of being frustrated in their intellectual interests, had made it necessary for her to take a lover. She was completely happy at the side of a wealthy husband who was her intellectual superior, with her two children, lazily and contentedly settled in her agreeable, broadly conventional, unruffled existence. But there is a flaccidity of atmosphere that affects the senses in a similar way to sultry weather or a storm, a well-regulated level of happiness that is more maddening than misfortune; and it is as disastrous for many women, because of their resignation to it, as a lasting discontent caused by despair. To have an overabundance is no less stimulating than to be hungry, and the secure certainty of her life aroused her curiosity about having an affair. There was no opposition in her existence. She was feather-bedded in every way, surrounded by anticipation of her needs, affection, a modicum of love, and domestic respect. Without her realising it this even tenor of life had never had to be adapted to outside things, but was always only the counterpart of an inner irrelevance. She felt somehow cheated of real life by this material well-being.

The hazy dreams of her adolescence, of great romance and ecstasy of feeling, which had been stilled by the friendly peacefulness of the early years of marriage and the playful charm of young motherhood, were now beginning, as she approached her thirties, to stir again. And like every woman she believed in her heart she was capable of great passion, without, however, associating the courage required to pay the real price of an affair – danger – with the will to experience it. At a moment of contentment, which she herself had no capacity to increase, this young man had approached her with his strong, unconcealed desire. Surrounded by the romance of art, he had entered her well-bred world, where the men usually respectfully honoured the 'beautiful lady' in her with mild jokes and little flirtatious compliments, without really seriously wanting the woman in her. She now felt deeply stirred for the first time since she was a girl. She had been drawn to him by perhaps nothing more than a shadow of sorrow that lay over his too interestingly arranged features. She was unable to discern if he was really as accomplished as was suggested by the technique of his art and that pensive air, wrapped in melancholy, from which he conjured up an impromptu (prepared well in advance). For her, feeling she was surrounded by over-fed, materialistic people, this melancholy was a glimpse of that higher world that looked at her colourfully out of books and moved her romantically at the theatre, which unconsciously she leaned over the edge of her everyday feelings to examine.

A compliment, born of the delight of the moment, and expressed perhaps with more warmth than decorum, made him look up at her from the piano, and that very first glance transfixed her. She was charmed and felt at once the sensual *frisson* that accompanies all fear. A conversation with him, in which everything shone and glowed as though with sub-terranean fire, so aroused and held her now intense curiosity that she did not avoid a further meeting at a public concert. They saw each other more frequently after that, and soon no longer by chance. That she, who hitherto had set little value on her musical judgment and rightly denied the importance of her artistic instinct, should mean much to him, a real artist, as judge and adviser – as he repeatedly assured her she did – was an aspiration that caused her rashly to trust him some weeks later, when he suggested he wanted her and her alone to come home and hear him play his newest composition. This was a proposition he perhaps intended half sincerely but, in fact, it was lost sight of in kisses and finally in her unintended sub-mission.

Her first reaction was one of alarm at this unanticipated turn towards the carnal. The mysterious thrill surrounding the relationship was abruptly broken; and the guilty conscience caused by this unplanned adultery was only partly quietened by the piquant vanity of deciding for herself, as she believed, for the first time to disavow the middle-class world in which she lived. The thrill of her own wickedness that shocked her for the first few days converted her vanity into a heightened sense of pride. But even that mysterious excitement was at its height only in the early stages. Her basic instinct rejected this man, especially his novelty value and the fact that he was different, which was really what had tempted her curiosity. The outlandish way he dressed, his unconventional home, the disorder of his finances, which swung eternally between excess and shortage, were antipathetic to her middle-class instincts. As with most women, she wanted the artist to be very romantic from afar and very polished as a personal acquaintance; a glittering beast of prey, but behind the iron bars of etiquette.

The passion that carried her away in his playing disturbed her in his physical presence. She couldn't help, in fact, subconsciously comparing the self-willed recklessness of those impetuous and pressing embraces with her husband's lovemaking, which was still shy and respectful after several years. But now she had once embarked on infidelity, she came back to her lover again and again. It didn't make her happy or disillusioned. She did it out of a certain feeling of commitment and of inertia in the face of what had become a habit. She was one of those women, frequently to be found among irresponsible flirts, whose inner conventionality is so strong that they bring an orderliness even to adultery, a kind of domesticity to loose living, and seek to cover the rarest feeling with a patient mask of banality. After only a few weeks this young man, her lover, fitted more or less neatly into her life. She granted him one day a week, as she did her parents-in-law. She gave up none of her established order for this new relationship, however, but merely added it, as it were, to her routine. He caused almost no changes in the comfortable workings of her existence. He was just an addition of moderate good fortune, like a third child or a car, and the affair soon seemed as ordinary as the permitted pleasures of marriage.

So the first time the affair had to be paid for by danger, its true price, she began to fuss and count the cost. It was her fate to have been pampered. Her family spoiled her and because of her advantageous financial position there was almost nothing she couldn't have if she wanted it. So even the first inconvenience of feeling sorry for herself seemed too much. She was immediately unwilling to give up any of her peace of mind, and was indeed ready to sacrifice her lover for her comfort, without a second thought.

Her lover's reply, an alarmed, upset, incoherent letter, was brought by a messenger the same afternoon. It was a frantic letter that implored her, complained, made accusations, and unsettled her again in her decision to end the affair; for this inordinate desire of his flattered her vanity, and his transport of despair delighted her. Her lover begged her in the most pressing language at all events to grant him one brief meeting, so that he could at least hear what he had done wrong. Had he offended her in some way without knowing it? And now she was stimulated by a new game: to sulk, and by refusing him without good reason to make herself even more precious to him. She was aware of being in the midst of an upset, and like any frigid person, that pleased her – being surrounded with the burning fire of passion without catching fire herself. So she arranged to meet him in a café where, she suddenly remembered, she had had a rendezvous with an actor when she was a young girl. It was a meeting she now, of course, considered childish, in the respect he had shown her and his lack of seriousness. How strange, she smiled to herself, that romance should blossom again in her life, when it had withered away in all her years of marriage. Now she was almost pleased about the brusque encounter of yesterday with that woman, for it had stimulated her feelings strongly again after they had lain dormant for so long. As a result, her nerves, which had been quite lightly relaxed, were vibrating again below the surface.

This time she put on a dark, inconspicuous dress and a different hat to confuse that creature's memory if she should chance to meet her. She already had a veil prepared to make herself unrecognisable, but a sudden fit of defiance made her put it aside. Why should she, a respected and highly-regarded married woman, not dare to go out, through fear of some person she hardly knew? Already fear in the face of danger was mixed with a strangely tempting fascination. She felt a dangerous, gripping desire that was ready to do battle, similar to someone running his fingers along the cold razor edge of a dagger or looking down the muzzle of a gun, where death sits compressed inside the black casing. The thrill of an affair brought some novelty into her sheltered life, and being close to one again tempted her. She felt a sensation that relaxed her nerves wonderfully and scattered electric sparks through her blood.

A fleeting feeling of anxiety came over her only during those first moments when she stepped out on the street. She felt a nervous, cold shiver go through her, like someone dipping her toes in the water to test it before committing herself fully to the waves. But this cold spasm went through her only for an instant. Then all at once she felt a rare surge of joy at being alive, and the urge to step out with a relaxed, positive step, so light, firm and lithe, that she had never experienced before. She was almost sorry that the café was so near, for some inclination drew her to continue walking rhythmically, following the mysterious, magnetic attraction of the adventure. But it was almost the time she had agreed for the rendezvous and she felt comfortably certain her lover was already waiting for her.

He was sitting in a corner as she entered and jumped up in a state of agitation that pleased and pained her simultaneously. She had to urge him to lower his voice, as a cascade of questions and remonstrance poured out of him from the passionate tumult of his inner excitement. She didn't make clear the real reason for her absence but played with vague hints that only further inflamed him. This time she remained deaf to his entreaties and hesitated even to make promises, because she sensed how this arbitrary unexplained withdrawal and rejection aroused him. And when she left him after half-an-hour's heated conversation, without offering the least sign of tenderness or promising anything, she glowed inwardly with a very peculiar feeling, one she had last had as a girl. It was as though there was a tiny, sharp flame deep within her waiting for the wind to whip up the fire until it engulfed her completely.

She quickly captured every glance from passers-by as she walked along. The unexpected effect of attracting such male attention so aroused her curiosity about her own face that she stopped suddenly in front of the mirror in a florist's window, to examine her own beauty framed in red roses and dew-laden violets. She flashed a radiant look at herself, lithe and young, a sensual, half-open mouth smiling back at her with satisfaction. As she walked on, her limbs seemed to have taken wing; a desire to be released physically, to dance or whirl about, broke the usual comfortable rhythm of her step. Now, reluctantly, she heard St Michael's church clock chime the hour as she hurried by, calling her home to her narrow, orderly world. She hadn't felt so carefree since she was a girl, or all her senses so alive. Neither the early days of her marriage nor the embraces of her lover had made her body glow in this way, and she couldn't bear to think she had to waste all this strange lightness, this sweet frenzy of the blood, on regular hours. Wearily she walked on. She stood hesitating once more outside the house, opening her lungs to breathe in again the fiery air, the confusion of the hour, so that she could feel deep in her heart the last ebbing wave of the affair.

Someone tapped her on the shoulder. She turned round. 'What ... what do you want this time?' she stammered, frightened to death as she suddenly saw the hated face. And she was even more horrified as she heard herself saying those fatal words, for she had intended not to acknowledge that creature again if she happened to meet her, to deny everything, to outface the blackmailer. Now it was too late.

'I've been waiting here for you for a good half-hour, Frau Wagner.'

Irene was taken aback when she heard her name. This woman knew her name and where she lived. Now all was lost: she was irretrievably delivered up to her. She had words on her lips, carefully prepared and calculated words, but her tongue wouldn't work and she couldn't utter a syllable.

'Half-an-hour I've been waiting, Frau Wagner.' The creature repeated her words, like a menacing reproach.

'What do you want ... what do you want of me, then?'

'You know very well, Frau Wagner,' – Irene cowered back again at the use of her name – 'you know exactly why I've come.'

'I haven't seen him again ... leave me alone now ... I won't see him again ... never.'

The woman waited unmoved until Irene could contain her agitation no longer. Then she said tartly, as though to an underling, 'Don't tell lies! I followed you to the café.' As she saw Irene shrink back she went on scornfully. 'I'm unemployed. They sacked me as they said there wasn't enough work, and because of the slump. Well, we have to make use of our time and go for a stroll, too, just like fine ladies.'

She said it with a cold malice that stabbed Irene's heart. She felt defenceless against the blunt brutality of this common woman. She grew more and more distraught at the fearful thought that the creature might begin to shout, or that her husband might appear, and then all would be lost. Quickly she fumbled in her muff, opened her silver purse and took out all the money she could hold. With loathing she thrust it into the woman's hand, which had been held out slowly and impudently already, in certain expectation of plunder.

But this time the bold hand didn't close humbly as soon as it felt the money, as it had before, but remained stiffly hovering in the air and open like a claw.

'Give me the purse, too, then, so I don't lose the money!' said the sneering, pouting mouth. The woman laughed lightly.

Irene looked her in the eye, but only for a second. She couldn't bear this impudent, vulgar mockery. She felt disgust flowing through her whole body like a burning pain. If only she could escape, be gone, and never see that face again! Turning away, she held out her expensive purse to the woman with a quick movement, and then ran up the steps, pursued by fear.

Her husband had not yet arrived home, so she could throw herself down on the sofa. She lay there motionless, as though struck by a hammer, except for a wild twitching which affected her fingers and made her arms tremble all the way up to her shoulders. But nothing in her body enabled her to defend herself against the raging force of terror that had been unleashed. Only when she heard her husband's voice outside did she make the utmost effort to pull herself together and slip into the other room, her movements automatic and her feelings numb.

Now dread sat with her in the house and would not stir. In the many empty hours in which pictures of the terrible encounter flooded back into her mind the hopelessness of her position became very clear to her. The woman knew her name, her address – she couldn't imagine how that could have happened – and now her first attempts had been so successful she would undoubtedly shrink from no measure to put her involvement to use for prolonged blackmail. The creature would be a nightmare burden on her life for years and years, not to be shaken off by even the most desperate efforts; for although Irene was wealthy and the wife of a man of substance she couldn't raise a sum sufficient to free herself once and for all from this woman without telling her husband. And besides – she knew from her husband's passing stories and lawsuits – agreements and promises made by such crafty and unprincipled persons were quite worthless. Disaster could be held at bay for one month or perhaps two, Irene reckoned. Then the artificial structure of her domestic happiness must collapse, and the certainty of bringing down the blackmailer with her own fall offered small satisfaction. For what were six months in prison for that creature who was certainly a loose woman and had probably already been convicted, compared with the life she would lose, in her mind the only possible one for her, and from which she already felt estranged? To begin a new existence, disgraced and discredited, seemed inconceivable, for until now life had showered its gifts on her and she had built no part of her own destiny herself. And then, her children were here, her husband, her home, all those things that, now she would be losing them, she realised for the first time were so much part and parcel of her inner life. Everything she had earlier taken for granted struck her all at once as terribly necessary. The thought that an unknown vagabond, lurking somewhere out in the street, had the power to destroy this warm unity with a single word, sometimes seemed inconceivable, indeed utterly unreal.

She knew now with horrible certainty that misfortune was unavoidable and escape impossible. But what ... what would happen? She fretted over this question from morning to night. A letter would arrive for her husband one of these days. She saw him already, coming in, pale, with an ominous expression, gripping her arm and asking her ... But then – what would happen then? What would he do? At this point the picture was obliterated suddenly in the darkness of a confused and dreadful fear. She was at a loss, and her guesses fell dizzily into a bottomless pit. One thing was horribly clear, though, among these brooding thoughts: how little she really knew her husband; how little she could anticipate his decisions in advance.

Her parents had suggested the marriage. She had raised no

objection and had married him with a degree of fondness that had not been disappointed in subsequent years. She had lived by his side for eight years of comfortable, stable happiness, she had borne his children, shared countless hours of his company in his house, but now when she asked herself how he might behave, it was clear to her how distant and unknown he had remained. She discovered in the fever of looking back, seeking to shed some light on the last few years, that she had never investigated his true character and now, years later, didn't even know if he was severe or easy-going, strict or soft. Arising from this serious anxiety about life caused by her guilty conscience, she had to admit, fatefully late, that she knew only the superficial, social side of his personality, and not the deeper side from which his decision would have to be hewn when the tragic hour came. Involuntarily she began to search for little signs and indications, and tried to recall what his opinions had been in talking of similar matters. She was painfully astonished to discover he had hardly ever spoken to her about his personal views, and admittedly, for her part, she had never turned to him with fundamental questions of this kind. Now for the first time she began to examine individual aspects of his entire life to see if they could clarify his character for her. At every little recollection her apprehension grew as she tried irresolutely to find an entry into the innermost areas of his heart.

She watched out now for his most insignificant remark and became very agitated and restless whenever he came in. She noticed his greeting not so much in his face as in his gestures — how he kissed her hand, or stroked her hair — this seemed to be evidence of a tenderness which (although she shrank demurely from more passionate behaviour) might indicate a deep inner disposition. He was always even-tempered when he spoke to her, never impatient or heated, and his whole bearing was one of calm affability. As she began to be uneasily aware, however, this behaviour was little different from the way he acted towards the servants and noticeably less loving than he was to the children, with whom he was altogether more lively, cheerful and even enthusiastic. He inquired today as usual in detail about household matters, as though to give her an opportunity of telling him of her preoccupations while concealing his own. And as she observed him, she discovered for the first time with how much respect he treated her, with how much restraint he strove to adjust to their daily conversations — she was suddenly appalled to recognise how insignificant and banal they were. He said not a word about himself, and her curiosity, yearning for reassurance, remained unsatisfied.

So she searched his face for answers, as his words did not betray him, while he sat in his armchair reading a book, his profile sharply etched by the electric light. It was as though she was looking into the face of a stranger, seeking to clear away the familiar and yet all at once unfamiliar signs of character that had been obscured by eight years of apathetic union. He had a high, refined forehead, as though shaped by strong intellectual activity within, but his mouth was firm and unyielding. Everything in his very masculine features, vigour and strength, was austere. She was astonished to discover he was quite handsome. With some admiration she contemplated his self-controlled seriousness and the visible austerity of his character. Until now, in her naïve way, she had always felt it was not very amusing and would have liked to exchange it for an ability to make conversation in company. His eyes, however, in which the true secret must be locked away, were looking down at his book and therefore prevented her from examining them. So she was able only to go on fixedly interrogating his profile, as though those sweeping lines might convey a single word that spoke of forgiveness or condemnation. The severity of that unfamiliar profile terrified her, but she now recognised for the first time that its decisiveness was remarkably handsome. Suddenly she felt pleasure in gazing at him; and longing and pride. Something tugged painfully at her heart at the awakening of this sentiment, an oppressive feeling of regret for something neglected, an almost sensual tension that she couldn't recall having ever experienced so strongly in her body before. Then he looked up from his book. Quickly she stepped back into the shadows to avoid arousing his suspicion by the burning question on her face.

For three days she did not leave the house. And soon she realised with disquiet that her sudden constant presence was already being noticed by the rest of the household. They remarked to her in general terms how exceptional it was for her to spend many hours or indeed whole days in her own rooms. Not much inclined to domesticity, released from the minor cares of household management by material independence, bored with her own company, her home was little more than a peaceful retreat. The shops, the theatre, social clubs with their lively receptions and their continuous stream of outward variety, were her favourite places, because their enjoyment required no serious effort. With her emotions dormant her senses felt frequently stimulated. Irene's attitude of mind was completely at one with that elegant stratum of the Viennese bourgeoisie, whose whole daily round appeared to consist of a secret agreement that all members of this invisible alliance should meet at the same time without fail to discuss the same interests; and they gradually elevated this eternal business of seeing and being seen to the purpose of their existence. Left to herself, isolated, and so used to indolent society, Irene lost every support and her interests became utterly unimportant without their normal nourishment. But even essential sensations revolt, and solitude degenerated quickly into a tense state of self-hate. She felt time weighing on her endlessly, and the hours lost any meaning without their usual employment. She walked about her rooms, idle and restless, as though she were in prison. She was cut off from the world outside, where her real life was. The blackmailer stood there with her threat like the avenging angel with his fiery sword.

Her children were the first to notice these changes, especially the boy, who was older. With embarrassing clarity he voiced his innocent astonishment at seeing Mama at home so much, while the servants just whispered and exchanged speculations about it with the governess. She tried without success to justify her conspicuous presence to some extent by devising a variety of random domestic tasks. But it was precisely the artificiality of her orders that revealed how superfluous she was in her own domain, having taken no interest in it for years. Wherever she wanted to take an active part she ran up against the opposition of other people, who rejected her unexpected endeavours as improper interference with established routine. Every position was occupied by an outsider, since she herself had lost the habit of organising her own house. So she didn't know what to do with herself or with time. Even her approach to the children was not a success, for they were suspicious that her sudden intense interest in them meant a new introduction of discipline, and she felt herself blushing with embarrassment when at one such attempt at supervision the seven-year-old boy cheekily asked her why she had stopped going out. Whenever she wanted to help she disturbed a system; and where she took an interest she aroused suspicion. Moreover, she wasn't astute enough to make her continuous presence less noticeable by intelligent self-effacement, staying quietly in one room reading a book or doing some task. She hurried about incessantly, driven from one room to another by the inner fear that converted every strong feeling into nervous tension. She started up whenever the telephone or the door-bell rang; and caught herself repeatedly peeping through the curtains out at the street, hungry for people, or at least a sight of them, longing for freedom and yet fearful of seeing among the passers-by the one face, staring up, that followed her into her dreams. She sensed how her peaceful existence was swiftly disintegrating and running through her fingers, and out of this enervated state grew the premonition that her life was going to be completely shattered.

Those three days imprisoned indoors seemed longer to her than the eight years of her marriage. She had, however, several weeks earlier accepted an invitation with her husband, and it was impossible to decline it now, abruptly, without strong grounds for doing so. And besides, if she was not to collapse she had to break this invisible metal grille of dread now erected round her life. She needed people, a few hours' break away from herself, from this suicidal loneliness of fear. Then, too, where would she be safer than with friends in someone else's house? Where would she be more secure from that unseen pursuit that dogged her steps? Just for one brief second did she shudder, and that was at the moment of leaving the house. Now for the first time since the encounter she came into contact again with the street, where that creature could be lurking anywhere. Involuntarily she took her husband's arm, closed her eyes and hurried the few steps across the pavement to the waiting car. Then, however, as she sat securely beside her husband while the vehicle sped through the empty, dimly-lit streets, the inner oppression she felt subsided; and as she walked up the steps of her host's house she knew she was safe. For a few hours she could be as she had been all the past year: carefree, happy, with the enhanced, conscious joy of someone who had left her prison walls for the sunshine. Here were ramparts against all pursuit. Hate could not enter. Here there were only people who were fond of her, respected and honoured her, well-dressed people without ulterior motives, glittering in the red flame of frivolity and engaged in a roundelay of pleasure that at last entwined itself round her too.

For now, as she walked in, she sensed from the glances she received that she was looking at her best, all the more beautiful because of that secure feeling she recognised and had missed for so long. How much good it did her after all those days of silence in which she had never stopped feeling the cutting edge of that single thought ploughing unproductively through her brain, where all was grief and pain! How good it was to hear flattering words again. They were like electric charges that crackled under her skin and stirred her blood. She stood and stared. It was as though something quivered uneasily in her breast and wanted to escape. And all at once she knew it was repressed laughter that wanted to be free. It shot out like a cork from a champagne bottle and overflowed into tiny, gurgling trills. She laughed and laughed, then was embarrassed by her bacchanalian high spirits, and started laughing again the next moment. Electricity flashed out of her nerves as they unwound; all her senses were strong, sound and aroused. For the first time in days she ate as though she was really hungry and drank as though she was dying of thirst.

Her parched spirit, longing for company, soaked up life and pleasure from everything. Music in the next room attracted her and worked its way into her blood. The dance began and before she knew it she was right in the middle of the crowd. She danced as she had never done in her life. All her cares were tossed aside in this swirling circle. The rhythm grew in her limbs and permeated her body with fiery movement. When the music stopped the silence hurt her. A snake of restlessness hissed round her trembling limbs. She jumped back into the whirl of the dance as though into a bath of cool, calming, supporting water. Until now she had always been just a moderate dancer, her steps too deliberate, too stiff and careful, but this frenzy of liberated joy released all physical constraints. An iron band of modesty and discretion that had hitherto held her wildest passions in check now snapped, and she felt unrestrained and thoroughly, blessedly set free. She was aware of arms and hands round her, touching and vanishing, words on the air, titillating laughter, music that penetrated her whole body. She was wound up to such a pitch that her clothes burned her and subconsciously she would have loved to have torn them off to enable her to experience this ecstasy deeper inside her naked body.

'Irene, what's the matter with you?' She turned round, her eyes wild and joyful, still elated by the embrace of her dancing partner. Her husband's astonished and steady gaze struck, cold and severe, into her heart. She was alarmed. Had she been too uninhibited? Had her delirium given something away?

'What ... what do you mean, Fritz?' she stammered, surprised by the sudden impact of his look which seemed to bore deeper into her all the time and had, she felt, already reached right down into her heart. She wanted to cry out under the searching determination of those eyes.

'That's strange, then,' he murmured at last. There was muffled amazement in his voice. She dared not ask what he meant. But a shudder ran through her limbs as he turned away from her without another word and she looked at his shoulders, broad, firm and large, topped by his strong, sinewy neck. 'Like a murderer's' flew through her mind insanely. The thought was soon driven away again. But now, as though she were seeing him for the first time, she discovered with dread that he, her own husband, was strong and dangerous.

The music started up again. A gentleman came over to her and she took his arm mechanically. But now everything had become difficult, and the light melody could no longer lift her stiffened limbs. An oppressive heaviness spread from her heart to her feet; every step hurt. And she had to ask her partner to release her.

As she walked away she instinctively looked round to see if her husband was about. She was startled. He was standing directly behind her as though he was waiting for her, and again he met her with a challenging look. What did he want? What did he already know? Unconsciously she adjusted the top of her dress as though she needed to hide her bare breast from him. His silence remained as stubborn as his expression.

'Are we going?' she asked anxiously.

'Yes.' His voice sounded severe and unfriendly. He went out. Again she saw his broad, threatening shoulders. Someone threw the travelling rug round her, but she was freezing. They were driven along beside each other in silence. She did not dare say a word. Dumbly she felt a new a danger. Now she was being hemmed in on both sides.

That night she had an oppressive dream. Some strange music was playing, there was a bright, high-ceilinged ballroom, she entered, a crowd mixed together in a multicoloured movement. Then a young man, whom she believed she knew but couldn't quite place, came up, took her arm, and she danced with him. She felt fine and supple, a single wave of music lifted her up so she wasn't aware of the floor any more, and in this way she danced through many rooms in which the little flames of chandeliers quite high up shone like stars, and mirrors on all the walls threw her own smiles back to her and bore them far away again in endless reflections. The dance became ever more lively, the music more fiery. She noticed how the young man clasped her closer to him, his hand grasping her bare arm until she had to sigh out loud with aching desire. And now, as her eyes drank in his, she thought she recognised him. She fancied he was an actor whom she had loved ecstatically from a distance when she was a young girl. She was about to speak his name with animation when he silenced her gentle cry with a glowing kiss. And so, their lips blended, their bodies coalesced into one, they flew through the rooms as though borne on a blessed wind. The walls rushed by, the ceiling seemed to have floated away, and she lost track of time, her limbs were immensely light and set free. Then suddenly someone was at her shoulder. She stopped, and with her the music; the lights went out, the walls came towards her darkly, and her partner disappeared.

'Give him back to me, you thief!' the horrible woman shouted, for it was she who made the walls reverberate and clutched her wrist with ice-cold fingers. Irene leapt back and heard herself scream, a frenzied, screeching sound of horror. The two of them grappled with each other but the woman was stronger. She tore Irene's pearl necklace off and with it half her dress, revealing her bare breast and arms under the hanging tatters. At once people arrived, streaming in from all the rooms in a crescendo of noise. They stared at her derisively, half-naked as she was, and the woman shrieked in a shrill voice, 'She has stolen him from me, adulteress, harlot!'

Irene didn't know where to hide, where to look, for everyone was closing in on her, curious; and hissing, distorted faces ogled at her nakedness. And now, as her eyes cast about giddily for rescue, she suddenly saw her husband standing motionless in the shadowy doorway, his right hand concealed behind his back. She screamed and ran away from him, running through one room after another, the avid crowd surging behind her. She felt her dress sliding down more and more; she could scarcely hold it up. Then a door opened in front of her. Eagerly she fled down the stairs to save herself. But the coarse woman with her woollen skirt and clutching hands was there again downstairs waiting for her. Irene jumped aside and ran madly on, but the other woman chased after her, and so the two of them pursued each other all night through long, silent streets, and the lamps bent down and grinned at them. She heard the woman's wooden shoes clattering behind her all the time, but whenever she came to a corner the woman was always there, too, to jump out at her; and again at the next corner, from behind all the houses, right and left, she was waiting to pounce. She was already there; it was terrifying how she multiplied. She was not to be outdistanced, she kept on jumping out and seizing her until Irene felt her knees giving way. There at last was her house. Irene rushed towards it, but as she wrenched the door open there stood her husband with a knife in his hand, his eyes drilling into her.

'Where have you been?' he asked flatly.

'Nowhere,' she heard herself say, and already there was strident laughter at her side.

'I saw her! I saw her!' the leering woman shouted, for there she was again suddenly standing beside her, laughing insanely. Then Irene's husband raised the knife.

'Help!' she cried out. 'Help!'

She started up, and her horrified gaze met her husband's. What ... what was that? She was in her room, the lamp over the bed was shining pale yellow. She was at home in her bed; she had only been dreaming. But what was her husband doing sitting on the edge of her bed looking at her as though she were ill? Who had put on the light, why was he sitting there, stock-still, looking so serious? Terror swept through her. Instinctively she glanced towards his right hand: no, he wasn't holding a knife. Slowly the stupefaction of sleep and the sheet-lightning of those images left her. She must have been dreaming, have shouted out in the course of it, and wakened him. But why was he looking at her so curiously, with such searching, relentless gravity?

She tried to smile. 'What ... what's the matter? Why are you looking at me like that? I think I had a nightmare.'

'Yes, you called out. I heard you from the other room.'

What did I say? What have I given away? She shuddered. What does he already know? She hardly dared meet his eyes again. But, strangely calm, he was looking down at her quite seriously.

'What's the matter, Irene? Something is going on. You've been quite different these last few days, as though you have a fever. You're tense, absent-minded, and call for help in your sleep.'

She tried to smile again.

'No,' he continued. 'You shouldn't hide things from me. Are you worried about something – is something distressing you? Everyone in the house has noticed how you've changed. You should trust me, Irene.'

He drew imperceptibly closer to her. She felt his fingers smoothing and stroking her arm; and his eyes had a strange light in them. She was overcome with a longing to throw herself into his strong arms, to cling to him, to confess everything, and not to let him go until he had forgiven her, now this minute, while he saw how she was suffering.

But the lamp was burning yellow, lighting up her face, and she felt ashamed. She was frightened to tell him.

'Don't worry, Fritz.' She tried to smile, while her whole body shivered right down to her bare toes. 'I'm just a little over-wrought. I'll be all right again soon.'

His arm, which was already round her shoulders, was quickly withdrawn. She shivered, as she saw him now, pale in the glassy light, his brow clouded with the deep shadows of dark thoughts. Slowly he stood up.

'I don't know. I've had a feeling these last few days that there's something you've been wanting to tell me. Something that concerns only you and me. We're on our own now, Irene.'

She lay there and didn't move, as though hypnotised by his serious sidelong glance. How good everything could be now, she felt. She needed only to say two words, two little words — forgive me — and he wouldn't ask her what for. But why was that light on, that strong, brassy, all-seeing light? She could have said it in the dark, she thought. But the light shattered her strength.

'So you really haven't anything to tell me, anything at all?'

How frightful was the temptation, how gentle his voice! She had never heard him speak like that. But the light, the lamp, that yellow, avid light!

She shrugged her shoulders. 'What's the matter with you?' She laughed, and was immediately alarmed by how high-pitched her voice was. 'Just because I'm not sleeping well, does that mean I have secrets from you? An affair, is that what you really mean?'

She was appalled herself how false, how dishonest the words sounded. Horror struck her to the very core at her own words. Involuntarily she looked away.

'Well — sleep well then.' He spoke abruptly and quite sharply. His voice had changed. It sounded like a threat or ill-tempered, menacing sarcasm.

Then he put out the light. She saw his pale shadow disappear through the door, without a sound, dull yellow, a ghost of the night. And as the door closed she felt as though she was being shut in a coffin. She felt withdrawn from the whole world, and empty. Only within her numbed body did her heart pound loudly and turbulently, pain upon pain in every beat.

The next day, when they were all together at luncheon — the

children had just been squabbling and peace had been restored only with difficulty – the maid brought in a letter. It was for Madame and the man was waiting for an answer. She looked in surprise at the unknown writing and quickly opened the envelope, only to go pale as soon as she read the first line. She jumped up immediately and was even more alarmed as she realised she had thoughtlessly betrayed herself to the others, who were all looking astonished at her impetuous behaviour.

The letter was short. Three lines: 'Please give the bearer of this letter one hundred crowns immediately.' There was no signature, no date, only this horrible, peremptory order in obviously disguised writing. Irene ran to her room to fetch the money, but she had mislaid the key to her cash-box. Feverishly she rooted about in one drawer after another until at last she found it. Trembling, she folded the banknote, put it in an envelope and gave it personally to the messenger waiting at the door. She did all that mindlessly, as though she was under hypnosis, without thinking of the possibility of delay. Then she returned to the dining-room – she had been gone scarcely two minutes.

No one spoke. She sat down, ill-at-ease and frightened. She was looking for some excuse to leave the table quickly, when she was absolutely horrified to observe – and it made her hand tremble so much that she had to put down the glass she was holding – that, blinded by the white heat of her agitation, she had left the letter lying open beside her plate. It would only have taken a slight movement for her husband to draw it across to him; one glance, perhaps, could have been sufficient to read the large and clumsily written lines. She was lost for words. Stealthily she crumpled up the note, but as she hid it, looking up she met her husband's stern gaze. It was a penetrating, severe, pained expression she had never seen on his face before. For several days now he had been giving her these sudden explosive looks of mistrust, which made her tremble inwardly and she didn't know how to ward off. It was with one such look that he had paralysed her limbs at the dance; it was the same look that had glinted in her sleep last night like a knife.

Was it something he knew or something he wished to know that was making him so severe, so hostile, so steely, so hurtful?

And while she strove to think what to say she was reminded of a long-forgotten anecdote her husband had once told her. He was counsel before an examining magistrate whose trick it was to scan the papers during the hearing as though he were short-sighted. Then at the really decisive question he would look up, quick as a flash, and strike like a dagger into the sudden fear of the accused. Through the piercing flash of concentrated attention the defendant lost his composure and weakly let fall the carefully sustained lie. Was her husband now trying such a dangerous subterfuge himself and was she the victim? She shuddered, all the more so because she knew how his great passion for the psychological far exceeded his interest in the juridical demands of his profession. He could be as absorbed by tracking down, exposing and drawing out information from a criminal as others are by gambling or sex. And on days when he was engaged in such psychological detective work it was as though his whole being glowed with inner inspiration. Burning nervous energy that often allowed him to light upon forgotten legal precedents in the night, became outwardly steely imperviousness. He ate and drank little, but he chain-smoked. He also spoke little in the hours before a trial. She had seen him once making his speech for the defence and she hadn't gone a second time. She had been so terrified at the threatening passion, the almost angry fire of his speech and the grim and bitter expression on his face. All at once she thought she recognised this again in the penetrating gaze under his menacingly frowning forehead.

All these forgotten memories were concentrated at this instant and turned away the words that formed on her lips. She was silent, and became all the more troubled the more she sensed how dangerous this silence was, and how badly she was letting slip the last plausible possibility to explain. She dared not raise her eyes again, but as she looked down she was even more frightened, for she saw her own hands, normally so calm and controlled, straying up and down on the table like little wild animals. Fortunately luncheon was soon over, the children jumped down and rushed off into the next room with their light, excited voices and the governess tried in vain to subdue their high spirits. Her husband stood up too and went into the adjoining room without speaking or looking round.

Scarcely was she alone than she brought out the fateful letter again. She ran her eye over the lines once more: 'Please give the bearer of this letter one hundred crowns immediately.' Then in a fury she tore it in pieces and crumpled up the remains to hurl them in the waste-paper basket. But a thought struck her and she stopped, bent over the stove and threw the paper into the hissing heat. She was calmed by the white flames, which leapt greedily to gobble up the threat.

At that moment she heard her husband's footsteps at the door as he returned. She started up quickly, her face red from the heat of the fire and from being caught in the act. The stove door was still open, betraying her. Clumsily she tried to hide it by standing in front of it. He walked over to the table and struck a match for his cigar. As the flame was near his face she thought she saw his nostrils twitching, always a sign that he was angry. Now he looked across at her calmly.

'I just wanted you to know that you aren't obliged to show me your letters. If you want to have secrets from me you are absolutely free to do so.'

She said nothing and dared not look at him. He waited a moment, vigorously exhaled a large cloud of cigar smoke, and went out of the room with a heavy tread.

She did not want to think about anything any more. She wanted just to live, to deaden her senses, to fill her heart with empty and meaningless occupations. She couldn't bear the house any longer. She felt impelled to go out, to be among people, or she would go mad with terror. She hoped the hundred crowns had bought her a few short days of freedom from the blackmailer. She decided to risk going out again for a walk, the more so because there were many things to be attended to, and above all because she needed to conceal the noticeable change in her behaviour from the household. She already had a definite way of escaping. With her eyes shut she plunged out of the front door into the stream of passers-by as though from a diving board. And once she had the solid paving stones under her feet and the warm flow of people around her she pressed forward as quickly as a lady might go without being conspicuous, in tense haste, headlong, her eyes looking fixedly at the ground, terrified in case she should meet some hostile gaze. If she was being watched, at least she did not wish to know it. And yet she realised she was thinking of nothing else, and took fright if by chance someone brushed past her. Her nerves vibrated painfully at every sound, every approaching step, every shadow that fell across her path. Only in a vehicle or someone else's house was she really able to breathe freely.

A gentleman greeted her. Looking up she recognised an old friend of the family, a genial, talkative man with a grey beard. She usually preferred to avoid him because he had a way of burdening you for an hour or more with his minor, and possibly only imaginary, physical ailments. But now she was sorry to have merely acknowledged his greeting instead of seeking his company, for a friend would indeed have been a defence against being spoken to unexpectedly by her blackmailer. She hesitated and would have turned round as an afterthought, but she had a feeling someone behind her was approaching quickly. Instinctively, without further thought, she hurried on. But with her sixth sense sharpened by her terrible fear she scented, as it were, someone trying to catch up with her. She walked even faster, but she knew she would not be able to escape her pursuer in the end. Her shoulder began to quiver in anticipation of the hand that would touch her any minute – the steps were coming closer – and the quicker she wanted to go the stiffer her knees became. Her pursuer was quite close now, and a voice called out, 'Irene!' urgently but gently. It was a voice she really had to heed.

But it was not, after all, the voice she feared, the dreaded messenger of misfortune. She breathed again and turned round: it was her lover, who almost ran into her, she had stopped so suddenly. His face was pale and showed all the signs of agitation, and now, under her disconcerted gaze, of embarrassment too. Unsurely he held out his hand in greeting, and let it drop again when she didn't offer him hers. She just stared at him for a couple of seconds, she was so surprised to see him. She had been so afraid these last few days she had quite forgotten him. But now that she saw his pale, questioning face close to, with that expression of perplexed emptiness in his eyes that is always a sign of irresolution, hot waves of anger suddenly foamed up in her. Her lips struggled for a word

187

and the tension in her face was so obvious that in his alarm he could only stammer her name.

'Irene, what's the matter?' When he saw her impatient attitude he added, already downcast, 'Tell me what I've done to upset you.'

She stared at him with scarcely controlled rage. 'What you've done?' She laughed bitterly. 'Nothing! Nothing at all! You've been kindness itself. Charm personified.'

He looked startled, and his mouth fell half open with astonishment, which made him look even more naïve and comical.

'But Irene ... Irene!'

'Don't make a scene here,' she ordered him brusquely. 'And stop playing games with me. She's bound to be watching somewhere near by, your fine friend, and then she'll attack me again ... '

'Who ... who will?'

She would have liked to strike him in the face — that effeminate, surprised, grimacing face — with her fist. She was already aware how tightly her hand was gripping her umbrella. Never had she so despised or hated anyone.

'But Irene ... Irene,' he stuttered, becoming even more confused. 'What have I done? All of a sudden you ... I've waited day and night for you ... I've been standing outside your house all day today, waiting just to be able to speak to you for a minute.'

'You've been waiting ... well, well ... you too.' Fury, she felt, was making her mad. It would do her so much good to be able to slap his face. But she restrained herself, gave him another withering look full of disgust, and at the same time considered whether or not she could spit the whole of her pent-up wrath in his face with abuse. Then she abruptly turned and forced herself on into the passing crowd, without looking back. He stood there with hand still outstretched, imploring her, helpless and quivering, until the general movement on the street caught him up. It carried him along as a current takes a falling leaf, which resists, tumbling and circling, and is finally swept away despite itself.

It suddenly struck her as quite false and meaningless that this man had once been her lover. She could remember nothing

—not the colour of his eyes, or the shape of his face—she couldn't imagine what any of his caresses felt like, and all she could hear of his words was that whining, effeminate, cringing, 'But Irene!' as he stammered his despair. She hadn't thought of him even once during all those days, or dreamt of him, even though he was so much the source of all her trouble. He was nothing to her, without attraction and barely a memory. She couldn't comprehend how her lips could once have come in contact with his. She felt she could swear she had never been his. What had driven her into his arms? What fearful madness had hounded her into an affair? Her own heart did not understand it any more and scarcely did her mind. She no longer knew anything about it; all that had happened was unfamiliar. She was a stranger to herself.

But hadn't everything else changed too, during the days of this terrible week? Corrosive fear had eaten into her life like nitric acid and separated its elements. All at once things had different weight, values were altered and relationships confused. It was as though she had only fumbled her way through life until now, with half-closed eyes and dulled feelings, and here, with terrifying speed, everything had become crystal clear. Right in front of her, a hair's breadth away, were things with which she had never concerned herself. She realised suddenly they had meaning in her real life while other things she had thought important vanished like smoke. Until now she had led an active social life, moved in the noisy, talkative company of well-to-do circles, and had really lived only for that. But now, after a week imprisoned in her own home, she felt no hardship in being deprived of such society, only aversion to the empty activity of the idle. Instinctively she measured this first strong feeling that had come over her against the superficiality of her previous inclinations and her considerable neglect of charity. She saw her past as though it were an abyss. Married eight years, under the delusion that she was moderately happy, she had never been drawn close to her husband, was a stranger to his fundamental character and no less a stranger to her children. Between her and them were employees—governesses and servants, taking all the small anxieties away from her. Now she began to be aware—looking closer into her children's lives—that they had more to commend them than the ardent glances of men and were more inspiring than any embrace. Slowly her life developed a new meaning. Everything fell into place and all at once turned towards her an earnestly significant face. Since she had known danger and with it genuine feeling, everything, including the most unfamiliar, began suddenly to come together. She perceived herself in everything, and the world, earlier as transparent as glass, became all at once the reflection of the dark expanse of her own shadow. She suddenly found reality wherever she looked, wherever she listened.

She sat with the children. The governess was reading them a fairy story about the princess who was allowed to look inside all the rooms in the palace except the one that was locked with a silver key. Nevertheless she opened it, to her own undoing. Was that not her own fate, that she, too, had stirred up what was forbidden and set misfortune in motion? She found deep wisdom in the little story, which only a week ago she would have ridiculed. There was a story in the newspaper of an officer who had been blackmailed into becoming a traitor. She shivered, and understood. Wouldn't she, too, do the impossible to obtain money, to buy a few days' peace, a semblance of happiness? Every line of print that spoke of suicide, every crime, every despair, now happened to her. Everything said 'I' to her, the dejected, the despairing, the seduced servant girl and the abandoned child; it was as though all these were her own fate. All at once she felt how rich life was and that no hour of her destiny could ever be poor again. Now, as everything drew to a close, she sensed a new beginning. And being so wonderfully caught up with the whole infinite world, should that reprobate female have the power to tear it to pieces with her coarse hands? Would all the nobility and sensitivity she now felt capable of for the first time be destroyed on account of this one offence?

And why – she fought blindly against a fate she unconsciously believed reasonable – why exactly did she have to be so terribly punished for a trifling transgression! How many women did she know, vain, forward, full of desire, who even bought themselves lovers? They made game of their husbands in their admirers' arms, and were perfectly at home living a lie. Dissimulation made them more beautiful, pursuit stronger, danger cleverer, whereas she weakly collapsed the first time she was afraid, at her first lapse.

But was she, then, really guilty? Deep down she felt that this man, this lover, was a stranger, that she had never given him anything out of her real life. She had taken nothing from him, given him nothing. Everything that was past and forgotten was not really her offence but that of another woman she couldn't understand and into whose mind she could never again think herself. Ought a transgression be punished that was already absolved by time?

Suddenly she was alarmed. She felt these were not at all her own thoughts. But who had said that? Someone in her circle, only recently, a day or two ago. She pondered over it, and her fright was not lessened when she recalled it was her own husband who had awakened these thoughts in her. He had returned from a trial, distressed and pale, and this normally taciturn man had impetuously said to her and some friends who happened to be there, 'Today an innocent man was convicted.' Questioned by those present he explained, while he was still upset, that a thief had been punished for a theft committed three years earlier; and how he felt this was wrong, because after three years the thief didn't really identify himself with the crime any more. They were punishing a different man and punishing him twice over, because he had already spent those three years imprisoned by his own fear, by the constant anxiety of being convicted.

With horror she remembered she had disagreed with him on that occasion. To her way of thinking, lacking experience of the outside world, a criminal was always merely a parasite living off middle-class material comfort and he had to be destroyed at any price. For the first time she now sensed how deplorable her argument had been, how charitable and fair her husband's. But would he be able to understand in her case, too, that it was the adventure she had loved, not the man? That her husband was to blame as well, for being too kind, for the languid comfort with which he had surrounded her life? Would he be able to be fair, acting as judge in his own case?

But fate saw to it that she should not indulge in pleasant hopes. The very next day another note arrived, another lash of the whip, that revived her fear. This time the demand was for two hundred crowns, which she gave without protest. This steep increase in the price, which she could afford without noticing it, horrified her, for although she came from a wealthy family she was not in a position to pay out large sums unobtrusively. And then, what good was it? She knew tomorrow it would be four hundred crowns and soon a thousand; always more, the more she gave, and then eventually when her money ran out, the anonymous letter, the débâcle. What she was buying was only time, a breathing space, two days' respite, or three, perhaps a week, but what horrible, useless time, full of torment and tension. For weeks now her sleep had been troubled with dreams that were as distressing as her waking hours. She lacked fresh air, freedom of movement, peace, occupation. She couldn't read any more, or do anything, pursued diabolically by her inner fear. She felt ill. Sometimes she had to sit down suddenly, her heart was beating so hard. All her limbs felt restless and heavy, filled with the leaden weight of fatigue that made them almost hurt but nevertheless prevented her from sleeping. Her whole existence was undermined by gnawing fear, her whole body poisoned, and in her heart she actually longed for this ill health finally to break out in some obvious pain, some really tangible, visible, clinical disease for which people had sympathy and understanding. In those hours of inner agony she envied the sick. How good it must be to lie in a hospital, in a white bed, between white walls, surrounded by compassion and flowers. People would come, everyone would be kind to her, and behind the cloud of suffering would be recovery, far in the distance like a great, benevolent sun. If someone was in pain at least he was allowed to cry out, but she must continuously play the tragi-comedy of cheerful good health, while every day and almost every hour found her in new and frightening situations. She had to smile and appear happy while her nerves were on edge. No one must suspect the ceaseless strain of this feigned gaiety, the heroic strength she expended on such everyday and yet futile self-control.

Only one of all those around her seemed, she fancied, to have some inkling of the fear that haunted her, and that was only because he was observing her. She felt, and the certainty of it constrained her to be doubly vigilant, that he was incessantly occupied with her, as she was with him. They prowled round day and night, as though circling one another to find out the other's secret and to keep their own hidden. Her husband had changed, too, recently. The threatening severity of those first inquisitorial days had softened into a sort of kindness and solicitude that reminded her unconsciously of when she was just married. He treated her like an invalid, with a care that bewildered her because she felt ashamed of so much undeserved love. She was afraid of it, too, because it might be a stratagem to snatch the secret from her relaxed hands in an unguarded moment. Since that night when he had spied on her while she slept, and that day when he had seen the letter in her hand, his suspicion seemed to have changed to pity. He invited her trust with a tenderness that sometimes calmed her and disposed her to be compliant, only for her distrust to return seconds later. Was it only a ruse, the examining judge's tempting bait for the accused, a safety net to gain her confidence, which was supposed to trap her confession and then be suddenly pulled away, leaving her defenceless and at his mercy? Or did he feel, too, that this growing situation of cat and mouse was unbearable, and his sympathy was so strong that he was secretly suffering as her distress became daily more obvious? She sensed with a distinct shock how he sometimes led her up, as it were, to the words that would release her, making it seductively easy for her to confess. She understood his aim and was glad and grateful for his kindness. But she discovered, too, that her sense of shame grew to the same extent as her inclination to tell him, and was stronger in preventing her from speaking than her mistrust had been earlier.

Once at this time he spoke to her face to face, quite frankly. She had just come into the house and heard loud voices in the hall: her husband's, sharp and vigorous, the irritable babble of the governess, and in between sounds of sobbing and crying. Her first feeling was one of terror. Whenever she heard loud voices or a commotion in the house she trembled with fear. Fear was her response to everything, to whatever was unusual, burning fear that the letter had arrived now, revealing the secret. Always, when she opened the door her first questioning glance went to everyone's face, to ascertain that nothing had happened in her absence, the catastrophe had not yet occurred while she was away. This time, as she was soon reassured to learn, it was only the children quarrelling; a little impromptu legal case. An aunt had brought the boy a present a few days earlier, a brightly decorated toy horse. This aroused the little girl's envy, for she had received a smaller gift. In vain she had sought to maintain her right to share it, and she coveted it so much that the boy had forbidden her to touch it at all. This first provoked the child's loud indignation and then a gloomy, resigned, stubborn silence. But the next morning the horse had suddenly disappeared, without trace, defying all the boy's efforts to find it. By chance it was discovered eventually in the stove, dismembered. The wooden parts were broken, the coloured covering was torn off, and the stuffing pulled out. Naturally suspicion fell on the little girl; the boy had run crying to his father to accuse the evil-doer. She was unable to produce a convincing explanation, and the trial was just beginning.

Irene was filled with violent envy. Why did the children always come to him with all their problems, and never to her? From the beginning they had entrusted all their disputes and complaints to her husband; until now she had preferred to be free of these little vexations, but for once she coveted them because she felt they contained love and trust.

The little law suit was soon settled. The child lied at first, admittedly with downcast eyes and a give-away tremble in her voice. The governess gave evidence against her. She had heard the little girl threaten in a temper to throw the horse out of the window. The child tried in vain to deny it. There was a little outburst of despairing sobs. Irene looked at her husband. It seemed to her as though he was sitting in judgment not on the child but on her own fate, for tomorrow perhaps she would be standing opposite him, trembling in the same way and with the same catch in her voice. Her husband looked stern at first, as long as the child persevered with her lie, undermining her position word by word, though without ever losing his temper when she denied something. Then, however, when the lies gave way to gloomy stubbornness, he spoke kindly to her. He explained plainly the basic need for the inquiry and to some extent excused her for doing such a dreadful thing without thinking, in the first fury of the moment. He also pointed out how she hadn't considered that it would in fact hurt her brother. And he explained so pleasantly and impressively to the increasingly uncertain child that what she had done was understandable but still wrong, that she eventually burst into tears and began to howl loudly. And soon out of the deluge of tears she finally stammered out the truth.

Irene rushed across to take the crying child in her arms, but the little girl pushed her away in a rage. Her husband also stopped her, warning her against too hasty sympathy, for he did not want the offence to go unpunished. He decreed the quite trivial punishment – which nevertheless was grievous for the child – that she was not to go to a party the next day, one she had been looking forward to for weeks. Wailing, the child heard his judgment. The boy began noisily to crow, but this untimely and spiteful exultation involved him instantly in the same punishment. For his delight in his sister's downfall he, too, was refused permission to go the children's party. Crestfallen, and consoled only by receiving the same punishment, the pair finally left the room and Irene was alone with her husband.

Now at last, she felt in a flash, was her opportunity to talk about her own offence under the guise of discussing the child's misdemeanour and admission. And a feeling of relief came over her, that at least she could made the confession in a concealed form and ask for compassion. If he took her speaking up for the child now in a kindly way, it would be a sign and she knew she would perhaps be able to dare to speak about herself.

'Tell me, Fritz,' she began, 'will you really not let the children go tomorrow? They'll be so unhappy, especially the little one. What she did wasn't really so dreadful. Why are you punishing her so hard? Aren't you just a little bit sorry for her?'

He looked at her. Then he sat down comfortably. He seemed obviously willing to discuss the subject further. A foreboding, pleasant yet disquieting, made her suspect he was going to argue it out with her. She waited for an end to the silence which he, possibly deliberately or deep in thought, particularly prolonged.

'You ask, am I sorry about it? I can only say, not any longer.

She's feeling better now she's been punished, even though it seems bitter to her too. Yesterday she was unhappy, while the poor horse lay broken in the stove and everyone in the house was looking for it. She was frightened all the time that some-one would – someone must – find it. Fear is more worrying than punishment, for the latter is something definite. Whether it is large or small it's better than awful uncertainty and that never-ending nightmare of stress. As soon as she knew what her punishment was, she was relieved. You shouldn't be upset by her tears: they were only bringing out what was earlier trapped inside her. And it's more damaging inside than out. If she wasn't a child or you could see right into her heart, I think you'd find she's really happy since she's been punished and had a good cry. She's certainly happier than she was yesterday when she had to go about looking carefree, and no one suspected her.'

She looked up. It was as though he was aiming his words at her. But he appeared not to notice it at all and, perhaps misunderstanding the movement she made, continued dogma-tically, 'It really is so, believe me. I know that from the law and investigations. The accused suffer most from hiding things, under the threat of discovery – under the awful pressure of having to sustain a lie against a thousand little hidden attacks. It's terrible to see such a case, where the judge already has everything in his hands, the guilt, the proof, perhaps even the sentence ready, and only the confession is missing. That's stuck inside the accused and won't come out however hard he pushes and pulls. It's dreadful to see how the defendant twists and turns because someone has to tear the "Yes" out of his resisting flesh as though with a fish-hook. Sometimes the word is sitting there right in his throat. An irresistible force propels it into the open, he chokes on it, he almost forms the word. Then an evil power takes control of him, an inexplicable feeling of defiance and fear, and gulps it down again. And the battle begins all over again. Sometimes the judges suffer more than the victims. Yet the accused always look on them as the enemy, when in reality they are helping them. And I, as their lawyer, their counsel for the defence, ought really to warn my clients not to confess, to consolidate and strengthen their lies. But deep down I dare not, because they suffer more from not

confessing than from admitting their guilt and being punished.
I really still don't understand how anyone can do something,
knowing the danger, and then not have the courage to admit it.
I find this minor fear in the face of saying one word more
deplorable than the crime itself.'

'Do you mean ... that it's always ... always just fear that
stops them? Couldn't it be they are ashamed ... ashamed to
speak up, to lay themselves bare in public?'

He looked up in astonishment. She did not usually offer a
reply. But what she said fascinated him.

'Is it shame, you say? That's only another form of fear, of
course ... but a better one. It's not fear of the sentence, but ...
yes, I understand.'

He had stood up, noticeably disturbed, and was pacing up
and down. The idea seemed to have sparked something off in
him and now it was catching alight and affecting him considerably. Suddenly he stopped.

'I admit ... shame in the face of people, before strangers ...
in front of the masses who devour other people's troubles from
the newspapers as though they were eating a sandwich. But
surely one could at least confess to someone close ... you
remember that arsonist I defended last year, who took such an
incredible liking to me? He told me everything, little anecdotes
from his childhood, all sorts of personal things. You see, he'd
definitely done it and been sentenced ... but he hadn't admitted it even to me. That was fear I could give him away, not
shame, for he trusted me really. I was the only person, I believe,
he'd found offering him any sort of friendship, so it wasn't
shame in front of a stranger ... what was it then, when he
could still trust me?'

'Perhaps,' — she had to turn away because he was looking so
directly at her and she felt her voice quavering — 'perhaps ...
one feels most shame when facing ... the person one feels
closest to.'

He stopped suddenly, as though struck by some inner force.

'You mean ... you mean then ...' and all at once his tone of
voice changed. It became quite soft and quiet — 'You mean that
Helen would have been able to admit her guilt more easily to
someone else, to her governess perhaps, someone she ... '

'I'm sure of it. She put up so much opposition to you only

because ... she values your opinion most ... because she loves you most.'

He did not move.

'Perhaps you're right ... yes, of course you are. It's strange I've never thought of that. It's so simple of course ... Perhaps I was too strict—but you know me, I don't mean it. But I'll go straightaway and tell her. Of course she may go to the party. I wanted only to punish her for being obstinate, for resisting, and ... for not trusting me. But you're right. I don't want you to think I can't forgive—I wouldn't want that—I wouldn't want you especially, Irene, to think that.'

He looked at her and she felt herself blushing under his gaze. Had he said that deliberately or not? Or was it just fortuitous —knavishly, dangerously accidental? Once again she felt dreadfully undecided.

'The sentence is quashed.' He seemed to become altogether more cheerful. 'Helen is set free, and I'm going to tell her so myself. Are you satisfied now? Or is there anything else you want? ... You ... you see, I'm in a generous mood today, perhaps because I'm pleased I've recognised an injustice in time. That's always a relief, Irene. Always.'

She believed she understood what this emphasis meant. Instinctively she drew nearer him and felt the words rising to the surface. He, too, took a step towards her as though he wanted quickly to take from her hands what was so obviously burdening her. Then she met his gaze and saw in it a longing for her to confess, for her to reveal some part of her inner feelings, a glowing impatience. And without warning her resolution collapsed. Her hands fell limply with fatigue and she turned away. It was no use. She would never be able to say it, those two words that would release her, that burned inside her and consumed her peace. The warning rolled like approaching thunder, but she knew she could not escape. In her heart of hearts she already yearned for what she had feared so long, the lightning flash that would deliver her: to be found out.

Her wish seemed likely to be fulfilled sooner than she expected. The battle had been going on now for a fortnight and Irene felt her strength running out. It was four days since she had heard from that creature, and fear had so penetrated her and coursed as one with her blood that she always jumped up hastily whenever the doorbell rang, so that she could intercept a blackmailing messenger in time herself. There was impatience, almost longing, in this eagerness, for with every payment she bought an evening's peace, a few quiet hours with the children, a walk. She could breathe freely for an evening, a day, go out shopping and visit friends. Admittedly, sleep was wise; it didn't allow such flimsy solace to deceive it about the constant imminent danger it knew for certain existed. It filled her at night with undermining, anxious dreams.

Once again when the bell rang she hurried out impetuously to open the door, even though she must have known her anxiety to arrive before the servant must arouse suspicion and easily invite hostile speculation. But how weak these little contradictions of prudent consideration were when at the sound of the telephone, of a step in the street behind her or the summons of the doorbell her whole body leapt as though struck by a whip. Once again she had heard the bell from her room and had rushed to the door. She opened it, and for a second looked astonished to see a lady she did not know. Then she stepped back in horror as she recognised the face she detested. It was the blackmailer, fitted out in new clothes and wearing an elegant hat.

'Oh, it's you Frau Wagner, I'm glad of that. I've something important to talk to you about.' And without waiting for an answer from the terrified Irene, whose trembling hand was clutching on to the door-handle, she stepped inside, put down her parasol, a showy red parasol, obviously a purchase with the proceeds of her earlier blackmailer's raids. She moved with impudent assurance, as though she felt appeased by inspecting the imposing interior. She walked uninvited towards the half-open door of the reception room. 'In here, is it?' she asked, with controlled scorn. As Irene, terrified and unable as yet to say a word, tried to turn away, she calmly added, 'If it isn't convenient now, we can settle it quite quickly.' Irene followed her in silence. The idea of the blackmailer in her own home, of this effrontery, which exceeded her worst expectations, left her speechless. She thought she was dreaming it all.

'You've got it very nice here, very nice.' The creature admired the room with an obviously relaxed air, as she sat down. 'My, this chair's comfy. And all those pictures. It makes me realise how poor the rest of us are. You're doing very well, very well indeed, Frau Wagner.'

Then, as she saw this criminal so comfortably settled in her own house, the torture was too much for Irene. She burst out in a rage. 'What do you want then, you blackmailer? You follow me right into my own home. But I'm not going to be frightened to death by you. I'm going to – '

'Not so loud, then.' The other woman interrupted her with offensive familiarity. 'The door's still open and the servants can hear you. It doesn't matter to me. My God, I take nothing back, and after all, it can't be worse in prison than it is now, the miserable life I lead. But you, Frau Wagner, ought to be more careful. I'll close the door first, in case you find it necessary to lose your temper again. But I'll tell you now, insults make no impression on me.'

Irene's strength, reinforced momentarily by anger, collapsed feebly once more before the woman's imperturbability. She stood there meekly, almost, and uneasy, like a child waiting to be given an exercise to do.

'Well, Frau Wagner, I'll come to the point. As you know, things aren't going too well for me. I've told you that already. And now I need money for the rent. I've been owing it for such a time, and I've other debts too. I'd like to get a bit straight at last. That's why I've come to you. I'm sure you'll help me out – well, with four hundred crowns, let's say.'

'I can't,' Irene stammered, appalled by the amount, which in fact she didn't have in ready money. 'I really don't have it. I've already given you three hundred crowns this month. Where do you think I can get it from?'

'Oh, you'll think of a way, if you put your mind to it. A lady as rich as you can always get money. As much as you want. But you must make up your mind and get it, and that's flat. So think about it, Frau Wagner, you'll find a way.'

'But I really don't have it. I'd give it to you gladly. But I just don't have that much. I could give you something ... a hundred crowns perhaps.'

'Four hundred crowns, I said. That's what I need.' She threw down the words bluntly as though outraged by Irene's unreasonableness.

'But I haven't got it!' Irene cried in despair. If her husband were to come in now, she thought. He could arrive at any moment. 'I swear to you I haven't got it.'

'Then try to raise it.'

'I can't.'

The creature looked Irene up and down as though she were a valuer.

'Well now, for example ... that ring there. If you pawned that it would be about right. I admit I'm not well up on jewellery. I've never really had any. But I believe you'd get four hundred crowns for that.'

'My ring!' exclaimed Irene. It was her engagement ring, the only one she never took off. It was a precious stone of great beauty and was consequently very valuable.

'Come on, then. Why not? I'll send you the pawn-ticket, then you can redeem it when you want to. You'll get it back. I won't keep it. What would a poor person like me do with a posh ring like that?'

'Why are you persecuting me? Why are you tormenting me? I can't ... I can't go on. You must understand that. Look, I've done what I can. You must get that clear. For pity's sake!'

'No one's had pity on me. I've been left to cave in with hunger, almost. Why should I be sorry for someone as rich as you, I'd like to know?'

Irene was on the point of replying angrily, when she heard a door bang outside – and her blood ran cold. That must be her husband back from the office. Without stopping to think she wrenched the ring from her finger and handed it to the woman, who quickly hid it away.

'Don't worry. I'm going.' The creature nodded as she noted the unspeakable fear in Irene's face and the tense way her ear was straining towards the hall, where a man's footsteps were clearly audible. She opened the door and smiled at Irene's husband as he came in. He glanced at her for a moment, did not appear to notice her particularly, and disappeared.

'A lady who wanted some information,' said Irene, making a last attempt at explanation as soon as the door had closed behind the creature. The worst moment was over. Her husband did not reply and went quietly into the dining-room, where luncheon was already on the table.

It seemed to Irene as though the spot on her finger that was usually covered by the cool band of the ring was on fire. Everyone must be looking at the bare flesh as though there was a brand-mark there. During the meal she did her best to keep her hand hidden, and while she did so she tried to shake off a remarkably strong feeling that her husband's eye was continually wandering over her hand, and following it wherever it went. She made a great effort to divert his attention and to keep the conversation flowing with endless questions. She talked and talked, to him, the children, and the governess, continuously fanning the little flames of conversation; but she kept running out of breath and the talk would be snuffed out again. She tried to seem to be in high spirits and to cajole the others into jollity. She teased the children and set them against each other, but they wouldn't quarrel and wouldn't laugh. She sensed there must be a false note in her brightness which unconsciously alienated the others. The more she tried the less the attempt succeeded. Eventually she grew tired and fell silent.

The others were silent, too. She heard only the light clatter of plates and the swelling voice of fear within her. Then, abruptly, her husband said, 'Where's your ring today, then?'

She winced. 'It's all over!' she said to herself. But her instinct still saved her. She felt she must summon up all her strength. She must find a phrase, a word. She must think up just one more lie, a final one.

'I ... I've sent it to be cleaned.'

And as though strengthened by the falsehood she continued resolutely, 'I'm collecting it the day after tomorrow.' The day after next. Now she was committed. The lie would be discovered, and she with it, if she didn't accomplish it. Now she had fixed the deadline herself, and all her chaotic fear was permeated by a new feeling, happiness of a sort, knowing the crisis was so close. The day after next: now she knew her time-limit and from this certainty she felt a curious calmness flow over her. A new strength was growing within her, the strength to live and the strength to die.

Knowing for certain the crisis was approaching at last, she began to feel unexpected clear-sightedness spreading through her. Nervous tension gave way miraculously to orderly deliberation. Fear was replaced by a feeling of utter peace, which was a stranger to her. Thanks to this she suddenly saw her entire life and its true value distinctly. She took stock of her life and, however heavy the burden, she perceived that if she could only sustain it and raise it to the new and heightened consciousness these days of fear had taught her, she could begin again, genuinely and positively, without lies. And she felt ready to do so. But to go on living, if she were divorced, an adulteress, defiled by scandal, she was too tired for that; and too tired also to continue this dangerous game of buying limited periods of peace of mind. She felt she could no longer consider further resistance. The end was in sight. She was threatened with betrayal by her husband, her children, everyone around her, and by herself. Flight was impossible from an adversary who appeared to be ubiquitous. And confession, that sure and certain help, was out of the question, she knew that now. There was only one way out — but there was no return from that. Life was still sweet. It was one of those irresistible spring days which sometimes burst violently from the depths of winter, a day of endless blue sky, whose uplifted canopy one contemplated with a sigh of relief after all the gloomy winter hours.

The children rushed in wearing light clothes they had put on for the first time that year, and she had to restrain herself not to respond with tears to their outburst of jubilation. As soon as the children's laughter with its painful response had died away, she prepared to carry out what she had definitely decided to do. First she would try to redeem her ring, then, however her fate was settled, no suspicion would fall on her memory, no one would have any visible proof of her guilt. No one, especially the children, would ever guess the terrible secret she had kept from them; it must appear to be an accident for which no one was responsible.

Then she went to a pawnshop to dispose of a piece of inherited jewellery she hardly ever wore, to arm herself with enough money to be able perhaps to buy back the all-betraying ring from that creature. Feeling more secure as soon as she had the ready money in her purse, she walked about on the off-chance of meeting the blackmailer, now longing deep down for what she had until yesterday feared most. The air was mild and there was a glimmer of sunshine over the houses. Something in the turbulent movement of the wind, which was sending the white clouds scudding across the sky, seemed to have penetrated the rhythm of the people. They were stepping out more briskly and cheerfully than they had in all the cheerless, dull winter days there had been up to now. And she thought she felt something of it herself. The thought of death, clutched at yesterday in passing but not let slip from her trembling hand, grew suddenly into a monstrosity and lowered her spirits. Was it possible, then, that a word from some disgusting woman could destroy all this — the houses out there with their gleaming façades, the traffic rushing by, the people laughing, and her blood pulsing within her? Could one word extinguish the eternal flame which caused the whole world to blaze in her living heart?

She walked on and on, her eyes no longer downcast, but openly searching, almost eager now to find the elusive woman. The prey now sought the hunter, and in the same way that a weaker hunted animal, feeling escape no longer possible, suddenly turns on its pursuer with the determination of despair, ready to stand and fight, she now longed to meet her torturer face to face and to struggle with that last strength the survival instinct bestows on the despairing. She deliberately stayed near the house where the blackmailer was usually in the habit of watching for her. Once she hurried across the street because some woman's dress reminded her of the creature she was seeking. The ring had long since ceased to be what she was fighting for. That was only a question of postponement and not of rescue. But she longed for this encounter as a sign of fate, as a decision between life and death by a higher power. It seemed to her that the recovery of the ring was out of her hands. But the creature was nowhere to be seen. She had disappeared in the maze of the great city like a rat into its hole.

Disappointed, but not yet giving up hope, she went home at midday, and immediately after luncheon resumed the fruitless search. She wandered through the streets again and, as she did not find the creature anywhere, the dread she had almost overcome rose up again. It was no longer the woman or the ring that troubled her but the dreadful mystery of all these events that did not make sense any more. This woman had obtained her name and address as though by magic. She knew how she disposed of her time and all about her domestic arrangements. She came at the most frightening and danger-ous moments only to disappear now without warning, when she was most sought after. She must be somewhere in this great bustling city, near by when it suited her, yet out of reach as soon as someone wanted her. The amorphous nature of the threat, the ephemeral proximity of the blackmailer, touching her life and yet intangible, rendered her — already exhausted as she was — powerless in the face of increasingly mystical fear. It was as though higher powers had devilishly conspired to ruin her. There was such a mockery of her weak-ness in this overpowering confusion of hostile events. Already tense, she paced up and down the same street, again and again, with feverish steps. Like a prostitute, she thought to herself. But the woman stayed out of sight. Only dusk now came creeping menacingly around. The early spring evening dis-solved the bright colour of the sky, making it drab and over-cast, and night fell quickly. Lights were lit in the streets, the stream of people surged quickly homewards; all life seemed to vanish in a dark current of movement. She walked up and down once or twice more, looking in hope along the street again, for the last time; then she turned for home. She was freezing.

Tired, she went upstairs. She heard the children being put to bed in the next room, but she avoided wishing them good night, saying goodbye to them once and for all, and having therefore to think about eternity. What would be the point of seeing them now? To feel serene happiness in their high-spirited kisses, love in their shining faces? To what purpose should she torture herself further with a joy that was already lost? She clenched her teeth: no, she didn't want to feel any more of life's sensations, any of the blessed gaiety she associ-ated with many memories, since she had to break all these bonds abruptly tomorrow. Now she wanted to think only about disagreeable things, things that were hateful and vulgar, about fate, the blackmailer, the scandal, about everything she was ridding herself of, about the disaster confronting her.

Her husband's return interrupted her oppressive and lonely thoughts. He was affable and lively, asking her many questions and trying to draw close to her through conversation. A certain nervousness made her feel she could do without this sudden intense solicitude, but she was reluctant to say anything when she recalled the exchange they had had the day before. Some inner fear held her back, from being bound by love, from letting herself be stopped by sympathy. He seemed to sense her resistance and was somewhat concerned. She, on the other hand, was afraid his anxiety would lead him to make a new approach and she wished him good night early. 'See you in the morning,' he answered. Then she retired.

The morning: how near that was and how infinitely far away! How terribly long and dark the sleepless night seemed to her. The noises outside gradually decreased and she saw the street lights, which were reflected in the room, go out. Sometimes she thought she could hear the sound of breathing from the other rooms near by, and feel the presence of her children, her husband, and the whole world, so near and yet so distant, which had already almost disappeared. At the same time, however, there was an indescribable and unnatural silence. It did not seem to come from her surroundings but from within herself, as though from a mysterious bubbling spring. She felt buried in an infinity of silence, the darkness of the invisible sky heavy on her breast. Sometimes the hours chimed loudly in the darkness, then the night became black and lifeless. But for the first time she felt she understood the significance of this endless, empty darkness. She thought no more now about departure and death, only of how she was running towards it and how she could be as unobtrusive as possible, so as to spare the children and herself the shame of a scandal. She thought of all the ways she knew that would lead her to death. She reviewed all the possible ways to commit suicide and suddenly remembered, with a kind of delicious terror, that during a painful illness when she couldn't sleep, the doctor had prescribed morphine. She had occasionally taken a few drops of the bitter-sweet poison from a little bottle. The contents, she had been told at the time, were enough to ensure a gentle sleep. Oh, not to be hounded any more: to be at peace, at peace in infinity – no longer to feel fear hammering in her heart! The thought of this gentle oblivion tugged continuously at the sleepless Irene. Already she imagined she felt the bitter taste on her lips and the soft clouding over of her mind. She gathered herself up quickly and put on the light. She soon found the little bottle, but it was now only half full and she was afraid it wouldn't be enough. Feverishly she searched all the drawers until she finally found the prescription that made it possible for larger quantities to be prepared. With a smile she folded the prescription as though it were a precious banknote: now she held death in her hand. Shivering with cold terror and yet feeling calmer, she wanted to go back to bed, but as she passed the mirror, now reflecting the light, she caught sight of herself approaching the dark frame, ghostly, pale, with cavernous eyes. In her white nightgown she looked as if she were wrapped in a shroud. Fear gripped her. She put out the light and fled, shivering, to the bed she had left. She lay awake until daylight.

The following morning she burned all her correspondence, put all sorts of little things in order, but she avoided as far as possible seeing the children and everything in general that was precious to her. All she wanted now was to prevent life from clinging on to her with desire and temptation, causing her to hesitate in a futile way and making it difficult for her to carry out her decision. Then she went out again to seek her fate for the last time and to meet the blackmailer. Again she walked restlessly up and down, but no longer with that growing feeling of tension. Something in her had already given up and she despaired of being able to go on fighting. She walked on and on for two hours as though from a sense of duty. The woman was nowhere to be seen. She no longer cared. She felt so lacking in energy she almost didn't want to meet her any more. She looked at the faces of the passers-by and they all seemed alien to her, dead and somehow withdrawn. Everything was somehow far away and lost, and no longer concerned her.

Only once did she have a shock. As she was looking round she thought she suddenly glimpsed her husband among the crowd on the other side of the street, watching her with that peculiar, severe, penetrating expression she had only recently come to know. Vexed, she peered across the street, but the figure quickly disappeared behind a passing carriage. She reassured herself with the thought that at this time of day he was always busy at the Courts. In the fever of her search she lost all sense of time and arrived home late for luncheon. He wasn't there either, however, but came in two minutes later looking, it seemed to her, a little disturbed.

She counted the hours until evening and was appalled to think how many there still were. How remarkable it was that so little time was needed for departure and how worthless everything seemed when you knew you couldn't take it with you. She began to feel somewhat drowsy. Mechanically she went out into the street again, going nowhere in particular, her mind a blank and her eyes unseeing. As she crossed the road a coachman reined in his horses at the last moment or she would surely have been hit by the shafts of the carriage. The driver let out a stream of abuse but she scarcely turned round. That would have been a way out or a reprieve. An accident would have spared her the decision. She walked on, wearily. It was pleasant not to think, but to feel within her only a vague sensation of finality, a haze that descended gradually and obscured everything.

As she looked up casually to see the name of the street, she shuddered: in her confused wandering she had arrived, quite by chance, almost outside the house of her former lover. Was this a sign? Perhaps he could help her even now. He must know that creature's address. She almost trembled with joy. Why couldn't she have thought of this before? It was so obvious. All at once her limbs recovered their agility, hope gave wings to her sluggish thoughts, which now flew about in confusion. He must go with her to the woman and make an end of the matter once and for all. He must put pressure on her to stop this blackmail. Perhaps a sum of money might persuade her to leave the city. She instantly regretted she had treated the poor fellow so badly the other day, but nevertheless she was sure he would help her. How odd that this salvation should come now, now, at the last moment.

She sped up the stairs and rang the bell. No one answered it. She listened: she thought she heard cautious steps behind the door. She rang again. Once more, silence. And there was that faint noise from inside again. She lost patience: she kept her finger on the bell—her life was at stake.

At last there was a real movement inside, the lock clicked and the door opened an inch.

'It's me,' she said hurriedly.

He opened the door now with alarm. 'It's you, Irene … Frau Wagner,' he stammered, visibly embarrassed, 'I was … forgive me … I wasn't expecting you. Please excuse my dress.' He indicated his shirtsleeves. His shirt was half open and he wore no tie.

'I must speak to you urgently … you must help me,' she said tensely, because he was keeping her standing in the corridor like a beggar. 'Won't you let me in and listen to me for a minute?' she added excitedly.

'I'm sorry,' he murmured, disconcerted, and with a sidelong glance 'I'm busy just now … I really can't … '

'You must listen to me. It's your fault. It's your duty to help me. You must get the ring back for me, you must. Or at least tell me her address. She follows me all the time, but now she's gone. You must, do you hear me, you must.'

He stared at her. She now realised her words were tumbling out incoherently.

'So that's it. You don't know … well, your mistress, your former mistress, that creature, saw me leave here, and since then she's followed me and blackmailed me. She's tormenting me to death. Now she's taken my ring, and I must have it back. I must have it back by tonight, I've said I'll have it by tonight … Will you please help me?'

'But … but I … '

'Will you or won't you?'

'But I really don't know this person. I don't know whom you mean. I've never had anything to do with blackmailers.' He was almost rude.

'So … you don't know her. She just invented it all. And she knows your name and my address. Perhaps it isn't true either that she's blackmailing me. Perhaps I'm only dreaming it.' She gave a shrill laugh. He felt uncomfortable. He thought for a moment she might have gone mad, the way her eyes were glittering. Her behaviour was disturbed and her words meaningless. He looked around anxiously.

'Please calm yourself, Frau Wagner ... I assure you, you are mistaken. It's quite impossible ... it must be. No, I don't understand it myself. I don't know women of that sort. The two liaisons I've had since I've been here, which as you know isn't long, are not of that kind. I won't mention names, but ... it's so ridiculous. I assure you, there must be a mistake.'

'So you won't help me, then?'

'Of course, if I can.'

'Then come with me. We'll go to her together.'

'To whom ... to whom then?' He had that awful feeling again that she must be insane, as she grasped him by the arm.

'To her. Will you come or won't you?'

'Of course ... of course,'—his suspicion was increased by the eager way she pressed him—'certainly, certainly.'

'Come on then—it's a matter of life and death to me!'

He had to stop himself from smiling. Then all at once he became formal.

'Excuse me, Frau Wagner, but it's not possible at the moment. I'm giving a piano lesson. I can't break it off just now.'

'I see ... So that's it.' She laughed in his face, 'So you give piano lessons in your shirtsleeves ... you liar, you.' And suddenly, struck by a thought, she pushed forward. He tried to hold her back. 'She's here then, the blackmailer, with you? You're playing the same game, when it comes down to it. Perhaps you're dividing between you what you have squeezed out of me. But I'll get my hands on her. I'm not afraid of anything any more,' she shouted. He held her back but she struggled with him, tore herself free and rushed to the bedroom door.

Someone, who had apparently been listening at the door, drew back. Irene stared dumbfounded at a woman she didn't know, whose dress looked somewhat disordered, and who hurriedly turned her face away. Her lover, who thought Irene had taken leave of her senses, stormed after her to stop her and prevent an unfortunate scene, but Irene was already retreating from the room. 'Excuse me,' she murmured. She was quite bewildered. She didn't understand any more. She felt only disgust, infinite disgust, and exhaustion.

'Excuse me,' she said again, as she saw him looking at her uneasily. 'You'll understand everything tomorrow ... tomor-

row . . . that is, I don't understand any more myself.' She spoke
to him as though to a stranger. She had no recollection that she
had once belonged to this man; she was hardly conscious of
her own body. Everything was now all much more confused
than before. She knew only that somewhere, someone was
telling lies. But she was too tired to think any more, too tired to
look any farther. She went down the stairs with her eyes
closed, like a condemned person to the scaffold. The street was
in darkness when she went out. It crossed her mind that
perhaps the woman was waiting for her on the other side.
Perhaps rescue was at hand at the last moment after all. She
thought she ought to put her hands together and pray to a
forgotten God. Oh, if only she could buy another month or
two, the few months until summer, and then spend it peacefully in the fields and meadows, out of the blackmailer's reach.
Just one summer, which would be so complete and full that it
would be worth a whole lifetime. Eagerly she scanned the
already dark street. On the other side she thought she could see
a figure lurking in a doorway, but as she stepped nearer it
shrank back into the entrance. For a moment she thought there
was some resemblance to her husband. For the second time
today she had the worrying feeling that he was watching her
here out in the street. She lingered to make sure, but the figure
had disappeared into the shadows. Disturbed, she walked on,
with a strange, tense feeling at the back of her neck, as though
someone's eyes were burning into her. She turned round once,
but no one was there.

The chemist's shop was not far. She went in, shivering
slightly. The dispenser took the prescription and made it up. In
the short time she was waiting her eyes took in everything, the
shiny scales, the neat weights, the little labels, and up in the
cupboards the rows of distillations with strange Latin names,
which she spelt out automatically as she cast her eye over
them. She heard the clock ticking, was conscious of the characteristic smell, that oily-sweet odour medicines have, and all at
once recalled how, as a child, she was always asking her
mother to let her fetch things from the chemist's because she
loved that smell and the strange sight of those many glittering
globes. This reminded her with great distress that she hadn't
said goodbye to her mother. The thought of the poor old lady

saddened her. What a shock it would be for her, thought Irene with horror. But the dispenser was already counting out the clear drops from a bulging round container into a little blue bottle. Transfixed, she watched death finding its way from the container into the phial. From there it would soon be flowing through her veins, and an icy feeling spread through her limbs. With her senses deadened, as though she were hypnotised in some way, she looked fixedly at his fingers as he now put the cork into the filled bottle, then sealed the dangerous opening with paper. Her whole mind was shackled and immobilised by gruesome thoughts.

'Two crowns, please,' said the dispenser.

Irene awoke from her trance and didn't know where she was. Then mechanically she put her hand into her purse to take out the money. Still in a dream, she looked at the coins without really identifying them, and unconsciously took a long time counting them out.

At this moment she felt her arm knocked sharply sideways and heard money clatter on the glass counter. A hand stretched out beside her and grasped the bottle.

Instinctively she turned round. And her expression froze. It was her husband standing there, his lips set in a grim line. His face was ashen and his forehead glistened with perspiration.

She felt faint and had to hold on to the counter. Instantly she realised that it had been him she had seen in the street and also a short time ago in the doorway. She really had already recognised him there from deep instinct, yet been confused at the moment.

'Come along,' he said in a hollow, choked voice. She looked at him blankly and wondered inwardly, in a quite muffled, buried world of her consciousness, that she obeyed him. She fell in step with him without knowing it.

They crossed the street together. They did not look at each other. He still had the bottle in his hand. Once he stopped and wiped the perspiration from his brow. Instinctively she stopped too, without wanting to or knowing she had. But she dared not look round at him. Neither of them spoke. The noise of the street hung heavily between them.

He let her go up the steps ahead of him. But immediately he was not walking beside her she became uncertain. She stopped and stood still. Then he took her arm. The contact recalled her to herself and she ran quickly up the last few steps.

She went to her room. He followed her. The walls gleamed darkly, the furniture could hardly be made out. They still didn't speak. He tore off the paper seal, opened the little bottle, poured away the contents. Then he threw it violently into a corner. She jumped at the sound of breaking glass.

The silence between them continued a long time. She felt how he was keeping his self-control; she felt it without looking at him. Eventually he walked over to her: close, and now really close. She could feel him breathing heavily and with her glassy, dulled look she saw the gleam in his eyes flashing out of the darkness of the room. She waited for him to lose his temper and shivered in the firm grip of his hand as he took hold of her. Irene's heart stood still; only her nerves vibrated, like highly tuned strings. Her whole being waited for punishment and she almost longed for him to fly into a rage. But he continued to say nothing, and with boundless astonishment she realised that his approach to her was a gentle one.

'Irene,' he said, and his voice sounded remarkably soft, 'how long are we going to torture ourselves like this?'

Then it erupted from her, convulsively, with an overwhelming force, like a single, mindless, animal cry. At last they burst out, the sobs and tears she had stored up and suppressed all these weeks. She seemed to be in the grip of some inner angry hand which shook her violently. She swayed as though she were drunk, and she would have fallen if he had not held her firmly.

'Irene.' He strove to soothe her. 'Irene, Irene.' He spoke her name more gently each time and tried to sound more consoling, as though he could calm the desperate turmoil of her convulsed nerves by the ever more tender tone of his words. But only uncontrolled bursts of sobbing answered him, waves of misery that rolled through her whole body. He led, he carried her trembling body to the sofa and laid her down on it. But she went on sobbing. The convulsive tears shook her limbs as though they were electric shocks; waves of dread and coldness seemed to run through her tormented body. After weeks of the most intolerable strain her nerves were in shreds, and agony coursed without restraint through her inert body.

Greatly agitated, he cradled her shuddering body, held her cold hands, kissed her clothes, her neck, first reassuringly and then tempestuously, in fear and passion, but the convulsions continued to run through her cowering form like a laceration, and from within the rising wave of tears, once released, rolled on. He felt how cold her face was and bathed in tears, and saw the veins hammering at her temples. He was overcome by unspeakable fear. He knelt down to whisper in her ear.

'Irene,' he began again, 'why are you crying? It's all over now. Why are you still torturing yourself? You must stop upsetting yourself. She won't come again, not any more.'

Her body was again convulsed and he held her tightly with both hands. He was frightened as he felt the despair that was tearing her tortured body apart, as though he had murdered her. He kissed her again and again and stammered out incoherent words of apology.

'No ... not any more ... I swear it ... I had no idea you'd be so frightened. I only wanted to recall you, bring you back to your responsibilities ... I only wanted you to leave him for good ... and come back to us. I really had no other choice when I learnt about it by chance ... I just couldn't say it to you myself ... I thought ... I kept on thinking, you would come back. That's why I sent that poor creature to push you. She's a poor thing, an out-of-work actress. She didn't want to do it really, but I did ... I see now it was wrong ... but I wanted you back. I've shown you all the time I was ready, that I wanted only to forgive. But you didn't understand me. I didn't want to drive you so far ... I've suffered more, too, seeing it all. I've watched every step you've taken. I appeal to you if only for the children's sake ... but now it's all over and done with. Everything will be all right again now.'

From an infinite distance she heard muffled words that sounded near, yet she didn't understand them. There was a roaring inside that drowned everything; her mind was in a turmoil that took away all feeling. She felt something touch her skin, kisses and caresses, and her own tears, now already cold; but inwardly her blood was tingling, full of a dull, roaring clamour that swelled violently and thundered now like frantic bells. She lost consciousness. When she came to in a confused state, she felt someone was undressing her. She saw her husband's face as through a bank of cloud, kind and concerned. Then she fell into the deep, dark, dreamless sleep she had been deprived of so long.

When she opened her eyes next morning, it was already light in the room. And she felt a shining light within herself, as though the clouds had lifted and her blood had been washed clean by a thunderstorm. She tried to remember what had happened to her, but everything seemed to be still a dream. This pounding sensation seemed to her unreal, light and free, like floating through space in sleep, and to be certain she was awake, she examined her own hands, touching them.

Instantly she started up: the ring was sparkling on her finger. All at once she was wide awake. Confused words, heard and yet not heard while she was half-unconscious, and an earlier ominous, oppressive feeling that had never quite dared to harden into thought and suspicion, both now suddenly wove themselves together into a clear relationship. She understood everything all at once — her husband's questions, her lover's astonishment — the whole net unrolled and she saw the awful mesh in which she had become ensnared. Bitterness and shame overwhelmed her, her nerves began to quiver again and she was almost sorry she had awakened from that dreamless, untroubled sleep.

Laughter rang out in the next room. The children were up and making a noise like waking birds at daybreak. She recognised the boy's voice clearly and noticed for the first time with astonishment how very much like his father's it was. A smile spread lightly across her lips and stayed there peacefully.

She lay there with eyes closed to savour more deeply everything that made her life and now, too, her happiness. She felt a slight ache within her, but it was a pain that held out hope, burning yet soothing, as wounds burn before they heal for ever.

LETTER FROM AN UNKNOWN WOMAN

WHEN the celebrated novelist R. returned to Vienna early in the morning after a refreshing three-day trip in the mountains, he bought a newspaper. He was reminded, as soon as he glanced at the date, that it was his birthday. It was his forty-first, he reflected rapidly, and was neither glad nor sorry at this observation. Cursorily he turned the crackling pages of the paper, and then took a taxi to his flat. His manservant told him there had been two visitors and some telephone calls while he was away, and brought him the accumulated post on a tray. Looking idly at what had been put before him, he opened one or two envelopes that interested him on account of who had sent them. He put aside for the time being one letter which looked too bulky, addressed in unfamiliar handwriting. Meanwhile tea had been brought. He leaned back comfortably in his armchair, glanced through the newspaper again, and some circulars; then he lit a cigar and picked up the letter he had put aside.

There were about two dozen hastily written pages in an unfamiliar, shaky, feminine hand, a manuscript rather than a letter. He examined the envelope again automatically, to see if a covering letter had been left inside. But it was empty, and as with the pages themselves, it carried no sender's address or signature. Strange, he thought, and took up the manuscript again. At the top, as an opening, it said: 'To you who never really knew me.' Surprised, he paused. Did that refer to him, or to an imaginary person? His curiosity was suddenly aroused. He began to read.

'My child died yesterday. For three days and nights I struggled with death over this small, fragile life. I sat by his bed for forty hours while influenza shook his poor body with its fever. I put cold compresses on his burning forehead and held his restless little hands day and night. On the third evening I was in a state of collapse. I couldn't keep my eyes open and involuntarily I fell asleep. I must have slept on the hard chair for three or four hours and during that time death took him. There he lies, the poor, sweet boy, in his narrow bed, just as he died; only someone has closed his eyes, those intelligent, dark eyes, and folded his hands over his white nightshirt.

'Four candles—one at each corner of the bed—burn brightly. I dare not look; I am afraid to move. When the candles flicker, shadows flit over his face and his closed lips, and it seems then as if his features move; and I can almost imagine he isn't dead, that he'll wake up again and say something childishly tender to me in his clear voice. But I know he is dead. I won't look again, so as not to revive my hopes, and be disappointed once more. I know, I know, my son died yesterday—now I have only you left in all the world, only you, who know nothing about me. You, who meanwhile amuse yourself all unawares or trifle with people and things; only you, who never knew me, and whom I always loved.

'I have taken the fifth candle and put it here on the table on which I am writing to you. I can't be alone with my dead child without pouring my heart out to someone. And to whom should I speak at this terrible time if not to you? To you who were everything to me, and still are? Perhaps I can't make myself completely clear to you, perhaps you won't understand me. My head is so heavy; my temples twitch and throb; my limbs ache. I think I am feverish. Perhaps I have influenza, too. It is spreading from door to door now; and that would be good, for then I would go with my child and not have to kill myself. Sometimes everything goes dark before my eyes. Perhaps I shall not be able to finish this letter—but I want to summon up all my strength, this once, just this once, to speak to you, my darling, who never knew me.

'I want to speak to you alone, to tell you everything for the first time. You ought to know all about my life. It has always belonged to you and you knew nothing about it. But you shall know my secret only when I am dead, when you won't have to answer me, if what is making my limbs go hot and cold really is the end. If I must go on living I shall tear up this letter and keep silent, as I have always done. But if you hold it in your hands you will know that a dead woman is telling you the story of her life; the life that was yours all her waking hours. Don't be afraid of my words. A dead woman no longer wants anything —not love, or pity, or comforting words. There is only one thing I ask of you and that is to believe everything I tell you, everything the pain that flies from me to you reveals. Believe my every word, I ask nothing more of you: one doesn't tell lies at the deathbed of an only child.

'I will reveal my whole life to you, a life which truly began only on the day I first knew you. Before that everything was simply obscure and confused, in that my memory never surfaced from some kind of cellar filled with dusty, dull things and people, covered in spiders' webs, that my heart no longer recognises. When you came into my life I was thirteen years old and lived in the same house you live in now, the same house in which you are holding this letter —my last living breath —in your hand. I lived on the same floor, immediately opposite the door of your flat. You will certainly not remember us at all, the poor widow of an accountant (she always wore mourning) and the thin, half-grown child —we were very quiet, of course, immersed in our petty-bourgeois poverty. Perhaps you never heard our name: we had no nameplate on our door and no one came to visit us, no one inquired after us. It is also so long ago, fifteen or sixteen years. No, you certainly won't remember it now, my darling, but I, oh I remember passionately every little detail. I remember as though it were today, the day, no, the hour, I first heard of you, first saw you. Why shouldn't I, for it was then the world began for me. Have patience, my darling, I want to tell you everything, everything from the beginning. Don't tire of listening to me for a little while, I beg you. I haven't grown tired of loving you all my life.

'Before you moved in to our house, odious, nasty, quarrelsome people lived in your flat. Poor as they were, they hated most of all having poverty-stricken neighbours like us, because we didn't want to have anything to do with their depraved, lower-class coarseness. The man was a drunkard and beat his wife. We were often wakened in the night by the noise of chairs being knocked over and the clatter of breaking plates. Once, after she had been beaten until she was bleeding, she ran out on to the stairs, her hair dishevelled, and with the drunken man bawling after her, until people opened their doors and threatened to call the police. My mother had avoided having anything to do with them from the start and forbade me to speak to the children, who as a result never missed an opportunity to take it out on me. When they met me in the street they shouted obscenities after me and once they threw such hard snowballs at me they made my forehead bleed. Everyone in the house instinctively disliked that family and breathed a sigh of relief when something happened to make them leave suddenly with their bits and pieces—I believe the husband was imprisoned for theft. For a few days a 'To Let' notice appeared on the front door, then it was taken down and the caretaker promptly let it be known that an author, a quiet bachelor, had taken the flat. That was how I heard your name for the first time.

'After a few days painters and decorators, cleaners and carpet layers came to renovate after the mess left by the former tenants. There was much hammering, banging, plastering and scraping but Mother was only too pleased, she said, that the unsavoury goings-on over the way had come to an end. I didn't actually see you—not even while you were moving in. All the work was supervised by your manservant. That small, grave, greyhaired gentleman's gentleman directed everything in a quiet, business-like, superior way. He impressed us all very much, firstly because in our suburban dwelling a gentleman's gentleman was something of a novelty, and then because he was so very polite to everybody, without in any way putting himself on a level with the servants, or descending to familiar gossip. From the very first he treated my mother as a lady, with respect, and he was always friendly and serious, even to a little shrimp like me. If he mentioned your name it was always with a certain reverence, with particular esteem. It was evident that he was attached to you far more than was usual with servants.

And how I have loved good old John for that, though I envied him because he could always be near you, and do things for you.

'I am telling you all this, my darling, all these little, almost silly things, so that you will understand how right from the start you were able to gain such power over the shy, timid child I was. Even before you actually came into my life, there was a prestige about you, an aura of opulence, of being special and mysterious. Everyone in the small suburban house waited impatiently for you to move in (people who live narrow lives are always curious about new neighbours), and I first felt this curiosity about you when I came home from school one afternoon and the furniture van was standing outside. The removal men had already taken up most of the heavy furniture and were carrying in a number of small things. I stood at the door to marvel at everything, for all your things were so very different from anything I had ever seen. There were Indian idols; pieces of Italian sculpture; large pictures in dazzling colours; and then, finally came the books, so many and so beautiful, I wouldn't have believed it possible. They were all piled up at the door, where the manservant took charge of them and carefully removed the dust from every single one with a feather duster. I loitered near the ever-growing pile with curiosity; the manservant didn't send me away, but neither did he encourage me. I didn't dare touch anything, although I would have loved to handle the soft leather of some of them. I just looked shyly at the titles on the spines; there were French and English books among them, and many in languages I didn't understand. I believe I would have looked at them all for hours but Mother called me in.

'I thought about nothing else but you all the evening; even before I knew you. I myself possessed only a dozen cheap tattered books with cardboard covers which I loved more than anything else and had read over and over again. And then I wondered what the man must be like who owned and had read all those wonderful books, who knew all those languages, and was so wealthy and knowledgeable at the same time. A sort of supernatural awe combined with the idea of all those books. I tried to picture you in my mind. You were an old man with glasses and a long, white beard, like our geography teacher, only much kinder, more handsome and gentler—I don't know why I was already sure then that you must be good-looking, when I still thought of you as an old man. That night, still without meeting you, I dreamt about you for the first time.

'The next day you moved in, but in spite of being on the look-out all the time, I wasn't able to catch a glimpse of you—which only increased my curiosity. At last, on the third day, I saw you; and what a tremendous surprise it was, to discover how different you were, so completely unrelated to my childish picture of a godfather. I had imagined a bespectacled, kindly, old man, and then you appeared—you, exactly as you still are today, unchangeable, on whom the years sit lightly! You were wearing fashionable, light-brown country clothes and ran up the stairs two at a time in your inimitable, easy, boyish way. You carried your hat in your hand so I was able to see, with amazement I could scarcely hide, your open, lively face and your youthful hair: really, I was taken aback to see how young, how handsome, how willow-slim and elegant you were. And isn't it strange: at that first moment I saw clearly what I and everyone else came to see in you so uniquely time and time again, but with some astonishment—that somehow you are two people in one, a passionate, happy-go-lucky young man given over to pleasure and adventure, and at the same time as far as your writing is concerned a relentless, serious, responsible, extremely well-read and educated man. Unconsciously I felt what everyone sensed about you, that you led a double life, a life which presented to the world a light-hearted, open face and an obscure life known only to yourself. I, the thirteen-year-old, magically attracted, felt this profound duality, this secret of your existence, at my first sight of you.

'Do you understand now, my darling, what a marvel, what an alluring enigma you must have been for me, as a child? Suddenly to discover that a man everyone held in respect because he wrote books, because he was famous in that great world outside, was a young, stylish, boyishly high-spirited, twenty-five-year-old! Do I have to tell you that from that day on nothing else in our house, in my entire wretched childish world, interested me except you, that the entire obduracy, the whole intense tenacity of a thirteen-year-old revolved more and more around your life, your existence? I watched you, I observed your routine, noticed the people who visited you; and all that only increased my curiosity about you, instead of diminishing it, for the two sides of your character were revealed by the diversity of those visitors. There were young people, friends of yours, with whom you laughed and were in high spirits; shabbily dressed students; and then again there were ladies who drove up in cars; once the Director of the Opera, the great conductor whom I had only looked at respectfully from afar on his rostrum. Then there were also young girls still attending commercial school, who scurried in the door looking embarrassed. Altogether there were many, very many, women. I didn't think anything about this particularly, not even when, as I was on my way to school one morning, I saw a heavily-veiled lady leave your flat. I was only thirteen and too innocent to know that the intense curiosity with which I watched and spied on you was already love.

'But I know exactly, my darling, the day and the hour when my heart was lost to you for ever. I had been for a walk with a schoolfriend and we were standing at the gate chatting. A car drew up, stopped, and you jumped from the running board in that impatient, buoyant way that thrills me about you even today, and made for the door. Instinctively I was impelled to open it for you and so I stepped in your path and we nearly collided. You looked at me with that warm, soft, covert expression, which was like a caress, smiled at me tenderly — yes, I can't put it any other way — and said in a very soft and almost intimate voice, "Thanks very much, young lady."

'That was all, darling; but from that moment when I met your gentle, caressing eyes, I was yours. Later, of course, it was not long before I discovered you look this way at every woman who passes by. You give them a glance intended to attract and trap them. It takes in everything they are wearing and at the same time strips them naked. It's the look of the born seducer. You give it to every shopgirl who serves you, every maid who opens the door for you. It signifies little more to you than desire and curiosity, but it shows simply that your fondness for women quite unconsciously makes your expression caring and warm, when it is turned on them. But I, the thirteen-year-old child, did not suspect this: it was as though I had been plunged into fire. I thought the tenderness was for me alone, and at that moment the woman in me, the adolescent, awoke and that woman was yours for ever.

"Who was that?" my friend asked.

'I couldn't answer straightaway. It was impossible to speak your name. At that one, unique moment your name was already sacred, had become my secret. "Oh, some man who lives in the house," I stammered awkwardly.

"Well why did you go so red then when he looked at you?"

'My friend teased me with all the mischievousness of an inquisitive child. And the thought that she was making fun of my secret made me blush even more. Feeling embarrassed, I was rude. "Stupid fool," I said angrily: I would have liked to have strangled her. But she only laughed louder and more scornfully, until I felt the tears well up in my eyes with impotent rage. I left her standing there and ran upstairs.

'I have loved you ever since that moment. I know women have often told you they love you, you pampered man! But believe me, no one has loved you as slavishly, with such dog-like devotion, as the creature I was, and have always been. Nothing on earth equals the unseen, hidden love of a child, because it is so without hope, so servile, so submissive, so observant and intense, as the covetous and unconsciously demanding love of a grown woman never is. Only lonely children can maintain their passion completely. The others rid themselves of emotion by chattering with their companions; they smooth it away in confidences. They have heard and read so much about love and know it is the fate of all. They play with it, as though it were a toy, they boast of it like boys with their first cigarette. But I had no one in whom to confide. No one advised or warned me; I was inexperienced and unsuspecting; I fell headlong into my destiny as into an abyss. Everything that grew and blossomed within me centred trustfully on you, and the dream of you. My father had long been dead; my mother was a stranger to me with her everlasting, wretched depression, and worries about her pension. The half-corrupted schoolgirls repelled me, as they played so unscrupulously with what was to me the ultimate passion. And so I turned everything that would normally have scattered and divided, towards you – my whole concentrated and ever-impatiently growing personality. You were to me – how shall I put it? No comparison is good enough — you were indeed everything, my whole life. Nothing existed unless it related to you. My whole existence made sense only if it was connected with you. You transformed my whole life. Until then apathetic and only average in school, I suddenly came first. I read a thousand books far into the night, because I knew you loved books. Much to my mother's astonishment I began to practise the piano with almost mulish tenacity, because I thought you were fond of music. I mended and pressed my clothes, just so that I would look neat and pleasing to you; I thought it terrible that my school overall (it was made out of one of my mother's dresses) had a square patch inserted on the left-hand side. I was afraid you might notice it and despise me. So I always covered it with my satchel when I ran up the stairs, trembling with fear in case you saw it. But how silly that was: you hardly ever looked at me again.

'But I, on the other hand, really did nothing all day but wait and watch for you. There was a small brass peep-hole in our door and through this round hole it was possible to see your door. That peep-hole — no, don't laugh, darling, even today I am not ashamed of the hours I spent! — was my eye on the world outside. During those months and years I sat whole afternoons there in the icy hall on the alert, a book in my hand, afraid my mother would be suspicious. I was like a taut string, vibrating if your presence touched it. I was always tense and agitated whenever I was near you, but you could no more have felt it than you did the tension of the spring in the watch you carried in your pocket. It patiently counts the hours for you in the darkness and ticks them off, accompanying you on your way with inaudible heartbeats, and you give it only a quick glance once in a million ticking seconds. I knew all about you, knew all your habits, all your suits and ties. I knew and soon made distinctions between your various friends and divided them into those I liked and those I disliked. From the time I was thirteen until I was sixteen my every hour was yours. Oh, what follies I committed! I kissed the door-handle your hand had touched, I picked up a cigarette end you had thrown away in the entrance, and it was sacred to me because your lips had touched it. In the evenings I ran down into the street a hundred times, on any pretext, to see in which of your rooms the light was burning, and so be party to your invisible presence. And during the weeks you were away—my heart always stopped with anguish when I saw John faithfully carrying your yellow travelling bag outside—in those weeks my life was desolate and without meaning. I went about sullen, bored and bad-tempered and had to take care all the time that Mother did not notice how my eyes were red with crying and from that see my despair.

'I know I am telling you about childish follies, extravagant over-enthusiasm. I ought to be ashamed of them but I am not ashamed, for my love for you was never purer and more passionate than at the time of those childish excesses. I could tell you for hours, for days, how I lived with you then. You scarcely knew me by sight, for if I met you on the stairs and could not avoid you, I ran past with my head lowered, afraid of meeting your ardent look, like someone jumping into water to avoid being scorched by fire. I could tell you about those long-since vanished years of yours for hours, for days on end, and unroll the entire calendar of your life; but I won't bore you, won't distress you. I'll confide to you only the most wonderful experience of my childhood; and please don't deride me because it is such a small thing. To me, as a child, it was of infinite importance. It must have been on a Sunday. You were away and your manservant was pulling the heavy carpets, which he had been beating, through the open door of the flat. The good fellow found it hard work and in a fit of rashness I went over and asked if I could help. He was astonished but let me do it, and so—if only I could find words to tell you with what awe-struck, indeed devout, reverence—I saw the inside of your flat. I saw your world, the writing-table at which your were accustomed to sit, with a blue crystal vase on it containing a few flowers, your bookcases, your pictures, your books. It was only a fleeting, surreptitious glance into your life, as the faithful John would certainly have prevented me from making a closer inspection. But with this one glance I absorbed the whole atmosphere and had nourishment for my endless dreams about you, waking or sleeping.

'These fleeting moments were the happiest of my childhood. I wanted to tell you about them so that you, who didn't know me, will at last begin to understand how a life ebbed and flowed with you. I wanted to tell you about them and about that other, most dreadful hour, which unhappily was so near. Because of you – I have already told you – I had forgotten everything else. I had paid no attention to my mother and concerned myself with no one. I didn't notice that an elderly gentleman, a businessman from Innsbruck, distantly related to my mother by marriage, was calling more often and staying longer. Indeed I was only too pleased that he sometimes took Mother to the theatre and I could then be alone, thinking of you and watching out for you – my greatest, my only happiness. Well, one day my mother called me to her room with a certain formality; she had something serious to say to me. I went pale and heard my heart start to pound: had she noticed something, guessed something? My first thought was of you, the secret that linked me with the world. But mother was herself embarrassed, she kissed me tenderly once or twice (which she hardly ever did), she sat me close beside her on the sofa and began hesitantly and shamefacedly to tell me that her relative, who was a widower, had made her an offer of marriage, and she had decided, mainly on my account, to accept. My heart beat very fast: only one thought came into my head, the thought of you. "But we'll stay here, won't we?" I just managed to say.

"No, we'll move to Innsbruck. Ferdinand has a beautiful house there."

'I didn't hear anything else. Everything went black before my eyes. Later I knew I had fainted. I heard mother quietly telling my future stepfather, who had been waiting behind the door, that I had suddenly thrown up my hands, stepped backwards and then fallen down like a lump of lead.

'I cannot describe to you what happened in the next few days, how I, an impotent child, resisted their all-powerful intentions. My hand still trembles as I write, thinking about it. I could not betray my real secret, so my resistance merely appeared obstinate, wicked and insolent. No one spoke to me any more about it; everything was done behind my back. They used the time I was at school to expedite the removal. When I came home, yet another piece of furniture had been removed or sold. I saw how the flat, and with it my life, was disintegrating. And then one day when I came home to lunch, the removal men had been and taken everything away. Packed suitcases and two camp beds for Mother and me stood in the empty rooms. We were to sleep there for one more night – the last – and travel to Innsbruck in the morning.

'I decided all of a sudden on this last day that I could not go on living without being near you. You were my only refuge. How I was thinking and whether I was capable of thinking clearly at that desperate time, I can never say. But I stood up, wearing my school clothes – Mother had gone out – and just as I was, on the spur of the moment, I went across to you. No, I didn't go: I was impelled towards your door as though mesmerised; my legs were stiff and I was trembling. I have already told you I didn't know clearly what I wanted: to fall at your feet and ask you to keep me as a maid, as a slave. I am afraid you will laugh at this innocent fanaticism of a fifteen-year-old, but – my darling, you wouldn't go on laughing if you knew how I stood there outside in the icy hall, rigid with fear and yet pushed forward by a power I could not comprehend, and how my trembling arm seemed to tear itself loose from my body, lifted itself up and – it was a struggle that lasted through an eternity of terrible seconds, pressed the doorbell. It still rings in my ear today, that shrill sound of the bell, and then the silence that followed, while my heart stood still and my blood froze, and I just listened to see if you would come to the door.

'But you didn't. Nobody came. You were obviously out that afternoon and John away on an errand; so I stumbled back into the desert of our empty flat, with the dead note of the bell reverberating in my ear, and threw myself exhausted on a travelling rug, worn out with the four steps I had taken, as though I had been walking for hours in deep snow. But beneath this exhaustion there still burned undiminished the determination to see you, to speak to you, before they tore me away. I swear there was nothing sexual in it. I was still ignorant, just because I thought of nothing but you. I wanted only to see you, to see you once more, to cling to you. The whole night, the whole long, frightful night, I waited for you, my darling. Scarcely had Mother gone to bed and fallen asleep than I crept into the hall to listen for your return. I waited the whole night, and it was a bitterly cold January night. I was tired, my limbs ached and there was no longer a chair to sit on. So I lay down on the cold floor, stretched out in the draught that came under the door. I lay there in my thin clothes, on the painfully cold floor, without putting on any covering. I didn't want to be warm for fear of falling asleep and not hearing your footsteps. Oh how painful it was, I had cramp in my feet, my arms shivered; I had to keep standing up, it was so cold in the frightful darkness. But I waited, waited, waited for you, as for my destiny.

'At last—it must have been two or three o'clock in the morning—I heard the lock turn in the front door and then steps coming up the stairs. The cold vanished, warmth spread over me, I opened the door softly meaning to throw myself upon you, to fall at your feet ... Oh I don't know what I should have done in my childish foolishness. The footsteps came nearer, candle-light flickered. Trembling, I held on to the door-handle. Was it you climbing the stairs?

'Yes, it was you, darling—but you were not alone. I heard a soft, sensual laugh, a rustling of silk, and your voice speaking quietly—you had come home with a woman. I don't know how I lived through that night. The next day, at about eight o'clock, they took me off to Innsbruck: I had no more energy to resist.

'My child died last night—now I shall be alone again, if I really must go on living. In the morning strangers will come, bulky men in black, bringing a coffin in which they will place my poor child, my only child. Perhaps friends will come, too, bringing wreaths, but of what use are flowers on a coffin? They will comfort me, and say a few words. Words, words! But how can they help me? I know I must be alone again. And there is nothing more terrible than to be alone with people all around. I experienced it before, in those endless two years from sixteen to eighteen in Innsbruck, where I lived with my family like a prisoner, an outcast. My stepfather, a very easy-going, taciturn man, was kind to me. My mother, as if to atone for an unwitting injustice, seemed ready to grant my every wish. Young people tried to be helpful but, fiercely stubborn, I rebuffed them. I didn't want to be happy, to be content away from you; I buried myself in a dark world of self-torment and loneliness. I did not wear the pretty clothes they bought me. I refused to go to concerts or the theatre, or to join in companionable excursions. I rarely left the house. Would you believe it, my darling, I didn't know ten streets in that small town, where I lived for two years? I grieved, and I wanted to; I wallowed in every deprivation I inflicted on myself while I thought about you. And then, I didn't want to allow anyone to turn me from my passion to live only for you. I sat alone at home, hour after hour, day after day, and did nothing but think of you; again and again I revived my hundred small recollections of you, every encounter, all the times I waited, and played over those little events as though I were in a theatre. It is because of the innumerable times I re-enacted every second of those days that my whole childhood has remained such a glowing memory. I feel every minute of those past years are as alive and active as if I had experienced them yesterday.

'I lived only through you in those days. I bought all your books; if your name appeared in the newspaper it was a red-letter day. Will you believe it when I tell you that I know every line of your books by heart, I have read them so often? If someone were to wake me in the night and quote one of your lines at random I could continue it, trance-like, even now, today, after thirteen years. Your every word was holy writ to me. The whole world existed only with reference to you. I read in the Viennese newspapers about concerts and first nights, thinking only which would have interested you, and when evening came, I accompanied you from afar: now he is entering the concert hall, now he is taking his seat. I dreamt that a thousand times, because I had seen you once at a concert.

'But why should I recount all this, this raving, self-destructive, so tragic, hopeless fanaticism of a forsaken child? What is the good of telling someone who never suspected it, never knew? Was I really still a child then? I was seventeen, eighteen — young men in the street began to turn and look at me, which only annoyed me. For love, or even flirting with the idea of it, with anyone other than you was so unimaginable, so unthinkable, so foreign to me, that even the temptation seemed to me like a crime. My passion for you remained constant; only it changed as I matured physically, as my senses awoke and became more ardent, more physical, more womanly. And what the innocent, unaroused child who had rung your doorbell could have had no inkling of, was now my only thought: to give myself to you, to surrender to you.

'People around me considered me shy, and said I was timid (I had kept my secret to myself). But I developed a firm resolve. All my thoughts and endeavours were stretched in one direction: back to Vienna, back to you. And I achieved my purpose, however foolish and incomprehensible it must have seemed to the others. My stepfather was well off. He looked on me as his own child. But I was bitterly obstinate and insisted I wanted to earn my own living, and eventually I succeeded in coming to Vienna as an employee in a large, ready-to-wear dress business belonging to a relative.

'Need I tell you where I went first when — at last! At last! — I arrived in Vienna on a foggy autumn day? I left my cases at the station, rushed on to a tram — how long that journey seemed. I resented every stop! — and ran to the house. There was a light in your window. My whole heart sang. The city had been so alien, so mindlessly tumultuous to me, but now it came alive, as I did again, when I felt your presence, you, my everlasting dream. I didn't realise that in fact I was just as far away from your consciousness, beyond valleys, mountains and rivers, as I was when only the thin, glass window-pane, showing a light, was between you and my radiant gaze. All I did was to go on staring up; there was a light, the house, you, there was my world. For two years I had dreamed of this hour, now my dream had come true. All that long, soft, misty evening I stood in front of your window until the light went out. Only then did I look for my own lodging.

'Every evening I stood in front of your house like that. I had to work until six o'clock. It was hard, tiring work, but I liked it, as the turmoil there prevented me from feeling my own so painfully. And straightaway, as soon as the iron shutters rolled down behind me, off I ran to my beloved destination. Only to see you again, only to meet you once more; that was all I wanted, just to be able to look on your face from a distance. After about a week I did meet you at last. In fact it was just at a moment when I least expected it: while I was looking up at your windows, you actually crossed the street. And in an instant I became a child, that thirteen-year-old, again. I felt the blood rush to my cheeks. Involuntarily, against my innermost longing to feel your eyes on me, I bowed my head and ran past you like lightning, as though someone was chasing me. Afterwards I felt ashamed at running away like a shy schoolgirl, as now I knew exactly what I wanted: I really wanted to meet you. I looked for you, I wanted you to recognise me after all the accursed, yearning years, to notice me, to love me.

'But for a long time you didn't notice me, although I stood in your street every evening, even in flurries of snow and in the sharp, cutting Viennese wind. I often waited for hours in vain. You would come out at last with friends. I saw you twice with women, and then I felt my adulthood, experienced that new, different feeling towards you in the way my heart would suddenly quicken, tearing me apart, when I saw a woman I didn't know walking so confidently arm in arm with you. I wasn't surprised, I knew already from my childhood days about those endless lady callers, but now, somehow, it hurt me physically. Something was aroused in me, hostility and desire at the same time, in the presence of this public physical familiarity with someone else. One day, childishly proud as I was, and perhaps still am, I stayed away from your house. But how awful that empty evening of defiance and revolt was. The next evening I stood once more humbly outside your house waiting, waiting, as it has long been my whole destiny to stand, outside your life which has been closed to me.

'At last, one evening, you noticed me. I had seen you coming from a distance and pulled myself together to prevent myself avoiding you. By chance the street was made narrower by a lorry that was unloading and you had to pass quite close to me. Your absent-minded glance skimmed over me so quickly and casually that hardly had you noticed how intently I was looking at you than it became that look you give all women – how the recollection terrified me! – tender, veiled yet unveiling, all-embracing and captivating – the look that awoke my passion for you as a child, and now did so for the first time as a woman. For one, perhaps two, seconds, your glance held mine in this way – I could not tear mine away, and did not want to – and then you had walked past me. My heart beat so fast that in spite of myself I had to slow my pace. When I turned round, overcome by irresistible curiosity, I saw you had stopped and were gazing in my direction. And by the way you were looking at me, with interest and speculation, I knew at once you did not recognise me.

'You did not recognise me then or ever — you have never recognised me. How can I describe the disappointment of those moments, my darling? That was the very first time I endured the fate of not being recognised by you, the first of many occasions I have lived through since, and a fate I shall die with — never, ever recognised by you. How can I describe that disappointment? Just consider, in those two years in Innsbruck, where I thought of you all the time and did nothing but imagine what our first reunion in Vienna would be like, my fancy ranged from the wildest to the most blissful possibilities, according to my mood. If I may put it this way, every fantasy passed through my mind. In my darkest moments I had imagined you would reject me, despise me for being too inferior, too ugly, too importunate. I suffered dreadful visions of all forms of your disfavour, coldness or indifference. But not in the darkest stirrings of my feelings, or in the uttermost awareness of my inferiority, had I ventured to consider this one most appalling possibility: that you had never actually noticed my existence.

'I understand now, of course — indeed you taught me to understand! — that a girl's or a woman's face must be extraordinarily changeable for a man, because it is mostly a mirror, now of a passion, now of childishness, now of exhaustion. It is gone as quickly as a reflection in a glass. You taught me that a man can easily forget a woman's face because her age changes with the light and shade, and her clothes provide a different setting from one occasion to the next. Those who are resigned to it are the truly wise. But I was a young girl then and couldn't understand how you could have forgotten. For somehow my excessive, endless preoccupation with you gave me the illusion that you must often be thinking of me and were waiting for me. How could I have gone on living, knowing for certain that I was nothing to you, that you never gave me the slightest thought? This realisation came to me from your glance, which showed that you had forgotten my existence and there was no thread of memory connecting your life to mine. That was my first plunge into reality, my first premonition of my destiny.

'You didn't recognise me on that occasion. And two days later when we met again and you looked at me as though you knew me, it was not that you recognised me as the one who loved you and whom you aroused, but simply as the pretty eighteen-year-old who passed you at the same place two days earlier. You looked at me with friendly surprise, a light smile playing round your mouth. You passed me again and slowed up immediately as before. I trembled, I was jubilant, I prayed you would speak to me. I felt you saw me as flesh and blood for the first time. I, too, walked slowly and did not avoid you. Suddenly, without turning round, I was conscious that you were behind me. I knew I would hear your dear voice speak directly to me for the first time. Anticipation paralysed me. My heart beat so fast I was afraid I would have to stop — there you were at my side. You spoke to me in your easy, cheerful way as though we were old friends — oh, you knew nothing about me, you never had any idea of what my life was like. You spoke to me in such a charming, free and easy manner that I was even able to answer you. We walked the whole length of the street together. Then you asked me if we might dine together. I agreed. How could I have refused you?

'We ate together in a small restaurant — do you still know where it was? No, of course not. You certainly won't distinguish it from other similar evenings, for who was I to you? One of hundreds, one flirtation in a never-ending chain. Why should you remember me? I said very little. I was so infinitely happy to have you near me, to hear you speak to me. I didn't want to waste a moment of it by asking questions or by foolish chatter. I shall never cease to be grateful to you for that hour. How fully you earned my warmest respect. How tender, how gentle, how tactful you were, entirely self-controlled, without trying to force caresses on me. And from the first moment you displayed such a confident, friendly intimacy that you would have won me, even if I had not already long been yours with all my heart and soul. Oh, you don't know what a monster you exorcised, when you didn't disillusion me after five years of childish anticipation.

'It was late; we had finished eating. At the restaurant door you asked me if I was in a hurry or not. How could I conceal from you that I was ready to give myself to you! I said

I had plenty of time. Then you asked me, after a moment's hesitation, if I would come home with you and talk. It was a foregone conclusion, feeling as I did, that I said, "With pleasure." I noticed at once that my prompt acceptance affected you somehow; you were either embarrassed or pleased. Anyway, you were visibly surprised. Of course, today I understand your astonishment. I know now it is usual for a woman, although she has a burning desire to give herself to a man, to hide her willingness, to feign alarm or indignation, which will only be calmed by urgent entreaties, lies, protestations and promises. I know that perhaps only professional prostitutes or naïve adolescents agree so readily to such an invitation. How could you know that for me it was only the outward expression, the outburst, of longing accumulated over a thousand lonely days. In any case, however, you were attracted and I began to interest you. As we walked along, talking, I felt you were somehow appraising me speculatively. Your instinct, your magically certain instinct about human nature, told you at once there was something unusual, some mystery, about this pretty, trusting girl. Your curiosity was awakened and I was aware from your indirect, searching questions, how you wanted to discover the secret of this mystery. But I was evasive. I preferred to appear stupid rather than reveal it.

'We went up to your flat. Forgive me, darling, when I say that you can't understand what that path, those stairs meant to me — how it disturbed me, such rapture, such frantic, agonising happiness — I nearly died. I can scarcely think of it now without crying; and I have no more tears. I only felt that every object there was steeped in my love. Everything was an emblem of my childhood and my longing: the gate, where I waited for you thousands of times; the stairs, which taught me to recognise your step and where I first saw you; the peephole, through which I spent my very soul looking for you; the mat in front of your door where I once knelt; the click of the key at which I always sprang up from my vigil. My whole childhood, all my passion, was centred on those few square yards. My whole life was there. And now it broke over me like a storm: I had achieved everything — everything — and I was going with you — you and I together — into your home, our home. Just think of it — it sounds banal, but I don't know how else to say it—outside your door lay reality, that dreary daily round that had been my whole existence; and at your door the magic kingdom of childhood began—Aladdin's Cave. Just think—that door, that threshold I now crossed with a feeling of intoxication, I had gazed at it a thousand times, with eyes aglow—and you will have an inkling, but only an inkling—you will never completely understand, my darling—what that tumultuous moment cost me.

'I spent the whole night with you. You had no idea that until then no man had touched me, caressed my body or seen it. But how could you possibly have suspected that, darling, since I offered you no resistance? I suppressed all modesty, all hesitation, only to prevent you from guessing the secret of my love for you, as you would certainly have been alarmed. You care only for the superficial, the frivolous, the inconsequential. You are afraid of becoming involved in anyone's destiny. You want to squander yourself on everyone, on the whole world; and to accept no sacrifice. If I tell you now, darling, that I was a virgin when I gave myself to you, I implore you, don't misunderstand me! I'm not complaining. You didn't entice me, deceive me, seduce me—I forced myself on you, threw myself into your arms, went out to meet my fate. Never, never will I accuse you. No, I shall always be grateful to you, for how rich that night was for me, how it sparkled with pleasure, how blissful it was when I opened my eyes in the darkness and knew you were by my side. I felt so much as if I were in heaven that I was surprised not to find the stars all around me. No, I have never regretted it, my darling, never wished those hours undone. I only know that as you slept, as I heard you breathing and felt your body and mine so close, I wept for joy in the darkness.

'In the morning I hurried away early. I had to go to work and, besides, I wanted to be away before your man came. I didn't want him to see me. When I stood there, dressed to go out, you took me in your arms and looked at me intently; was it a faint and distant memory that stirred in your mind, or was it that, because I was so happy, you thought I looked beautiful? Then you kissed me. I freed myself gently from your embrace and was ready to leave. You then asked, "Would you like to take some flowers with you?" I said I would. You took four white roses from the blue crystal vase on the writing-table (how I knew that vase from the one glance I stole in childhood!) and gave them to me. I kissed them for days on end.

'We had first arranged another evening together. I came to your flat, and again it was wonderful. You gave me a third night. Then you said you had to go away — oh how I had hated those journeys, from my childhood on! — and you promised to tell me as soon as you returned. I gave you a *poste restante* address — I didn't want to give you my real name. I kept my secret. On parting, you gave me roses again — on parting!

'Every day for two weeks I asked — but no, what's the point of describing to you the agony of waiting, of despair? I'm not complaining. I love you as you are, passionate and forgetful, generous and unfaithful. I love you exactly as you have always been and as you still are. You had been back a long time. I saw it from your lighted windows. You didn't write to me. I have no letters from you to read in my final hours, not a line from you, to whom I gave my life. I waited, waited in desperation, but you didn't send for me. Not a line did you write ... not a line ...

'My child died yesterday — he was your child, too. He was your child, too, darling, conceived on one of those three nights: I swear it, and one doesn't tell lies in the shadow of death. It was our child, I give you my solemn word, for no man touched me from the time I gave myself to you until the child was wrested from my womb. Your touch sanctified me. How could I possibly have shared you, who were all the world to me, with others who only lightly brushed against my life in passing? He was our child, darling, the child of my conscious love and your carefree, abundant, almost instinctive embraces; our child, our son, our only child.

'You will ask now — perhaps you are shocked, perhaps merely surprised — you ask, my darling, why I concealed this child from you all these years. Why do I tell you about him only today, as he lies here sleeping in the darkness, asleep for ever, about to leave me for ever, never to return? But how could I have told you? You would never have believed me, the eager stranger who was all too willing to spend three nights with you and offered no resistance in giving herself. Yes, obviously willing. You would never have believed that the

nameless woman of a fleeting encounter was faithful to you
—to you, who were unfaithful. You would never have
accepted the child as your own without misgivings. Even if
what I said might have seemed plausible you would never have
been able to put aside the secret suspicion that I was trying to
foist another man's child on you, because you were wealthy.
You would always have been suspicious of me. There would
have been a shadow, a dreadful, hovering shadow of mistrust
between us. I wouldn't have wanted that. Besides, I know you.
I know you so well, perhaps better than you know yourself. I
know it would have been embarrassing for you, who prefer
love to be carefree, superficial and frivolous, suddenly to find
you were a father, immediately responsible for another life.
The real you can breathe only while you are free, and you
would have felt somehow restricted with me. You would have
hated me for this obligation—yes, I know you would—against
your own conscious will. I would have been an encumbrance
and you would have hated me, perhaps only for an hour or
two, or perhaps only for fleeting moments, but in my pride I
wanted you to think of me all your life without being worried.
I preferred to take everything on myself rather than be a
burden to you; to be the only one among all your women you
always think of with affection and gratitude. But, to be sure,
you have never thought of me. You have forgotten me.

'I'm not complaining, my darling. No, I'm not complaining.
Forgive me if a drop of bitterness occasionally falls from my
pen. My child—ours—lies here dead beneath the flickering
candles. I have shaken my clenched fists at God and called Him
murderer, my feelings are so confused and perplexed. Excuse
the lamentations; forgive me! I am well aware you are a good
man and helpful at heart. You help anyone who asks you, even
the remotest stranger. But your generosity is so peculiar. It lies
open to anyone who can take it, as much as a man can carry.
Your generosity is large, infinitely large, but it is—excuse
me—it is lazy. It has to be asked for, has to be taken. You help
if someone calls for help, requests it. You help from a sense of
guilt, from weakness, and not gladly. Let's be honest about
it—you don't like the needy and the afflicted any more than
you do your companions in good fortune. And people like you,
even the most charitable, are difficult to ask for help.

'Once, when I was still a child, looking through the peephole, I saw how you gave something to a beggar who had rung your doorbell. You gave promptly, and indeed generously, even before he had asked, but you handed it to him with a certain anxiety and haste; so that he would go away again quickly. It was as though you were afraid to look at him. I have never forgotten your uneasy, reticent way of helping, retreating from being thanked. That's why I've never turned to you. Of course, I knew you would have stood by me at the time even without being certain it was your child. You would have comforted me, given me money, plenty of money. But it would always have been only with concealed impatience to shake off an embarrassment. I think you would even have tried to persuade me to have an abortion. That was what I dreaded most – for what would I not have done if you wanted it! How could I have refused you anything? But this child was everything to me. It was yours; it was you all over again: not the happy, carefree you whom I had no power to keep, but you given to me for ever – so I thought – implanted in my womb, bound up with my life. Now, at last, I had captured you. I could feel your life growing in my blood; I would be able to nourish you, suckle you, cuddle you, kiss you, whenever my heart yearned to do so. You see, darling, that's why I was so happy when I had your child, and why I didn't tell you about it: because now you could never run away from me. I admit, darling, they were not months only of happiness, as I had anticipated in my mind. They were also months of greyness and torment, full of loathing for the baseness of mankind. It wasn't easy for me. I couldn't go to work in the later months in case my relatives became aware of my condition and sent the news home. I wouldn't ask my mother for money – so I kept body and soul together until my time came by selling the few bits of jewellery I possessed. A week before the confinement a washerwoman stole my last few crowns from a cupboard, so I had to go to the maternity hospital. The child, your child, was born there – in the midst of the squalor of penury – where only the very poor, the outcast and the forgotten drag themselves in their need. It was a deadly place: everything was alien, completely alien. We were strangers to one another, lying there in our loneliness, and hating each other thoroughly. We were thrown together only by misfortune, by the same anguish, in that stifling, overcrowded room full of screaming and moaning, chloroform and blood. I experienced there what degradation, what spiritual and physical shame has to be endured by the poverty-stricken. I experienced it in the company of prostitutes and the sick, who created a baseness out of a common fate; in the cynicism of the young doctors who stripped the bedclothes off the defenceless women with an ironic smile and pretended to examine them scientifically; in the avarice of the nurses. Oh, there a person's shame was crucified with looks and scourged with words. The chart with one's name on it is the only indication that one still exists. For what lies in the bed is only a quivering piece of flesh to be handled by the inquisitive, an object to be exhibited and studied. Oh, women with husbands waiting lovingly for them to bestow children on the home, they don't know what it means to give birth to a child alone, defenceless, as though you were being experimented on! And even today if I read the word 'Hell' in a book, I can't help thinking immediately of that slaughterhouse full of shame, that overcrowded, steaming room, filled with groans, hysterical laughter and bloodcurdling screams, where I suffered.

'Forgive me, forgive me for speaking of these things. I mention them only this once, but I shall never do so again. I have kept silent for eleven years and soon I shall be mute for all eternity. I had to proclaim it once, just once, how dearly I bought this child, who was all my joy and who now lies dead. I had already forgotten those hours. They were long forgotten in laughter, in the child's voice, in my delight. But now that he is dead, the torment has come alive again, and I had to cry out to you from the depths of my soul just this once. But I'm not blaming you—only God, only God, who made that torment futile. I swear I don't blame you, and I have never risen up in anger against you. Even at the time my womb was contorted in labour, when my body burned with shame under the devouring gaze of the students, even at the moment when the pain rent my soul, I never accused you before God. I have never regretted those nights, never gainsaid my love for you. I have always loved you, always blessed the hour you came into my life. And if I had to go through the hell of those hours again, and knew in advance what awaited me, I would do it, my darling, not once but a thousand times!

'Our child died yesterday – you never knew him. Your most casual glance never lighted on this small, blossoming human being, your creation, even in a fleeting chance meeting. I kept myself hidden from you for a long time as soon as I had the child. My longing for you became less painful. Indeed I think I loved you less ardently. At least I didn't suffer so much from my love, once I had the gift of the child. I didn't want to divide myself between you and him, so I didn't give myself to you who were happy and out of my life, but to this child, who needed me. He had to be fed, and I could kiss him and take him in my arms. I appeared to have been rescued from the disturbance you caused me, from my fate, saved by this replica of you. Moreover, he was truly mine. Only seldom now, very seldom, were my emotions directed humbly towards your home. I did just one thing, though. I always sent you a bouquet of white roses on your birthday, exactly like those you gave me after our first night of love. Have you ever asked yourself, in the last ten, eleven, years, who sent them? Have you remembered at all the girl to whom you once gave roses like those? I don't know and never shall. It was enough for me to send them to you out of the blue; that once a year the memory of that hour should be allowed to flower.

'You never knew our poor child. I blame myself now for keeping him from you, for you would have loved him. You never knew him, the poor boy, never saw him smile, when he gently opened his eyes, his dark, intelligent eyes – your eyes! – and then cast a bright, happy light over me, over all the world. Oh, he was so cheerful, so lovable: all your easy grace was repeated in him in a child-like way. Your quick, lively imagination was renewed in him. He could play with things for hours, totally absorbed, as you play with life, and then sit earnestly again, his brow furrowed, with his books. He grew more and more like you. He soon also began noticeably to develop that double blend of seriousness and frivolity so characteristic of you. And the more he resembled you, the more I loved him. He was a good pupil. He chattered away in French like a little magpie, and his exercise books were the neatest in the class. How good-looking he was, how smart in his black velvet suit or his little white sailor-jacket. He was always the best dressed wherever he went. When I walked with him along the beach at Grado, women stopped and stroked his long, fair hair. At Semmering, when he went tobogganing, people looked round after him admiringly. He was so handsome, so gentle, so helpful. When he became a boarder at the Theresianum last year he wore his uniform and the little sword like an eighteenth-century page-boy—now he has nothing on but his little nightshirt, the poor child, lying there with pale lips and folded hands.

'But you will ask me perhaps how I could bring him up in such luxury, how I managed to allow him this lively, happy, well-to-do life. Dearest, I speak to you out of the darkness. I'm not ashamed. I will tell you. But don't be shocked, darling—I sold myself. I was not exactly what one calls a whore, a prostitute, but I sold myself. I had rich friends, rich lovers: at first I sought them out, then they sought me. I was—did you ever notice it?—very beautiful. Everyone to whom I gave myself grew fond of me, they all thanked me, they were all devoted, they all loved me—all but you, all but you, my darling!

'Do you despise me now because I have disclosed that I sold myself? No, I know you won't despise me. I know you understand everything and will also understand I did it only for you, for your other self, for your child. In that room in the maternity hospital I had once experienced the horror of poverty. I knew that in this world the poor are always the downtrodden, the under-privileged, the victims, and no matter what the cost I didn't want your child, your bright, good-looking child, to grow up down there in the dregs, the apathy and the vulgarity of the street, in the polluted air of a backyard. His gentle mouth should not learn the language of the gutter. His white skin should not know the rough, crumpled linen of the poor. Your child should have all the riches, all the comfort in the world; he should rise to your level, live in your world. For that reason, for that alone, my darling, I sold myself. It was no sacrifice for me, for what is generally called honour and dishonour meant nothing to me. You didn't love me, you, the only one to whom my body belonged. So I was indifferent to what happened to it. Men's caresses, even their deepest passion, didn't move me profoundly, although I had to respect some of them, and pity for their unrequited love often upset me when I thought of my own fate. They were all good to me, those I knew, they all pampered me, all respected me. There was one in particular, an elderly man, a titled widower, who loved me like a daughter. He was the one who used his influence to have the fatherless child, your child, accepted for the Theresianum. Three or four times he asked me to marry him — I could have been a countess today, mistress of an enchanting castle in the Tyrol, without a care in the world. For the boy would have had a kindly father who worshipped him and I would have had a peace-loving, distinguished and good man by my side. I didn't do it: however much he pressed me, however much I hurt him by my refusal. Perhaps I was foolish, for had I accepted I would now be living a quiet, secure life somewhere, my beloved son with me, but—why shouldn't I admit it to you—I didn't want to bind myself. I wanted to be free, free for you all the time. Deep down I unconsciously continued to cherish the old childish dream that you would perhaps call me to your side again, even if only for an hour. And I threw everything away for the possibility of that one hour—only to be free for you at your first call. Hadn't my whole life, from the time I was awakened from childhood, consisted of nothing but waiting; waiting for your pleasure?

'And that hour really came. But you didn't know it, you didn't suspect it, my darling! You didn't recognise me on that occasion either—never, never, never have you recognised me! I often used to meet you earlier, in theatres, at concerts, in the Prater, in the street—every time my heart jumped but you looked straight past me. I was certainly a different person outwardly; the shy child had become a woman, beautiful, they said, dressed in expensive clothes and surrounded by admirers. How could you recognise in me the shy girl in the subdued light of your bedroom? Sometimes one of the gentlemen I was accompanying would greet you. You would acknowledge him and look up at me, but your glance was that of a polite stranger, one of approval but never of recognition, distant, terribly distant. Once—I still remember it—I felt real anguish at this lack of recognition, although I was almost used to it by that time. I was sitting in a box at the opera with a friend and you were in the next box. The lights were lowered for the overture. I couldn't see your face any more, but I felt your breath as close to me as I did that night we were together. Your hand, your delicate, gentle hand, rested on the velvet division between our boxes. And I was overcome by an infinite longing to bend forward and humbly kiss the hand I loved so much, whose gentle caress I had once felt, but which belonged now to a stranger. The music swirled excitedly around me, the craving became ever more powerful, and so intensely were my lips drawn towards your beloved hand that I had to take a grip on myself, tear myself forcibly away. After the first act I asked my friend to take me away. I couldn't bear it any longer, having you so distant and so near in the darkness.

'But the time came, once more, one last time in my shambles of a life. It was almost a year ago, on the day after your birthday. Strange: I had been thinking of you all day, as I always celebrated your birthday as a feast day. I had gone out very early in the morning and bought the white roses I sent you every year in memory of an hour you had forgotten. In the afternoon I drove with the boy to the café Demel and in the evening we went to the theatre. I wanted him also to feel that this day was some kind of mysterious, youthful holiday without, of course, his knowing its significance. The next day I spent with my lover of that time, a wealthy young manufacturer from Brünn, with whom I had been living for the previous two years. He worshipped me and spoiled me, and also wanted to marry me, as the other men did. I refused him as I refused the others, without any apparent reason, although he showered me and the child with gifts and was himself a lovable man, in his slightly dull, submissive kindness.

We went together to a concert where we met some high-spirited friends and we all had supper in a restaurant in the Ringstrasse. In the midst of the laughter and chatter there, I suggested we should go on to a dance hall, to the Tabarin. I usually loathed that kind of establishment, with its forced, alcohol-induced gaiety, like all 'gallivanting', and I normally always resisted such propositions. This time, however — it was as though some inexplicable magic power within me suddenly led me despite myself to throw out the suggestion in the midst of everyone's happy, agreeable excitement – I had, all at once, an unaccountable desire, as if I felt something special awaited me there. Everyone stood up quickly, as usual ready to please me, and we went over to the dance hall and drank champagne. Swiftly I was overcome with a frenzied, almost physically painful exhilaration, such as I have never known. I drank one glass after another, joined in the singing of bawdy songs, and felt almost compelled to dance or shout for joy. But abruptly – it was as though something icy cold or something burning hot at that instant touched my heart – I was torn apart: you were sitting at the next table with some friends, watching me with an admiring and covetous look: that look that always stirred me to my innermost depths. For the first time in ten years you looked at me again with all the unconsciously passionate power of your being. I trembled. I nearly dropped the glass I had in my hand. Fortunately my friends round the table didn't notice my confusion: they were lost in the noise of laughter and music.

'Your look became more and more ardent and set me on fire. I didn't know if you had finally recognised me at last; or did you desire me afresh as someone else, as a stranger? The blood rushed to my cheeks; I answered my friends absent-mindedly. It must have been obvious to you how your gaze disturbed me. With an inconspicuous movement of your head that my friends wouldn't notice, you signalled to me to come out to the entrance hall for a moment. Then you paid the bill ostentatiously, took leave of your friends and departed; but not before you again gave a sign you would wait for me outside. I trembled as if I were cold, or in a fever. I couldn't speak, I couldn't control my quickened pulse. It so happened that two Negroes began at that moment an unusual new dance, clattering their heels and uttering shrill cries. Everyone turned to look at them and I took advantage of it. I stood up, told my friends I'd be back soon and went out to you.

'There you stood in the entrance hall, in front of the cloak-room, waiting for me. Your face lit up as I arrived. You hurried towards me with a smile. I saw immediately that you didn't recognise me, neither the child of long ago nor the young girl. Once again you approached me as a new, unknown person. "Have you an hour to spare for me too?" you asked me confidentially. I felt from the certainty of your manner you took me for one of those women who could be bought for an evening.

"Yes," I said, agreeing in the same tremulous and yet matter-of-course affirmative way as the young girl of more than a decade before in that darkened street.

"When could we meet, then?" you asked.

"Whenever you like," I replied – I was shameless where you were concerned. You looked at me a little surprised, with the same suspicious curiosity as on the earlier occasion when the promptness of my consent had astonished you.

"What about now?" you asked, a little hesitantly.

"Yes," I said, "all right."

'I was about to go to the cloakroom to fetch my coat when it struck me that my friend had the ticket for both our coats, which had been handed in together. It wasn't possible to go back and ask him for it without a proper excuse. On the other hand, I had no wish to sacrifice the hour with you that I had longed for for years. So I didn't hesitate for a second: I merely put my shawl over my evening dress and went out into the damp, misty night, without troubling about my coat, without considering the kind, well-meaning man who had been keeping me. I had made him look a ridiculous fool in front of his friends. After two years, his mistress ran off the first time a stranger whistled. Oh, I knew in my heart exactly how base, how ungrateful I was; what an infamy I was committing towards an honourable friend. I felt my behaviour was absurd and in my madness I had mortally offended a good man for ever. I felt I had torn my life in two – but what was friendship to me, what was my existence compared with my impatience to feel your lips on mine once again; to hear your words softly whispered in my ear. That's how much I loved you, I can tell you now, now everything is past and done with. And I believe if you were to call me from my deathbed I would suddenly find the strength to get up and go with you.

'There was a taxi at the door and we drove to your home. I heard your voice again, felt you amorously near me and was as dazzled, as childishly overjoyed, as overwhelmed as before. How I climbed those stairs again after more than ten years – no, no, I can't describe it. At that instant I felt everything twice over, the past and the present; and I was always conscious only of you. Little had changed in your room. There were a few more pictures and more books, here and there different furniture, but everything seemed really familiar. The vase with the roses in it stood on the writing-table — my roses I had sent you the day before on your birthday as a memento of a woman you didn't remember, didn't recognise even now, although she was beside you, holding hands with you and exchanging kisses. I was gratified, however, to see you had looked after the flowers. In that way you had a trace of my life, a breath of my love around you.

'You took me in your arms. Once again I spent a whole heavenly night with you. But you didn't even recognise my naked body. Overjoyed, I accepted your experienced caresses and saw that your passion made no distinction between a loved one and a whore; that you gave yourself wholly to your desire with all the unthinking, extravagant intensity of your being. You were so tender and gentle with me, the chance dance-hall encounter, so refined and so sincerely respectful, and at the same time so passionate in enjoying the woman. Dizzy from the old happiness, I sensed again the unique duality of your nature, the conscious, intellectual passion and the sensual, which had already enslaved me as a child. I have never known a man make love with such complete surrender to the moment, such a radiant outpouring of his deepest emotion — only to efface the memory in everlasting, almost inhuman forgetfulness. But I also forgot myself. Who was I, then, lying in the darkness beside you? Was I the eager child of days gone by; was I the mother of your child; was I the unknown woman? Oh, it was all so familiar; it had all been gone through before. Yet everything was ecstatically new that passionate night. And I prayed it would never end.

'But morning came. We got up late and you invited me to have breakfast with you. We chatted together and drank the tea which an unseen servant's hand had discreetly set out in the dining-room. Again you spoke with the entirely frank, cordial confidence natural to you. Again you asked no indiscreet questions, and showed no curiosity about what kind of person I was. You didn't ask my name, or where I lived. Once again I was only an affair for you, anonymous, an hour of passion that dissolves without trace in the haze of forgetfulness. You told me you now intended to go on a long journey – for two or three months to North Africa. I trembled in the midst of my happiness, for the words were already hammering in my ears: it's all over, all over and forgotten! I wanted to fall at your feet and cry out, "Take me with you, recognise me at last, finally, in the end, after so many years!" But I was still so shy, so cowardly, so like a slave, so weak in your presence. All I could say was, "I'm sorry."

'You looked at me with a smile. "Are you really sorry?"

'A sudden anger seized me. I stood up and looked at you, long and hard. Then I said, "The man I loved was always going away too." I looked at you straight between the eyes. "Now, now, he'll recognise me!" My whole being urged you, trembling.

'But you smiled at me and said by way of consolation, "But we always come back."

"Yes," I replied, "You come back. But by then you've forgotten."

'There must have been something unusual, something vehement in the way I spoke. For you stood up then, too, and looked at me in surprise and very affectionately. You put your arm round my shoulders. "One doesn't forget what is good. I shan't forget you," you said, and as you said it you looked at me searchingly, as if you wanted to imprint my image on your mind. And as I felt your penetrating look, searching, examining, taking in the whole of me, I believed at last, finally, the spell of blindness was broken. "He will recognise me, he will recognise me!" My whole soul trembled at the thought.

'But you didn't recognise me. No, you didn't. Never had I been more of a stranger to you than I was at that moment, for otherwise – otherwise you could never have done what you did a few minutes later. You had kissed me, kissed me again passionately. My hair was disarranged and I had to put it right. And as I stood in front of the mirror I saw reflected in it – and I thought I would faint with shame and horror – I saw you push some large banknotes discreetly into my muff. I don't know how I managed to stop myself, then, from crying out, from slapping your face – I who had loved you since childhood and was the mother of your child – you were paying me for the night! To you I was a tart from the Tabarin, nothing more. You paid me, paid me! It wasn't enough that you had forgotten me. Now I had to be humiliated.

'I gathered up my belongings quickly. I wanted to leave at once. The pain was too great. I snatched up my hat. It was on the writing-table beside the vase with the white roses, my roses. Then I was seized with an utterly irresistible urge: I would try once more to make you remember. "Would you give me one of your white roses?"

"With pleasure," you said, immediately picking one out.

"But perhaps a woman gave them to you, a woman who loves you?" I said.

"Possibly," you answered. "I don't know. Someone gave them to me but I don't know who it was. That's why I like them so much."

'I looked at you. "Perhaps they're also from someone you've forgotten!"

'You looked astonished. I gazed at you fixedly. My expression begged you: "Recognise me, recognise me at last!" But your eyes smiled in a friendly way and had no recognition in them. You kissed me again. But you didn't recognise me.

'I hurried to the door for I was aware of the tears welling up in my eyes and I didn't want you to see them. I went out in such haste that I almost collided with your manservant, John, in the hall. Speedily and discreetly he stepped aside, opened the front door to let me out, and then — are you listening? — in that one, single second, as I looked at him, with tears streaming from my eyes, looked at the now elderly man, a light of recognition suddenly came into his eyes. In that one instant, do you hear me? In that one instant the old man knew who I was. He hadn't seen me since I was a child. I could have fallen on my knees before him and kissed his hands for that recognition. But I just quickly pulled from my muff the money you had scourged me with, and slipped in into his hands. He trembled and looked at me in alarm — at that moment he perhaps understood more about me than you did in your whole life. Everyone, everyone indulged me, everyone was good to me — only you, you alone forgot me. Only you, you alone, never recognised me!

. . .

'My child is dead, our child – now I have no one else in the world to love but you. But who are you to me, you who never, ever recognise me, who pass over me as though you were crossing a stream, and tread on me as though I were a stone? You go on and on and leave me to wait for ever. Once I thought I could hold on to you, ever elusive as you are, in the child. But he was your child. Overnight he has cruelly gone from me, on a journey; he has forgotten me and will never come back. I am alone again, more alone than ever. I have nothing, nothing of yours – no child any more, no word, no written line, no mementoes. And if anyone were to mention my name, it wouldn't mean anything to you. Why shouldn't I gladly die, since I am dead to you? Why not move on, since you are gone from me? No, darling, I am not reproaching you. I don't want to toss my misery into your cheerful home. Don't be afraid that I'll ever embarrass you again. Forgive me, but I must pour my soul out to you at this hour, when the child lies there dead and forlorn. I must speak to you just this once – then I'll go back silently into my obscurity, as I have always been silent where you are concerned. But you won't hear this cry as long as I am alive – you'll receive this testament from me only when I'm dead – from one who loved you more than anyone else and whom you didn't recognise; from one who always waited for you but for whom you never sent. Perhaps, perhaps you will call me then, and for the first time I shall be unfaithful to you; I shan't hear you any more, from the dead. I leave you no picture and no token, as you left nothing to me. You'll never recognise me, never. It was my fate in life; it will also be my fate in death. I won't send for you in my last hour. I am going without your knowing my name or what I look like. It will be easy for me to die since you won't feel it from afar. I couldn't die if my death were to cause you pain.

'I can't go on writing any longer. My head is so heavy ... my limbs ache, I'm feverish. I think I must lie down now. Perhaps it will soon be over; perhaps fate will be kind to me for once and I won't have to see them take the child away ... I can't write any more. Farewell, darling. Farewell. Thank you. It was good as it was, in spite of everything. I'll be grateful to you until my last breath. I'm all right: I've told you everything, you know now, no, you can only guess, how much I loved you. You have no encumbrance from that love. I won't fail you — that comforts me. Nothing will be changed in your splendid, pleasant life. My death will not affect you ... that comforts me, my darling.

'But who ... who will send you white roses now on your birthday? Oh, the vase will be empty, the little breath, the tiny trace of my life that once a year wafted around you will also be blown away! Darling, listen, I ask you — it's my first and last request to you — do it for my sake. Every birthday — it's a day after all when everyone thinks of himself — buy some roses and put them in the vase. Do it, darling, do it, as others have a mass said once a year in memory of a dead loved one. But I don't believe in God any more and don't want a mass. I believe only in you, I love you, and want to go on living only in you ... Oh, only one day in the year, as I lived near you ... completely, totally silent. I ask you to do it, darling. It's my first request and the last. Thank you ... I love you, I love you. Farewell.'

His hands were shaking as he put the letter down. Then he meditated for a long time. Some confused recollection of a child next door, of a young girl, a woman in the nightclub, came to the surface, but it was a dim and muddled memory, like a stone sparkling and flickering without definition at the bottom of a running stream. Shadows flitted to and fro, yet no picture formed. He felt recollections of emotion, but still he didn't remember. It seemed to him that he had dreamt about all these figures, dreamt often and deeply, but even so only dreamt.

His glance fell on the blue vase in front of him on the writing-table. It was empty; the first time for years it had been empty on his birthday. He gave a start: it seemed to him as if a door had been flung open suddenly by an invisible hand, and a cold current of air from another world flowed into his peaceful room. He became conscious of a death and conscious of undying love. Something struck a chord in his innermost soul, and he strove ardently to reach out in spirit towards the unseen presence, as though he were hearing distant music.

MORE ABOUT PENGUINS, PELICANS AND PUFFINS

For further information about books available from Penguins please write to Dept EP, Penguin Books Ltd, Harmondsworth, Middlesex UB7 ODA.

In the U.S.A.: For a complete list of books available from Penguins in the United States write to Dept DG, Penguin Books, 299 Murray Hill Parkway, East Rutherford, New Jersey 07073.

In Canada: For a complete list of books available from Penguins in Canada write to Penguin Books Canada Ltd, 2801 John Street, Markham, Ontario L3R 1B4.

In Australia: For a complete list of books available from Penguins in Australia write to the Marketing Department, Penguin Books Australia Ltd, P.O. Box 257, Ringwood, Victoria 3134.

In New Zealand: For a complete list of books available from Penguins in New Zealand write to the Marketing Department, Penguin Books (N.Z.) Ltd, P.O. Box 4019, Auckland 10.

In India: For a complete list of books available from Penguins in India write to Penguin Overseas Ltd, 706 Eros Apartments, 56 Nehru Place, New Delhi 110019.

LOTTE IN WEIMAR
Thomas Mann

Forty-four years after their youthful association, Lotte Kestner, real-life heroine of Goethe's famous novel *The Sorrows of Werther*, makes a pilgrimage to Weimar to see Goethe.

To her surprise, Lotte is greeted as a celebrity. And, as she talks to Goethe's friends and his son, Goethe emerges intellectually as lively as ever, revising *Faust*, writing poetry, managing the theatre, theorizing on art, colour, geology, racism ... even arranging the Prince's rout.

The little provincial court of Weimar – a post-Waterloo Athens, agog with gossip and cerebral activity – is brilliantly re-created. But *Lotte in Weimar* is memorable, above all, for Mann's masterly portrayal of a creative genius, polymath and politician, and his influence on his contemporaries.

BERLIN ALEXANDERPLATZ
Alfred Döblin

Berlin Alexanderplatz was part of the heady flowering of Weimar culture.

In it Alfred Döblin described the grimy street life of Berlin in the last years of the republic, when the Nazi gangs were growling in the background and poverty stalked the streets.

'*Berlin Alexanderplatz*, the parodic, picaresque tale of an ex-murderer's progress through underworld Berlin, surviving disaster after disaster to achieve a kind of exhausted rebirth at the end, was much influenced by *Ulysses* ... it is a violent, funny book, with an enormous, almost freakish range' – Michael Ratcliffe in *The Times*

'*Alexanderplatz* is one of the great experimental fictions of the first half of our century, the German equivalent of *Ulysses* and Dos Passos' *U.S.A.*' – *Time Out*

MAN OF STRAW
Heinrich Mann

'Each of us is as nothing, but massed in ranks as Neo-Teutons ... we taper up like a pyramid to a point at the top where Power itself stands, graven and dazzling ...'

First published in 1918, *Man of Straw* is a sharp indictment of the Wilhelmine regime, and a chilling warning against the joint elevation of militarism and commercial values. The 'man of straw' is Diederich Hessling, embodiment of the corrupt society in which he moves; his brutish progression through life forms the central theme of the book.

Heinrich Mann (brother of Thomas) was imprisoned for his radical and outspoken views, and spent a long exile from the country at which he aimed his bitter satire. Yet his vision has a universal clarity which, with hindsight, seems little short of miraculous for its period, and the political content of his writings is forged from a biting wit and a poignant awareness of what elements constitute the worst excesses of man.

THE RADETZKY MARCH
Joseph Roth

Strauss's Radetzky March, signature tune of one of Europe's most powerful regimes, presides over Joseph Roth's account of three generations of the Trotta family in the years preceding the Austro-Hungarian collapse in 1918.

Grandfather, son and grandson are equally dependent on the empire: the first for his ennoblement; the second for the civil virtues that make him a meticulous servant of an administration whose failure he can neither comprehend nor survive; the third for the family standards of conduct to which he cannot attain but by which he is too enfeebled to rebel.

Published when he was prominent in the émigré intellectual opposition to the Nazis, with their new breed of expansionism, *The Radetzky March* helps to place Joseph Roth among this century's greatest German-speaking writers.

What others have said about
The Drowned World:

"We have something without precedent . . . a novel by a science fiction author that can be judged by the highest standards . . . Mr. Ballard may turn out to be the most imaginative of Wells' successors."

—*Kingsley Amis*

"A serious writer, almost a visionary, with much to tell us about the hell of the human predicament."

—*The Guardian*

"Ballard is the kind of author whose work generally proves addictive to the sympathetic reader, for his is indeed a unique voice."

—David Pringle, *Science Fiction: The 100 Best Novels*

The Drowned World

J. G. Ballard was born in Shanghai, China, of English parents in 1930, and lived there until he was fifteen. After the attack on Pearl Harbor he was interned by the Japanese in a civilian prison camp. He moved to England in 1946, and after leaving school he read medicine at King's College, Cambridge. Thereafter he worked variously as a copy-writer, a Covent Garden porter and, after a spell in Canada with the RAF, an editor of technical and scientific journals. His first short story appeared in 1956, and in 1962 he published *The Drowned World*, a brilliant first novel that won him instant critical acclaim and had a dramatic effect on the state of science fiction. His other books include *The Terminal Beach, The Crystal World, Vermilion Sands* and *The Unlimited Dream Company*.

Ballard has been held up as the originator of the so-called 'New Wave' that challenged the American science fiction of the 1950s, but his work can be appreciated by a wide readership as literature of the highest order. He has been hailed by Kingsley Amis as 'one of the brightest stars in post-war fiction'.

J.G. BALLARD

T·H·E

DROWNED WORLD

Carroll & Graf Publishers, Inc.
New York

Reprinted by arrangement with the Robin Straus Agency, Inc.

First Carroll & Graf edition 1987
Second printing 1989

Carroll & Graf Publishers, Inc.
260 Fifth Avenue
New York, NY 10001

ISBN: 0-88184-324-5

Manufactured in the United States of America

CONTENTS

CHAPTER ONE

ON THE BEACH AT THE RITZ

Soon it would be too hot. Looking out from the hotel balcony shortly after eight o'clock, Kerans watched the sun rise behind the dense groves of giant gymnosperms crowding over the roofs of the abandoned department stores four hundred yards away on the east side of the lagoon. Even through the massive olive-green fronds the relentless power of the sun was plainly tangible. The blunt refracted rays drummed against his bare chest and shoulders, drawing out the first sweat, and he put on a pair of heavy sunglasses to protect his eyes. The solar disc was no longer a well-defined sphere, but a wide expanding ellipse that fanned out across the eastern horizon like a colossal fire-ball, its reflection turning the dead leaden surface of the lagoon into a brilliant copper shield. By noon, less than four hours away, the water would seem to burn.

Usually Kerans woke at five, and reached the biological testing station in time to do at least four or five hours' work before the heat became intolerable, but this morning he found himself reluctant to leave the cool, air-curtained haven of the hotel suite. He had spent a couple of hours over breakfast alone, and then completed a six-page entry in his diary, deliberately delaying his departure until Colonel Riggs passed the hotel in his patrol boat, knowing that by then it would be too late to go to the station. The Colonel was always eager for an hour of conversation, particularly when sustained by a few rounds of aperitif, and it would be at least eleven-thirty before he left, his thoughts solely upon lunch at the base.

For some reason, however, Riggs had been delayed. Presumably he was carrying out a longer sweep than usual of the adjacent lagoons, or perhaps was waiting for Kerans to arrive at the testing station. For a moment Kerans wondered whether to try to reach him on the radio transmitter installed by the signals unit in the lounge, but the console was buried under a pile of books, its battery flat. The corporal in charge of the radio station at the base had protested to Riggs when his cheerful morning round-up of old pop songs and local news—an attack by two iguanas on the helicopter the previous night, the latest temperature and humidity readings—had been cut off abruptly half-way through the first instalment. But Riggs recognised Kerans' unconscious attempt to sever his links with the base—the careful haphazardness of the pyramid of books hiding the set contrasted too obviously with Kerans' otherwise meticulous neatness—and tolerantly accepted his need to isolate himself.

Leaning on the balcony rail, the slack water ten storeys below reflecting his thin angular shoulders and gaunt profile, Kerans watched one of the countless thermal storms rip through a clump of huge horse-tails lining the creek which led out of the lagoon. Trapped by the surrounding buildings and the inversion layers a hundred feet above the water, pockets of air would heat rapidly, then explode upwards like escaping balloons, leaving behind them a sudden detonating vacuum. For a few seconds the steam clouds hanging over the creek dispersed, and a vicious miniature tornado lashed across the 60-feet-high plants, toppling them like matchsticks. Then, as abruptly, the storm vanished and the great columnar trunks subsided among one another in the water like sluggish alligators.

Rationalising, Kerans told himself that he had been wise to remain in the hotel—the storms were erupting more and more frequently as the temperature rose—but he knew that his real motive was his acceptance that little now remained to be done. The biological mapping had become a pointless game, the new flora following exactly the emergent lines anticipated twenty years earlier, and he was sure that no

8

one at Camp Byrd in Northern Greenland bothered to file his reports, let alone read them.

In fact, old Dr. Bodkin, Kerans' assistant at the station, had slyly prepared what purported to be an eye-witness description by one of Colonel Riggs' sergeants of a large sail-backed lizard with a gigantic dorsal fin which had been seen cruising across one of the lagoons, in all respects indistinguishable from the Pelycosaur, an early Pennsylvanian reptile. Had the report been taken at its face value— heralding the momentous return of the age of the great reptiles—an army of ecologists would have descended on them immediately, backed by a tactical atomic weapons unit and orders to proceed south at a steady twenty knots. But apart from the routine acknowledgement signal nothing had been heard. Perhaps the specialists at Camp Byrd were too tired even to laugh.

At the end of the month Colonel Riggs and his small holding unit would complete their survey of the city (had it once been Berlin, Paris or London?, Kerans asked himself) and set off northward, towing the testing station with them. Kerans found it difficult to believe that he would ever leave the penthouse suite where he had lived for the past six months. The Ritz's reputation, he gladly agreed, was richly deserved—the bathroom, for example, with its black marble basins and gold-plated taps and mirrors, was like the side-chapel of a cathedral. In a curious way it satisfied him to think that he was the last guest who would stay at the hotel, identifying what he realised was a concluding phase of his own life—the northward odyssey through the drowned cities in the south, soon to end with their return to Camp Byrd and its bracing disciplines—and this farewell sunset of the hotel's long splendid history.

He had commandeered the Ritz the day after their arrival, eager to exchange his cramped cabin among the laboratory benches at the testing station for the huge, high-ceilinged state-rooms of the deserted hotel. Already he accepted the lavish brocaded furniture and the bronze art

9

nouveau statuary in the corridor niches as a natural background to his existence, savouring the subtle atmosphere of melancholy that surrounded these last vestiges of a level of civilisation now virtually vanished forever. Too many of the other buildings around the lagoon had long since slipped and slid away below the silt, revealing their gimcrack origins, and the Ritz now stood in splendid isolation on the west shore, even the rich blue moulds sprouting from the carpets in the dark corridors adding to its 19th-century dignity.

The suite had originally been designed for a Milanese financier, and was lavishly furnished and engineered. The heat curtains were still perfectly sealed, although the first six storeys of the hotel were below water-level and the load walls were beginning to crack, and the 250-amp. air-conditioning unit had worked without a halt. Although it had been unoccupied for ten years little dust had collected over the mantelpieces and gilt end-tables, and the triptych of photographic portraits on the crocodile-skin desk—financier, financier and sleek well-fed family, financier and even sleeker fifty-storey office block—revealed scarcely a blemish. Luckily for Kerans, his predecessor had left in a hurry, and the cupboards and wardrobes were packed with treasure, ivory-handled squash rackets and hand-printed dressing gowns, the cocktail bar stocked with an ample supply of what were now vintage whiskies and brandies.

A giant Anopheles mosquito, the size of a dragon-fly, spat through the air past his face, then dived down towards the floating jetty where Kerans' catamaran was moored. The sun was still hidden behind the vegetation on the eastern side of the lagoon, but the mounting heat was bringing the huge predatory insects out of their lairs all over the moss-covered surface of the hotel. Kerans was reluctant to leave the balcony and retreat behind the wire-mesh enclosure. In the early morning light a strange mournful beauty hung over the lagoon; the sombre green-black fronds of the gymnosperms, intruders from the Triassic past, and the half-submerged white-faced buildings of the 20th century still reflected together in the dark mirror of the water, the two interlocking worlds apparently suspended at some junction in time, the illusion momentarily broken when a giant water-spider cleft the oily surface a hundred yards away.

In the distance, somewhere beyond the drowned bulk of a large Gothic building half a mile to the south, a diesel engine coughed and surged. Kerans left the balcony, closing the wire door behind him, and went into the bathroom to shave. Water had long ceased to flow through the taps, but Kerans maintained a reservoir in the plunge bath, carefully purified in a home-made still on the roof and piped in through the window.

Although he was only forty, Kerans' beard had been turned white by the radio-fluorine in the water, but his bleached crew-cut hair and deep amber tan made him appear at least ten years younger. A chronic lack of appetite, and the new malarias, had shrunk the dry leathery skin under his cheekbones, emphasising the ascetic cast of his face. As he shaved he examined his features critically, feeling the narrowing planes with his fingers, kneading the altered musculature which was slowly transforming its contours and revealing a personality that had remained latent during his previous adult life. Despite his introspective manner, he now seemed more relaxed and equable than he could remember, his cool blue eyes surveying himself with ironic detachment. The slightly self-conscious absorption in his own world, with its private rituals and observances, had passed. If he kept himself aloof from Riggs and his men this was simply a matter of convenience rather than of misanthropy.

On the way out he picked a monographed cream silk shirt from the stack left in the wardrobe by the financier, and slipped into a pair of neatly pressed slacks with a Zürich label. Sealing the double doors behind him—the suite was effectively a glass box inside the outer brick walls—he made his way down the staircase.

He reached the landing stage as Colonel Riggs' cutter, a converted landing craft, pulled in against the catamaran. Riggs stood in the bows, a trim dapper figure, one booted foot up on the ramp, surveying the winding creeks and hanging jungles like an old-time African explorer.

"Good morning, Robert," he greeted Kerans, jumping down on to the swaying platform of fifty-gallon drums lashed inside a wooden frame. "Glad you're still here. I've got a job on my hands you can help me with. Can you take the day off from the station?"

Kerans helped him on to the concrete balcony that had once jutted from a seventh-floor suite. "Of course, Colonel. As a matter of fact, I have already."

Technically Riggs had overall authority for the testing station and Kerans should have asked his permission, but the relationship between the two men was without ceremony. They had worked together for over three years, as the testing station and its military escort moved slowly northward through the European lagoons, and Riggs was content to let Kerans and Bodkin get on with their work in their own fashion, sufficiently busy himself with the jobs of mapping the shifting keys and harbours and evacuating the last inhabitants. In the latter task he often needed Kerans' help, for most of the people still living on in the sinking cities were either psychopaths or suffering from malnutrition and radiation sickness.

In addition to running the testing station, Kerans served as the unit's medical officer. Many of the people they came across required immediate hospitalisation before being flown out in the helicopter to one of the large tank-landing craft ferrying refugees up to Camp Byrd. Injured military personnel marooned on an office block in a deserted swamp, dying recluses unable to separate their own identities from the cities where they had spent their lives, disheartened freebooters who had stayed behind to dive for loot—all these Riggs good humouredly but firmly helped back to safety, Kerans ready at his elbow to administer an analgesic or tranquilliser. Despite his brisk military front, Kerans found the Colonel intelligent and sympathetic, and with a concealed reserve of droll humour. Sometimes he wondered whether to test this by telling the Colonel about Bodkin's Pelycosaur, but on the whole decided against it.

The sergeant concerned in the hoax, a dour conscientious Scotsman called Macready, had climbed up on to the wire cage that enclosed the deck of the cutter and was carefully sweeping away the heavy fronds and vines strewn across it. None of the three other men tried to help him; under their heavy tans their faces looked pinched and drawn, and they sat inertly in a row against a bulkhead. The continuous heat and the massive daily doses of antibiotics drained all energy from them.

As the sun rose over the lagoon, driving clouds of steam into the great golden pall, Kerans felt the terrible stench of the water-line, the sweet compacted smells of dead vegetation and rotting animal carcases. Huge flies spun by, bouncing off the wire cage of the cutter, and giant bats raced across the heating water towards their eyries in the ruined buildings. Beautiful and serene from his balcony a few minutes earlier, Kerans realised that the lagoon was nothing more than a garbage-filled swamp.

"Let's go up on to the deck," he suggested to Riggs, lowering his voice so that the others would not hear. "I'll buy you a drink."

"Good man. I'm glad to see you've really caught on to the grand manner." Riggs shouted at Macready: "Sergeant, I'm going up to see if I can get the Doctor's distillation unit to work." He winked at Kerans as Macready acknowledged this with a sceptical nod, but the subterfuge was harmless. Most of the men carried hip-flasks, and once they secured the sergeant's grudging approval they would bring them out and settle down placidly until the Colonel returned.

Kerans climbed over the window-sill into the bedroom overlooking the jetty. "What's your problem, Colonel?"

"It's not *my* problem. If anything, in fact, it's yours."

They trudged up the staircase, Riggs slapping with his baton at the vines entwined around the rail "Haven't you got the elevator working yet? I always thought this place was overrated." However, he smiled appreciatively when they stepped into the clear ivory-cool air of the penthouse, and

13

sat down thankfully in one of the gilt-legged Louis XV armchairs. "Well, this is very gracious. You know, Robert, I think you have a natural talent for beachcombing. I may move in here with you. Any vacancies?"

Kerans shook his head, pressing a tab in the wall and w-iting as the cocktail bar disgorged itself from a fake bookcase. "Try the Hilton. The service is better."

The reply was jocular, but much as he liked Riggs he preferred to see as little of him as possible. At present they were separated by the intervening lagoons, and the constant clatter of the galley and armoury at the base were safely muffled by the jungle. He had known each of the twenty men in the unit for at least a couple of years, but with the exception of Riggs and Sergeant Macready, and a few terse grunts and questions in the sick-bay, he had spoken to none of them for six months. Even his contacts with Bodkin he kept to a minimum. By mutual consent the two biologists had dispensed with the usual pleasantries and small-talk that had sustained them for the first two years during their sessions of cataloguing and slide preparation at the laboratory.

This growing isolation and self-containment, exhibited by the other members of the unit and from which only the buoyant Riggs seemed immune, reminded Kerans of the slackening metabolism and biological withdrawal of all animal forms about to undergo a major metamorphosis. Sometimes he wondered what zone of transit he himself was entering, sure that his own withdrawal was symptomatic not of a dormant schizophrenia, but of a careful preparation for a radically new environment, with its own internal landscape and logic, where old categories of thought would merely be an encumbrance.

He handed a large Scotch to Riggs, then took his own over to the desk, self-consciously removed some of the books stacked over the radio console.

"Ever try listening to that thing?" Riggs asked, playfully introducing a hint of reproof into his voice.

14

"Never," Kerans said. "Is there any point? We know all the news for the next three million years."

"You don't. Really, you should switch it on just now and then. Hear all sorts of interesting things." He put his drink down and sat forward. "For example, this morning you would have heard that exactly three days from now we're packing up and leaving for good." He nodded when Kerans looked around in surprise. "Came through last night from Byrd. Apparently the water-level is still rising; all the work we've done has been a total waste—as I've always maintained, incidentally. The American and Russian units are being recalled as well. Temperatures at the Equator are up to one hundred and eighty degrees now, going up steadily, and the rain belts are continuous as high as the 20th parallel. There's more silt too——"

He broke off, watching Kerans speculatively. "What's the matter? Aren't you relieved to be going?"

"Of course," Kerans said automatically. He was holding an empty glass, and walked across the room, intending to put it on the bar, instead found himself absent-mindedly touching the clock over the mantelpiece. He seemed to be searching the room for something. "Three days, you said?"

"What do you want—three million?" Riggs grinned broadly. "Robert, I think you secretly want to stay behind."

Kerans reached the bar and filled his glass, collecting himself. He had only managed to survive the monotony and boredom of the previous year by deliberately suspending himself outside the normal world of time and space, and the abrupt return to earth had momentarily disconcerted him. In addition, he knew, there were other motives and responsibilities.

"Don't be absurd," he replied easily. "I simply hadn't realised that we might withdraw at such short notice. Naturally I'm glad to be going. Though I admit I have enjoyed being here." He gestured at the suite around them. "Perhaps it appeals to my *fin de siècle* temperament. Up at Camp Byrd I'll be living in half a mess-tin. The nearest I'll

15

ever get to this sort of thing will be 'Bouncing with Beethoven' on the local radio show."

Riggs roared at this display of disgruntled humour, then stood up, buttoning his tunic. "Robert, you're a strange one."

Kerans finished his drink abruptly. "Look, Colonel, I don't think I'll be able to help you this morning after all. Something rather urgent has come up." He noticed Riggs nodding slowly. "Oh, I see. That was your problem. *My* problem."

"Right. I saw her last night, and again this morning after the news came through. You'll have to convince her, Robert. At present she refuses point-blank to go. She doesn't realise that this time is the end, that there'll be no more holding units. She may be able to hang on for another six months, but next March, when the rain belts reach here, we won't even be able to get a helicopter in. Anyway, by then no one will care. I told her that and she just walked away."

Kerans smiled bleakly, visualising the familiar swirl of hip and haughty stride. "Beatrice can be difficult sometimes," he temporised, hoping that she hadn't offended Riggs. It would probably take more than three days to change her mind and he wanted to be sure that the Colonel would still be waiting. "She's a complex person, lives on many levels. Until they all synchronise she can behave as if she's insane."

They left the suite, Kerans sealing the air-locks and setting the thermostat alarms so that the air would be a pleasant eighty degrees in two hours' time. They made their way down to the landing-stage, Riggs pausing occasionally to savour the cool gilded air in one of the public drawing-rooms overlooking the lagoon, hissing at the snakes which glided softly among the damp, fungus-covered settees. They stepped into the cutter and Macready slammed the door of the cage behind them.

Five minutes later, the catamaran gliding and swirling behind the cutter, they set off from the hotel across the lagoon. Golden waves glimmered up into the boiling air,

16

and the ring of massive plants around them seemed to dance in the heat gradients like a voodoo jungle.

Riggs peered sombrely through the cage. "Thank God for that signal from Byrd. We should have got out years ago. All this detailed mapping of harbours for use in some hypothetical future is absurd. Even if the solar flares subside it will be ten years before there's any serious attempt to reoccupy these cities. By then most of the bigger buildings will have been smothered under the silt. It'll take a couple of divisions to clear the jungle away from this lagoon alone. Bodkin was telling me this morning that already some of the canopies—of non-lignified plants, mark you—are over two hundred feet high. The whole place is nothing but a confounded zoo."

He took off his peaked cap and rubbed his forehead, then shouted across the mounting roar of the two outboard diesels: "If Beatrice stays here much longer she *will* be insane. By the way, that reminds me of another reason why we've got to get out." He glanced across at the tall lonely figure of Sergeant Macready at the tiller, staring fixedly at the breaking water, and at the pinched haunted faces of the other men. "Tell me, Doctor, how do you sleep these days?"

Puzzled, Kerans turned to look at the Colonel, wondering whether the question obliquely referred to his relationship with Beatrice Dahl. Riggs watched him with his bright intelligent eyes, baton flexed between his neat hands. "Very soundly," he replied carefully. "Never better. Why do you ask?"

But Riggs merely nodded and began to shout instructions at Macready.

CHAPTER TWO

THE COMING OF THE IGUANAS

Screeching like a dispossessed banshee, a large hammer-nosed bat soared straight out of one of the narrow inlets off the creek and swerved straight towards the cutter.

Its sonar confused by the labyrinth of giant webs spun across the inlet by the colonies of wolf spiders, it missed the wire hood above Kerans' head by only a few feet, and then sailed away along the line of submerged office blocks, gliding in and out of the huge sail-like fronds of the fern-trees sprouting from their roofs. Suddenly, as it passed one of the projecting cornices, a motionless stone-headed creature snapped out and plucked the bat from the air. There was a brief piercing squawk and Kerans caught a glimpse of the crushed wings clamped in the lizard's jaws. Then the reptile shrank back invisibly among the foliage.

All the way down the creek, perched in the windows of the office blocks and department stores, the iguanas watched them go past, their hard frozen heads jerking stiffly. They launched themselves into the wake of the cutter, snapping at the insects dislodged from the air-weed and rotting logs, then swam through the windows and clambered up the staircases to their former vantage-points, piled three deep across each other. Without the reptiles, the lagoons and the creeks of office blocks half-submerged in the immense heat would have had a strange dream-like beauty, but the iguanas and basilisks brought the fantasy down to earth. As their seats in the one-time boardrooms indicated, the reptiles had taken over the city. Once again they were the dominant form of life.

Looking up at the ancient impassive faces, Kerans could understand the curious fear they roused, re-kindling archaic memories of the terrifying jungles of the Paleocene, when the reptiles had gone down before the emergent mammals, and sense the implacable hatred one zoological class feels towards another that usurps it.

At the end of the creek they entered the next lagoon, a wide circle of dark green water almost half a mile in diameter. A lane of red plastic buoys marked a channel towards an opening on the far side. The cutter had a draught of little more than a foot, and as they moved along through the flat water, the sun slanting down behind them opening up the submerged depths, they could see the clear outlines of five- and six-storey buildings looming like giant ghosts, here and there a moss-covered roof breaking the surface as the swell rolled past it.

Sixty feet below the cutter a straight grey promenade stretched away between the buildings, the remains of some former thoroughfare, the rusting humped shells of cars still standing by the kerb. Many of the lagoons in the centre of the city were surrounded by an intact ring of buildings, and consequently little silt had entered them. Free of vegetation, apart from a few drifting clumps of Sargasso weed, the streets and shops had been preserved almost intact, like a reflection in a lake that has somehow lost its original.

The bulk of the city had long since vanished, and only the steel-supported buildings of the central commercial and financial areas had survived the encroaching flood waters. The brick houses and single-storey factories of the suburbs had disappeared completely below the drifting tides of silt. Where these broke surface giant forests reared up into the burning dull-green sky, smothering the former wheatfields of temperate Europe and North America. Impenetrable Mato Grossos sometimes three hundred feet high, they were a nightmare world of competing organic forms returning rapidly to their Paleozoic past, and the only avenues of transit for the United Nations military units were through the lagoon systems that had superimposed themselves on the former cities. But even these were now being clogged with silt and then submerged.

Kerans could remember the unending succession of green twilights that had settled behind them as he and Riggs moved slowly northward across Europe, leaving one city after another, the miasmic vegetation swamping the narrow canals and crowding from roof-top to roof-top.

Now they were to abandon yet another city. Despite the massive construction of the main commercial buildings, it consisted of little more than three principal lagoons, surrounded by a nexus of small lakes fifty yards in diameter and a network of narrow creeks and inlets which wound off, roughly following the original street-plan of the city, into the outlying jungle. Here and there they vanished altogether or expanded into the steaming sheets of open water that were the residues of the former oceans. In turn these gave way to the archipelagoes that coalesced to form the solid jungles of the southern massif.

The military base set up by Riggs and his platoon, which harboured the biological testing station, was in the most southerly of the three lagoons, sheltered by a number of the tallest buildings of the city, thirty-storey blocks in what had once been the down-town financial sector.

As they crossed the lagoon the yellow-striped drum of the floating base was on its sun-ward side, almost obscured in the reflected light, the rotating blades of the helicopter on its roof throwing brilliant lances across the water at them. Two hundred yards down shore was the smaller white-painted hull of the biological testing station, moored against a broad hump-backed building which had formerly been a concert hall.

Kerans gazed up at the rectangular cliffs, enough of the windows intact to remind him of the illustrations of sun-dazzled promenades at Nice, Rio and Miami he had read about as a child in the encyclopaedias at Camp Byrd. Curiously, though, despite the potent magic of the lagoon worlds and the drowned cities, he had never felt any interest in their contents, and never bothered to identify in which of the cities he was stationed.

Dr. Bodkin, twenty-five years his senior, had actually lived in several of them, both in Europe and America, and spent most of his spare time punting around the remoter water-ways, searching out former libraries and museums. Not that they contained anything other than his memories.

Perhaps it was this absence of personal memories that made Kerans indifferent to the spectacle of these sinking civilisations. He had been born and brought up entirely within what had once been known as the Arctic Circle—now a sub-tropical zone with an annual mean temperature of eighty-five degrees—and had come southward only on joining one of the ecological surveys in his early 30's. The vast swamps and jungles had been a fabulous laboratory, the submerged cities little more than elaborate pedestals.

Apart from a few older men such as Bodkin there was no-one who remembered living in them—and even during Bodkin's childhood the cities had been beleaguered citadels, hemmed in by enormous dykes and disintegrated by panic and despair, reluctant Venices to their marriage with the sea. Their charm and beauty lay precisely in their emptiness, in the strange junction of two extremes of nature, like a discarded crown overgrown by wild orchids.

The succession of gigantic geophysical upheavals which had transformed the Earth's climate had made their first impact some sixty or seventy years earlier. A series of violent and prolonged solar storms lasting several years caused by a sudden instability in the Sun had enlarged the Van Allen belts and diminished the Earth's gravitational hold upon the outer layers of the ionosphere. As these vanished into space, depleting the Earth's barrier against the full impact of solar radiation, temperatures began to climb steadily, the heated atmosphere expanding outwards into the ionosphere where the cycle was completed.

All over the world, mean temperatures rose by a few degrees each year. The majority of tropical areas rapidly became uninhabitable, entire populations migrating north or south from temperatures of a hundred and thirty and a hundred and forty degrees. Once-temperate areas became tropical, Europe and North America sweltering under continuous heat waves, temperatures rarely falling below a hundred degrees. Under the direction of the United Nations, the colonisation began of the Antarctic plateau and of the northern borders of the Canadian and Russian continents.

Over this initial period of twenty years a gradual adjustment of life took place to meet the altered climate. A

21

slackening of the previous tempo was inevitable, and there was little spare energy available to cut back the encroaching jungles of the equatorial region. Not only was the growth of all plant forms accelerated, but the higher levels of radio-activity increased the rate at which mutations occurred. The first freak botanical forms appeared, recalling the giant tree-ferns of the Carboniferous period, and there was a drastic upsurge of all lower plant and animal forms.

The arrival of these distant forbears was overlayed by the second major geophysical upheaval. The continued heating of the atmosphere had begun to melt the polar ice-caps. The entrained ice-seas of the Antarctic plateau broke and dissolved, tens of thousands of glaciers around the Arctic Circle, from Greenland and Northern Europe, Russia and North America, poured themselves into the sea, millions of acres of permafrost liquefied into gigantic rivers.

Here again the rise of global water-levels would have been little more than a few feet, but the huge discharging channels carried with them billions of tons of top-soil. Massive deltas formed at their mouths, extending the continental coastlines and damming up the oceans. Their effective spread shrank from two-thirds of the world's area to only slightly more than half.

Driving the submerged silt before them, the new seas completely altered the shape and contours of the continents. The Mediterranean contracted into a system of inland lakes, the British Isles was linked again with northern France. The Middle West of the United States, filled by the Mississippi as it drained the Rocky Mountains, became an enormous gulf opening into the Hudson Bay, while the Caribbean Sea was transformed into a desert of silt and salt flats. Europe became a system of giant lagoons, centred on the principal low-lying cities, inundated by the silt carried southwards by the expanding rivers.

During the next thirty years the pole-ward migration of populations continued. A few fortified cities defied the rising water-levels and the encroaching jungles, building elaborate sea-walls around their perimeters, but one by one these were breached. Only within the former Arctic and Antarctic Circles was life tolerable. The oblique incidence of the sun's rays provided a shield against the more powerful radiation. Cities on higher ground in mountainous areas nearer the Equator had been abandoned, despite their cooler temperatures, because of the diminished atmospheric protection.

It was this last factor which provided its own solution to the problem of re-settling the migrant populations of the new Earth. The steady decline in mammalian fertility, and the growing ascendancy of amphibian and reptile forms best adapted to an aquatic life in the lagoons and swamps, inverted the ecological balances, and by the time of Kerans' birth at Camp Byrd, a city of ten thousand in Northern Greenland, it was estimated that fewer than five million people were still living on the polar caps.

The birth of a child had become a comparative rarity, and only one marriage in ten yielded any offspring. As Kerans sometimes reminded himself, the genealogical tree of mankind was systematically pruning itself, apparently moving backwards in time, and a point might ultimately be reached where a second Adam and Eve found themselves alone in a new Eden.

Rigg noticed him smiling to himself at this conceit. "What's amusing you, Robert? Another of your obscure jokes? Don't try to explain it to me."

"I was just casting myself in a new rôle." Kerans looked out over the ramp at the office blocks sliding past twenty feet away, the wash from the cutter splashing through the open windows along the water-line. The sharp tang of wet lime contrasted freshly with the over-sweet odours of the vegetation. Macready had taken them into the shadow of the buildings and it was pleasantly cool behind the breaking spray.

Across the lagoon he could see the portly bare-chested figure of Dr. Bodkin on the starboard bridge of the testing station, the Paisley cummerbund around his waist and the green celluloid shade shielding his eyes making him look like a riverboat gambler on his morning off. He was plucking the orange-sized berries from the ferns overhanging the station and tossing them up at the chittering marmosets dangling from the branches above his head, egging them on with playful shouts and whistles. Fifty feet away, on a projecting cornice, a trio of iguanas watched with stony disapproval, whipping their tails slowly from side to side in a gesture of impatience.

Macready swung the tiller, and they pivoted in a fan of spray into the lee of a tall white-faced building which lifted a full twenty storeys out of the water. The roof of an adjacent smaller block served as a jetty, next to which was moored a rusty white-hulled power cruiser. The raked perspex windows of the driving cabin were cracked and stained, and the exhaust vents leaked a scaly oil on to the water.

As the cutter jockeyed in behind the power cruiser under Macready's expert hand, they clambered over to the wire door, jumped down on to the jetty and crossed a narrow metal gangway that led into the apartment block. The walls of the corridor were slick with moisture, huge patches of mould feeding on the plaster, but the elevator was still working, powered by an emergency diesel. They rose slowly towards the roof, and stepped out on to the upper level of the duplex, then walked down a service corridor to the outer deck.

Directly below them was the lower level, a small swimming pool with a covered patio, bright deck-chairs drawn up in the shade by the diving board. Yellow venetian blinds masked the windows around three sides of the pool, but through the vanes they could see the cool shadows in the interior lounge, the glint of cut-glass and silver on the occasional tables. In the dim light under the striped blue awning at the rear of the patio was a long chromium counter, as inviting as an air-conditioned bar seen from a dusty street, glasses and decanters reflected in a diamond-paned mirror. Everything in this private haven seemed clean and discreet, thousands of miles away from the fly-blown vegetation and tepid jungle water twenty storeys below.

Beyond the far end of the pool, screened by an ornamental balcony, was a wide, open view of the lagoon, the city emerging from the encroaching jungle, flat sheets of silver water expanding towards the green blur along the southern horizon. Massive silt banks lifted their backs through the surface, a light yellow fur along their spines marking the emergence of the first giant bamboo groves.

The helicopter rose from its platform on the roof of the base and arced upwards into the air towards them, the pilot swinging the tail as he changed direction, then roared overhead, two men in the open hatchway searching the rooftops with binoculars.

Beatrice Dahl lay back on one of the deck-chairs, her long oiled body gleaming in the shadows like a sleeping python. The pink-tipped fingers of one hand rested lightly on an ice-filled glass on a table beside her, while the other hand turned slowly through the pages of a magazine. Wide blue-black sunglasses hid her smooth sleek face, but Kerans noted the slightly sullen pout of her firm lower lip. Presumably Riggs had annoyed her, forcing her to accept the logic of his argument.

The Colonel paused at the rail, looking down at the beautiful supple body with ungrudging approval. Noticing him, Beatrice pulled off her sunglasses, then tightened the loose back-straps of her bikini under her arms. Her eyes glinted quietly.

"All right, you two, get on with it. I'm not a strip show."

Riggs chuckled and trotted down the white metal stairway, Kerans at his heels, wondering how he was going to persuade Beatrice to leave her private sanctuary.

"My dear Miss Dahl, you should be flattered that I keep coming to see you," Riggs told her, lifting back the awning and sitting down on one of the chairs. "Besides, as the military governor of this area"—here he winked playfully at Kerans—"I have certain responsibilities towards you. And vice versa."

Beatrice regarded him briefly with a jaundiced eye and reached out to turn up the volume of the radiogram behind her. "Oh God . . ." She muttered some further, less polite imprecation under her breath and looked up at Kerans. "And what about you, Robert? What brings you out so early in the day?"

Kerans shrugged, smiling at her amiably. "I missed you."

"Good boy. I thought perhaps that the *gauleiter* here had been trying to frighten you with his horror stories."

"Well, he has, as a matter of fact." Kerans took the magazine propped against Beatrice's knee and leafed through it idly. It was a forty-year-old issue of Paris *Vogue*, from its icy pages evidently kept somewhere in cold storage. He dropped it on the green-tiled floor. "Bea, it looks as if we'll all have to leave here in a couple of days' time. The Colonel and his men are pulling out for good. We can't very well stay on after he's gone."

"We?" she repeated dryly. "I didn't know there was any chance of your staying behind?"

Kerans glanced involuntarily at Riggs, who was watching him steadily. "There isn't," he said firmly. "You know what I mean. There'll be a lot to do in the next forty-eight hours. Try not to complicate things by making a last emotional stand."

Before the girl could cut back at Kerans, Riggs added smoothly: "The temperature is still going up, Miss Dahl, you won't find it easy to stand one hundred and thirty degrees when the fuel for your generator runs out. The big Equatorial rain belts are moving northward, and they'll be here in a couple of months. When they leave, and the cloud cover goes, the water in that pool—" he indicated the tank of steaming, insect-strewn fluid—" will damn' nearly boil. What with the Type X Anopheles, skin cancers and the iguanas shrieking all night down below, you'll get precious little sleep." Closing his eyes, he added pensively: "That is, assuming that you still want any."

At this last remark the girl's mouth fretted slightly. Kerans realised that the quiet ambiguity in Riggs' voice when he asked how the biologist slept had not been directed at his relationship with Beatrice.

The Colonel went on: "In addition, some of the human scavengers driven northward out of the Mediterranean lagoons won't be too easy to deal with."

Beatrice tossed her long black hair over one shoulder. "I'll keep the door locked, Colonel."

Irritated, Kerans snapped: "For God's sake, Beatrice, what are you trying to prove? These self-destructive impulses may be amusing to play with now, but when we've gone they won't be so funny. The Colonel's only trying to help you—he doesn't really give a hoot whether you stay behind or not."

Riggs let out a brief laugh. "Well, I wouldn't say that. But if the thought of my personal concern worries you so much you can just put it down to duty."

"That's interesting, Colonel. I've always understood that our duty was to stay on here as long as possible and make every sacrifice necessary to that end. Or at least"—here the familiar gleam of sharp humour crossed her eyes—"that was the reason my grandfather was given when the Government confiscated most of his property." She noticed Riggs peering over his shoulder at the bar. "What's the matter, Colonel? Looking for your punka-wallah? I'm not going to get you a drink, if that's what you're after. I think you men only come up here to booze."

Riggs stood up. "All right, Miss Dahl. I give in. I'll see you later, Doctor." He saluted Beatrice with a smile. "Some time tomorrow I'll send the cutter over to collect your gear, Miss Dahl."

When Riggs had gone Kerans lay back in his chair, watching the helicopter circle over the adjacent lagoon. Now and then it dived along the water's edge, the down-draught from its rotor blades beating through the flapping fronds of the fern-trees, driving the iguanas across the roof-tops. Beatrice brought a drink from the bar and sat down on the chair at his feet.

"I wish you wouldn't analyse me in front of that man, Robert." She handed him the drink and then leaned against his knees, resting her chin on one wrist. Usually she looked sleek and well-fed, but her expression today seemed tired and wistful.

"I'm sorry," Kerans apologised. "Perhaps I was really analysing myself. Riggs' ultimatum came as a bit of a surprise; I wasn't expecting to leave so soon."

"You are going to leave, then?"

Kerans paused. The automatic player in the radiogram switched from Beethoven's Pastoral to the Seventh, Toscanini giving way to Bruno Walter. All day, without a break, it played through the cycle of nine symphonies. He searched for an answer, the change of mood, to the sombre opening motif of the Seventh, overlaying his indecision.

"I suppose I want to, but I haven't yet found an adequate reason. Satisfying one's emotional needs isn't enough. There's got to be a more valid motive. Perhaps these sunken lagoons simply remind me of the drowned world of my uterine childhood—if so, the best thing is to leave straight away. Everything Riggs says is true. There's little hope of standing up to the rainstorms and the malaria."

He placed his hand on her forehead, feeling her temperature like a child's. "What did Riggs mean when he said you wouldn't sleep well? That was the second time this morning he mentioned it."

Beatrice looked away for a moment. "Oh, nothing. I've just had one or two peculiar nightmares recently. A lot of people get them. Forget it. Tell me, Robert, seriously—if I decide to stay on here, would you? You could share this apartment."

Kerans grinned. "Trying to tempt me, Bea? What a question. Remember, not only are you the most beautiful woman here, but you're the only woman. Nothing is more essential than a basis for comparison. Adam had no aesthetic sense, or he would have realised that Eve was a pretty haphazard piece of work."

"You are being frank today." Beatrice stood up and went

28

over to the edge of the pool. She swept her hair back off her forehead with both hands, her long supple body gleaming against the sunlight. "But is there as much urgency as Riggs claims? We've got the cruiser."

"It's a wreck. The first serious storm will split it open like a rusty can."

Nearing noon, the heat on the terrace had become uncomfortable and they left the patio and went indoors. Double venetian blinds filtered a thin sunlight into the low wide lounge, and the refrigerated air was cool and soothing. Beatrice stretched out on a long pale-blue elephant hide sofa, one hand playing with the fleecy pile of the carpet. The apartment had been one of her grandfather's *pieds à terre*, and Beatrice's home since her parents' death shortly after her birth. She had been brought up under the supervision of the grandfather, who had been a lonely, eccentric tycoon (the sources of his wealth Kerans had never established: when he asked Beatrice, shortly after he and Riggs stumbled upon her penthouse eyrie, she replied succinctly: "Let's say he was in money") and a great patron of the arts in his earlier days. His tastes leaned particularly towards the experimental and bizarre, and Kerans often wondered how far his personality and its strange internal perspectives had been carried forward into his grand-daughter. Over the mantelpiece was a huge painting by the early 20th-century Surrealist, Delvaux, in which ashen-faced women danced naked to the waist with dandified skeletons in tuxedos against a spectral bone-like landscape. On another wall one of Max Ernst's self-devouring phantasmagoric jungles screamed silently to itself, like the sump of some insane unconscious.

For a few moments Kerans stared quietly at the dim yellow annulus of Ernst's sun glowering through the exotic vegetation, a curious feeling of memory and recognition signalling through his brain. Far more potent than the Beethoven, the image of the archaic sun burned against his mind, illuminating the fleeting shadows that darted fitfully through its profoundest deeps.

"Beatrice."

She looked up at him as he walked across to her, a light frown crossing her eyes. "What's the matter, Robert?"

Kerans hesitated, suddenly aware that, however brief and imperceptible, a moment of significant time had elapsed, carrying him forward with its passage into a zone of commitment from which he would not be able to withdraw.

"You realise that if we let Riggs go without us we don't merely leave here later. We *stay*."

CHAPTER THREE

TOWARDS A NEW PSYCHOLOGY

BERTHING THE CATAMARAN against the landing stage, Kerans shipped the outboard and then made his way up the gangway into the base. As he let himself through the screen hatch he looked back over his shoulder across the lagoon, and caught a brief glimpse through the heat waves of Beatrice standing at her balcony rail. When he waved, however, she characteristically turned away without responding.

"One of her moody days, Doctor?" Sergeant Macready stepped from the guard cubicle, a trace of humour relaxing his beak-like face. "She's a strange one, all right."

Kerans shrugged. "These tough bachelor girls, you know, Sergeant. If you're not careful they frighten the wits out of you. I've been trying to persuade her to pack up and come with us. With a little luck I think she will."

Macready peered shrewdly at the distant roof of the apartment house. "I'm glad to hear you say so, Doctor," he ventured noncommittally, but Kerans was unable to decide if his scepticism was directed at Beatrice or himself.

Whether or not they finally stayed behind, Kerans had resolved to maintain the pretence that they were leaving— every spare minute of the next three days would be needed to

30

consolidate their supplies and steal whatever extra equipment they required from the base stores. Kerans had still not made up his mind—once away from Beatrice his indecision returned (ruefully he wondered if she was deliberately trying to confuse him, Pandora with her killing mouth and witch's box of desires and frustrations, unpredictably opening and shutting the lid)—but rather than stumble about in a state of tortured uncertainty, which Riggs and Bodkin would soon diagnose, he decided to postpone a final reckoning until the last moment possible. Much as he loathed the base, he knew that the sight of it actually sailing off would act as a wonderful catalyst for emotions of fear and panic, and any more abstract motives for staying behind would soon be abandoned. A year earlier, he had been accidentally marooned on a small key while taking an unscheduled geomagnetic reading, the departure siren muffled by his headphones as he crouched over his instruments in an old basement bunker. When he emerged ten minutes later and found the base six hundred yards away across a widening interval of flat water he had felt like a child parted forever from its mother, barely managed to control his panic in time to fire a warning shell from his flare pistol.

"Dr. Bodkin asked me to call you as soon as you arrived, sir. Lieutenant Hardman hasn't been too happy this morning."

Kerans nodded, glancing up and down the empty deck. He had taken lunch with Beatrice, knowing that the base was deserted in the afternoons. Half the crew were away with either Riggs or the helicopter, the rest asleep in their bunks, and he had hoped to carry out a private tour of the stores and armoury. Now unluckily, Macready, the Colonel's ever-alert watch-dog, was hanging about at his heels, ready to escort him up the companion-way to the sick-bay on B-Deck.

Kerans studiously examined a pair of Anopheles mosquitoes which had slipped through the wire hatch behind him. "They're still getting in," he pointed out to Macready. "What's happened to the double screening you were supposed to be putting up?"

Swatting at the mosquitoes with his forage cap, Macready looked around uncertainly. A secondary layer of screening around the wire mesh enclosing the base had long been one of Colonel Riggs' pet projects. At times he would tell Macready to detail a squad to carry out the work, but as this involved sitting on a wooden trestle in the open sunlight in the centre of a cloud of mosquitoes only a few token sections around Riggs' cabin had been completed. Now that they were moving northward the utility of the project had faded, but Macready's Presbyterian conscience, once roused, refused to let him rest.

"I'll get the men on to it this evening, Doctor," he assured Kerans, pulling a ball-pen and note-book from his hip pocket.

"No hurry, Sergeant, but if you've nothing better to do. I know the Colonel's very keen." Kerans left him squinting along the metal louvres and walked off down the deck. As soon as he was out of sight he stepped through the first doorway.

C-Deck, the lowest of the three decks comprising the base, contained the crew's quarters and galley. Two or three men lay about among their tropical gear in the cabins, but the recreation-room was empty, a radio playing to itself by the table-tennis tournament board in the corner. Kerans paused, listening to the strident rhythms of the guitar music, over-layed by the distant blare of the helicopter circling over the next lagoon, then made his way down the central stair-well which led to the armoury and workshops housed in the pontoon.

Three-quarters of the hull was occupied by the 2,000-h.p. diesels which powered the twin screws, and by the oil and aviation fuel tanks, and the workshops had been temporarily transferred during the final aerial sweeps to two vacant offices on A-Deck, beside the officers' quarters, so that the mechanics could service the helicopter with the maximum speed.

The armoury was closed when Kerans entered, a single light burning in the technical corporal's glass-walled booth. Kerans gazed around the heavy wooden benches and cabinets lined with carbines and submachine-guns. Steel rods through the trigger guards locked the weapons into their cases, and he idly touched the heavy stocks, doubting whether he could handle any of the weapons even if he stole one. In a drawer at the testing station was a Colt .45 and fifty rounds issued to him three years earlier. Once a year he made an official return on the ammunition discharged—in his case none—and exchanged the unused shells for a fresh issue, but he had never tried to fire the pistol.

On his way out he scanned the dark green ammunition boxes stacked around the wall below the cabinets, all of them double-padlocked. He was passing the booth when the light through the door illuminated the dusty labels on a row of metal cartons below one of the work benches.

'Hy-Dyne.' On an impulse Kerans stopped, pushed his fingers through the wire cage and brushed the dust off a label, tracing the formula with his fingers. 'Cyclo-trimethylene-trinitramine: Gas discharge speed—8,000 metres/second.'

Speculating on the possible uses of the explosive—it would be a brilliant *tour de force* to sink one of the office buildings into the exit creek after Riggs had left, blocking any attempt to return—he leaned his elbows on the bench, playing absent-mindedly with a 4-inch-diameter brass compass that had been left for repair. The calibrated annulus was loose and had been rotated a full 180 degrees, the point emphasised with a chalked cross.

Still thinking about the explosive, and the possibility of stealing detonators and fuse-wire, Kerans rubbed away the blunt chalk marks and then lifted the compass and weighed it in his hand. Leaving the armoury, he began to climb the stairway, uncaging the compass and letting the pointer dance and float. A sailor walked past along C-Deck, and Kerans quickly slipped the compass into his jacket pocket.

Suddenly, as he visualised himself throwing his weight on to the handles of a plunger box and catapulting Riggs, the base and the testing station into the next lagoon, he stopped and steadied himself against the rail. Smiling ruefully at the absurdity of the fantasy, he wondered why he had indulged it.

Then he noticed the heavy cylinder of the compass dragging at his jacket. For a moment he peered down at it thoughtfully.

"Look out, Kerans," he murmured to himself. "You're living on two levels."

Five minutes later, when he entered the sick-bay on B-Deck, he found more urgent problems facing him.

Three men were being treated for heat ulcers in the dispensary, but the main twelve-bed ward was empty. Kerans nodded to the corporal issuing penicillin band-aids and walked through to the small single ward on the starboard side of the deck.

The door was closed, but as he turned the handle he could hear the restless heaving motion of the cot, followed by a fractious muttering from the patient and Dr. Bodkin's equable but firm reply. For a few moments the latter continued to speak in a low even monologue, punctuated by a few shrugging protests and concluded by an interval of tired silence.

Lieutenant Hardman, the senior pilot of the helicopter (now being flown by his co-pilot, Sergeant Daley) was the only other commissioned member of the survey unit, and until the last three months had served as Riggs' deputy and chief executive officer. A burly, intelligent but somewhat phlegmatic man of about 30, he had quietly kept himself apart from the other members of the unit. Something of an amateur naturalist, he made his own descriptive notes of the changing flora and fauna, employing a taxonomic system of his own devising. In one of his few unguarded moments he had shown the notebooks to Kerans, then abruptly withdrawn into himself when Kerans tactfully pointed out that the classifications were confused.

For the first two years Hardman had been the perfect buffer between Riggs and Kerans. The rest of the crew took their cue from the Lieutenant, and this had the advantage, from Kerans' point of view, that the group never developed that sense of happy cohesion a more extravert second-in-command might have instilled, and which would have soon made life unbearable. The loose fragmentary relationships aboard the base, where a replacement was accepted as a fully paid up member of the crew within five minutes and no one cared whether he had been there two days or two years, was largely a reflection of Hardman's temperament. When he organised a basket-ball match or a regatta out on the lagoon there was no self-conscious boisterousness, but a laconic indifference to whether anyone took part or not.

Recently, however, the more sombre elements in Hardman's personality had begun to predominate. Two months earlier he complained to Kerans of intermittent insomnia—often, from Beatrice Dahl's apartment, Kerans would watch him long after midnight standing in the moonlight beside the helicopter on the roof of the base, looking out across the silent lagoon—and then took advantage of an attack of malaria to excuse himself from flying duty. Confined to his cabin for up to a week on end, he steadily retreated into his private world, going through his old notebooks and running his fingers, like a blind man reading Braille, across the glass display cases with their few mounted butterflies and giant moths.

The malaise had not been difficult to diagnose. Kerans recognised the same symptoms he had seen in himself, an accelerated entry into his own 'zone of transit', and left the Lieutenant alone, asking Bodkin to call in periodically.

Curiously, however, Bodkin had taken a more serious view of Hardman's illness.

Pushing back the door, Kerans stepped quietly into the darkened room, pausing in the corner by the ventilator shaft as Bodkin raised a monitory hand towards him. The blinds over the windows were drawn, and to Kerans' surprise the air-conditioning unit had been switched off. The air pumped in through the ventilator was never more than twenty degrees below the ambient temperatures of the lagoon, and the air-conditioner normally kept the room at

35

an even 70 degrees. Bodkin had not only switched this off but plugged a small electric fire into the shaver socket over the hand-basin mirror. Kerans remembered him building the fire in the laboratory at the testing station, fitting a dented paraboloid mirror around the single filament. Little more than a couple of watts in strength, the fire seemed to emit an immense heat, blazing out into the small room like a furnace mouth, and within a few seconds Kerans felt the sweat gathering around his neck. Bodkin, sitting on the metal bedside chair with his back to the fire, was still wearing his white cotton jacket, stained by two wide patches of sweat that touched between his shoulder blades, and in the dim red light Kerans could see the moisture beading off his head like drops of white-hot lead.

Hardman lay slumped back on one elbow, his broad chest and shoulders filling the backrest, big hands holding the leads of a pair of headphones clasped to his ears. His narrow, large-jawed face was pointed towards Kerans, but his eyes were fixed on the electric fire. Projected by the parabolic bowl, a circular disc of intense red light three feet in diameter covered the wall of the cabin, Hardman's head at its centre, like an enormous glowing halo.

A faint scratching noise came from a portable record-player on the floor at Bodkin's feet, a single three-inch disc spinning on its turntable. Generated mechanically by the pick-up head, the almost imperceptible sounds of a deep slow drumming reached Kerans, lost as the record ended and Bodkin switched off the player. Quickly he jotted something down on a desk-pad, then turned off the electric fire and put on the bedside lamp.

Shaking his head slowly, Hardman pulled off the head-phones and handed them to Bodkin.

"This is a waste of time, Doctor. These records are insane; you can put any interpretation you like on them." He settled his heavy limbs uncomfortably in the narrow cot. Despite the heat, there was little sweat on his face and bare chest, and he watched the fading embers of the electric fire as if reluctant to see them vanish.

36

Bodkin stood up and put the record-player on his chair, wrapping the headphones around the case. "Perhaps that's the point, Lieutenant—a sort of aural Rorshach. I think the last record was the most evocative, don't you agree?"

Hardman shrugged with studied vagueness, evidently reluctant to co-operate with Bodkin and concede even the smallest point. But despite this Kerans felt that he had been glad to take part in the experiment, using it for his own purposes.

"Maybe," Hardman said grudgingly. "But I'm afraid it didn't suggest a concrete image."

Bodkin smiled, aware of Hardman's resistance but prepared for the moment to give in to him. "Don't apologise, Lieutenant; believe me, that was our most valuable session so far." He waved to Kerans. "Come in, Robert, I'm sorry it's so warm—Lieutenant Hardman and I have been conducting a small experiment together. I'll tell you about it when we go back to the station. Now"—he pointed to a contraption on the bedside table which appeared to be two alarm clocks clipped back to back, crude metal extensions from the hands interlocking like the legs of two grappling spiders—"keep this thing running as long as you can, it shouldn't be too difficult, all you have to do is re-set both alarms after each twelve-hour cycle. They'll wake you once every ten minutes, just enough time for you to get sufficient rest before you slide off the pre-conscious shelf into deep sleep. With luck there'll be no more dreams."

Hardman smiled sceptically, glancing up briefly at Kerans. "I think you're being over-optimistic, Doctor. What you really mean is that I won't be *aware* of them." He picked up a well-thumbed green file, his botanical diary, and began to turn the pages mechanically. "Sometimes I think I have the dreams continuously, every minute of the day. Perhaps we all do."

His tone was relaxed and unhurried, despite the fatigue which had drained the skin around his eyes and mouth, making his long jaw seem even more lantern-like. Kerans realised that the malaise, whatever its source, had barely touched the central core of the man's ego. The element of tough self-sufficiency in Hardman was as strong as ever, if anything stronger, like a steel blade springing against a fencing post and revealing its sinews.

Bodkin dabbed at his face with a yellow silk handkerchief, watching Hardman thoughtfully. His grimy cotton jacket and haphazard attire, coupled with his puffy, quinine-tinted skin, misleadingly made him look like a seedy quack, masking a sharp and unresting intelligence. "Perhaps you're right, Lieutenant. In fact, some people used to maintain that consciousness is nothing more than a special category of the cytoplasmic coma, that the capacities of the central nervous system are as fully developed and extended by the dream life as they are during what we call the waking state. But we have to adopt an empirical approach, try whatever remedy we can. Don't you agree, Kerans?"

Kerans nodded. The temperature in the cabin had begun to fall, and he felt himself breathing more freely. "A change of climate will probably help as well." There was a dull clatter outside as one of the metal scows being hauled up in its davits clanged against the hull. He added: "The atmosphere in these lagoons is pretty enervating. Three days from now when we leave I think we'll all show a marked improvement."

He assumed that Hardman had been told of their imminent departure, but the Lieutenant looked up at him sharply, lowering his notebook. Bodkin began to clear his throat and abruptly started talking about the danger of draughts from the ventilator. For a few seconds Kerans and Hardman watched each other steadily, and then the Lieutenant nodded briefly to himself and resumed his reading, carefully noting the time from the bedside clocks.

Angry with himself, Kerans went over to the window, his back turned to the others. He realised that he had told Hardman deliberately, unconsciously hoping to elicit precisely this response, and knowing full well why Bodkin had withheld the news. Without the shadow of a doubt he had warned Hardman, telling him that whatever tasks he had to carry out, whatever internal perspectives to bring to a common focus, this should be completed within three days.

Kerans looked down irritably at the alarm device on the table, resenting his diminishing control over his own motives. First the meaningless theft of the compass, and now this act of gratuitous sabotage. However varied his faults, in the past he had always believed them to be redressed by one outstanding virtue—a complete and objective awareness of the motives behind his actions. If he was sometimes prone to undue delays this was a result, not of irresolution, but of a reluctance to act at all where complete self-awareness was impossible—his affair with Beatrice Dahl, tilted by so many conflicting passions, from day to day walked a narrow tight-rope of a thousand restraints and cautions.

In a belated attempt to reassert himself, he said to Hardman: "Don't forget the clock, Lieutenant. If I were you, I'd set the alarm so that it rings continuously."

Leaving the sick-bay, they made their way down to the jetty and climbed into Kerans' catamaran. Too tired to start the motor, Kerans slowly pulled them along the overhead hawser stretched between the base and the testing station. Bodkin sat in the bows, the record player held between his knees like a briefcase, blinking in the bright sunlight that spangled the broken surface of the sluggish green water. His plump face, topped by an untidy grey thatch, seemed preoccupied and wistful, scanning the surrounding ring of half-submerged buildings like a weary ship's chandler being rowed around a harbour for the thousandth time. As they neared the testing station the helicopter roared in overhead and alighted, its impact tilting the base and dipping the hawser into the water, then tautening it and cascading a brief shower across their shoulders. Bodkin cursed under his breath, but they were dry within a few seconds. Although it was well after four o'clock, the sun filled the sky, turning it into an enormous blow-torch and forcing them to lower their eyes to the water-line. Now and then, in the glass curtain-walling of the surrounding buildings, they would see countless reflections of the sun move across the surface in huge sheets of fire, like the blazing facetted eyes of gigantic insects.

A two-storey drum some fifty feet in diameter, the testing station had a dead weight of twenty tons. The lower deck contained the laboratory, the upper the two biologists' quarters and the chartroom and offices. A small bridge traversed the roof, and housed the temperature and humidity registers, rainfall gauge and radiation counters. Clumps of dried air-weed and red kelp were encrusted across the bitumened plates of the pontoon, shrivelled and burnt by the sun before they could reach the railing around the laboratory, while a dense refuse-filled mass of sargassum and spirogyra cushioned their impact as they reached the narrow jetty, oozing and subsiding like an immense soggy raft.

They entered the cool darkness of the laboratory and sat down at their desks below the semicircle of fading programme schedules which reached to the ceiling behind the dais, looking down over the clutter of benches and fume cupboards like a dusty mural. The schedules on the left, dating from their first year of work, were packed with detailed entries and minutely labelled arrow sprays, but those on the right thinned out progressively, until a few pencilled scrawls in giant longhand loops sealed off all but one or two of the ecological corridors. Many of the cardboard screens had sprung off their drawing pins, and hung forwards into the air like the peeling hull-plates of a derelict ship, moored against its terminal pier and covered with gnomic and meaningless graffiti.

Idly tracing a large compass dial with his finger in the dust on the desk-top, Kerans waited for Bodkin to provide some explanation for his curious experiments with Hardman. But Bodkin settled himself comfortably behind the muddle of box-files and catalogue trays on his desk, then opened the record player and removed the disc from the table, spinning it reflectively between his hands.

Kerans began: "I'm sorry I let slip that we were leaving in three days' time. I hadn't realised you'd kept that from Hardman."

Bodkin shrugged, dismissing this as of little importance. "It's a complex situation, Robert. Having gone a few steps towards unravelling it, I didn't want to introduce another slip-knot."

"But why not tell him?" Kerans pressed, hoping obliquely to absolve himself of his slight feeling of guilt. "Surely the prospect of leaving might well jolt him out of his lethargy?"

Bodkin lowered his glasses to the end of his nose and regarded Kerans quizzically. "It doesn't seem to have had that effect on you, Robert. Unless I'm very much mistaken, you look rather un-jolted. Why should Hardman's reactions be any different?"

Kerans smiled. "Touché, Alan. I don't want to interfere, having more or less dropped Hardman into your lap, but what exactly are you and he playing about with—why the electric heater and alarm clocks?"

Bodkin slid the gramophone record into a rack of miniature discs on the shelf behind him. He looked up at Kerans and for a few moments watched him with the mild but penetrating gaze with which he had observed Hardman, and Kerans realised that their relationship, until now that of colleagues confiding completely in each other, had become closer to that of observer and subject. After a pause Bodkin glanced away at the programme charts, and Kerans chuckled involuntarily. To himself he said: Damn the old boy, he's got me up there now with the algae and nautiloids; next he'll be playing his records at me.

Bodkin stood up and pointed to the three rows of laboratory benches, crowded with vivaria and specimen jars, pages from notebooks pinned to the fume hoods above them.

"Tell me, Robert, if you had to sum up the last three years' work in a single conclusion, how would you set about it?"

Kerans hesitated, then gestured off-handedly. "It wouldn't be too difficult." He saw that Bodkin expected a serious answer, and composed his thoughts. "Well, one could simply say that in response to the rises in temperature, humidity and radiation levels the flora and fauna of this planet are beginning to assume once again the forms they displayed the last time such conditions were present—roughly speaking, the Triassic period."

"Correct." Bodkin strolled off among the benches. "During the last three years, Robert, you and I have examined something like five thousand species in the animal kingdom, seen literally tens of thousands of new plant varieties. Everywhere the same pattern has unfolded, countless mutations completely transforming the organisms to adapt them for survival in the new environment. Everywhere there's been the same avalanche backwards into the past—so much so that the few complex organisms which have managed to retain a foothold unchanged on the slope look distinctly anomalous—a handful of amphibians, the birds, and *Man*. It's a curious thing that although we've carefully catalogued the backward journeys of so many plants and animals, we've ignored the most important creature on this planet."

Kerans laughed. "I'll willingly take a small bow there, Alan. But what are you suggesting—that *Homo sapiens* is about to transform himself into Cro-Magnon and Java Man, and ultimately into *Sinanthropus*? Unlikely, surely. Wouldn't that merely be Lamarckism in reverse?"

"Agreed. I'm *not* suggesting that." Bodkin leaned against one of the benches, feeding a handful of peanuts to a small marmoset caged in a converted fume cupboard. "Though obviously after two or three hundred million years *Homo sapiens* might well die out and our little cousin here become the highest form of life on the planet. However, a biological process isn't completely reversible." He pulled the silk handkerchief out of his pocket and flicked it at the marmoset, which flinched away tremulously. "If *we* return to the jungle we'll dress for dinner."

He went over to a window and gazed out through the mesh screen, the overhang of the deck above shutting out all but a narrow band of the intense sunlight. Steeped in the vast heat, the lagoon lay motionlessly, palls of steam humped over the water like elephantine spectres.

"But I'm really thinking of something else. Is it only the external landscape which is altering? How often recently most of us have had the feeling of déjà vu, of having seen all this before, in fact of remembering these swamps and lagoons all too well. However selective the conscious mind may be, most biological memories are unpleasant ones, echoes of danger and terror. Nothing endures for so long as fear. Everywhere in nature one sees evidence of innate releasing mechanisms literally millions of years old, which have lain dormant through thousands of generations but retained their power undiminished. The field-rat's inherited image of the hawk's silhouette is the classic example—even a paper silhouette drawn across a cage sends it rushing frantically for cover. And how else can you explain the universal but completely groundless loathing of the spider, only one species of which has ever been known to sting? Or the equally surprising—in view of their comparative rarity—hatred of snakes and reptiles? Simply because we all carry within us a submerged memory of the time when the giant spiders were lethal, and when the reptiles were the planet's dominant life form."

Feeling the brass compass which weighed down his pocket, Kerans said: "So you're frightened that the increased temperature and radiation are alerting similar IRM's in our own minds?"

"Not in our minds, Robert. These are the oldest memories on Earth, the time-codes carried in every chromosome and gene. Every step we've taken in our evolution is a milestone inscribed with organic memories—from the enzymes controlling the carbon dioxide cycle to the organisation of the brachial plexus and the nerve pathways of the Pyramid cells in the mid-brain, each is a record of a thousand decisions taken in the face of a sudden physico-chemical crisis. Just as psychoanalysis reconstructs the original traumatic situation in order to release the repressed material, so we are now

43

being plunged back into the archaeopsychic past, uncovering the ancient taboos and drives that have been dormant for epochs. The brief span of an individual life is misleading. Each one of us is as old as the entire biological kingdom, and our bloodstreams are tributaries of the great sea of its total memory. The uterine odyssey of the growing foetus recapitulates the entire evolutionary past, and its central nervous system is a coded time scale, each nexus of neurones and each spinal level marking a symbolic station, a unit of neuronic time.

"The further down the CNS you move, from the hind-brain through the medulla into the spinal cord, you descend back into the neuronic past. For example, the junction between the thoracic and lumbar vertebrae, between T-12 and L-1, is the great zone of transit between the gill-breathing fish and the air-breathing amphibians with their respiratory rib-cages, the very junction where we stand now on the shores of this lagoon, between the Paleozoic and Triassic Eras."

Bodkin moved back to his desk, and ran his hand over the rack of records. Listening distantly to Bodkin's quiet, unhurried voice, Kerans toyed with the notion that the row of parallel black discs was a model of a neurophonic spinal column. He remembered the faint drumming emitted by the record-player in Hardman's cabin, and its strange under-tones. Perhaps the conceit was closer to the truth than he imagined?

Bodkin went on: "If you like, you could call this the Psychology of Total Equivalents—let's say 'Neuronics' for short—and dismiss it as metabiological fantasy. However, I am convinced that as we move back through geophysical time so we re-enter the amnionic corridor and move back through spinal and archaeopsychic time, recollecting in our unconscious minds the landscapes of each epoch, each with a distinct geological terrain, its own unique flora and fauna, as recognisable to anyone else as they would be to a traveller in a Wellsian time machine. Except that this is no scenic railway, but a total reorientation of the personality. If we let these buried phantoms master us as they re-appear we'll be

44

swept back helplessly in the flood-tide like pieces of flotsam." He picked one of the records from the rack, then pushed it away with a gesture of uncertainty. "This afternoon I may have been taking a risk with Hardman, using the heater to simulate the sun and raise the temperature well into the 120's, but it was worth a chance. For the previous three weeks his dreams were almost driving him out of his mind, but during the last few days he's been much less disturbed, almost as if he were accepting the dreams and allowing himself to be carried back without retaining any conscious control. For his own sake I want to keep him awake as long as possible—the alarm clocks may do it."

"If he remembers to keep them set," Kerans commented quietly.

Outside in the lagoon the sounds of Riggs' cutter droned past. Stretching his legs, Kerans walked over to the window, and watched the landing craft swing in a diminishing arc around the base. While it berthed by the jetty Riggs held an informal conference with Macready across the gangway. Several times he pointed to the testing station with his baton, and Kerans assumed that they were preparing to tow the station over to the base. But for some reason the imminent departure left him unmoved. Bodkin's speculations, however nebulous, and his new psychology of Neuronics, offered a more valid explanation for the metamorphosis taking place in his mind than any other. The tacit assumption made by the UN directorate—that within the new perimeters described by the Arctic and Antarctic Circles life would continue much as before, with the same social and domestic relationships, by and large the same ambitions and satisfactions—was obviously fallacious, as the mounting flood-water and temperature would show when they reached the so-called polar redoubts. A more important task than mapping the harbours and lagoons of the external landscape was to chart the ghostly deltas and luminous beaches of the submerged neuronic continents.

"Alan," he asked over his shoulder, still watching Riggs stamping about on the landing jetty, "why don't you draft a report to Byrd? I think you should let them know. There's always a chance of——"

But Bodkin had gone. Kerans listened to his feet clump slowly up the stairway and disappear into his cabin, the fatigued tread of a man too old and too experienced to care whether or not his warnings were heeded.

Kerans went back to his desk and sat down. From his jacket pocket he withdrew the compass and placed it in front of him, cradling it between his hands. Around him the muted sounds of the laboratory formed a low background to his mind, the furry puttering of the marmoset, the tick of a recording spool somewhere, the grating of a revolving rig estimating a creeper's phototropism.

Idly Kerans examined the compass, swinging the bearing gently in its air-bath and then aligning the pointer and scale. He tried to decide why he had taken it from the armoury. Normally it was installed in one of the motor launches, and its disappearance would soon be reported, probably involve him in the petty humiliation of admitting its theft.

Caging the compass, he rotated it towards himself, without realising it sank into a momentary reverie in which his entire consciousness became focused on the serpentine terminal touched by the pointer, on the confused, uncertain but curiously potent image summed up by the concept 'South', with all its dormant magic and mesmeric power, diffusing outwards from the brass bowl held in his hands like the heady vapours of some spectral grail.

CHAPTER FOUR

THE CAUSEWAYS OF THE SUN

THE NEXT DAY, for reasons Kerans was fully to understand only much later, Lieutenant Hardman disappeared.

After a night of deep, dreamless sleep Kerans rose early

and had breakfasted by seven o'clock. He then spent an hour on the balcony, sitting back in one of the beach chairs in a pair of white latex shorts, the sunlight expanding across the dark water bathing his lean ebony body. Overhead the sky was vivid and marbled, the black bowl of the lagoon, by contrast, infinitely deep and motionless, like an immense well of amber. The tree-covered buildings emerging from its rim seemed millions of years old, thrown up out of the Earth's magma by some vast natural cataclysm, embalmed in the gigantic intervals of time that had elapsed during their subsidence.

Pausing by the desk to run his fingers over the brass compass gleaming in the darkness of the suite, Kerans went into the bedroom and changed into his khaki drill uniform, a minimal concession to Riggs' preparations for departure. The Italian sportswear was now hardly de rigueur, and it would only rouse the Colonel's suspicions if he were seen sauntering about in a pastel-coloured ensemble with a Ritz hallmark.

Although he accepted the possibility that he would remain behind, Kerans found himself reluctant to make any systematic precautions. Apart from his fuel and food supplies, for which he had been dependent during the previous six months on Colonel Riggs' largesse, he had also needed an endless succession of minor spares and replacements, from a new watchface to a complete re-wiring of the lighting system in the suite. Once the base and its workshop had left he would soon find himself saddled with an accumulating series of petty annoyances, and with no accommodating technical sergeant to remove them.

For the convenience of the stores staff, and to save himself unnecessary journeys to and from the base, Kerans had stockpiled a month's forward supplies of canned food in the suite. Most of this consisted of condensed milk and luncheon meat, virtually inedible unless supplemented by the delicacies stored away in Beatrice's deep freeze. It was this capacious locker, with its reserves of pâté de foie gras and filet mignon, which Kerans counted upon to keep them going, but at the most there was a bare three months' stock. After that they would have to live off the land, switch their menu to wood soup and steak iguana.

Fuel raised more serious problems. The reserve tanks of diesel oil at the Ritz held little more than 500 gallons, sufficient to operate the cooling system for at most a couple of months. By closing down the bedroom and dressing room and moving into the lounge, and by raising the ambient temperature to ninety degrees, he would with luck double its life, but once the supplies were exhausted the chances of supplementing them were negligible. Every reserve tank and cache in the gutted buildings around the lagoons had long since been siphoned dry by the waves of refugees moving northward during the past thirty years in their power boats and cabin cruisers. The tank on the catamaran outboard motor carried three gallons, enough for thirty miles, or a return trip a day for a month between the Ritz and Beatrice's lagoon.

For some reason, however, this inverted Crusoeism—the deliberate marooning of himself without the assistance of a gear-laden carrack wrecked on a convenient reef—raised few anxieties in Kerans' mind. As he let himself out of the suite he left the thermostat at its usual eighty-degree setting, despite the fuel the generator would waste, reluctant to make even a nominal concession to the hazards facing him after Riggs' departure. At first he assumed that this reflected a shrewd unconscious assessment that his good sense would prevail, but as he started the outboard and drove the catamaran through the cool oily swells towards the creek into the next lagoon he realised that this indifference marked the special nature of the decision to remain behind. To use the symbolic language of Bodkin's schema, he would then be abandoning the conventional estimates of time in relation to his own physical needs and entering the world of total, neuronic time, where the massive intervals of the geological time-scale calibrated his existence. Here a million years was the shortest working unit, and problems of food and clothing became as irrelevant as they would have been to a Buddhist contemplative lotus-squatting before an empty rice-bowl under the protective canopy of the million-headed cobra of eternity.

Entering the third lagoon, an oar raised to fend off the ten-foot-long blades of a giant horse-tail dipping its leaves into the mouth of the creek, he noticed without emotion that a party of men under Sergeant Macready had hoisted the anchors of the testing station and were towing it slowly towards the base. As the gap between the two closed, like curtains drawing together after the end of a play, Kerans stood in the stern of the catamaran under the dripping umbrella of leaves, a watcher in the wings whose contribution to the drama, however small, had now completely ended.

In order not to attract attention by re-starting the engine, he pushed out into the sunlight, the giant leaves sinking to their hilts in the green jelly of the water, and paddled slowly around the perimeter of the lagoon to Beatrice's apartment block. Intermittently the roar of the helicopter dinned across the water as it carried out its tarmac check, and the swells from the testing station drummed against the prows of the catamaran and drove on through the open windows on his right, slapping around the internal walls. Beatrice's power cruiser creaked painfully at its moorings. The engine room had flooded and the stern was awash under the weight of the two big Chrysler engines. Sooner or later one of the thermal storms would catch the craft and anchor it forever fifty feet down in one of the submerged streets.

When he stepped out of the elevator the patio around the swimming pool was deserted, the previous evening's glasses still on the tray between the reclining chairs. Already the sunlight was beginning to fill the pool, illuminating the yellow sea-horses and blue tridents that patterned its floor. A few bats hung in the shadows below the gutter over Beatrice's bedroom window, but they flew off as Kerans sat down, like vampiric spirits fleeing the rising day.

Through the blinds Kerans caught a glimpse of Beatrice moving about quietly, and five minutes later she walked into the lounge, a black towel in a single twist around her midriff. She was partly hidden in the dim light at the far end of the room, and seemed tired and withdrawn, greeting him with a half-hearted wave. Leaning one elbow against the bar, she made a drink for herself, stared blankly at one of the Delvaux and returned to her bedroom.

When she failed to reappear Kerans went in search of her. As he pushed back the glass doors the hot air trapped inside the lounge hit his face like fumes vented from a crowded galley. Several times within the past month the generator had failed to respond immediately to the thermostat, and the temperature was well into the nineties, probably responsible for Beatrice's lethargy and ennui.

She was sitting on the bed when Kerans entered, the tumbler of whiskey resting on her smooth knees. The thick hot air in the room reminded Kerans of Hardman's cabin during the experiment Bodkin had conducted on the pilot. He went to the thermostat on the bedside table and jerked the tab down from seventy to sixty degrees.

"It's broken down again," Beatrice told him matter-of-factly. "The engine kept stopping."

Kerans tried to take the glass from her hands but she steered it away from him. "Leave me alone, Robert," she said in a tired voice. "I know I'm a loose, drunken woman, but I spent last night in the time jungles and I don't want to be lectured."

Kerans scrutinised her closely, smiling to himself in a mixture of affection and despair. "I'll see if I can repair the motor. This bedroom smells as if you've had an entire penal battalion billeted with you. Take a shower, Bea, and try to pull yourself together. Riggs is leaving tomorrow, we'll need our wits about us. What are these nightmares you're having?"

Beatrice shrugged. "Jungle dreams, Robert," she murmured ambiguously. "I'm learning my ABC again. Last night was the delta jungles." She gave him a bleak smile, then added with a touch of malicious humour: "Don't look so stern, you'll be dreaming them too, soon."

"I hope not." Kerans watched distastefully as she raised

the glass to her lips. "And pour that drink away. Scotch breakfasts may be an old Highland custom, but they're murder on the liver."

Beatrice waved him away. "I know. Alcohol kills slowly, but I'm in no hurry. Go away, Robert."

Kerans gave up and turned on his heel. He took the stairway from the kitchen into the store-room below, found a torch and the tool-set, and began to work on the generator.

Half an hour later, when he emerged on to the patio, Beatrice had apparently recovered completely from her torpor and was intently painting her nails with a bottle of blue varnish.

"Hello, Robert, are you in a better mood now?"

Kerans sat down on the tiled floor, wiping the last traces of grease off his hands. Crisply he punched the firm swell of her calf, then fended away the revenging heel at his head. "I've cured the generator; with luck you won't have any more trouble. It's rather amusing; the timing device on the two-stroke starting engine had gone wrong, it was actually running backwards."

He was about to explain the irony of the joke at full length when a loud-hailer blared from the lagoon below. The sounds of sudden excited activity had sprung up from the base; engines whined and accelerated, davits shrilled as the two reserve motor launches were lowered into the water, there was a medley of voices shouting and feet racing down gangways.

Kerans rose and hurried around the pool to the rail. "Don't tell me they're leaving today——? Riggs is clever enough to try that in the hope of catching us unprepared."

Beatrice at his side, the towel clasped to her breasts, they looked down at the base. Every member of the unit appeared to have been mobilised, and the cutter and the two launches surged and jockeyed around the landing jetty. The drooping rotors of the helicopter were circling slowly, Riggs and Macready about to embark. The other men were lined up on the jetty, waiting their turn to climb into the three craft.

51

Even Bodkin had been roused from his bunk, and was standing bare-chested on the bridge of the testing station, shouting up at Riggs.

Suddenly Macready noticed Kerans at the balcony rail. He spoke to the Colonel, who picked up an electric megaphone and walked forwards across the roof.

"KER-ANS! ! DOC-TOR KER-ANS! !"

Giant fragments of the amplified phrases boomed among the rooftops, echoing off the aluminium in-falls set into the sheets of windows. Kerans cupped his ears, trying to distinguish what the Colonel was shouting, but the sounds were lost in the mounting roar of the helicopter. Then Riggs and Macready climbed into the cabin, and the pilot began to semaphore at Kerans through the cockpit windscreen.

Kerans translated the morse signals, then turned quickly from the rail and began to carry the deck-chairs into the lounge.

"They're going to pick me up here," he told Beatrice as the helicopter rose from its pedestal and lifted diagonally across the lagoon. "You'd better get dressed or out of sight. The slip-steam will strip your towel away like tissue paper. Riggs has got enough to contend with now."

Beatrice helped him furl the awning, and stepped into the lounge as the flickering shadow of the helicopter filled the patio, the down-draught fanning across their shoulders.

"But what's happened, Robert? Why is Riggs so excited?"

Kerans shielded his head from the engine roar and stared out across the green-ringed lagoons stretching towards the horizon, a sudden spasm of anxiety twisting one corner of his mouth.

"He's not excited, just worried stiff. Everything is beginning to collapse around him. Lieutenant Hardman has disappeared!"

Like an immense putrescent sore, the jungle lay exposed below the open hatchway of the helicopter. Giant groves of gymnosperms stretched in dense clumps along the roof-tops of the submerged buildings, smothering the white rectangular outlines. Here and there an old concrete water tower protruded from the morass, or the remains of a makeshift jetty still floated beside the hulk of a collapsing office block, overgrown with feathery acacias and flowering tamarisks. Narrow creeks, the canopies overhead turning them into green-lit tunnels, wound away from the larger lagoons, eventually joining the six hundred-yard-wide channels which broadened outwards across the former suburbs of the city. Everywhere the silt encroached, shoring itself in huge banks against a railway viaduct or crescent of offices, oozing through a submerged arcade like the fetid contents of some latter-day Cloaca Maxima. Many of the smaller lakes were now filled by the silt, yellow discs of fungus-covered sludge from which a profuse tangle of competing plant forms emerged, walled gardens in an insane Eden.

Clamped securely to the cabin handrail by the nylon harness around his waist and shoulders, Kerans gazed down at the unfolding landscape, following the waterways unwinding from the three central lagoons. Five hundred feet below, the shadow of the helicopter raced across the mottled green surface of the water, and he focused his attention on the area immediately around it. An immense profusion of animal life filled the creeks and canals: water-snakes coiled themselves among the crushed palisades of the waterlogged bamboo groves, colonies of bats erupted out of the green tunnels like clouds of exploding soot, iguanas sat motionlessly on the shaded cornices like stone sphinxes. Often, as if disturbed by the noise of the helicopter, a human form seemed to dart and hide among the water-line windows, then revealed itself to be a crocodile snapping at a waterfowl, or one end of a subsiding log dislodged from the buffeted tree-ferns.

Twenty miles away the horizon was still obscured by the early morning mists, huge palls of golden vapour that hung from the sky like diaphanous curtains, but the air over the city was clear and vivid, the exhaust vapour of the helicopter

53

sparkling as it receded in a long undulating signature. As
they moved away from the central lagoons in their outward
spiral sweep Kerans leaned against the hatchway and
watched the glistening display, abandoning his search of the
jungle below.

The chances of seeing Hardman from the air were
infinitesimal. Unless he had taken refuge in a building
near the base he would have been forced to travel along the
water-ways, where he had the maximum possible protection
from aerial observation under the overhanging fern trees.

In the starboard hatchway Riggs and Macready
continued their vigil, passing a pair of binoculars to and fro.
Without his peaked cap, his thin sandy hair blown forwards
over his face, Riggs looked like a ferocious sparrow, his
little jaw jutting fiercely at the open air.

He noticed Kerans gazing up at the sky and shouted:
"Seen him yet, Doctor? Don't dawdle now, the secret of a
successful sweep is one hundred percent cover, one hundred
percent concentration."

Accepting the rebuke, Kerans scanned the tilting disc of
the jungle again, the tall towers of the central lagoon
pivoting around the hatchway. Hardman's disappearance
had been discovered by a sick-bay orderly at 8 o'clock that
morning, but his bed was cold and he had almost certainly
left the previous evening, probably soon after the final ward-
roll at 9.30. None of the smaller scows hitched to the jetty
rail had gone, but Hardman could easily have lashed
together a couple of the empty fuel drums stored in a pile by
the C-Deck hold and lowered them noiselessly into the
water. However crude, such a craft would paddle smoothly
and carry him ten miles away by day-break, somewhere on
the perimeter of a search area of some seventy-five square
miles, every acre of which was honeycombed by derelict
buildings.

Unable to see Bodkin before being winched aboard the
helicopter, Kerans could only speculate about Hardman's
motives for leaving the base, and whether these were part of
a grander design maturing slowly in the Lieutenant's mind

or merely a sudden meaningless reaction to the news that they were leaving the lagoons for the north. Kerans' initial excitement had evaporated, and he felt a curious sense of relief, as if one of the opposing lines of force that encircled him had been removed by Hardman's disappearance and the tension and impotence contained in the system suddenly released. If anything, however, the task of remaining behind would now be even more difficult.

Unshackling his harness, Riggs stood up with a gesture of exasperation and handed the binoculars to one of the two soldiers squatting on the floor at the rear of the cabin.

"Open searches are a waste of time over this type of terrain," he shouted at Kerans. "We'll go down somewhere and have a careful look at the map, you can have a shot at reading Hardman's psychology."

They were about ten miles north-west of the central lagoons, the towers almost obscured in the mists along the horizon. Five miles away, directly between them and the base, was one of the two motor launches, cruising down an open channel, its white wake fading across the glassy sheet of the water. Blocked by the urban concentration to the south, less silt had penetrated into the area, and the vegetation was lighter, more expanses of unbroken water between the principal lines of buildings. Altogether the zone below them was empty and uncongested, and Kerans felt convinced, though for no rational reason, that Hardman would not be found in the north-west sector.

Riggs climbed up into the cockpit and a moment later the speed and inclination of the helicopter altered. They began to make a shallow dive, swinging down to within a hundred feet of the water, glided in and out of the wide canals looking for a convenient roof-top on which to perch. Finally they picked out the humped back of a half-submerged cinema and let down slowly on to the square firm roof of the neo-Assyrian portico.

For a few minutes they steadied their legs, gazing out over the expanses of blue water. The nearest structure was an isolated department store two hundred yards away, and the open vistas reminded Kerans of Herodotus' description of the landscape in Egypt at floodtime, with its rampart cities like the islands of the Aegean Sea.

Riggs opened his map wallet and spread the polythene print across the cabin floor. Resting his elbows on the edge of the hatchway, he put his finger on their present landing stage.

"Well, Sergeant," he told Daley, "we seem to be half-way back to Byrd. Apart from wearing out the engine we haven't achieved much."

Daley nodded, his small serious face hidden inside the fibre-glass helmet. "Sir, I think our only chance is to carry out low-level inspections over a few selected runs. There's just a hope we might see something—a raft or an oil patch."

"Agreed. But the problem is"—here Riggs drummed on the map with his baton—"where? Hardman is very probably no more than two or three miles from the base. What's your guess, Doctor?"

Kerans shrugged. "I don't really know what Hardman's motives are, Colonel. Latterly he'd been in Bodkin's charge. It may be . . ."

His voice began to trail off, and Daley cut in with another suggestion, distracting Riggs' attention. For the next five minutes the Colonel, Daley and Macready argued about possible routes Hardman had taken, marking only the wider water-ways as if Hardman were navigating a pocket battleship. Kerans looked around at the water eddying slowly past the cinema. A few branches and clumps of weed drifted along on the northward current, the bright sunlight masking the molten mirror of the surface. The water drummed against the portico beneath his feet, beating slowly against his mind, and setting up a widening circle of interference patterns as if crossing it at an opposite direction to its own course of flow. He watched a succession of wavelets lapping at the sloping roof, wishing that he could leave the Colonel and walk straight down into the water, dissolve himself and the ever-present phantoms which attended him like sentinel birds in the cool bower of its magical calm, in the luminous, dragon-green, serpent-haunted sea.

Suddenly he realised without any shadow of doubt where Hardman was to be found.

He waited for Daley to finish. ". . . I knew Lieutenant Hardman, sir, flew nearly five thousand hours with him, he's obviously had a brain-storm. He wanted to get back to Byrd, must have decided he couldn't wait any longer, not even two days. He'll have headed north, be resting somewhere along these open channels out of the city."

Riggs nodded doubtfully, apparently unconvinced but prepared to accepted the Sergeant's advice in default of any other.

"Well, you may be right. I suppose it's worth trying. What do you think, Kerans?"

Kerans shook his head. "Colonel, it's a complete waste of time searching the areas north of the city. Hardman wouldn't have come up here; it's too open and isolated. I don't know whether he's on foot or paddling a raft, but he certainly isn't going north—Byrd is the last place on Earth he wants to return to. There's only one direction in which Hardman is heading—south." Kerans pointed to the nexus of channels which flowed into the central lagoons, tributaries of a single huge water-way three miles south of the city, its passage indented and diverted by the giant silt banks. "Hardman will be somewhere along there. It probably took him all night to reach the main channel, and I should guess that he's resting in one of the small inlets before he moves on tonight."

He broke off and Riggs stared hard at the map, peaked cap pulled down over his eyes in a gesture of concentration.

"But why south?" Daley protested. "Once he leaves the channel there's nothing but solid jungle and open sea. The temperature is going up all the time—he'll *fry*."

Riggs looked up at Kerans. "Sergeant Daley has a point, Doctor. Why should Hardman choose to travel south?"

Looking out across the water again, Kerans replied in a flat voice: "Colonel, there isn't any other direction."

57

Riggs hesitated, then glanced at Macready, who had stepped back from the group and was standing besides Kerans, his tall stooped figure silhouetted like a gaunt crow against the water. Almost imperceptibly he nodded to Riggs, answering the unspoken question. Even Daley put a foot up on the cockpit entry step, accepting the logic of Kerans' argument and the shared understanding of Hardman's motives once Kerans had made them explicit.

Three minutes later the helicopter was speeding off at full manifold pressure towards the lagoons in the south.

As Kerans had prophesied, they found Hardman among the silt flats.

Descending to three hundred feet above the water, they began to rake up and down the distal five-mile length of the main channel. The huge banks of silt lifted above the surface like the backs of yellow sperm whales. Wherever the hydrodynamic contours of the channel gave the silt banks any degree of permanence, the surrounding jungle spilled from the rooftops and rooted itself in the damp loam, matting the whole morass into an immovable structure. From the hatchway Kerans scrutinised the narrow beaches under the outer edge of the fern trees, watching for the tell-tale signs of a camouflaged raft or makeshift hut.

After twenty minutes, however, and a dozen careful sweeps of the channel, Riggs turned from the hatchway with a rueful shake of his head.

"You're probably right, Robert, but it's a hopeless job. Hardman's no fool, if he wants to hide from us we'll never find him. Even if he were leaning out of a window and waving, ten to one we wouldn't see him."

Kerans murmured in reply, watching the surface below. Each of the tracking runs was about a hundred yards to the starboard of the previous one, and for the last three runs he had been watching the semicircular crescent of what appeared to be a large apartment block standing in the angle between the channel and the southern bank of a small creek which ran off into the surrounding jungle. The upper eight or nine storeys of the block stood above the water, enclosing a low mound of muddy-brown silt. The surface streamed with water draining away from a collection of shallow pools covering it. Two hours earlier the bank had been a sheet of wet mud, but by ten o'clock, as the helicopter flew over, the mud was beginning to dry and grow firm. To Kerans, shielding his eyes from the reflected sunlight, its smooth surface appeared to be scored by two faint parallel lines, about six feet apart, that led across to the jutting roof of an almost submerged balcony. As they swept overhead he tried to see under the concrete slab, but its mouth was choked with refuse and rotting logs.

He touched Riggs' arm and pointed to the tracks, so immersed in tracing their winding progress to the balcony that he almost failed to notice the equally distinct pattern of imprints emerging in the drying surface between the lines, spaced some four feet apart, unmistakably the footsteps of a tall powerful man hauling a heavy load.

As the noise of the helicopter's engine faded out on the roof above them, Riggs and Macready bent down and inspected the crude catamaran hidden behind a screen of bocage under the balcony. Fashioned from two drop-tanks lashed to either end of a metal bed-frame, its twin grey hulls were still streaked with silt. Clumps of mud from Hardman's feet crossed the room opening on to the balcony and disappeared through the suite into the adjacent corridor.

"This is it without a doubt—agree, Sergeant?" Riggs asked, stepping out into the sunlight to look up at the crescent of apartment blocks. A chain of autonomous units, they were linked by short causeways between the elevator wells at the end of each building. Most of the windows were broken, the cream facing tiles covered by huge patches of fungus, and the whole complex looked like an over-ripe camembert cheese.

Macready knelt down by one of the hulls, cleaning away the silt, then traced out the code number painted across the bow. "UNAF 22-H-549—that's us, sir. The drop tanks were being cleared out yesterday, we'd stored them on C-Deck. He must have taken a spare bed from the sick-bay after ward-roll."

"Good." Rubbing his hands together with pleasure, Riggs stepped over to Kerans, smiling jauntily, his self-confidence and good humour fully restored. "Excellent, Robert. Superb diagnostic skill. You were quite right, of course." He peered shrewdly at Kerans, as if speculating on the real sources of this remarkable insight, invisibly marking him off. "Cheer up, Hardman will be grateful to you when we take him back."

Kerans stood on the edge of the balcony, the slope of caking silt below him. He looked up at the silent curve of windows, wondering which of the thousand or so rooms would be Hardman's hiding-place. "I hope you're right. You've still got to catch him."

"Don't worry. We will." Riggs began to shout up at the two men on the roof, helping Daley lash down the helicopter. "Wilson, keep a look-out from the south-west end; Caldwell, you work your way across to the north. Keep an eye on both sides, he might try to swim for it."

The two men saluted and moved off, their carbines held at their hips. Macready cradled a Thompson gun in the crook of his arm, and as Riggs unbuttoned the flap of his holster Kerans said quietly: "Colonel, we're not tracking down a wild dog."

Riggs waved this aside. "Relax, Robert, it's just that I don't want my leg bitten off by some sleeping croc. Though as a matter of interest"—here he flashed Kerans a gleaming smile—"Hardman has got a ·45 Colt with him."

Leaving Kerans to digest this, he picked up the electric megaphone.

"*Hardman!! This is Colonel Riggs!!*" He bellowed Hardman's name at the silent heat, then winked at Kerans and added: "*Dr. Kerans wants to talk to you, Lieutenant!!*"

Focused by the crescent of buildings, the sounds echoed away across the swamps and creeks, booming distantly over the great empty mudflats. Around them everything glistened in the immense heat, and the men on the roof fretted nervously under their forage caps. A thick cloacal stench exuded from the silt flat, a corona of a million insects pulsing and humming hungrily above it, and a sudden spasm of nausea knotted Kerans' gullet, for a moment dizzying him. Pressing a wrist tightly to his forehead, he leaned back against a pillar, listening to the echoes reverberate around him. Four hundred yards away two white-faced clock towers protruded through the vegetation, like the temple spires of some lost jungle religion, and the sounds of his name—"*Kerans . . . Kerans . . . Kerans*"—reflected off them seemed to Kerans to toll with an intense premonition of terror and disaster, the meaningless orientation of the clock hands identifying him, more completely than anything he had previously experienced, with all the confused and minatory spectres that cast their shadows more and more darkly through his mind, the myriad-handed mandala of cosmic time.

His name still echoed faintly in his ears as they began their search of the building. He took up his position at the stairwell at the centre of each corridor while Riggs and Macready inspected the apartments, keeping a look-out as they climbed the floors. The building had been gutted. All the floorboards had rotted or been ripped out, and they moved slowly along the tiled inlays, stepping warily from one concrete tie-beam to another. Most of the plaster had slipped from the walls and lay in grey heaps along the skirting boards. Wherever sunlight filtered through, the bare lathes were intertwined with creeper and wire-moss, and the original fabric of the building seemed solely supported by the profusion of vegetation ramifying through every room and corridor.

Through the cracks in the floors rose the stench of the greasy water swirling through the windows below. Disturbed for the first time in many years, the bats which hung from the tilting picture rails flew frantically for the windows, dispersing with cries of pain in the brilliant sunlight. Lizards scuttered and darted through the floor cracks, or

61

skated desperately around the dry baths in the bathrooms.

Exacerbated by the heat, Riggs' impatience mounted as they climbed the floors and had covered all but the top two without success.

"Well, where is he?" Riggs rested against the stair-rail, gesturing for quiet, and listened to the silent building, breathing tightly through his teeth. "We'll stand easy for five minutes, Sergeant. Now's the time for caution. He's somewhere around here."

Macready slung his Thompson over his shoulder and climbed to the fan-light on the next landing which let in a thin breeze. Kerans leaned against the wall, the sweat pouring across his back and chest, temples thudding from the exertion of mounting the stairs. It was 11.30, and the temperature outside was well over 120 degrees. He looked down at Riggs' flushed pink face, admiring the Colonel's self-discipline and single-mindedness.

"Don't look so condescending, Robert. I know I'm sweating like a pig, but I haven't had as much rest as you lately."

The two men exchanged glances, each aware of the conflict of attitude towards Hardman, and Kerans, in an effort to resolve the rivalry between them, said quietly: "You'll probably catch him now, Colonel."

Searching for somewhere to sit, he walked off down the corridor and pushed back the door into the first apartment.

As he unlatched the door the frame collapsed weakly into a litter of worm-eaten dust and timbers, and he stepped across it to the wide french windows overlooking the balcony. A little air funnelled through, and Kerans let it play over his face and chest, surveying the jungle below. The promontory on which the crescent of apartment houses stood had at one time been a small hill, and a number of the buildings visible beneath the vegetation on the other side of the silt flat were still above the flood-waters. Kerans stared at the two clock towers jutting up like white obelisks above the fern fronds. The yellow air of the noon high seemed to press down like a giant translucent counterpane on the leafy spread, a thousand motes of light spitting like diamonds

62

whenever a bough moved and deflected the sun's rays. The obscured outline of a classical portico and colonnaded façade below the towers suggested that the buildings were once part of some small municipal centre. One of the clock-faces was without its hands; the other, by coincidence, had stopped at almost exactly the right time—11.35. Kerans wondered whether the clock was not in fact working, tended by some mad recluse clinging to a last meaningless register of sanity, though if the mechanism were still operable Riggs might well perform that role. Several times, before they abandoned one of the drowned cities, he had wound the two-ton mechanism of some rusty cathedral clock and they had sailed off to a last carillon of chimes across the water. For nights afterwards, in his dreams Kerans had seen Riggs dressed as William Tell, striding about in a huge Dalinian landscape, planting immense dripping sundials like daggers in the fused sand.

Kerans leaned against the window, waiting as the minutes passed and left behind the clock fixed at 11.35, overtaking it like a vehicle in a faster lane. Or was it not stationary (guaranteed though it would be to tell the time with complete, unquestionable accuracy twice a day—more than most time-pieces) but merely so slow that its motion *appeared* to be imperceptible? The slower a clock, the nearer it approximated to the infinitely gradual and majestic progression of cosmic time—in fact, by reversing a clock's direction and running it backwards one could devise a time-piece that in a sense was moving even more slowly than the universe, and consequently part of an even greater spatio-temporal system.

Kerans' amusement at this notion was distracted by his discovery among the clutter of debris on the opposite bank of a small cemetery sloping down into the water, its leaning headstones advancing to their crowns like a party of bathers. He remembered again one ghastly cemetery over which they had moored, its ornate Florentine tombs cracked and sprung, corpses floating out in their unravelling winding-sheets in a grim rehearsal of the Day of Judgement.

Averting his eyes, he turned away from the window, with a jolt realised that a tall black-bearded man was standing motionlessly in a doorway behind him. Startled, Kerans stared uncertainly at the figure, with an effort reassembling his thoughts. The big man stood in a slightly stooped but relaxed pose, his heavy arms loosely at his sides. Black mud caked across his wrists and forehead, and clogged his boots and the fabric of his drill trousers, for a moment reminding Kerans of one of the resurrected corpses. His bearded chin was sunk between his broad shoulders, the impression of constraint and fatigue heightened by the medical orderly's blue denim jacket several sizes too small which he wore, the corporal's stripe pulled up over the swell of his deltoid muscles. The expression on his face was one of hungry intensity, but he gazed at Kerans with sombre detachment, his eyes like heavily banked fires, a thin glow of interest in the biologist the only outward show of the energy within.

Kerans waited until his eyes adjusted themselves to the darkness at the rear of the room, looking involuntarily at the bedroom doorway through which the bearded man had stepped. He reached out one hand to him, half-afraid of breaking the spell between them, warning him not to move, and elicited in return an expression of curiously understanding sympathy, almost as if their roles were reversed.

"Hardman!" Kerans whispered.

With a galvanic leap, Hardman flung himself at Kerans, his big frame blocking off half the room, feinted just before they collided and swerved past, before Kerans could regain his balance had jumped out on to the balcony and climbed over the rail.

"*Hardman!*" As one of the men on the roof shouted the alarm Kerans reached the balcony. Hardman swung himself like an acrobat down the drain-pipe to the parapet below. Riggs and Macready dived into the room. Holding on to his hat, Riggs pivoted out over the rail, swore as Hardman disappeared into the apartment.

"Good man, Kerans. You nearly held him!" Together they ran back into the corridor and raced down the stairway,

where a group of sedate 19th-century municipal buildings looked down on an ornate fountain. Wild orchids and magnolia entwined themselves around the grey ionic columns of the old courthouse, a miniature sham-Parthenon with a heavy sculptured portico, but otherwise the square had survived intact the assaults of the previous fifty years, its original floor still well above the surrounding water level. Next to the courthouse with the faceless clock tower, was a second colonnaded building, a library or museum, its white pillars gleaming in the sunlight like a row of huge bleached bones.

Nearing noon, the sun filled this antique forum with a harsh burning light, and Hardman stopped and looked back uncertainly at the men following him, then stumbled up the steps into the courthouse. Signalling to Kerans and Caldwell, Macready backed away among the statues in the square and took up his position behind the bowl of the fountain.

"Doctor, it's too dangerous now! He may not recognise you. We'll wait until the heat lifts; he can't move from there. Doctor——"

Kerans ignored him. He advanced slowly across the cracked flagstones, both forearms up over his eyes, and placed one foot insecurely on the first step. Somewhere among the shadows he could hear Hardman's exhausted breathing, pumping the scalding air into his lungs.

Shaking the square with its noise, the helicopter soared slowly overhead, and Riggs and Wilson hurried up the steps into the museum entrance, watching as the tail rotor turned the machine in a diminishing spiral. Together the noise and the heat drummed at Kerans' brain, bludgeoning him like a thousand clubs, clouds of dust billowing around him. Abruptly the helicopter began to lose lift, with an agonised acceleration of its engine slid out of the air into the square, then picked up just before it touched the ground. Ducking away, Kerans sheltered with Macready behind the fountain, while the aircraft jerked about over their heads. As it revolved, the tail rotor lashed into the portico of the courthouse, in an explosion of splintered marble the helicopter porpoised and plunged heavily on to the cobbles, the shattered tail propeller rotating eccentrically. Cutting his engine, Daley sat back at his controls, half stunned by the impact with the ground and trying helplessly to remove his harness.

Frustrated at this second attempt to catch Hardman, they crouched in the shadows below the portico of the museum, waiting for the noon high to subside. As if illuminated by immense searchlights, a vast white glare lit the grey stone of the buildings around the square, like an over-exposed photograph, reminding Kerans of the chalk-white colonnade of an Egyptian necropolis. As the sun mounted to its zenith the reflected light began to glimmer upwards from the paving stones. Periodically, while he tended Wilson and settled him with a few grains of morphine, Kerans could see the other men as they kept up their watch for Hardman, fanning themselves slowly with their forage caps.

Ten minutes later, shortly after noon, he looked up at the square. Completely obscured by the light and glare, the buildings on the other side of the fountain were no longer continuously visible, looming in and out of the air like the architecture of a spectral city. In the centre of the square, by the edge of the fountain, a tall solitary figure was standing, the pulsing thermal gradients every few seconds inverting the normal perspectives and magnifying him fleetingly. Hardman's sun-burnt face and black beard were now chalk-white, his mud-stained clothes glinting in the blinding sunlight like sheets of gold.

Kerans pulled himself to his knees, waiting for Macready to leap forward at him, but the Sergeant, with Riggs beside him, was huddled against a pillar, his eyes staring blankly at the floor in front of them, as if asleep or entranced.

Stepping away from the fountain, Hardman moved slowly across the square, in and out of the shifting curtains of light. He passed within twenty feet of Kerans, who knelt hidden behind the column, one hand on Wilson's shoulder, quietening the man's low grumbling. Skirting the helicopter, Hardman reached the far end of the courthouse and there left the square, walking steadily up a narrow incline towards the silt banks which stretched along the shore a hundred yards away.

Acknowledging his escape, the intensity of the sunlight diminished fractionally.

"Colonel Riggs!"

Macready plunged down the steps, shielding his eyes from the glare, and pointed off across the silt flat with his Thompson. Riggs followed him, hatless, his thin shoulders pinched together, tired and dispirited.

He put a restraining hand on Macready's elbow. "Let him go, Sergeant. We'll never catch him now. There doesn't seem to be much point, anyway."

Safely two hundred yards away, Hardman was still moving strongly, undeterred by the furnace-like heat. He reached the first crest, partly hidden in the huge palls of steam which hung over the centre of the silt flat, fading into them like a man disappearing into a deep mist. The endless banks of the inland sea stretched out in front of him, merging at their edges into the incandescent sky so that to Kerans he seemed to be walking across dunes of white-hot ash into the very mouth of the sun.

For the next two hours he sat quietly in the museum, waiting for the cutter to arrive, listening to Riggs' irritated grumbling and Daley's lame excuses. Drained by the heat, Kerans tried to sleep, but the occasional crack of a carbine jolted through his bruised brain like the kick of a leather boot. Attracted by the sounds of the helicopter, a school of iguana had approached, and the reptiles were now sidling around the edges of the square, braying at the men on the steps of the museum. Their harsh shrieking voices filled Kerans with a dull fear that persisted even after the cutter's arrival and their return journey to the base. Sitting in the comparative coolness under the wire hood, the green banks of the channel sliding past, he could hear their raucous barks.

At the base he settled Wilson in the sick-bay, then sought out Dr. Bodkin and described the events of the morning, referring in passing to the voices of the iguanas. Enigmatically, Bodkin only nodded to himself, then remarked: "Be warned, Robert; you may hear them again."

About Hardman's escape he made no comment.

Kerans' catamaran was still moored across the lagoon, so he decided to spend the night in his cabin at the testing station. There he passed a quiet afternoon, nursing a light fever in his bunk, thinking of Hardman and his strange southward odyssey, and of the silt banks glowing like luminous gold in the meridian sun, both forbidding and inviting, like the lost but forever beckoning and unattainable shores of the amnionic paradise.

CHAPTER FIVE

DESCENT INTO DEEP TIME

LATER THAT NIGHT, as Kerans lay asleep in his bunk at the testing station, the dark waters of the lagoon outside drifting through the drowned city, the first of the dreams came to him. He had left his cabin and walked out on to the deck, looking down over the rail at the black luminous disc of the lagoon. Dense palls of opaque gas swirled across the sky only a few hundred feet overhead, through which he could just discern the faint glimmering outline of a gigantic sun. Booming distantly, it sent dull glows pulsing across the lagoon, momentarily lighting the long limestone cliffs which had taken the place of the ring of white-faced buildings.

Reflecting these intermittent flares, the deep bowl of the water shone in a diffused opalescent blur, the discharged light of myriads of phosphorescing animalcula, congregating in dense shoals like a succession of submerged haloes.

Between them the water was thick with thousands of entwined snakes and eels, writhing together in frantic tangles that tore the surface of the lagoon.

As the great sun drummed nearer, almost filling the sky itself, the dense vegetation along the limestone cliffs was flung back abruptly, to reveal the black and stone-grey heads of enormous Triassic lizards. Strutting forward to the edge of the cliffs, they began to roar together at the sun, the noise gradually mounting until it became indistinguishable from the volcanic pounding of the solar flares. Kerans felt, beating within him like his own pulse, the powerful mesmeric pull of the baying reptiles, and stepped out into the lake, whose waters now seemed an extension of his own bloodstream. As the dull pounding rose, he felt the barriers which divided his own cells from the surrounding medium dissolving, and he swam forwards, spreading outwards across the black thudding water. . . .

He woke in the suffocating metal box of his cabin, his head splitting like a burst marrow, too exhausted to open his eyes. Even as he sat on the bed, splashing his face in the luke-warm water from the jug, he could still see the vast inflamed disc of the spectral sun, still hear the tremendous drumming of its beat. Timing them, he realised that the frequency was that of his own heartbeats, but in some insane way the sounds were magnified so that they remained just above the auditory threshold, reverberating dimly off the metal walls and ceiling like the whispering murmur of some blind pelagic current against the hull-plates of a submarine.

The sounds seemed to pursue him as he opened the cabin door and moved down the corridor to the galley. It was shortly after 6 a.m. and the testing station stirred with a faint hollowed silence, the first flares of the false dawn illuminating the dusty reagent benches and the crates stacked under the fan-lights in the corridor. Several times Kerans paused and tried to shrug off the echoes that persisted in his ears, uneasily wondering what was the real identity of his new pursuers. His unconscious was rapidly becoming a well-stocked pantheon of tutelary phobias and obsessions, homing on to his already over-burdened psyche like lost telepaths. Sooner or later the archetypes themselves would become restive and start fighting each other, anima against persona, ego against id. . . .

Then he remembered that Beatrice Dahl had seen the same dream and pulled himself together. He went out on to the deck and looked across the slack water of the lagoon at the distant spire of the apartment block, trying to decide whether to borrow one of the scows moored to the jetty and drive over to her. Having now experienced one of the dreams, he realised the courage and self-sufficiency Beatrice had displayed, brushing off the least show of sympathy.

And yet Kerans knew that for some reason he had been reluctant to give Beatrice any real sympathy, cutting his questions about the nightmares as short as possible and never offering her treatment or sedative. Nor had he tried to follow up any of Bodkin's or Riggs' oblique remarks about the dreams and their danger, almost as if he had known that he would soon be sharing them, and accepted them as an inevitable element of his life, like the image of his own death each of them carried with him in the secret places of his heart. (Logically—for what had a more gloomy prognosis than life?—every morning one should say to one's friends: 'I grieve for your irrevocable death', as to anyone suffering from an incurable disease, and was the universal omission of this minimal gesture of sympathy the model for their reluctance to discuss the dreams?)

Bodkin was sitting at the table in the galley when Kerans entered, placidly drinking coffee brewed in a large cracked saucepan on the stove. His shrewd quick eyes watched Kerans unobtrusively as he lowered himself into a chair and massaged his forehead slowly with a febrile hand.

"So you're one of the dreamers now, Robert. You've beheld the fata morgana of the terminal lagoon. You look tired. Was it a deep one?"

Kerans managed a rueful laugh. "Are you trying to frighten me, Alan? I wouldn't know yet, but it felt deep enough. God, I wish I hadn't spent last night here. There are no nightmares at the Ritz." He sipped pensively at the hot coffee. "So that's what Riggs was talking about. How many of his men are seeing these dreams?"

"Riggs himself doesn't, but at least half the others. And Beatrice Dahl, of course. I've been seeing them for a full three months. It's basically the same recurrent dream in all cases." Bodkin spoke in a slow unhurried voice, with a softer tone than his usual blunt delivery, as if Kerans had now become a member of a select inner group. "You've held out for a long time, Robert, it's quite a tribute to the strength of your preconscious filters. We were all beginning to wonder when you'd arrive." He smiled at Kerans. "Figuratively, of course. I've never discussed the dreams with anyone. Except for Hardman, and there, poor chap, the dreams were having him." As an afterthought he added: "You spotted the sun : pulse equation? Hardman's gramophone record was a play-back of his own pulse, amplified in the hope of precipitating the crisis then and there. Don't think I sent him out into those jungles deliberately."

Kerans nodded and gazed out through the window at the rounded bulk of the floating base moored alongside. High up on the top deck Sergeant Daley, the helicopter co-pilot, was standing motionless by the rail, staring across the cool early morning water. Perhaps he too had just woken from the same corporate nightmare, was filling his eyes with the olive-green spectrum of the lagoon in the forlorn expectation of erasing the burning image of the Triassic sun. Kerans looked down at the dark shadows below the table, seeing again the faint glimmer of the phosphorescing pools. Distantly in his ears he could hear the sun drumming over the sunken water. As he recovered from his first fears he realised that there was something soothing about its sounds, almost reassuring and encouraging like his own heartbeats. But the giant reptiles had been terrifying.

He remembered the iguanas braying and lungeing across the steps of the museum. Just as the distinction between the latent and manifest contents of the dream had ceased to be valid, so had any division between the real and the super-real in the external world. Phantoms slid imperceptibly from nightmare to reality and back again, the terrestrial and psychic landscapes were now indistinguishable, as they had been at Hiroshima and Auschwitz, Golgotha and Gomorrah.

Sceptical of the remedy, he said to Bodkin: "You'd better lend me Hardman's alarm clock, Alan. Or better still, remind me to take a phenobarbitone tonight."

"Don't," Bodkin warned him firmly. "Not unless you want the impact doubled. Your residues of conscious control are the only thing holding up the dam." He buttoned his cotton jacket around his shirtless chest. "That wasn't a true dream, Robert, but an ancient organic memory millions of years old."

He pointed to the ascending rim of the sun through the groves of gymnosperms. "The innate releasing mechanisms laid down in your cytoplasm millions of years ago have been awakened, the expanding sun and the rising temperature are driving you back down the spinal levels into the drowned seas submerged beneath the lowest layers of your unconscious, into the entirely new zone of the neuronic psyche. This is the lumbar transfer, total biopsychic recall. We really *remember* these swamps and lagoons. After a few nights you won't be frightened of the dreams, despite their superficial horror. That's why Riggs has received orders for us to leave."

"The Pelycosaur . . . ?" Kerans asked.

Bodkin nodded. "The joke was on us. The reason they didn't take the report seriously at Byrd was that our's wasn't the first to be reported."

Footsteps sounded up the companionway and moved briskly along the metal deck outside. Colonel Riggs pushed back the double swing doors, freshly scrubbed and breakfasted.

He waved his baton at them amiably, eyeing the litter of unwashed cups and his two reclining subordinates.

"God, what a pig hole. Morning to you both. We've got a busy day ahead of us so let's get our elbows off the table.

74

I've fixed the departure time for twelve hundred hours tomorrow, and there'll be a final embarkation stand-by at ten hundred. I don't want to waste any more fuel than I have to, so dump everything you can overboard. You all right, Robert?"

"Perfectly," Kerans replied flatly, sitting up.

"Glad to hear it. You look a bit glassy. Right, then. If you want to borrow the cutter to evacuate the Ritz . . ."

Kerans listened to him automatically, watching the sun as it rose magnificently behind the gesticulating outline of the Colonel. What completely separated them now was the single fact that Riggs had not seen the dream, not felt its immense hallucinatory power. He was still obeying reason and logic, buzzing around his diminished, unimportant world with his little parcels of instructions like a worker bee about to return to the home nest. After a few minutes he ignored the Colonel completely and listened to the deep subliminal drumming in his ears, half-closed his eyes so that he could see the glimmering surface of the lake dapple across the dark underhang of the table.

Opposite him Bodkin appeared to be doing the same, his hands folded over his navel. During how many of their recent conversations had he in fact been miles away?

When Riggs left, Kerans followed him to the door. "Of course, Colonel, everything will be ready in good time. Thank you for calling."

As the cutter moved off across the lagoon he went back to his chair. For a few minutes the two men stared across the table at each other, the insects outside bouncing off the wire mesh as the sun lifted into the sky. At last Kerans spoke.

"Alan, I'm not sure whether I shall be leaving."

Without replying, Bodkin took out his cigarettes. He lit one carefully, then sat back smoking it calmly. "Do you know where we are?" he asked after a pause. "The name of this city?" When Kerans shook his head he said: "Part of it used to be called London; not that it matters. Curiously enough, though, I was born here. Yesterday I rowed over to the old University quarter, a mass of little creeks, actually found the laboratory where my father used to teach. We left here when I was six, but I can just remember being taken to meet him one day. A few hundred yards away there was a planetarium, I saw a performance once—that was before they had to re-align the projector. The big dome is still there, about twenty feet below water. It looks like an enormous shell, fucus growing all over it, straight out of *The Water Babies*. Curiously, looking down at the dome seemed to bring my childhood much nearer. To tell the truth, I'd more or less forgotten it—at my age all you have are the memories of memories. After we left here our existence became completely nomadic, and in a sense this city is the only home I've ever known——" He broke off abruptly, his face suddenly tired.

"Go on," Kerans said evenly.

CHAPTER SIX

THE DROWNED ARK

THE TWO MEN MOVED quickly along the deck, their padded soles soundless on the metal plates. A white midnight sky hung across the dark surface of the lagoon, a few stationary clumps of cumulus like sleeping galleons. The low night sounds of the jungle drifted over the water; occasionally a marmoset gibbered or the iguanas shrieked distantly from their eyries in the submerged office blocks. Myriads of insects festered along the water-line, momentarily disturbed as the swells rolled in against the base, slapping at the canted sides of the pontoon.

Kerans began to cast off the restraining lines one by one, taking advantage of the swells to lift the loops off the rusting bollards. As the station slowly pivoted away he looked up anxiously at the dark bulk of the base. Gradually the three nearside blades of the helicopter came into view above the top deck, then the slender tail rotor. He paused before releasing the last line, waiting for Bodkin to give the all-clear from the starboard bridge.

The tension on the line had doubled, and it took Kerans several minutes to work the metal loop up the curving lip of the bollard, the successive swells giving him a few inches of slack as the station tilted, followed a moment later by the base. Above him he could hear Bodkin whispering impatiently—they had swung right around into the narrow interval of water behind them and were now face on to the lagoon, the single light in Beatrice's penthouse burning on its pylon. Then he cleared the lip and lowered the heavy cable into the slack water three feet below, watching it cleave back towards the base.

Freed of its attendant burden, and with its centre of gravity raised by the helicopter on its roof, the huge drum rolled over a full five degrees from the vertical, then gradually regained its balance. A light in one of the cabins went on, then flicked off again after a few moments. Kerans seized the boat-hook on the deck beside him as the interval of open water widened, first to twenty yards, then to fifty. A low current moved steadily through the lagoons, and would carry them back along the shore to their former mooring.

Holding the station off from the buildings they skirted, now and then crushing the soft fern trees sprouting through the windows, they soon covered two hundred yards, slowing as the current diminished around the curve, and finally lodged in a narrow inlet about a hundred feet square in size.

Kerans leaned over the rail, looking down through the dark water at the small cinema theatre twenty feet below the surface, its flat roof luckily uncluttered by elevator-heads or fire escapes. Waving to Bodkin on the deck above, he stepped in through the laboratory and made his way past the specimen tanks and sinks to the companionway leading down to the float.

Only one stop-cock had been built into the base of the float, but as he turned the handwheel a powerful jet of cold foaming water gushed up around his legs. By the time he returned to the lower deck, to make a final check of the

77

laboratory, water was already spilling ankle-deep through the scuppers, sluicing among the sinks and benches. He quickly released the marmoset from its fume cupboard and pushed the bushy-tailed mammal through one of the windows. The station went down like an elevator, and he waded waist-deep to the companionway and climbed up to the next deck where Bodkin was exultantly watching the windows of the adjacent office blocks rise into the air.

They settled about three feet below deck level, on a flat keel with a convenient access point by the starboard bridge. Dimly below they could hear trapped air bubbling from the retorts and glass-ware in the laboratory, and a frothy stain spread across the water from a submerged window by one of the reagent benches.

Kerans watched the indigo bubbles fade and dissolve, thinking of the huge semi-circle of programme charts sinking below the water as he left the laboratory, a perfect, almost vaudevillean comment on the biophysical mechanisms they sought to describe, and which perhaps symbolised the uncertainties that lay ahead now that he and Bodkin had committed themselves to remaining behind. They were now entering the *aqua incognita*, with only a few rule-of-thumb principles to guide them.

From the typewriter in his cabin Kerans took a sheet of paper, pinned it firmly to the door of the galley. Bodkin appended his signature to the message, and the two men went out on to the deck again and lowered Kerans' catamaran into the water.

Paddling slowly, the outboard shipped, they glided off across the black water, soon disappearing among the dark blue shadows along the edge of the lagoon.

As the down-draught from its blades fanned furiously across the swimming pool, tearing at the striped awning of the patio, the helicopter circled deafeningly over the penthouse, plunging and diving as it searched for a landing point. Kerans smiled to himself as he watched it through the plastic vanes over the lounge windows, confident that the tottering pile of kerosene drums he and Bodkin had pyramided over the roof would safely deter the pilot. One or two of the drums toppled down on to the patio and splashed into the pool, and the helicopter veered away and then came in more slowly, hovering steadily.

The pilot, Sergeant Daley, swung the fuselage around so that the hatch door faced the lounge windows, and the hatless figure of Riggs appeared in the doorway, two of the soldiers holding on to him as he bellowed into an electric megaphone.

Beatrice Dahl ran across to Kerans from her observation post at the far end of the lounge, cupping her ears from the din.

"Robert, he's trying to talk to us!"

Kerans nodded, the Colonel's voice completely lost in the engine roar. Riggs finished and the helicopter leaned backwards and soared away across the lagoon, taking the noise and vibration with it.

Kerans put his arm around Beatrice's shoulders, the bare oiled skin smooth under his fingers. "Well, I think we have a pretty good idea what he was saying."

They went out on to the patio, waving up to Bodkin, who had appeared from the elevator-house and was straightening the drums. Below them, on the opposite side of the lagoon, the upper deck and bridge of the scuttled testing station protruded from the water, a flotsam of hundreds of pieces of old note-paper eddying away from it. Standing by the rail, Kerans pointed to the yellow hull of the base moored by the Ritz in the furthest of the three central lagoons.

After a futile attempt to re-float the station, Riggs had set off at noon as planned, sending the cutter over to the apartment house where he assumed the two biologists were hiding. Finding the elevator out of order, his men had refused the alternative of a twenty-storey climb up the stairway— already a few iguanas had made their homes on the lower landings—so Riggs had finally tried to reach them with the helicopter. Balked there, he was now crashing the Ritz.

"Thank God he's left," Beatrice said fervently. "For some reason he really got on my nerves."

"You made that pretty plain. I'm surprised he didn't take a pot shot at you."

"But, darling, he was insufferable. All that stiff upper lip stuff and dressing for dinner in the jungle—a total lack of adaptability."

"Riggs was all right," Kerans remarked quietly. "He'll probably get by." Now that Riggs had gone he was aware of how dependent he had been on the Colonel's buoyancy and good humour. Without him the morale of the unit would have disintegrated in an instant. It remained to be seen whether Kerans could imbue his own little trio with the same degree of confidence and sense of purpose. Certainly it was up to him to be the leader; Bodkin was too old, Beatrice too self-immersed.

Kerans glanced at the thermo-alarm he wore next to his wrist-watch. It was after 3.30, but the temperature was still a hundred and ten degrees, the sun beating against his skin like a fist. They joined Bodkin and went into the lounge.

Resuming the action conference interrupted by the helicopter, Kerans said: "You've got about a thousand gallons left in the roof tank, Bea, enough for three months—or let's say two as we can expect it to get a lot hotter—and I recommend you to close down the rest of the apartment and move into here. You're on the north side of the patio so the elevator-house will protect you from the heavy rains when they come in on the southerly storms. Ten to one the shutters and air-seals along the bedroom walls will be breached. What about food, Alan? How long will the stocks in the deep freeze last?"

Bodkin pulled a distasteful face. "Well, as most of the lambs' tongues in aspic have been eaten they now consist chiefly of bully beef, so you could say 'indefinitely'. However, if you're actually planning to eat the stuff—six months. But I'd prefer iguana."

"No doubt the iguana would prefer us. All right then, that seems pretty fair. Alan will be over in the station until the level rises, and I'll be holding out at the Ritz. Anything else?"

Beatrice wandered away around the sofa towards the bar.

"Yes, darling. Shut up. You're beginning to sound like Riggs. The military manner doesn't suit you."

Kerans threw her a mock salute and strolled over to look at the painting by Ernst at the far end of the lounge, while Bodkin gazed down at the jungle through the window. More and more the two scenes were coming to resemble each other, and in turn the third nightscape each of them carried within his mind. They never discussed their dreams, the common zone of twilight where they moved at night like the phantoms in the Delvaux painting.

Beatrice had sat down on the sofa with her back to him, and shrewdly Kerans guessed that the present unity of the group would not be long maintained. Beatrice was right; the military manner did not suit him, his personality was too passive and introverted, too self-centred. More important, though, they were entering a new zone, where the usual obligations and allegiances ceased to operate. Now that they had made their decision the bonds between them had already begun to fade, and it was not simply for reasons of convenience that they would live apart. Much as he needed Beatrice Dahl, her personality intruded upon the absolute freedom he required for himself. By and large, each of them would have to pursue his or her own pathway through the time jungles, mark their own points of no return. Although they might see one another occasionally, around the lagoons or at the testing station, their only true meeting ground would be in their dreams.

CHAPTER SEVEN

CARNIVAL OF ALLIGATORS

SPLIT BY AN immense roar, the early morning silence over the lagoon shattered abruptly, and a tremendous blare of noise battered past the windows of the hotel suite. With an effort Kerans pulled his reluctant body from his bed and stumbled across the books scattered on the floor. He kicked back the mesh door on to the balcony in time to see a huge white-hulled hydroplane speed by around the lagoon, its two long stepped planes cleaving perfect slices of glittering spray. As the heavy wash slapped against the wall of the hotel, breaking up the colonies of water spiders and disturbing the bats nesting among the rotting logs, he caught a glimpse of a tall, broad-shouldered man in the cockpit, wearing a white helmet and jerkin, standing upright at the controls.

He drove the hydroplane with an easy nonchalant swagger, accelerating the two powerful propeller turbines mounted in front of him as the craft hit the broad swells across the lagoon, so that it plunged and dived like a power-boat wrestling through giant rollers, throwing up gales of rain-bowing spray. The man rolled with the surging motion of the craft, his long legs supple and relaxed, like a charioteer completely in command of a spirited team.

Hidden by the calamites which now spilled across the balcony—the effort of cutting them back had long seemed pointless—Kerans watched him unobserved. As the craft sped by on its second circuit, Kerans had a glimpse of a rakish profile, bright eyes and teeth, an expression of exhilarated conquest.

The silver studs of a cartridge belt flashed around his waist, and when he reached the far side of the lagoon there was a series of short explosions. Signal shells burst over the water into ragged red umbrellas, the fragments spitting down across the shore.

In a final lunge of energy, its engines screaming, the hydroplane swerved out of the lagoon and gunned away down the canal to the next lagoon, its wash thrashing at the foliage. Kerans gripped the balcony rail, watching the disturbed restless water of the lagoon trying to re-settle itself, the giant cryptograms and scale trees along the shore tossed and flurried by the still surging air. A thin pall of red vapour drifted away to the north, fading with the diminishing sounds of the hydroplane. The violent irruption of noise and energy, and the arrival of this strange white-suited figure, momentarily disconcerted Kerans, jerking him roughly from his lassitude and torpor.

In the six weeks since Riggs' departure he had lived almost alone in his penthouse suite at the hotel, immersing himself more and more deeply in the silent world of the surrounding jungle. The continued increase in temperature—the thermo-alarm on the balcony now registered a noon high of one hundred and thirty degrees—and the enervating humidity made it almost impossible to leave the hotel after ten o'clock in the morning; the lagoons and the jungle were filled with fire until four o'clock, by when he was usually too tired to do anything but return to bed.

All day he sat by the shuttered windows of the suite, listening from the shadows to the shifting movement of the mesh cage, as it expanded and contracted in the heat. Already many of the buildings around the lagoon had disappeared beneath the proliferating vegetation; huge club-mosses and calamites blotted out the white rectangular faces, shading the lizards in their window lairs.

Beyond the lagoon the endless tides of silt had begun to accumulate in enormous glittering banks, here and there over-topping the shore-line, like the immense tippings of some distant gold-mine. The light drummed against his brain, bathing the submerged levels below his consciousness, carrying him downwards into warm pellucid depths where the nominal realities of time and space ceased to exist. Guided by his dreams, he was moving backwards through the emergent past, through a succession of ever stranger land-scapes, centred upon the lagoon, each of which, as Bodkin had said, seemed to represent one of his own spinal levels. At times the circle of water was spectral and vibrant, at others slack and murky, the shore apparently formed of shale, like the dull metallic skin of a reptile. Yet again the soft beaches would glow invitingly with a glossy carmine sheen, the sky warm and limpid, the emptiness of the long stretches of sand total and absolute, filling him with an exquisite and tender anguish.

83

He longed for this descent through archaeopsychic time to reach its conclusion, repressing the knowledge that when it did the external world around him would have become alien and unbearable.

Sometimes he restlessly made a few entries in his botanical diary about the new plant forms, and during the first weeks called several times on Dr. Bodkin and Beatrice Dahl. But both were increasingly preoccupied with their own descents through total time. Bodkin had become lost in his private reverie, punting aimlessly around the narrow creeks in search of the submerged world of his childhood. Once Kerans came across him resting on an oar in the stern of his small metal scow and gazing vacantly at the unyielding buildings around him. He had stared straight through Kerans, failing to acknowledge his call.

However, with Beatrice, despite their superficial estrangement, there was an intact underlying union, a tacit awareness of their symbolic roles.

More signal shells burst over the distal lagoon, containing the station and Beatrice's apartment house, and Kerans shielded his eyes as the bright fire-balls studded the sky. A few seconds later, several miles away among the silt banks to the south, there was a series of answering bursts, faint puffs that soon dispersed.

So the stranger driving the hydroplane was not alone. At the prospect of this imminent invasion Kerans pulled himself together. The distance separating the answering signals was wide enough to indicate that there was more than one group, and that the hydroplane was merely a scout vehicle.

Sealing the mesh door behind him, he stepped back into the suite, pulling his jacket off the chair. Out of habit he went into the bathroom and stood in front of the mirror, absently feeling the week-old stubble on his face. The hair was white as pearl, and with his ebony tan and introspective eyes gave him the appearance of a refined and cultivated beachcomber. A bucketful of dingy water had leaked in from the wrecked still on the roof, and he scooped some out and splashed his face, a token toilet performed, as far as he could see, solely out of habit.

Using the metal-tipped boat-hook to drive away two small iguanas idling on the jetty, he slid the catamaran into the water and cast off, the little outboard carrying him steadily through the sluggish swells. Huge clumps of algae stirred below the craft, and stick-beetle and water spider raced around its prows. It was a few minutes after seven o'clock, and the temperature was only eighty degrees, comparatively cool and pleasant, the air free of the enormous clouds of mosquitoes which would later be roused from their nests by the heat.

As he navigated the hundred-yard-long creek leading into the southern lagoon more signal rockets were exploding overhead, and he could hear the hydroplane zooming to and fro, occasionally glimpse the white-suited figure at its controls as it flashed past. Kerans cut the outboard at the entrance to the lagoon and glided quietly through the overhanging fern fronds, watching for water snakes disturbed from the branches by the surging wash.

Twenty-five yards along the shore he berthed the catamaran among the horse-tails growing on the shelving roof of a department store, waded up the sloping concrete to a fire escape on the side of the adjacent building. He climbed the five storeys to the flat roof-top and lay down behind a low pediment, glancing up at the nearby bulk of Beatrice's apartment house.

The hydroplane was circling noisily by an inlet on the far side of the lagoon, the driver plunging it backwards and forwards like a horseman reining his steed. More flares were going up, some only a quarter of a mile away. As he watched Kerans noticed a low but mounting roar, a harsh animal sound not unlike that emitted by the iguanas. It drew nearer, mingled with the drone of engines, followed by the noise of vegetation being torn and buffeted. Sure enough, along the course followed by the inlet, the huge fern trees and calamites were flung down one after the other, their branches waving as they fell like vanquished standards. The whole jungle was being torn apart. Droves of bats erupted into the air and scattered frantically across the lagoon, their screeching masked by the accelerating turbines of the hydroplane and the exploding star-shells.

Abruptly, the water in the mouth of the inlet rose several feet into the air, what seemed to be an enormous log-jam crushed down it, tearing the vegetation away, and burst out into the lagoon. A miniature niagara of foaming water cascaded outwards, impelled by the pressure of the tidal bore behind it, on which rode several square black-hulled craft similar to Colonel Riggs' cutter, paint peeling from the giant dragon eyes and teeth slashed across their bows. Manned by a dozen dusky-skinned figures in white shorts and singlets, the scows jockeyed out towards the centre of the lagoon, the last of the star-shells still going up from their decks in the general mêlée and excitement.

Half-deafened by the noise, Kerans stared down at the vast swarm of long brown forms swimming powerfully through the seething water, their massive tails lashing the foam. By far the largest alligators he had seen, many of them over twenty-five feet long, they jostled together ferociously as they fought their way into the clear water, churning in a pack around the now stationary hydroplane. The white-suited man was standing in the open hatchway, hands on hips, gazing exultantly at this reptilian brood. He waved lazily at the crews of the three scows, then gestured in a wide circle at the lagoon, indicating that they would anchor there.

As his Negro lieutenants re-started their engines and drifted off towards the bank, he surveyed the surrounding buildings with a critical eye, his strong face raised almost jauntily to one side. The alligators congregated like hounds around their master, the wheeling cries of the dense cloud of sentinel birds overhead, Nile plover and stone curlew, piercing the morning air. More and more of the alligators joined the pack, cruising shoulder to shoulder in a clock-wise spiral, until at least two thousand were present, a massive group incarnation of reptilian evil.

With a shout, the pilot swung back to his controls, the two thousand snouts lifting in recognition. The propellers kicked into life and lifted the hydroplane forward across the water. Its sharp planes ploughing straight across the hapless creatures in their path, it drove away towards the communicating creek into the next lagoon, the great mass of alligators surging along behind it. A few detached themselves and cruised off in pairs around the lagoon, ferreting among the submerged windows and driving off the iguanas who had come out to watch. Others glided among the buildings and took up their positions on the barely covered roof-tops. Behind them, in the centre of the lagoon, the beaten water churned uneasily, occasionally throwing up the snow-white belly of a dead alligator crushed by the hydroplane.

As the advancing armada headed towards the creek on his left, Kerans scrambled down the fire escape and splashed down the sloping roof to the catamaran. Before he could reach it the heavy wash set up by the hydroplane had rocked the craft adrift, and it floated off into the oncoming mass. Within a few seconds it was engulfed, upended by the press of alligators fighting to get into the creek and cut to pieces in their snapping jaws.

A large caiman bringing up the rear spotted Kerans waist-deep among the horse-tails and veered towards him, its eyes steadying. Its rough scaly back and the crest along its tail flexed powerfully as it surged through the water. Quickly Kerans retreated up the slope, slipping once to his shoulders, reached the fire escape as the caiman lumbered out of the shallows on its short hooked legs and lunged at his leaping feet.

Panting, Kerans leaned on the rail, looking down at the cold unblinking eyes which regarded him dispassionately.

"You're a well-trained watchdog," he told it ungrudgingly. He eased a loose brick from the wall and launched it with both hands at the knob on the end of the caiman's snout, grinning as it bellowed and backed off, snapping irritably at the horse-tails and a few drifting spars of the catamaran.

After half an hour, and a few minor duels with the retreating iguanas, he managed to cross the intervening two hundred yards of shoreline and reach Beatrice's apartment house. She met him as he stepped out of the elevator, wide-eyed with alarm.

"Robert, what's happening?" She put her hands on his shoulders and pressed her head against his damp shirt. "Have you seen the alligators? There are thousands of them!"

"*Seen* them—I was damn' nearly eaten by one on your doorstep." Kerans released himself and hurried over to the window, pushed back the plastic vanes. The hydroplane had entered the central lagoon and was circling it at speed, the shoal of alligators following in its wake, those at the tail breaking off to station themselves at points around the shore. At least thirty or forty had remained in the lagoon below, and were cruising about slowly in small patrols, occasionally swerving on a careless iguana.

"Those devilish things must be their watch-guards," Kerans decided. "Like a tame troupe of tarantulas. Nothing better, when you come to think of it."

Beatrice stood beside him, nervously fingering the collar of the jade silk shirt she wore over her black swim-suit. Although the apartment was beginning to look ramshackle and untidy, Beatrice continued to tend her own appearance devotedly. On the few occasions when Kerans called she would be sitting on the patio or before a mirror in her bedroom, automatically applying endless layers of patina, like a blind painter forever retouching a portrait he can barely remember for fear that otherwise he will forget it completely. Her hair was always dressed immaculately, the make-up on her mouth and eyes exquisitely applied, but her withdrawn, isolated gaze gave her the waxen, glacé beauty of an inanimate mannequin. At last, however, she had been roused.

"But who are they, Robert? That man in the speed-boat frightens me. I wish Colonel Riggs was here."

"He'll be a thousand miles away by now, if he hasn't already reached Byrd. Don't worry, Bea. They may look a piratical crew, but there's nothing we can give them."

A large three-decker paddle-boat, paddles set fore and aft, had entered the lagoon, and was slowly moving over to the three scows drawn up a few yards from where Riggs' base had been moored. It was loaded with gear and cargo, decks crammed with large bales and canvas-swathed machinery, so that there was only six inches of freeboard amidships.

Kerans guessed that this was the group's depot ship, and that they were engaged, like most of the other freebooters still wandering through the Equatorial lagoons and archipelagos, in pillaging the drowned cities, reclaiming the heavy specialised machinery such as electrical power generators and switchgear that had been perforce abandoned by the governments. Nominally such looting was highly penalised, but in fact the authorities were only too eager to pay a generous price for any salvage.

"Look!"

Beatrice gripped Kerans' elbow. She pointed down at the testing station, where the rumpled, shaggy-haired figure of Dr. Bodkin stood on the roof, waving slowly at the men on the bridge of the paddle-boat. One of them, a bare-chested Negro in white slacks and a white peaked cap, began to shout back through a hailer.

Kerans shrugged. "Alan's right. We've everything to gain by showing ourselves. If we help them they'll soon push off and leave us alone."

Beatrice hesitated, but Kerans took her arm. The hydroplane, now free of its entourage, was crossing the central lagoon on its return, leaping lightly through the water on a beautiful wake of foam.

"Come on. If we get down to the jetty in time he'll probably give us a lift."

CHAPTER EIGHT

THE MAN WITH THE WHITE SMILE

His handsome saturnine face regarding them with a mixture of suspicion and amused contempt, Strangman lounged back under the cool awning that shaded the poop deck of the depot ship. He had changed into a crisp white suit, the silk-like surface of which reflected the gilt plate of his high-backed Renaissance throne, presumably dredged from some Venetian or Florentine lagoon, and invested his strange personality with an almost magical aura.

"Your motives seem so complex, Doctor," he remarked to Kerans. "But perhaps you've given up hope of understanding them yourself. We shall label them the total beach syndrome and leave it at that."

He snapped his fingers at the steward standing in the shadows behind him and selected an olive from the tray of small chow. Beatrice, Kerans and Bodkin sat in a semi-circle on the low couches, alternately chilled and roasted as the erratic air-conditioner above them varied its perimeter. Outside, half an hour before noon, the lagoon was a bowl of fire, the scattered light almost masking the tall apartment house on the opposite bank. The jungle was motionless in the immense heat, the alligators hiding in whatever shade they could find.

None the less, several of Strangman's men were messing about in one of the scows, unloading some heavy diving equipment under the direction of a huge hunchbacked Negro in a pair of green cotton shorts. A giant grotesque parody of a human being, now and then he took off his eye-patch to bellow abuse at them, and the mingled grunts and curses drifted across the steaming air.

"But tell me, Doctor," Strangman pressed, apparently

dissatisfied with Kerans' answers, "when do you finally propose to leave?"

Kerans hesitated, wondering whether to invent a date. After waiting an hour for Strangman to change, he had offered their greetings to him and tried to explain why they were still there. However, Strangman seemed unable to take the explanation seriously, swinging abruptly from amusement at their naïvety to sharp suspicion. Kerans watched him carefully, reluctant to make even the smallest false move. Whatever his real identity, Strangman was no ordinary freebooter. A curious air of menace pervaded the depot ship, its crew and their master. Strangman in particular, with his white smiling face, its cruel lines sharpening like arrows when he grinned, disturbed Kerans.

"We haven't really considered the possibility," Kerans said. "I think we all hope to stay on indefinitely. We have small stocks of supplies."

"But, my dear man," Strangman remonstrated, "the temperature will soon be up to nearly two hundred degrees. The entire planet is rapidly returning to the Mesozoic Period."

"Precisely," Dr. Bodkin cut in, rousing himself for a moment from his introspection. "And in so far as we are part of the planet, a piece of the main, we too are returning. This is our zone of transit, here we are re-assimilating our own biological pasts. That's why we have chosen to remain here. There is no ulterior motive, Strangman."

"Of course not, Doctor. I completely respect your sincerity." Shifts of mood seemed to cross and re-cross Strangman's face, making him look in turn irritable, amiable, bored and abstracted. He listened to an air-line pumping from the scow, then asked: "Dr. Bodkin, did you live in London as a child? You must have many sentimental memories to recapture, of the great palaces and museums." He added: "Or are the only memories you have pre-uterine ones?"

Kerans looked up, surprised at the ease with which Strangman had mastered Bodkin's jargon. He noticed that

Strangman was not only watching Bodkin shrewdly, but also waiting for any reaction from himself and Beatrice.

But Bodkin gestured vaguely. "No, I'm afraid I remember nothing. The immediate past is of no interest to me."

"What a pity," Strangman rejoined archly. "The trouble with you people is that you've been here for thirty million years and your perspectives are all wrong. You miss so much of the transitory beauty of life. I'm fascinated by the immediate past—the treasures of the Triassic compare pretty unfavourably with those of the closing years of the Second Millenium."

He leaned around on one elbow and smiled at Beatrice, who sat with her hands discretely covering her bare knees, like a mouse observing a particularly fine cat. "And what about you, Miss Dahl? You look a little melancholy. A touch of time-sickness, perhaps? The chronoclasmic bends?" He chuckled, amused by this sally, and Beatrice said quietly:

"We're usually rather tired here, Mr. Strangman. By the way, I don't like your alligators."

"They won't hurt you." Strangman leaned back and surveyed the trio. "It's all very strange." Over his shoulder he rapped a short command at the steward, then sat frowning to himself. Kerans realised that the skin of his face and hands was uncannily white, devoid altogether of any pigmentation. Kerans' heavy sunburn, like that of Beatrice and Dr. Bodkin, made him virtually indistinguishable from the remainder of the Negro crew, and the subtle distinctions between the mulattoes and quadroons had vanished. Strangman alone retained his original paleness, the effect emphasised by the white suit he had chosen.

The bare-chested Negro in the peaked cap appeared, sweat rilling across his powerful muscles. He was about six feet in height, but the rolling breadth of his shoulders made him seem stocky and compact. His manner was deferential and observant, and Kerans wondered how Strangman managed to maintain his authority over the crew, and why they accepted his harsh, callous tone.

Strangman introduced the Negro curtly. "This is the

Admiral, my chief whip. If I'm not around when you want me, deal with him." He stood up, stepping down from the dais. "Before you leave, let me take you on a brief tour of my treasure ship." He extended an arm gallantly to Beatrice, who took it timorously, his eyes glinting and rapacious.

At one time, Kerans surmised, the depot ship had been a gambling steamer and floating vice den, moored beyond the five-mile limit outside Messina or Beirut, or in the shelter of some estuarine creek under the blander, more tolerant skies south of the equator. As they left the deck a squad of men were lowering an ancient ornamental gangway to the water's edge, its banisters of peeling gilt shaded by a white clapboard marquee painted with gold tassels and drapery, creaking about on its pulleys like a funicular gazebo. The interior of the ship was decorated in a similar pastiche baroque. The bar, now dark and closed, at the forward end of the observation deck was like the stern castle of a ceremonial galleon, naked gilt caryatids supporting its portico. Semi-columns of fake marble formed little loggias that led away to the private alcoves and dining rooms, while the divided central stairway was a bad film set of Versailles, an aerial riot of dusty cupids and candelabra, the grimy brass overlayed with mould and verdigris.

But the former roulette wheels and chemin de fer tables had gone, and the scarred parquet flooring was covered with a mass of crates and cartons, piled up against the wire-mesh windows so that only a faint reflection of the light outside seeped through. Everything was well packed and sealed, but on an old mahogany chart table in one corner Kerans saw a collection of bronze and marble limbs and torsos, fragments of statuary waiting to be sorted.

Strangman paused at the bottom of the staircase, tearing off a strip of fading tempera from one of the murals. "The place is falling to bits. Hardly up to the standard of the Ritz, Doctor. I envy your good sense."

Kerans shrugged. "It's a low-rent area now." He waited

as Strangman unlocked a door, and they entered the main
storehold, a dim stifling cavern packed with large wooden
crates, the floor strewn with sawdust. They were no longer
in the refrigerated section of the ship, and the Admiral and
another sailor followed them closely, continually hosing
them with ice-cold air from a faucet on the wall. Strangman
snapped his fingers and the Admiral quickly began to
pull away the canvas wrappings draped between the
crates.

In the thin light Kerans could just see the glimmering
outline of a huge ornamented altarpiece at the far end of the
hold, fitted with elaborate scroll-work and towering dolphin
candelabra, topped by a neo-classical proscenium which
would have covered a small house. Next to it stood a dozen
pieces of statuary, mostly of the late Renaissance, stacks of
heavy gilt frames propped against them. Beyond these were
several smaller altar-pieces and triptychs, an intact pulpit in
panelled gold, three large equestrian statues, a few strands
of sea-weed still entwined in the horses' manes, several
pairs of enormous cathedral doors, embossed in gold and
silver, and a large tiered marble fountain. The metal shelves
around the side of the hold were loaded with smaller
bric-à-brac: votive urns, goblets, shields and salvers,
pieces of decorative armour, ceremonial inkstands and the
like.

Still holding Beatrice's arm, Strangman gestured expan-
sively a few yards ahead. Kerans heard him say "Sistine
Chapel" and "Medici Tomb", but Bodkin muttered:
"Aesthetically, most of this is rubbish, picked for the gold
content alone. Yet there's not much of that. What *is* the
man up to?"

Kerans nodded, watching Strangman in his white suit, the
bare-legged Beatrice beside him. Suddenly he remembered
the Delvaux painting, with its tuxedoed skeletons. Strangman's chalk-white face was like a skull, and he had
something of the skeletons' jauntiness. For no reason he
began to feel an intense distaste for the man, his hostility
more generalised than personal.

"Well, Kerans, what do you think of them?" Strangman pivoted at one end of the aisle and swung back, barking at the Admiral to cover the exhibits again. "Impressed, Doctor?"

Kerans managed to take his eyes off Strangman's face and glanced at the looted relics.

"They're like bones," he said flatly.

Baffled, Strangman shook his head. "Bones? What on earth are you talking about? Kerans, you're insane! Bones, good God!"

As he let out a martyred groan, the Admiral took up the refrain, first saying the word quietly to himself as if examining a strange object, then repeating it more and more rapidly in a sort of nervous release, his broad face gibbering with laughter. The other sailor joined in, and together they began to chant it out, convulsed over the fire hose like snake dancers.

"Bones! Yes, man, dem's all bones! Dem bones dem bones dem . . .!"

Strangman watched them angrily, the muscles of his face locking and unlocking like manacles. Disgusted with this display of rudeness and bad temper, Kerans turned to leave the hold. In annoyance Strangman rushed after him, pressed the palm of his hand in Kerans' back and propelled him along the aisle out of the hold.

Five minutes later, as they drove off in one of the scows, the Admiral and half a dozen other members of the crew lined the rail, still chanting and dancing. Strangman had regained his humour, and stood coolly in his white suit, detached from the others, waving ironically.

CHAPTER NINE

THE POOL OF THANATOS

DURING THE NEXT two weeks, as the southern horizon became increasingly darkened by the approaching rain-clouds, Kerans saw Strangman frequently. Usually he would be driving his hydroplane at speed around the lagoons, his white lounge suit exchanged for overalls and helmet, supervising the work of the salvage teams. One scow, with six men, was working in each of the three lagoons, the divers methodically exploring the sunken buildings. Occasionally the placid routines of descent and pump would be interrupted by the sounds of rifle fire as an alligator venturing too near the divers was despatched.

Sitting in the darkness in his hotel suite, Kerans was far away from the lagoon, content to let Strangman dive for his loot as long as he would soon leave. More and more the dreams had begun to encroach on his waking life, his conscious mind becoming increasingly drained and withdrawn. The single plane of time on which Strangman and his men existed seemed so transparent as to have a negligible claim to reality. Now and then, when Strangman came to call on him, he would emerge for a few minutes on to this tenuous plane, but the real centre of his consciousness was elsewhere.

Curiously, after his initial irritation, Strangman had developed a sneaking liking for Kerans. The biologist's quiet, angular mind was a perfect target for Strangman's dry humour. At times he would subtly mimic Kerans, earnestly taking his arm during one of their dialogues and saying in a pious voice: "You know, Kerans, leaving the sea two hundred million years ago may have been a deep trauma from which we've never recovered . . ."

On another occasion he sent two of his men over in a skiff to the lagoon; on one of the largest buildings on the opposite bank they painted in letters thirty feet high:

TIME ZONE

Kerans took this banter in good part, ignoring it when the divers' lack of success made it more acerbic. Sinking backwards through the past, he waited patiently for the coming of the rain.

It was after the diving party arranged by Strangman that Kerans first realised the true nature of his fear of the man.

Ostensibly the party had been devised by Strangman as a social function to bring the three exiles together. In his laconic, off-hand way Strangman had begun to lay siege to Beatrice, deliberately cultivating Kerans as a means of securing an easy entrée to her apartment. When he discovered that the members of the trio rarely saw each other he evidently decided on an alternative approach, bribing Kerans and Bodkin with the promise of his well-stocked cuisine and cellar. Beatrice, however, always refused these invitations to luncheon and midnight breakfast—Strangman and his entourage of alligators and one-eyed mulattoes still frightened her—and the parties were invariably cancelled.

But the real reason for his 'diving gala' was more practical. For some time he had noticed Bodkin punting around the creeks of the former university quarter—often the old man, much to his amusement, would be trailed around the narrow canals by one of the dragon-eyed scows, manned by the Admiral or Big Caesar and camouflaged with fern fronds, like a lost carnival float—and attributing his own motives to others, assumed that Bodkin was searching for some long-buried treasure. The focus of his suspicions finally became fixed on the submerged planetarium, the one underwater building to which there was easy access. Strangman posted a permanent guard over the little lake, some two hundred yards to the south of the central lagoon, which contained the planetarium, but when Bodkin failed to appear at the dead of night in flippers and aqualung Strangman lost patience and decided to anticipate him.

"We'll pick you up at seven tomorrow morning," he told Kerans. "Champagne cocktails, cold buffet, we'll really find out what old Bodkin has got hidden down there."

"I can tell you, Strangman. Just his lost memories. They're worth all the treasure in the world to him."

But Strangman had let out a peal of sceptical laughter, roared away in the hydroplane and left Kerans hanging helplessly to the switchbacking jetty.

Promptly at seven the next morning the Admiral had come for him. They collected Beatrice and Doctor Bodkin and then repaired to the depot ship, where Strangman was completing his preparations for the dive. A second scow was filled with diving equipment—both aqualung and suit—pumps and a telephone. A diving cage hung from the davit, but Strangman assured them that the lake was free of iguanas and alligators and there was no need to remain in the cage underwater.

Kerans was sceptical of this, but for once Strangman was as good as his word. The lake had been cleared completely. Heavy steel grilles had been lowered into the water at the submerged entrances, and armed guards sat with harpoons and shot-guns astride the booms. As they entered the lake and moored against a shaded waterside balcony on the eastern side the last of a series of grenades was being tossed into the water, the sharp pulsing explosions spewing up a flotsam of stunned eels, shrimp and somasteroids, which were promptly raked away to one side.

The cauldron of submerged foam dispersed and cleared, and from their seats by the rail they looked down at the wide-domed roof of the planetarium, wreathed in strands of fucus, as Bodkin had said, like a giant shell-palace from a childhood fairy tale. The circular fanlight at the apex of the dome was covered by a retractable metal screen, and an attempt had been made to lift one of the sections, but to

Strangman's chagrin they had long since rusted into place. The main entrance of the dome was at the original street level, too far down to be visible, but a preliminary reconnaissance had revealed that they would be able to enter without difficulty.

As the sunlight rose across the water Kerans gazed down into the green translucent depths, at the warm amnionic jelly through which he swam in his dreams. He remembered that despite its universal superabundance he had not fully immersed himself in the sea for ten years, and mentally recapitulated the motions of the slow breast-stroke that carried him through the water while he slept.

Three feet below the surface a small albino python swam past, searching for a way out of the enclosure. Watching its strong head swerve and dart as it evaded the harpoons, Kerans felt a momentary reluctance to entrust himself to the deep water. On the other side of the lake, behind one of the steel grilles, a large estuarine crocodile was wrestling with a group of sailors trying to drive it off. Big Caesar, his great legs clamped to the narrow sill of the boom, kicked savagely at the amphibian, which snapped and lunged at the spears and boat-hooks. Over thirty feet long, it was well over ninety years old, and measured six or seven feet in chest diameter. Its snow-white under-belly reminded Kerans that he had seen a curiously large number of albino snakes and lizards since Strangman's arrival, appearing from the jungle as if attracted by his presence. There had even been a few albino iguanas. One had sat on his jetty the previous morning, watching him like an alabaster lizard, and he had automatically assumed that it bore a message from Strangman.

Kerans looked up at Strangman, who stood in his white suit in the bows of the vessel, watching expectantly as the crocodile thrashed and slammed against the grille, almost toppling the giant Negro into the water. Strangman's sympathies were all too obviously with the crocodile, but not for any reasons of sportsmanship or from a sadistic desire to see one of his principal lieutenants gored and killed.

Finally, amid a confusion of shouts and curses, a shot-gun

was passed to Big Caesar, who steadied himself and discharged both barrels into the hapless crocodile below his feet. With a bellow of pain, it backed away into the shallows, its tail smacking the water.

Beatrice and Kerans looked away, waiting for the coup de grâce to be administered, and Strangman swarmed along the rail in front of them, eager for a better vantage-point.

"When they're trapped or dying they smack the water as an alarm signal to each other." He put a forefinger on Beatrice's cheek, as if trying to make her face the spectacle. "Don't look so disgusted. Kerans! Damn it, show more sympathy for the beast. They've existed for a hundred million years; they're among the oldest creatures on the planet."

After the animal had been dispatched he still stood elatedly by the rail, bouncing on the balls of his feet, as if hoping that it would resuscitate itself and make a come-back. Only when the decapitated head was hoisted away on the end of a boat-hook did he turn with a spasm of irritation to the business of the dive.

Under the supervision of the Admiral, two of the crew made a preliminary dive in aqualungs. They climbed down the metal ladder into the water and glided away towards the sloping curve of the dome. They examined the fan-light, then tested the semicircular ribs of the building, pulling themselves across the dome by the cracks in the surface. After their return a third sailor descended, with suit and line. He clumped slowly across the cloudy floor of the street below, the thin light reflected off his helmet and shoulders. As the lines wound out, he entered the main doorway and disappeared from view, communicating by telephone with the Admiral, who sang out his commentary for all to hear in a rich fruity baritone: "In de pay-box . . . now in de main lounge. . . . Jomo says de seats in de church, Captain Strang', but de altar gone."

Everyone was leaning over the rail, waiting for Jomo to reappear, but Strangman was slumped back moodily in his chair, face clamped in one hand.

"Church!" he snorted derisively. "God! Send someone else down. Jomo's a bloody fool."

"Yes, Captain."

More divers descended, and the first champagne cocktails were brought round by the steward. Intending to dive himself, Kerans sipped lightly at the heady effervescence.

Beatrice touched his elbow, her face watchful. "Are you going down, Robert?"

Kerans smiled. "To the basement, Bea. Don't worry. I'll use the big suit; it's perfectly safe."

"I wasn't thinking of that." She looked up at the expanding ellipse of the sun just visible over the roof-top behind them. The olive-green light refracted through the heavy fern-fronds filled the lake with a yellow, swampy miasma, drifting over the surface like vapour off a vat. A few moments earlier the water had seemed cool and inviting, but now had become a closed world, the barrier of the surface like a plane between two dimensions. The diving cage was swung out and lowered into the water, its red bars blurred and shimmering, so that the entire structure was completely distorted. Even the men swimming below the surface were transformed by the water, their bodies as they swerved and pivoted turned into gleaming chimeras, like exploding pulses of ideation in a neuronic jungle.

Far below them, the great dome of the planetarium hove out of the yellow light, reminding Kerans of some cosmic space vehicle marooned on Earth for millions of years and only now revealed by the sea. He leaned behind Beatrice and said to Bodkin: "Alan, Strangman's searching for the treasure you've hidden down there."

Bodkin smiled fleetingly. "I hope he finds it," he said mildly. "The entire ransom of the Unconscious is waiting for him if he can."

Strangman was standing in the bows of the craft, interrogating one of the divers who had surfaced and was now being helped out of his suit, water streaming off his copper skin across the deck. As he barked his questions he noticed

Bodkin and Kerans whispering to each other. Brows knitting, he stalked across the deck to where they were sitting, watching them suspiciously through half-closed eyes, and then sidled behind them like a guard eyeing a trio of potentially troublesome prisoners.

Toasting him with his champagne cocktail, Kerans said jocularly: "I was just asking Dr. Bodkin where he'd hidden his treasure, Strangman."

Strangman paused, staring at him coldly as Beatrice laughed uneasily, hiding her face inside the wing collars of her beach shirt. He put his hands on the back of Kerans' wicker chair, his face like white flint. "Don't worry, Kerans," he snapped softly. "I know where it is, and I don't need your help to find it." He swung round on Bodkin. "Do I, Doctor?"

Shielding one ear from the cutting edge of his voice, Bodkin murmured: "I think you probably do know, Strangman." He pushed his chair back into the shrinking shade. "When does the gala begin?"

"*Gala?*" Strangman glanced about irritably, apparently forgetting that he had introduced the term himself. "There are no bathing beauties here, Doctor; this isn't the local aquadrome. Wait a minute, though, I mustn't be ungallant and forget the beautiful Miss Dahl." He bowed over her with an unctuous smile. "Come, my dear, I'll make you queen of the aquacade, with an escort of fifty divine crocodiles."

Beatrice looked away from his gleaming eyes. "No, thanks, Strangman. The sea frightens me."

"But you must. Kerans and Dr. Bodkin expect you to. And I. You'll be a Venus descending to the sea, made twice beautiful by your return." He reached down to take her hand and Beatrice flinched from him, frowning with repugnance at his oleaginous smirk. Kerans pivoted in his seat and held her arm.

"I don't think this is Beatrice's day, Strangman. We only swim in the evenings, under a full moon. It's a question of mood, you know."

He smiled at Strangman as the latter tightened his grip on Beatrice, his face like a white vampire's, as if becoming exasperated beyond all measure.

Kerans stood up. "Look, Strangman, I'll take her place. All right? I'd like to go down and have a look at the planetarium." He waved Beatrice's alarms aside. "Don't worry, Strangman and the Admiral will take good care of me."

"Of course, Kerans." Strangman's good humour had returned, instantly he radiated a benevolent willingness to please, only the slightest hint in his eyes of his pleasure at having Kerans within his clutches. "We'll put you in the big suit, then you can talk to us over the loudspeaker. Relax, Miss Dahl; there's no danger. Admiral! Suit for Dr. Kerans! Chop, chop!"

Kerans exchanged a brief warning glance with Bodkin, then looked away when he saw Bodkin's surprise at the alacrity with which he had volunteered. He felt curiously light-headed, though he had barely touched his cocktail.

"Don't go down for too long, Robert," Bodkin called after him. "The temperature of the water will be high, at least ninety-five degrees; you'll find it very enervating."

Kerans nodded, then followed Strangman's eager stride to the forward deck. A couple of men were hosing down the suit and helmet, while the Admiral and Big Caesar, and the sailors resting on the pump-wheels, watched Kerans approach with noncommittal interest.

"See if you can get down into the main auditorium," Strangman told him. "One of the boys managed to find a slit in an exit door, but the frame had rusted solid." He examined Kerans with a critical eye as he waited for the helmet to be lowered over his head. Designed for use only within the first five fathoms, it was a complete perspex bowl, braced by two lateral ribs, and affording maximum visibility. "It suits you, Kerans, you look like the man from inner space." The rictus of a laugh twisted his face. "But don't try to reach the Unconscious, Kerans; remember it isn't equipped to go down that far!"

Clumping slowly to the rail, the sailors carrying the lines after him, Kerans paused to wave cumbersomely to Beatrice and Dr. Bodkin, then mounted the narrow ladder and lowered himself slowly towards the slack green water below. It was shortly after eight o'clock and the sun shone directly on to the tacky vinyl envelope that enclosed him, clamming damply against his chest and legs, and he looked forward with pleasure to cooling his burning skin. The surface of the lake was now completely opaque. A litter of leaves and weed floated slowly around it, occasionally disrupted by bubbles of trapped air erupting from the interior of the dome.

To his right he could see Bodkin and Beatrice with their chins on the rail, watching him expectantly. Directly above, on the roof of the scow, stood the tall gaunt figure of Strangman, tails of his jacket pushed back, arms akimbo, the light breeze lifting his chalk-white hair. He was grinning soundlessly to himself, but as Kerans' feet touched the water shouted something which Kerans heard dimly relayed over the headphones. Immediately the hiss of air through the intake valves in the helmet increased and the internal circuit of the microphone came alive.

The water was hotter than he expected. Instead of a cool revivifying bath, he was stepping into a tank filled with warm, glutinous jelly that clamped itself to his calves and thighs like the foetid embrace of some gigantic protozoan monster. Quickly he lowered himself to his shoulders, then took his feet off the rungs and let his weight carry him slowly downwards into the green-lit deep, hand over hand along the the rail, and paused at the two-fathom mark.

Here the water was cooler, and he flexed his arms and legs thankfully, accustoming his eyes to the pale light. A few small angel fish swam past, their bodies gleaming like silver stars in the blue blur that extended from the surface to a depth of five feet, a 'sky' of light reflected from the millions of dust and pollen particles. Forty feet away from him loomed the pale curved hull of the planetarium, far larger and more mysterious than it had seemed from the surface, like the stern of an ancient sunken liner. The once polished aluminium roof had become dull and blunted, molluscs and bivalves clinging to the narrow ledges formed by the transverse vaulting. Lower down, where the dome rested on the square roof of the auditorium, a forest of giant fucus floated delicately from their pedestals, some of the fronds over ten feet tall, exquisite marine wraiths that fluttered together like the spirits of a sacred neptunian grove.

Twenty feet from the bottom the ladder ended, but Kerans was now almost at equilibrium with the water. He let himself sink downwards until he was holding the tips of the ladder above his head with his fingers, then released them and glided away backwards towards the lake floor, the twin antennae of his air-line and telephone cable winding up the narrow well of light reflected by the disturbed water to the silver rectangular hull of the scow.

Cut off by the water from any other sounds, the noise of the air pump and the relayed rhythms of his own respiration drummed steadily in his ears, increasing in volume as the air pressure was raised. The sounds seemed to boom around him in the dark olive-green water, thudding like the immense tidal pulse he had heard in his dreams.

A voice grated from his headphones: "Strangman here, Kerans. How's the grey sweet mother of us all?"

"Feels like home. I've nearly reached the bottom now. The diving cage is over by the entrance."

He sank to his knees in the soft loam which covered the floor, and steadied himself against a barnacled lamp-post. In a relaxed, graceful moon-stride he loped slowly through the deep sludge, which rose from his footprints like clouds of disturbed gas. On his right were the dim flanks of the buildings lining the side-walk, the silt piled in soft dunes up to their first-floor windows. In the intervals between the buildings the slopes were almost twenty feet high, and the retaining grilles were locked into them like huge portcullises.

Most of the windows were choked with debris, fragments of furniture and metal cabinets, sections of floorboards, matted together by the fucus and cephalopods.

The diving cage swung slowly on its cable five feet off the street, a selection of hacksaws and spanners loosely tied to the floor. Kerans approached the doorway of the planetarium, steering the lines behind him and occasionally pulled lightly off his feet when they became over-extended.

Like an immense submarine temple, the white bulk of the planetarium stood before him, illuminated by the vivid surface water. The steel barricades around the entrance had been dismantled by the previous divers, and the semicircular arc of doors which led into the foyer was open. Kerans switched on his helmet lamp and walked through the entrance. He peered carefully among the pillars and alcoves, following the steps which led up into the mezzanine. The metal railings and chromium display panels had rusted, but the whole interior of the planetarium, sealed off by the barricades from the plant and animal life of the lagoons, seemed completely untouched, as clean and untarnished as on the day the last dykes had collapsed.

Passing the ticket booth, he propelled himself slowly along the mezzanine, and paused by the rail to read the signs over the cloakroom doors, their luminous letters reflecting the light. A circular corridor led around the auditorium, the lamp throwing a pale cone of light down the solid black water. In the faint hope that the dykes would be repaired, the management of the planetarium had sealed a second inner ring of barricades around the auditorium, locked into place by padlocked cross-bars which had now rusted into immovable bulkheads.

The top right-hand corner panel of the second bulkhead had been jemmied back to provide a small peep-hole into the auditorium. Too tired by the water pressing on his chest and abdomen to lift the heavy suit, Kerans contented himself with a glimpse of a few motes of light gleaming through the cracks in the dome.

On his way to fetch a hacksaw from the diving cage, he

noticed a small doorway at the top of a short flight of steps behind the ticket box, apparently leading over the auditorium, either a cine-projectionist's booth or the manager's office. He pulled himself up the handrail, the metal cleats of his weighted boots skating on the slimy carpet. The door was locked, but he drove his shoulders against it and the two hinges parted easily, the door gliding away gracefully across the floor like a paper sail.

Pausing to free his lines, Kerans listened to the steady pumping in his ears. The rhythm had changed perceptibly, indicating that a different pair of operators had taken over the job. They worked more slowly, presumably unaccustomed to pumping air at the maximum pressure. For some reason, Kerans felt a slight stirring of alarm. Although fully aware of Strangman's malice and unpredictability, he felt confident that he would not try to kill him by so crude a method as blocking the air supply. Both Beatrice and Bodkin were present, and although Riggs and his men were a thousand miles away there was always the chance that some specialist Government unit might pay a flying visit to the lagoons. Unless he killed Beatrice and Bodkin as well—which seemed unlikely, for a number of reasons (he obviously suspected them of knowing more about the city than they admitted)— Strangman would find Kerans' death more trouble than it was worth.

As the air hissed reassuringly through his helmet, Kerans moved forward across the empty room. A few shelves sagged from one wall, a filing cabinet loomed in a corner. Suddenly, with a shock of alarm, he saw what appeared to be a man in an immense ballooning space-suit facing him ten feet away, white bubbles streaming from his frog-like head, hands raised in an attitude of menace, a blaze of light pouring from his helmet. "Strangman!" he shouted at it involuntarily.

"Kerans! What is it?" Strangman's voice, closer than the whisper of his own consciousness, cut across his panic. "Kerans, you fool . . .!"

"Sorry, Strangman." Kerans pulled himself together, and advanced slowly towards the approaching figure. "I've just seen myself in a mirror. I'm up in the manager's office or control-room, I'm not sure which. There's a private stairway from the mezzanine, may be an entrance into the auditorium."

"Good man. See if you can find the safe. It should be behind the picture frame directly over the desk."

Ignoring him, Kerans placed his hands on the glass surface and swung the helmet sharply from left to right. He was in the control booth overlooking the auditorium, his image reflected in the glass sound-proof panel. In front of him was the cabinet which had once held the instrument console, but the unit had been removed, and the producer's swing-back seat faced out unobstructed like an insulated throne of some germ-obsessed potentate. Almost exhausted by the pressure of the water, Kerans sat down in the seat and looked out over the circular auditorium.

Dimly illuminated by the small helmet lamp, the dark vault with its blurred walls cloaked with silt rose up above him like a huge velvet-upholstered womb in a surrealist nightmare. The black opaque water seemed to hang in solid vertical curtains, screening the dais in the centre of the auditorium as if hiding the ultimate sanctum of its depths. For some reason the womb-like image of the chamber was reinforced rather than diminished by the circular rows of seats, and Kerans heard the thudding in his ears uncertain whether he was listening to the dim subliminal requiem of his dreams. He opened the small panel door which led down into the auditorium, disconnecting the telephone cable from his helmet so that he would be free of Strangman's voice.

A light coating of silt covered the carpeted steps of the aisle. In the centre of the dome the water was at least twenty degrees warmer than it had been in the control-room, heated by some freak of convection, and it bathed his skin like hot balm. The projector had been removed from the dais, but the cracks in the dome sparkled with distant points of light, like the galactic profiles of some distant universe. He gazed up at this unfamiliar zodiac, watching it merge before his eyes like the first vision of some pelagic Cortez emerging from the oceanic deeps to glimpse the immense Pacifics of the open sky.

Standing on the dais, he looked around at the blank rows of seats facing him, wondering what uterine rite to perform for the invisible audience that seemed to watch him. The air pressure inside his helmet had increased sharply, as the men on the deck lost contact with him by telephone. The valves boomed off the sides of the helmet, the silver bubbles darted and swerved away from him like frantic phantoms.

Gradually, as the minutes passed, the preservation of this distant zodiac, perhaps the very configuration of constellations that had encompassed the Earth during the Triassic Period, seemed to Kerans a task more important than any other facing him. He stepped down from the dais and began to return to the control-room, dragging the air-line after him. As he reached the panel door he felt the line snake out through his hands, and with an impulse of anger seized a loop and anchored it around the handle of the door. He waited until the line tautened, then wound a second loop around the handle, providing himself with a radius of a dozen feet. He walked back down the steps and stopped half-way down the aisle, head held back, determined to engrave the image of the constellations on his retina. Already their patterns seemed more familiar than those of the classical constellations. In a vast, convulsive recession of the equinoxes, a billion sidereal days had reborn themselves, re-aligned the nebulae and island universes in their original perspectives.

A sharp spur of pain drove itself into his eustachian tube, forcing him to swallow. Abruptly he realised that the intake valve of the helmet supply was no longer working. A faint hiss seeped through every ten seconds, but the pressure had fallen steeply. Dizzying, he stumbled up the aisle and tried to free the air-line from the handle, certain now that Strangman had seized the opportunity to fabricate an accident. Breath exploding, he tripped over one of the steps, fell awkwardly across the seats with a gentle ballooning motion.

As the spotlight flared across the domed ceiling illuminating the huge vacant womb for the last time, Kerans felt the warm blood-filled nausea of the chamber flood in upon him. He lay back, spreadeagled across the steps, his hand pressed numbly against the loop of line around the door handle, the soothing pressure of the water penetrating his suit so that the barriers between his own private blood stream and that of the giant amnion seemed no longer to exist. The deep cradle of silt carried him gently like an immense placenta, infinitely softer than any bed he had ever known. Far above him, as his consciousness faded, he could see the ancient nebulae and galaxies shining through the uterine night, but eventually even their light was dimmed and he was only aware of the faint glimmer of identity within the deepest recesses of his mind. Quietly he began to move towards it, floating slowly towards the centre of the dome, knowing that this faint beacon was receding more rapidly than he could approach it. When it was no longer visible he pressed on through the darkness alone, like a blind fish in an endless forgotten sea, driven by an impulse whose identity he would never comprehend. . .

Epochs drifted. Giant waves, infinitely slow and enveloping, broke and fell across the sunless beaches of the time-sea, washing him helplessly in its shallows. He drifted from one pool to another, in the limbos of eternity, a thousand images of himself reflected in the inverted mirrors of the surface. Within his lungs an immense inland lake seemed to be bursting outwards, his rib-cage distended like a whale's to contain the oceanic volumes of water.

"Kerans. . . ."

He looked up at the bright deck, at the brilliant panoply of light on the canvas shade above him, at the watchful ebony face of the Admiral sitting across his legs and pumping his chest in his huge hands.

"Strangman, he . . ." Choking on the expressed fluid in his throat, Kerans let his head loll back on to the hot deck, the sunlight stinging his eyes. A circle of faces looked down at him intently—Beatrice, her eyes wide with alarm, Bodkin frowning seriously, a motley of brown faces under khaki képis. Abruptly a single white grinning face interposed itself. Only a few feet from him, it leered like an obscene statue.

"Strangman, you——"

The grin broke into a winning smile. "No, I didn't, Kerans. Don't try to pin the blame on me. Dr. Bodkin will vouch for that." He waggled a finger at Kerans. "I warned you not to go down too far."

The Admiral stood up, evidently satisfied that Kerans had recovered. The deck seemed to be made of burning iron, and Kerans pulled himself up on one elbow, sat weakly in the pool of water. A few feet away, creased in the scuppers, the suit lay like a deflated corpse.

Beatrice pushed through the circle of onlookers, and crouched down beside him. "Robert, relax, don't think about it now." She put her arm around his shoulders, glancing up watchfully at Strangman. He stood behind Kerans, grinning with pleasure, hands on hips.

"The cable seized . . ." Kerans cleared his head, his lungs like two bruised, tender flowers. He breathed slowly, soothing them with the cool air. "They were pulling it from above. Didn't you stop . . ."

Bodkin stepped forward with Kerans' jacket and draped it across his shoulders. "Easy, Robert; it doesn't matter now. Actually, I'm sure it wasn't Strangman's fault; he was talking to Beatrice and I when it happened. The cable was hooked round some obstruction, it looks as if it was a complete accident."

"No, it wasn't, Doctor," Strangman cut in. "Don't perpetuate a myth, Kerans will be much more grateful for the truth. He anchored that cable himself, quite deliberately. Why?" Here Strangman tapped the air magisterially. "Because he *wanted* to become part of the drowned world."

He began to laugh to himself, slapping his thighs with amusement as Kerans hobbled weakly to his chair. "And the joke is that he doesn't know whether I'm telling the truth or not. Do you realise that, Bodkin? Look at him; he genuinely isn't sure! God, what irony!"

"Strangman!" Beatrice snapped at him angrily, overcoming her fears. "Stop saying that! It might have been an accident."

Strangman shrugged theatrically. "It *might*," he repeated with great emphasis. "Let's admit that. It makes it more interesting—particularly for Kerans. '*Did I or did I not try to kill myself?*' One of the few existential absolutes, far more significant than 'To be or not to be?', which merely underlines the uncertainty of the suicide, rather than the eternal ambivalence of his victim." He smiled down patronisingly at Kerans as the latter sat quietly in his chair, sipping at the drink Beatrice had brought him. "Kerans, I envy you the task of finding out—if you can."

Kerans managed a weak smile. From the speed of his recovery he realised that he had suffered only mildly from the drowning. The remainder of the crew had moved away to their duties, no longer interested.

"Thank you, Strangman. I'll let you know when I have the answer."

On the way back to the Ritz he sat silently in the stern of the scow, thinking to himself of the great womb-chamber of the planetarium and the multi-layered overlay of its associations, trying to erase from his mind the terrible 'either/or' which Strangman had correctly posed. Had he unconsciously locked the air-pipe, knowing that the tension in the cable would suffocate him, or had it been a complete accident, even, possibly, an attempt by Strangman to injure him? But for the rescue by the two skin divers (perhaps he had counted on them setting out after him when the telephone cable was disconnected) he would certainly have found the answer. His reasons for making the dive at all remained obscure. There was no doubt that he had been impelled by a curious urge to place himself at Strangman's mercy, almost as if he were staging his own murder.

During the next few days the conundrum remained unsolved. Was the drowned world itself, and the mysterious quest for the south which had possessed Hardman, no more than an impulse to suicide, an unconscious acceptance of the logic of his own devolutionary descent, the ultimate neuronic synthesis of the archaeopsychic zero? Rather than try to live with yet another enigma, and more and more frightened of the real role that Strangman played in his mind, Kerans systematically repressed his memories of the accident. Likewise, Bodkin and Beatrice ceased to refer to it, as if accepting that an answer to the question would solve for them many of the other mysterious enigmas which now alone sustained them, delusions which, like all the ambiguous but necessary assumptions about their own personalities, they would only sacrifice with reluctance.

CHAPTER TEN

SURPRISE PARTY

"KERANS...!"

Roused by the deep blare of the hydroplane as it approached the landing stage, Kerans stirred fretfully, his head lolling from side to side on the stale pillow. He focused his eyes on the bright green parallelogram which dappled the ceiling above the venetian blinds, listening to the engines outside reverse and accelerate, then with an effort pulled himself off the bed. It was already after 7.30, an hour later than he had woken a month earlier, and the brilliant sunlight reflected off the lagoon thrust its fingers into the darkened room like a ravenous golden monster.

With a pang of annoyance he noticed that he had forgotten to switch off the bedside fan before going to sleep. He had begun to fall asleep now at unpredictable moments, sometimes sitting half-upright on the bed while unlacing his shoes. In an attempt to conserve his fuel he had closed down the bedroom and moved the heavy gilt-framed double bed into the lounge, but its associations with sleep were so powerful that he was soon forced to move it back again.

"Kerans . . .!"

Strangman's voice echoed warningly down the corridor below. Kerans limped slowly to the bathroom, managed to splash his face by the time Strangman let himself into the suite.

Tossing his helmet on to the floor, Strangman produced a decanter of hot black coffee and a canned gorgonzola green with age.

"A present for you." He examined Kerans' dulled eyes with an amiable frown. "Well, how are things in deep time?"

Kerans sat on the edge of the bed, waiting for the booming of the phantom jungles in his mind to fade. Like an endless shallows, the residues of the dreams stretched away below the surface of the reality around him. "What brings you here?" he asked flatly.

Strangman put on an expression of deep injury.

"Kerans, I *like* you. You keep forgetting that." He turned up the volume of the air-conditioner, smiling at Kerans, who gazed watchfully at the wry, perverted leer. "Actually I have another motive—I want you to have dinner with me tonight. Don't start shaking your head. I have to keep coming here; it's time I returned your hospitality. Beatrice and old Bodkin will be there; it should be pretty swagger— fire-work displays, bongo drums *and* a surprise."

"What exactly?"

"You'll see. Something really spectacular, believe me. I don't do things by halves. I'd have those 'gators dancing on the tips of their tails if I wanted to." He nodded solemnly. "Kerans, you're going to be impressed. And it may even do you some good mentally, stop this crazy time machine of yours." His mood changed, becoming distant and abstracted. "But I musn't poke fun at you, Kerans. I couldn't

114

bear a tenth of the personal responsibility you've shouldered. The tragic loneliness, for example, of those haunted Triassic swamps." He picked a book off the air-conditioner, a copy of Donne's poems, and extemporised a line: "World within world, each man an island unto himself, swimming through seas of archipelagos. . . ."

Fairly certain that he was fooling, Kerans asked: "How's the diving going?"

"Frankly, not very well. The city's too far north for much to have been left. But we've discovered a few interesting things. You'll see tonight."

Kerans hesitated, doubting whether he would have enough energy to make small talk with Dr. Bodkin and Beatrice—he had seen neither of them since the debacle of the diving party, though every evening Strangman drove over in his hydroplane to Beatrice's apartment house (what success he had Kerans could only guess, but Strangman's references to her—"Women are like spiders, they sit there watching you and knitting their webs" or "She keeps talking about *you*, Robert, confound her"—indicated a negative response.)

However, the particular twist of emphasis in Strangman's voice suggested that Kerans' attendance was obligatory, and that he would not be allowed to refuse. Strangman followed him into the lounge, waiting for a reply.

"It's rather short notice, Strangman."

"I'm terribly sorry, Kerans, but as we know each other so well I felt sure you wouldn't mind. Blame it on my manic-depressive personality. I'm always seizing on wild schemes."

Kerans found two gold-plated porcelain coffee cups and filled them from the decanter. Know each other so well, he repeated to himself ironically. I'm damned if I know you at all, Strangman. Racing around the lagoons like the delinquent spirit of the drowned city, apotheosis of all its aimless violence and cruelty, Strangman was half-buccaneer, half-devil. Yet he had a further neuronic role, in which he seemed almost a positive influence, holding a warning mirror up to Kerans and obliquely cautioning him about the future he had chosen. It was this bond that kept them together, for otherwise Kerans would long since have left the lagoons and moved southwards.

"I assume this isn't a farewell celebration?" he asked Strangman. "You aren't leaving us?"

"Kerans, of course not," Strangman remonstrated. "We've only just got here. Besides," he added sagely, "where would we go? There's nothing much left now—I can tell you, I sometimes feel like Phlebas the Phoenician. Though that's really your role, isn't it?

> A current under sea
> Picked his bones in whispers. As he rose and fell
> He passed the stages of his age and youth
> Entering the whirlpool."

He continued to pester Kerans until the latter accepted his invitation, then made off jubilantly. Kerans finished the coffee in the decanter, when he began to recover drew the venetian blinds and let in the bright sunlight.

Outside, in his chair on the veranda, a white monitor lizard sat and regarded him with its stony eyes, waiting for something to happen.

As he rode across the lagoon to the paddle-ship that evening, Kerans speculated on the probable nature of Strangman's "surprise", hoping that it would not be some elaborate practical joke. The effort of shaving off his beard and putting on a white dinner jacket had tired him.

Considerable preparations were obviously afoot in the lagoon. The depot ship had been moored about fifty yards from shore, strung with awnings and coloured lights, and the two remaining scows were working systematically along the banks, driving the alligators into the central lagoon.

Kerans pointed to a big caiman thrashing about in a circle of boat-hooks, and said to Big Caesar: "What's on the menu tonight—roast alligator?"

The giant hunch-backed mulatto at the helm of the scow shrugged with studied vagueness. "Strang' got a big show tonight, Mistah Kerans, a real big show. You see."

Kerans left his seat and leaned on the bridge. "Big Caesar, how long have you known the Captain?"

"Long time, Mistah Kerans. Ten years, maybe twenty."

"He's a strange one, all right," Kerans continued. "His moods change so quickly—you must have noticed that, working for him. Sometimes he frightens me."

The big mulatto smiled cryptically. "You right there, Mistah Kerans," he rejoined with a chuckle. "You really right."

But before Kerans could press him a megaphone jabbed at them across the water from the bridge of the depot ship.

Strangman met each one of his guests as they arrived at the head of the gangway. In high spirits, he managed a sustained mood of charm and good cheer, complimenting Beatrice elaborately on her appearance. She wore a full-length blue brocade ball dress, the turquoise mascara around her eyes making her look like some exotic bird of paradise. Even Bodkin had contrived to trim his beard and salvage a respectable linen jacket, an old piece of crepe around his neck a ragged concession to a black tie. Like Kerans, however, they both seemed glazed and remote, joining in the conversation over dinner automatically.

Strangman, however, failed to notice this, or if he did was too elated and preoccupied to care. Whatever his motives, he had obviously gone to considerable trouble to stage his surprise. A fresh canvas awning had been broken out like a crisp white sail over the observation deck, flared at its rim in the form of an inverted marquee to give them an uninterrupted view over the lagoon and sky. A large circular dining table stood by the rail, low divans in the Egyptian style, with spiral gilt and ivory bolsters, disposed around it. A clutter of unmatched but none the less brilliant pieces of gold and silver dining plate decorated the table, much of it of huge proportions—the ormolu finger-bowls were the size of face baths.

Strangman had rifled his treasure house below in an access of profligacy—several pieces of blackened bronze statuary stood about behind the table bearing salvers of fruit and

orchids, and an immense canvas by some painter of the
school of Tintoretto had been propped against the funnels
and screened the service hatches, looming down over the
table like a mural. Its title was "The Marriage of Ester and
King Xerxes", but the pagan treatment and the local
background of the Venetian lagoon and the Grand Canal
palazzos, coupled with the Quinquecento décor and costume,
made it seem more like "The Marriage of Neptune and
Minerva", no doubt the moral Strangman intended to point.
King Xerxes, a wily, beak-nosed elderly Doge or Venetian
Grand-Admiral, already seemed completely tamed by his
demure, raven-haired Ester, who had a faint but none the
less perceptible likeness to Beatrice. As he cast his eye over
the crowded spread of the canvas with its hundreds of
wedding guests, Kerans suddenly saw another familiar
profile—the face of Strangman among the hard cruel smiles
of the Council of Ten—but when he approached the painting
the similarity vanished.

The marriage ceremony was being celebrated aboard a
galleon moored against the Doge's Palace, and its elaborate
rococo rigging seemed to merge directly into the steel hawsers
and bracing lines of the depot ship. Apart from the kindred
settings, emphasised by the two lagoons and the buildings
rising from the water, Strangman's motley crew might
themselves have stepped straight from the canvas, with its
jewelled slaves and Negro captain of gondoliers.

Sipping his cocktail, Kerans said to Beatrice: "Do you
see yourself there, Bea? Obviously, Strangman hopes you'll
subdue the flood-waters with the same skill Ester used to
pacify the King."

"Correct, Kerans!" Strangman stepped over to them from
the bridge. "You have it exactly." He bowed to Beatrice.
"I hope you accept the compliment, my dear?"

"I'm very flattered, Strangman, of course." Beatrice
moved over to the painting, examining her double, then
turned in a swirl of brocade and stood by the rail, staring
out over the water. "But I'm not sure whether I want to be
cast in that role, Strangman."

"But you are, Miss Dahl, inescapably." Strangman gestured the steward over to Bodkin, who was sitting in a quiet reverie, then slapped Kerans on the shoulder. "Believe me, Doctor, you'll soon see——"

"Good. I'm getting a little impatient, Strangman."

"What, after thirty million years you can't wait five minutes? I'm obviously bringing you back to the present."

Throughout the meal Strangman supervised the succession of wines, taking advantage of his absences from the table to confer with the Admiral. With the final brandies before them, Strangman sat down apparently for the last time, winking broadly at Kerans. Two of the scows had moved over to the inlet by the far side of the lagoon and disappeared into its mouth, while the third took up its position in the centre, from where it released a small firework display.

The last sunlight still lay over the water, but had faded sufficiently for the bright catherine wheels and rockets to flicker and dazzle, their sharp explosions etched clearly against the tinted crepuscular sky. The smile on Strangman's face grew broader and broader, until he lay back on his chesterfield grinning soundlessly to himself, the red and green flashes illuminating his saturnine features.

Uncomfortably, Kerans leaned forward to ask him when their surprise would materialise, but Strangman anticipated him.

"Well, haven't you noticed?" He glanced around the table. "Beatrice? Dr. Bodkin? You three are slow. Come out of deep time for a moment."

A curious silence hung over the ship, and involuntarily Kerans leaned against the rail to brace himself in case Strangman was about to set off an underwater explosive charge. Glancing down at the deck below, he suddenly saw the twenty or thirty members of the crew, looking motionlessly at the lagoon, their ebony faces and white singlets flickering with the ghostly light, like the crew of a spectral ship.

Puzzled, Kerans searched the sky and lagoon. The dusk had come in rather more quickly than he expected, the curtain walls of the buildings opposite sinking into shadow. At the same time the sky remained clear and visible in the sunset, the tops of the surrounding vegetation brilliantly tinted.

A low drumming sounded somewhere in the distance, the air-pumps which had worked all day and whose noise had been masked by the pyrotechnic display. Around the ship the water had become strangely slack and lifeless, the low swells that usually disturbed it absent. Wondering whether an exhibition of underwater swimming had been arranged for a troupe of trained alligators, he peered down at the surface.

"Alan! Look, for heaven's sake! Beatrice, can you see?" Kerans kicked back his chair and leapt to the rail, pointing down in amazement at the water. "The level is going down!"

Looming just below the dark pellucid surface were the dim rectangular outlines of the submerged buildings, their open windows like empty eyes in enormous drowned skulls. Only a few feet from the surface, they drew closer, emerging from the depths like an immense intact Atlantis. First a dozen, then a score of buildings appeared to view, their cornices and fire escapes clearly visible through the thinning refracting glass of the water. Most of them were only four or five storeys high, part·of a district of small shops and offices enclosed by the taller buildings that had formed the perimeter of the lagoon.

Fifty yards away the first of the roofs broke surface, a blunted rectangle smothered with weeds and algae, across which slithered a few desperate fish. Immediately half a dozen others appeared around it, already roughly delineating a narrow street. The upper line of windows emerged, water spilling from their ledges, fucus draped from the straggling wires that sagged across the roadways.

Already the lagoon had vanished. As they sank slowly downwards, settling into what seemed to be a large open square, they were now looking across a diffuse straggle of roof-tops, punctuated by eroded chimneys and spires, the flat sheet of the surface transformed into a jungle of cubist blocks, at its boundaries merging into the higher ground of the enveloping vegetation. What remained of the water had formed into distinct channels, dark and sombre, eddying away around corners and into narrow alleyways.

"Robert! Stop it! It's horrible!" Kerans felt Beatrice seize his arm, her long blue nails biting through the fabric of his dinner jacket. She gazed out at the emerging city, an expression of revulsion on her tense face, physically repelled by the sharp acrid smells of the exposed water-weeds and algae, the damp barnacled forms of rusting litter. Veils of scum draped from the criss-crossing telegraph wires and tilting neon signs, and a thin coating of silt cloaked the faces of the buildings, turning the once limpid beauty of the under-water city into a drained and festering sewer.

For a moment Kerans fought to free his mind, grappling with this total inversion of his normal world, unable to accept the logic of the rebirth before him. First he wondered whether there had been a total climatic reversal that was shrinking the formerly expanding seas, draining the submerged cities. If so, he would have to make his way back to this new present, or be marooned millions of years away on the beach of some lost Triassic lagoon. But deep within his mind the great sun pounded dimly with a strength still undiminished, and beside him he heard Bodkin mutter:

"Those pumps are powerful. The water is going down by a good two or three feet a minute. We're not far from the bottom now. The whole thing's fantastic!"

Laughter rocked out into the darkening air as Strangman rolled about mirthfully on the chesterfield, dabbing his eyes with a napkin. Released from the tension of staging the spectacle, he was now exulting in the three bewildered faces at the rail. On the bridge above him, the Admiral watched with dry amusement, the fading light glinting across his bare chest like a gong. Two or three men below were taking in the mooring lines, holding the orientation of the ship in the square.

The two scows which had moved over to the creek mouth during the firework display were floating behind a massive boom, and a foaming mass of water poured from the twin vents of a huge pumping system. Then the rooftops obscured their view across the interval, and the people on the deck were looking up at the blanched buildings of the square. Only fifteen or twenty feet of water remained, and a hundred yards away down one of the side streets they could see the third scow wending tentatively below the trailing wires.

Strangman controlled himself and came over to the rail. "Perfect, don't you agree, Dr. Bodkin? What a jest, a really superb spectacle! Come on, Doctor, don't look so piqued. Congratulate me! It wasn't too easy to arrange."

Bodkin nodded and moved away along the rail, his face still stunned. Kerans asked: "But how did you seal off the perimeter? There's no continuous wall around the lagoon."

"There is now, Doctor. I thought you were the expert in marine biology. The fungi growing in the swamp mud outside consolidated the entire mass; for the last week there's only been one point of influx; took us five minutes to dam it up."

He gazed out brightly at the emerging streets in the dim light around them, the humped backs of cars and buses appearing through the surface. Giant anemones and starfish flopped limply in the shallows, collapsing kelp straggled out of windows.

Numbly, Bodkin said: "Leicester Square."

His laughter vanishing, Strangman swung on him, his eyes peering rapaciously at the neon-covered porticos of the hulks of former cinemas and theatres.

"So you *do* know your way around here, Doctor! A pity you couldn't have helped us before, when we were getting nowhere." He slammed the rail with an oath, jarring Kerans' elbow. "By God, though, we're really in business now!" With a snarl he flung himself away from them, kicking back the dining table, shouting up at the Admiral.

Beatrice watched him disappear below with alarm, a slender hand on her throat. "Robert, he's insane. What are we going to do?—He'll drain all the lagoons."

Kerans nodded, thinking about the transformation of Strangman which he had witnessed. With the reappearance of the submerged streets and buildings his entire manner had changed abruptly. All traces of courtly refinement and laconic humour had vanished; he was now callous and vulpine, the renegade spirit of the hoodlum streets returning to his lost playground. It was almost as if the presence of the water had anaesthetised him, smothering his true character so that only the surface veneer of charm and moodiness remained.

Behind them the shadow of an office block fell across the deck, drawing a diagonal curtain of darkness over the huge painting. A few figures, Ester and the Negro captain of gondoliers, still remained, and a single white face, a beardless member of the Council of Ten. As Strangman had prophesied, Beatrice had performed her symbolic role, Neptune had deferred and withdrawn.

Kerans looked up at the round bulk of the testing station, poised on the cinema behind them like an enormous boulder on the edge of a cliff. Apparently eighty to ninety feet higher, the tall buildings around the lagoon perimeter now cut off half the sky, enclosing them in a dim canyon-floor world.

"It doesn't matter that much," Kerans temporised. He steadied her against his arm as the ship touched bottom and rolled slightly, crushing a small car under the port bow. "When he's finished stripping the stores and museums they'll leave. Anyway, the rain-storms will be here in a week or two."

Beatrice cleared her throat distastefully, wincing as the first bats flickered among the roof-tops, darting from one dripping eave to another. "But it's all so hideous. I can't believe that anyone ever lived here. It's like some imaginary city of Hell. Robert, I *need* the lagoon."

"Well, we could leave and move south across the silt flats. What do you think, Alan?"

Bodkin shook his head slowly, still staring out blankly at the darkened buildings around the square. "You two go, I must stay here."

Kerans hesitated. "Alan," he warned him gently. "Strangman has everything he needs now. We're useless to him. Soon we'll simply be unwelcome guests."

But Bodkin ignored him. He looked down at the streets, hands clasping the rail like an old man at the counter of some vast store, shopping for the memories of his childhood.

The streets had almost been drained. The approaching scow ran aground on the sidewalk, pushed off again and then stuck finally on a traffic island. Led by Big Caesar, the three-man crew jumped down into the waist-deep water and waded noisily towards the depot ship, splashing water excitedly into the open shop-fronts.

With a jolt the paddle-ship settled itself firmly on the bottom, cheers and shouts going up from Strangman and the rest of the crew as they fended off the snapping overhead wires and tilted telegraph poles. A small dinghy was thrown into the water, and to a chorus of fists pounding a drumbeat on the rail the Admiral rowed Strangman across the shallow pool to the fountain in the centre of the square. Here Strangman debarked, pulled a flare pistol from a pocket of his dinner jacket and with an exultant shout began to fire salvo after salvo of coloured star-shells into the air overhead.

CHAPTER ELEVEN

"THE BALLAD OF MISTAH BONES"

HALF AN HOUR LATER Beatrice, Kerans and Dr. Bodkin were able to walk out into the streets. Huge pools of water still lay about everywhere, leaking from the ground floors of the buildings, but they were little more than two or three feet deep. There were clear stretches of pavement over a hundred yards long, and many of the further streets were completely drained. Dying fish and marine plants expired in the centre of the roadways, and huge banks of black sludge were silted up into the gutters and over the sidewalks, but fortunately the escaping waters had cut long pathways through them.

Strangman at their head, racing along in his white suit, firing star-shells into the dark streets, the crew charged off in a bellowing pack, those in front balancing a rum keg on their upturned palms, the others brandishing an assortment of bottles, machetes and guitars. A few derisive shouts of 'Mistah Bones!' faded around Kerans as he helped Beatrice down off the gangway, and then the trio were left alone in the silence of the huge stranded paddle-ship.

Glancing up uncertainly at the high distant ring of the jungle looming out of the darkness like the encircling lip of an extinct volcanic cone, Kerans led the way across the pavement to the nearest buildings. They stood in the entrance to one of the huge cinemas, sea urchins and cucumbers flickering faintly across the tiled floor, sand dollars flowering in the former ticket booth.

Beatrice gathered her skirt in one hand, and they moved slowly down the line of cinemas, past cafés and amusement arcades, patronised now only by the bivalves and molluscs. At the first corner they turned away from the sounds of revelry coming from the other side of the square, and walked westwards down the dim dripping canyons. A few star-shells continued to explode overhead, and the delicate glass sponges in the doorways glowed softly as they reflected the pink and blue light.

"Coventry Street, Haymarket . . ." Kerans read off the rusting street signs. They stepped quickly into a doorway as Strangman and his pack charged back across the square in a blaze of light and noise, machetes slashing at the rotting boards over the shop-fronts.

"Let's hope they find something that satisfies them," Bodkin murmured. He searched the crowded skyline, as if looking for the deep black water that had once covered the buildings.

For several hours they wandered like forlorn elegant ghosts through the narrow streets, occasionally meeting one of the roistering crew, ambling drunkenly along the centre of the roadway with the remains of some fading garment in one hand, a machete in the other. A few small fires had been started in the centre of the street junctions, groups of two or three men warming themselves over the flaring tinder.

Avoiding these, the trio made their way across the nexus of streets to the south shore of the sometime lagoon, where Beatrice's apartment house rose up into the darkness, the penthouse lost among the stars.

"You'll have to walk the first ten storeys," Kerans told Beatrice. He pointed to the deep bank of silt which reached upwards in a damp concave slope to the fifth floor windows, part of an immense massif of coagulated loam which, as Strangman had described, now encircled the lagoon and formed an impenetrable dyke against the encroaching sea. Down the side-streets they could see the great viscous mass lifting over the roof-tops, flowing through the gutted buildings, which in turn helped to rigidify them.

Here and there the perimeter of the dyke moored itself to a heavier obstruction—a church or government office— and diverged from its circular path around the lagoon. One of these evaginations followed the route they had taken on their way to the diving party, and Kerans felt his step quicken as they approached the planetarium. He waited impatiently as the others idled in front of the empty display windows of the old department stores, or gazed at the black slime oozing down the escalators below the office blocks into sluggish pools across the street.

Even the smallest of the buildings had been barricaded before being abandoned, and a makeshift clutter of steel screens and grilles collapsed across the doorways, hiding whatever might lie behind them. Everything was covered with a fine coating of silt, smothering whatever grace and character had once distinguished the streets, so that the entire city seemed to Kerans to have been resurrected from its own sewers. Were the Day of Judgement to come, the armies of the dead would probably rise clothed in the same filthy mantle.

"Robert." Bodkin held his arm, pointing down the

darkened street ahead of them. Fifty yards away, its metal dome outlined faintly in the fragmentary light of the distant signal rockets, stood the sombre, shadow-draped hull of the planetarium. Kerans stopped, recognising the orientation of the surrounding roadway, the sidewalks and street lamps, then walked forward, half uncertain, half curious, towards this pantheon which held so many of his terrors and enigmas.

Sponges and red kelp sagged limply across the sidewalk outside the entrance as they approached, picking their way carefully over the banks of mud that lined the street. The groves of wraith-like fucus which had wreathed the dome now flopped limply over the portico, their long draining fronds hanging over the entrance like a ragged awning. Kerans reached up and pushed aside the fronds, then peered cautiously into the interior of the darkened foyer. Thick black mud, hissing faintly as its contained marine life expired in a slow deflation of air-bladders and buoyancy sacs, lay everywhere, over the ticket booths and the stairway to the mezzanine, across the walls and door-panels. No longer the velvet mantle he remembered from his descent, it was now a fragmenting cloak of rotting organic forms, like the vestments of the grave. The once translucent threshold of the womb had vanished, its place taken by the gateway to a sewer.

Kerans began to walk forwards across the foyer, remembering the deep twilight bower of the auditorium and its strange zodiac. Then he felt the dark fluid rilling out across the mud between his feet, like the leaking blood-stream of a whale.

Quickly he took Beatrice's arm, and retraced their steps down the street. "I'm afraid the magic has gone," he re-remarked flatly. He forced a laugh. "I suppose Strangman would say that the suicide should never return to the scene of his crime."

Attempting to take a shorter route, they blundered into a winding cul-de-sac, managed to step back in time as a small caiman lunged at them from a shallow pool. Darting between the rusting shells of cars, they regained the open street, the alligator racing behind them. It paused by a lamp post on the edge of the sidewalk, tail whipping slowly, jaws flexing, and Kerans pulled Beatrice after him. They broke into a run and had covered ten yards when Bodkin slipped and fell heavily into a bank of silt.

"Alan! Hurry!" Kerans started to go back for him, the caiman's head pivoting towards them. Marooned behind in the lagoon, it seemed bewildered and ready to attack anything.

Suddenly there was a roar of gunfire, the flames stabbing across the roadway. Flares held above their heads, a group of men appeared around a corner. In front of them was the white-faced figure of Strangman, followed by the Admiral and Big Caesar, shot-guns at their shoulders.

Strangman's eyes glittered in the flare light. He made a small bow towards Beatrice, then saluted Kerans. Its spine shattered, the alligator thrashed impotently in the gutter, revealing its yellow underbelly, and Big Caesar drew his machete and began to hack at its head.

Strangman watched it with evil pleasure. "Loathsome brute," he commented, then pulled from his pocket a huge rhinestone necklace, still encrusted with algae, and held it out to Beatrice.

"For you, my dear." Deftly, he strung the strands around her neck, regarding the effect with pleasure. The entwined weeds among the sparkling stones against the white skin of her breast made her look like some naiad of the deep. "And all the other jewels of this dead sea."

With a flourish he was off again, the flares vanishing in the darkness with the shouts of his men, leaving them alone in the silence with the white jewels and the decapitated alligator.

During the next days events proceeded to even greater madness. Increasingly disorientated, Kerans would wander alone through the dark streets at night—by day it became unbearably hot in the labyrinth of alleyways—unable to tear himself away from his memories of the old lagoon, yet at the same time locked fast to the empty streets and gutted buildings.

After his first surprise at seeing the drained lagoon he began to sink rapidly into a state of dulled inertia, from which he tried helplessly to rouse himself. Dimly he realised that the lagoon had represented a complex of neuronic needs that were impossible to satisfy by any other means. This blunting lethargy deepened, unbroken by the violence around him, and more and more he felt like a man marooned in a time sea, hemmed in by the shifting planes of dissonant realities millions of years apart.

The great sun beating in his mind almost drowned out the sounds of the looting and revelry, the roars of explosives and shot-guns. Like a blind man he stumbled in and out of the old arcades and entrances, his white dinner suit stained and grimy, jeered at by the sailors as they charged by him, playfully buffeting his shoulders. At midnight he would wander feverishly through the roistering singers in the square and sit beside Strangman at his parties, hiding back under the shadow of the paddle-ship, watching the dancing and listening to the beat of the drums and guitars, overlayed in his mind by the insistent pounding of the black sun.

He abandoned any attempt to return to the hotel—the creek was blocked by the pumping scows, and the intervening lagoon seethed with alligators—and during the day either slept in Beatrice's apartment on the sofa or sat numbly in a quiet alcove on the gaming deck of the depot ship. Most of the crew would be asleep among the crates or arguing over their spoils, waiting with surly impatience for the dusk, and they left him alone. By an inversion of logic it was safer to stay close to Strangman than to try to continue his previous separate regimen. Bodkin attempted this, withdrawing in a growing state of shock to the testing station—now reached by a precipitous climb up a dilapidated fire escape—but on one of his midnight forays out into the streets of the university quarter behind the planetarium he had been seized by a group of sailors and roughly manhandled. By attaching himself to Strangman's entourage Kerans had at least conceded his absolute authority over the lagoons.

Once he managed to force himself to visit Bodkin, found him resting quietly in his bunk, cooled by a home-made fan and the fading air-conditioner. Like himself, Bodkin seemed to be isolated on a small spur of reality in the centre of the time sea.

"Robert," he murmured through his swollen lips, "get away from here. Take her, the girl"—here he searched for the name—"Beatrice, and find another lagoon."

Kerans nodded, hunching himself inside the narrow cone of cool air projected by the air-conditioner. "I know, Alan, Strangman's insane and dangerous, but for some reason I can't leave yet. I don't know why, but there's something here—those naked streets." He gave up cloudily. "What is it? There's a strange incubus on my mind. I must lift it first."

Bodkin managed to sit up weakly. "Kerans, listen. Take her and go. Tonight. Time doesn't exist here now."

In the laboratory below, a pallid brown scum was draped over the great semicircle of progress charts, Bodkin's dismembered neuronic zodiac, and veiled the stranded benches and fume cupboards. Kerans made a half-hearted attempt to replace the charts that had fallen to the floor, then gave up and spent the next hour washing his silk dinner jacket in a pool of water left behind in one of the sinks.

Perhaps in imitation of himself, several of the crew now also sported tuxedos and black ties. A pantechnicon full of evening wear sealed inside watertight tin envelopes had been found in one of the warehouses. Egged on by Strangman, half a dozen of the sailors dressed themselves up, bow ties around their bare necks, and pranced through the streets in tremendous glee, tails flaring and knees high-kicking, like a troupe of lunatic waiters at a dervish carnival.

After the initial abandon, the looting began to take on a more serious note. Whatever his private reasons, Strangman was solely interested in objets d'art, and after a careful reconnaissance identified one of the city's principal museums. But, to his annoyance, the building had been stripped, and his only salvage was a large mosaic which his men removed tile by tile from the entrance hall and laid out like a vast jig-saw on the observation deck of the depot ship.

This disappointment prompted Kerans to warn Bodkin that Strangman might try to vent his spleen on him, but when he climbed up to the testing station early the next evening he found that Bodkin had gone. The air-conditioner had exhausted its fuel, and Bodkin, deliberately it seemed, had opened the windows before he left, so that the entire station steamed like a cauldron.

Curiously, Bodkin's disappearance gave Kerans little concern. Immersed in himself, he merely assumed that the biologist had followed his own advice and moved out to one of the lagoons to the south.

Beatrice, however, was still there. Like Kerans, she had sunk into a private reverie. Kerans rarely saw her during the day, when she would be locked into her bedroom, but at midnight, when it became cool, she would always come down from her penthouse among the stars and join Strangman at his parties. She sat numbly beside him in her blue evening dress, her hair studded with three or four of the tiaras Strangman had looted from the old jewellery vaults, her breasts smothered under a mass of glittering chains and crescents, like a mad queen in a horror drama.

Strangman treated her with a strange deference, not unmarked by a polite hostility, almost as if she were a tribal totem, a deity whose power was responsible for their continued good fortune but none the less resented. Kerans tried to stay near her, within her orbit of protection, and the evening after Bodkin's disappearance leaned across the cushions to say: "Alan's gone. Old Bodkin. Did he see you before he left?"

But Beatrice stared out over the fires burning in the square, without looking at him said in a vague voice: "Listen to the drumming, Robert. How many suns are there, do you think?"

Wilder now than Kerans had ever seen him, Strangman danced about the camp-fires, sometimes forcing Kerans to join him, inciting the bongo drummers to ever faster rhythms. Then, exhausted, he would slump back on his divan, his thin white face like blue chalk.

Leaning on one elbow, he stared sombrely at Kerans, squatting on a cushion behind him.

"Do you know why they fear me, Kerans? The Admiral, Big Caesar and the others. Let me tell you my secret." Then, in a whisper: "Because they think I'm dead."

In a spasm of laughter, he rocked back into the divan, shaking helplessly, "Oh, my God, Kerans! What's the matter with you two? Come out of that trance." He looked up as Big Caesar approached, doffing the dried alligator's head which he wore like a hood over his own. "Yes, what is it? A special song for Doctor Kerans? Capital! Did you hear that, Doctor? Let's go then, with *The Ballad of Mistah Bones!*"

Clearing his throat, with much prancing and gesticulation, the big Negro began, his voice deep and guttural.

"Mistah Bones, he loves dried men,
  Got himself a banana girl; three prophets sly,
  She played him all crazy, drowned him in the snake
                                                  wine,
  Never heard so many swamp birds,
  That old boss alligator.

Rum Bones, he went skull fishing,
  Down off Angel Creek, where the dried men run,
  Took out his turtle stone, waited for the chapel boat,
  Three prophets landing.
  Some bad joss.

Rum Bones, he saw the loving girl,
  Gave his turtle stone for two bananas,
  He had that banana girl like a hot mangrove;
  Prophets saw him,
  No dried men coming for Rum Bones.

Rum Bones, he danced for that loving girl,
  Built a banana house for her loving bed——"

With a sudden shout, Strangman leapt from the divan,

raced past Big Caesar into the centre of the square, pointing up at the perimeter wall of the lagoon high above them. Outlined against the setting sky was the small square figure of Dr. Bodkin, picking his way slowly across the wooden barrage that held back the creek waters outside. Unaware that he had been seen by the party below, he carried a small wooden box in one hand, a faint light fizzing from a trailing wire.

Wide awake, Strangman bellowed: "Admiral! Big Caesar! Get him! He's got a bomb!"

In a wild scramble the party dissolved, with the exception of Beatrice and Kerans everyone raced off across the square. Shot-guns slammed left and right, and Bodkin paused uncertainly, the fuse wire sparking about his legs. Then he turned and began to edge back along the barrage.

Kerans jumped to his feet and ran after the others. As he reached the perimeter wall star-shells were bursting into the air, spitting magnesium fragments across the roadway. Strangman and the Admiral were leaping up a fire escape, Big Caesar's shot-gun slamming out over their heads. Bodkin had left the bomb in the centre of the dam and was racing away over the roof-tops.

Straddling the final ledge, Strangman leapt up on to the barrage, in a dozen strides reached the bomb and kicked it out into the centre of the creek. As the splash died away a cheer of approval went up from those below. Catching his breath, Strangman buttoned his jacket, then slipped a short-barrelled ·38 from his shoulder holster. A thin smile glittered on his face. Whipping on the cries of his followers, he set out after Bodkin as he scaled his way painfully up the pontoon of the testing station.

Kerans listened numbly to the final shots, remembering Bodkin's warning and the possibility, for which he bore him no grudge as he had chosen to ignore it, of being swept away himself with Strangman and his crew. He walked slowly back to the square, where Beatrice still sat on the heap of cushions, the alligator head on the ground in front of her.

As he reached her he heard the footsteps behind him slowing menacingly, a strange silence fall over the pack.

He swung around to see Strangman saunter forward, a smirk twisting his lips. Big Caesar and the Admiral were at his shoulder, their shot-guns exchanged for machetes. The rest of the crew fanned out in a loose semicircle, watching expectantly, obviously pleased to see Kerans, the aloof medicine-man of a rival juju, get his just deserts.

"That was rather stupid of Bodkin, don't you think, Doctor? Dangerous too, as a matter of fact. We could damn' nearly have all been drowned." Strangman paused a few feet from Kerans, eyeing him moodily. "You knew Bodkin pretty well, I'm surprised you didn't anticipate that. I don't know whether I should take any more chances with mad biologists."

He was about to gesture to Big Caesar when Beatrice jumped to her feet and rushed over to Strangman.

"Strangman! For heaven's sake, one's enough. Stop it. We won't hurt you! Look, you can have all these!"

With a wrench she unclasped the mass of necklaces, tore the tiaras from her hair and flung them at Strangman. Snarling with anger, Strangman kicked them into the gutter, and Big Caesar stepped past her, the machete swinging upward.

"Strangman!" Beatrice threw herself at Strangman, stumbled and almost dragged him to the ground by his lapels. "You white devil, can't you leave us alone?"

Strangman twisted her away, breath seething through his clenched teeth. He gazed wildly at the dishevelled woman down on her knees among the jewels, and was about to wave Big Caesar on when a sudden intention tremor flickered across his right cheek. He slapped at it with his open hand, trying to brush it away like a fly, then flexed his facial muscles in an ugly grimace, unable to master the spasm. For a moment his face was twisted in a grotesque gape, like a man struggling in lock-jaw. Aware of his master's indecision, Big Caesar hesitated, and Kerans moved backwards into the shadows under the depot ship.

"All right! God, what a . . .!" Strangman muttered something thickly to himself and straightened his jacket, the point grudgingly conceded. The tic had faded. He nodded slowly at Beatrice, as if warning her that any future intercessions would be ignored, then barked sharply at Big Caesar. The machetes were tossed aside, but before Beatrice could protest again the entire pack threw itself on Kerans with a series of whoops and yells, hands flailing and clapping.

Kerans tried to sidestep them, uncertain from the circle of grinning faces whether this was merely some elaborate form of horse-play intended to discharge the tension that Bodkin's murder had generated, and at the same time administer a salutary reproof. He skipped around Strangman's divan as the pack closed in, found his escape blocked by the Admiral, who was feinting from side to side in his white tennis shoes like a dancer. Suddenly he sprang forwards and kicked Kerans' feet from under him. Kerans sat down heavily on the divan, and a dozen, oily brown-skinned arms seized him around the neck and shoulders and somersaulted him backwards on to the cobbled ground. He struggled helplessly to free himself, had a glimpse through the panting bodies of Strangman and Beatrice watching from the distance. Taking her arm, Strangman drew her firmly towards the gangway.

Then a large silk cushion was stuffed into Kerans' face, and hard palms began to pound a drum-beat across the back of his neck.

CHAPTER TWELVE

THE FEAST OF SKULLS

"*THE FEAST of Skulls!*"

Goblet raised in the flare-light, its amber contents spilling over his suit, Strangman let out an exultant shout, with a flourish leapt down from the fountain as the tumbril cart swerved across the cobbled square. Propelled by six sweating, bare-chested sailors bent double between its shafts, it rattled and jolted through the quickening embers of the charcoal fires, a dozen hands helping it on its way, and to a final accelerating crescendo on the drums struck the edge of the dais and tipped its white gleaming cargo across the boards at Kerans' feet. Immediately a chanting circle formed around him, hands beat out an excited rantando, white teeth flashed and snapped at the air like demoniac dice, hips swivelled and heels stamped. The Admiral dived forward and cleared a way through the whirling torsos, and Big Caesar, a steel trident held in front of him with a huge bale of red kelp and fucus transfixed on its barbs, lurched on to the dais and with a grunting heave tossed the dripping fronds into the air over the throne.

Kerans swayed forward helplessly as the sweet, acrid weeds cascaded around his head and shoulders, the lights of the dancing flares reflected in the gilt arm-rests of the throne. As the rhythm of the drums beat around him, almost exorcising the deeper pulse booming faintly in the base of his mind, he let his weight hang against the leather thongs around his wrists, indifferent to the pain as he sank in and out of consciousness. At his feet, at the base of the throne, the broken white harvest of bones gleamed with their ivory whiteness: slender tibias and femurs, scapulas like worn trowels, a mesh of ribs and vertebrae, even two lolling skulls. The light flickered across their bald pates and winked in the empty eye sockets, leaping from the bowls of kerosene borne by the corridor of statues which led towards the throne across the square. The dancers had formed themselves into a long undulating line, and with Strangman prancing at their head began to weave in and out of the marble nymphs, the drummers around the fires pivotting in their seats to follow their progress.

Given a momentary respite as they circled the square, Kerans lolled against the velvet back-rest, pulling automatically at his clamped wrists. The kelp trailed around his neck and shoulders, falling over his eyes from the tin crown Strangman had clamped to his brow. Almost dry, the kelp exuded its sweaty stench, and covered his arms so that only a few ragged strips of his dinner jacket were visible. At the edge of the dais, beyond the litter of bones and rum bottles, were more drifts of the weed, and a debris of conches and dismembered starfish with which they had pelted him before finding the mausoleum.

Twenty feet behind him towered the dark bulk of the depot ship, a few lights still burning on its decks. For two nights the parties had continued, the tempo mounting hour by hour, Strangman apparently determined to exhaust his crew. Kerans drifted helplessly in a half-conscious reverie, his pain dulled by the rum forced down his throat (evidently the final indignity, drowning Neptune in an even more magical and potent sea), mild concussion cloaking the scene before him in a mist of blood and scotomata. Dimly he was aware of his torn wrists and bruised body, but he sat patiently, stoically acting out the role of Neptune into which he had been cast, accepting the refuse and abuse heaped upon him as the crew discharged their fear and hatred of the sea. In that role, too, or its caricature which he performed, lay his only safety. Whatever his motives, Strangman still seemed reluctant to kill him, and the crew reflected this hesitation, always disguising their insults and tortures in the form of grotesque and hilarious jokes, protecting themselves when they pelted him with sea-weed by half-pretending to make an offering to an idol.

The snake of dancers reappeared and formed itself into a changing circle around him. Strangman detached himself from its centre—he was obviously reluctant to come too close to Kerans, perhaps afraid that the bleeding wrists and forehead would make him realise the crudity of the jape—and Big Caesar came forward, his huge knobbed face like an inflamed hippo's. Lumbering about to the rhythm of the bongos, he selected a skull and femur from the pile of bones around the throne, began to beat out a tattoo for Kerans, tapping the varying thicknesses of the temporal and occipital lobes to pick out a crude cranial octave. Several others joined in, and with a rattle of femur and tibia, radius and ulna, a mad dance of the bones ensued. Weakly, only half aware of the grinning, insulting faces pressed to within a foot or two of his own, Kerans waited for this to subside, then leaned back and tried to shield his eyes as a salvo of star-shells burst overhead and for a moment illuminated the depot ship and the surrounding buildings. This signalled the end of the festivity and the start of another night's work. With a shout, Strangman and the Admiral pulled apart the dancing group. The cart was hauled away, metal rims ringing over the cobbles, and the kerosene flares were extinguished. Within a minute the square was dark and empty, a few gutted fires sputtering among the cushions and drums, intermittently reflected in the gilt limbs of the throne and the white bones encircling it.

Now and then, at intervals through the night, a small group of looters would reappear, wheeling their booty in front of them, a bronze statue or a section of portico, hoist them into the ship and then vanish again, ignoring the motionless figure hunched on the throne among the shadows. By now Kerans was asleep, unaware of his fatigue and hunger, waking for a few minutes before dawn at the coolest ebb of the night to shout for Beatrice. He had not seen her since his capture after Bodkin's death, and assumed that Strangman had locked her away within the depot ship.

At last, after the exploding night with its bravura of drums and star-shells, the dawn lifted over the shadow-filled square, drawing behind it the immense golden canopy of the sun. Within an hour the square and the drained streets around it were silent, only a distant whir of an air-conditioner in the depot ship reminding Kerans that he was not alone. Somehow, by a manifest miracle, he had survived the previous day, sitting out unprotected in the full noon heat, shaded by only the cloak of weeds trailing from his crown. Like a stranded Neptune, he looked out from this pavilion of seaweed at the carpet of brilliant light covering the bones and garbage. Once he had been aware of a hatchway opening on to a deck above, and sensed that Strangman had come from his cabin to observe him—a few minutes later several

138

uckets of icy water were tossed down on to him. He sipped feverishly at the cold drops falling from the weeds into his mouth like frozen pearls. Immediately afterwards he sank off into a profound torpor, waking after dusk just before the night's festivities were to begin.

Then Strangman had come down in his pressed white suit and examined him critically, in a strange access of pity suddenly murmured: "Kerans, you're still alive. How do you do it?"

It was this remark which sustained him through the second day, when the white carpet at noon lay over the square in incandescent layers a few inches apart, like the planes of parallel universes crystallised out of the continuum by the immense heat. Across his skin the air burned like a flame. He stared listlessly at the marble statues, and thought of Hardman, moving through the pillars of light on his way towards the mouth of the sun, disappearing over the dunes of luminous ash. The same power which guarded Hardman seemed to have revealed itself within Kerans, in some way adjusting his metabolism so that he could survive the unbroken heat. Still he was watched from the deck above. Once a large salamander three feet long had darted among the bones towards him, its insane teeth like flints of obsidian flexing slowly as it scented Kerans, and a single shot had roared out from the deck, smashing the lizard into a writhing bloodied mess at his feet.

Like the reptiles which sat motionlessly in the sunlight, he waited patiently for the day to end.

Again Strangman seemed baffled to find him, swaying in an exhausted delirium, but still alive. A flicker of nervousness creased his mouth, and he glanced irritably at Big Caesar and the crew waiting around the dais in the torchlight, apparently as surprised as himself. When Strangman began to whoop and shout for drums the response was markedly less prompt.

Determined to break Kerans' power for once and for all, Strangman ordered two additional casks of rum lowered from the depot-ship, hoping to drive from his men's minds their unconscious fear of Kerans and the paternal guardian of the sea he now symbolised. Soon the square was filled with noisy stumbling figures, tipping their jugs and bottles to their lips, tap dancing on the drum-skins. Accompanied by the Admiral, Strangman moved swiftly from one party to another, inciting them to further acts of extravagance. Big Caesar donned the alligator head and tottered about the square on his knees, a whooping troupe of drummers behind him.

Wearily Kerans waited for the climax. At Strangman's instructions the throne was lifted from the dais and lashed to the cart. Kerans lay back limply against the head-rest, looking up at the dark flanks of the buildings as Big Caesar heaped the bones and sea-weed around his feet. With a shout from Strangman the drunken procession set off, a dozen men fighting to get between the shafts of the tumbril, throwing it from left to right across the square and knocking down two of the statues. Amid a chorus of excited orders from Strangman and the Admiral, who raced along beside the wheels, trying helplessly to restrain it, the cart rapidly gathered speed and veered away into a side-street, careened along the pavement before demolishing a rusty lamp-standard. Bludgeoning the curly pates of the men around him with his massive fists, Big Caesar fought his way to the front of the shafts, seized one in each hand and enforced a more leisurely progress.

High above their heads, Kerans sat in the rocking throne, the cool air slowly reviving him. He watched the ceremony below with semi-conscious detachment, aware that they were moving systematically down every street in the drained lagoon, almost as if he were an abducted Neptune forced against his will to sanctify those sections of the drowned city which had been stolen from him by Strangman and reclaimed.

But gradually, as the exertion of pulling the cart cleared their heads and made them move in step, the men between the shafts began to sing what sounded like the lay of an old

Haitian cargo cult, a deep crooning melody that again underlined their ambivalent attitude towards Kerans. In an effort to re-establish the real purpose of the outing, Strangman began to shout and brandish his flare pistol, after a short scrimmage made them reverse the direction of the cart so that they pushed it instead of pulled. As they passed the planetarium Big Caesar leapt up on to the cart, clinging to the throne like an immense ape, picked up the alligator's head and clamped it down over Kerans' shoulders.

Blinded and almost suffocated by the foetid stench of the crudely skinned hide, Kerans felt himself flung helplessly from side to side as the tumbril gained speed again. The men between the shafts, unaware of their direction, raced along the street, panting after Strangman and the Admiral, Big Caesar pursuing them with a rain of blows and kicks. Almost out of control, the cart swerved and lurched, narrowly missed wrecking itself on a traffic island, then straightened up and accelerated down an open stretch of roadway. As they neared a corner Strangman suddenly shouted to Big Caesar. Without looking, the huge mulatto flung his weight on the right-hand shaft and the cart pivoted and bounded up on to the sidewalk. For fifty yards it raced along helplessly, several of the men tripping over each other's legs and falling to the ground, then in a scream of axle iron and timber collided with the wall and pitched on to its side.

Torn from its mooring, the throne was flung half-way across the street into a low mud bank. Kerans lay face downwards, his impact with the ground softened by the damp silt, freed of the alligator head, but still trapped in his seat. Two or three of the crew were spread-eagled around him and picked themselves up, and an upended wheel of the cart rumbled slowly in the air.

Staggering helplessly with laughter, Strangman slapped Big Caesar and the Admiral on the back, soon had the rest of the crew jabbering excitedly to each other. They gathered around the wrecked cart, then went over to look at the upturned throne. Strangman rested one foot upon it majestically, rocking the shattered head-rest. Holding the pose long enough to convince his followers that Kerans' power was now truly spent, he holstered his flare pistol and ran away down the street, beckoning the others after him. With a chorus of jeers and shouts, the pack made off.

Pinioned below the inverted throne, Kerans stirred painfully. His head and right shoulder were half buried in the bank of caking silt. He flexed his wrists against the loosened thongs, but they were still too tight for him to free his hands.

Shifting his weight on to his shoulders, he tried to pull the throne over by his arms, then noticed that the left-hand arm-rest had snapped from its vertical support. Slowly he pressed his blunted fingers under the arm-rest and began to work the thongs loop by loop over the ragged stump of the support protruding from the mortice joint.

When his hand freed itself, he let it fall limply to the ground, then massaged his bruised lips and cheeks, and kneaded the stiffened muscles of his chest and stomach. He twisted himself on to his side and picked at the knot clamping his right wrist to the other rest, in the brief flares of light from the star-shells loosened the thongs and freed himself.

For five minutes he lay inertly under the dark hulk of the throne, listening to the distant voices recede into the alleys beyond the depot ship. Gradually the flares faded, and the street became a silent canyon, the roof-tops faintly illuminated by the fading phosphorescent glow of the dying animalcula, which cast a web-like silver veil over the drained buildings and turned them into the expiring corner of an ancient spectral city.

Crawling from below the throne, he rose uncertainly to his feet, stumbled across the sidewalk and leaned against the wall, his head pounding from the exertion. He pressed his face against the cool still-damp stone, staring down the street into which Strangman and his men had disappeared.

Abruptly, before his eyes closed involuntarily, he saw two figures approaching, one familiarly white-suited, the other tall and bow-shouldered, walking swiftly down the street towards him.

"Strangman . . . !" Kerans whispered. His fingers gripped the loose mortar, and he stiffened into the shadows which covered the wall. The two men were a hundred yards away, but he could see Strangman's brisk, purposive stride, Big Caesar's loping step behind him. Something gleamed as it caught a ray of light shining down an intersection, a stab of silver that swung from Big Caesar's hand.

Searching the darkness, Kerans edged along the wall, almost cut his hands on a ragged angle of plate glass in a store window. A few yards away was the entrance to a large arcade, running through the block until it joined a parallel street fifty yards to the west. Black silt a foot deep covered its floor, and Kerans crouched down as he climbed the shallow steps, then ran slowly through the dark tunnel to the far end of the arcade, the soft silt muffling his limping footsteps.

He waited behind a pillar at the rear entrance, steadying himself as Strangman and Big Caesar reached the throne. The machete in the mulatto's giant hand seemed little more than a razor. Strangman raised one hand warningly before touching the throne. Carefully he scanned the streets and walls of windows, his lean white jaw illuminated in the moonlight. Then he gestured sharply at Big Caesar and kicked the throne over with his foot.

As their oaths rang out into the air, Kerans drew himself back behind the pillar, then tiptoed quickly across the street towards a narrow alleyway that ran off into the labyrinthine nexus of the University quarter.

Half an hour later he took up his position on the top floor of a fifteen-storey office block that formed part of the perimeter wall of the lagoon. A narrow balcony ringed the suite of offices, at its rear leading to a fire escape that trailed off across the lower roofs into the jungle beyond, finally swallowed by the giant retaining banks of silt. Thin pools of water which had condensed from the afternoon heat mists lay across the plastic floors, and after climbing the central stairwell Kerans lay down and bathed his face and mouth in the cool liquid, slowly soothing his wounded wrists.

No search-party came after him. Rather than concede complete defeat—the only interpretation most of the crew would put upon Kerans' disappearance, Strangman had evidently decided to accept his escape as a fait accompli and forget him, assuming that Kerans would set off for the lagoons in the south. Through the night the looting parties continued to rove the streets, each succeeding find signalised by a display of rockets and pyrotechnics.

Kerans rested until dawn, lying in a pool of water, letting it soak through the ragged strips of the silk dinner jacket that still clung to him, washing away the stench of the sea-weed and silt. An hour before dawn he pulled himself to his feet, tore off his jacket and shirt and stuffed them down a crack in the wall. He unscrewed a glass light bracket that was intact, carefully scooped up the water from one of the clean pools on the floor below. He had collected about a quart by the time the sun was lifting over the eastern perimeter of the lagoon. Two corridors down he trapped a small lizard in the washroom, killed it with a loose brick. He lit a fire of tinder with a lens of chipped glass, roasted the fillets of dark stringy meat until they were tender. The small steaks melted in his cracked mouth with the exquisite tenderness of warm fat. Recovering his strength, he climbed back to the top floor and retired to a service cubicle behind the elevator shaft. After wedging the door with a few lengths of rusty banister rail, he settled down in the corner and waited for the evening.

The last sunlight was fading over the water as Kerans paddled his raft below the fronds of the fern trees dipping into the water around the lagoon, the blood and copper bronzes of the afternoon sun giving way to deep violets and indigo. Overhead the sky was an immense funnel of sapphire and purple, fantasticated whorls of coral cloud marking the descent of the sun like baroque vapour trails. A slack oily swell disturbed the surface of the lagoon, the water clinging to the leaves of the ferns like translucent wax. A hundred yards away it slapped lazily against the shattered remains of the jetty below the Ritz, throwing up a few broken spars of timber. Still restrained by the loose net of mooring lines, the fifty-gallon drums floated together like a group of hump-backed alligators. Luckily, the alligators Strangman had posted around the lagoon were still in their nests among the buildings, or had dispersed into the neighbouring creeks in search of food as the iguanas retreated before them.

Kerans paused before paddling out across the exposed face of the derelict bank adjacent to the Ritz, scanning the shoreline and the exit creek for any of Strangman's sentries. The concentration needed to build the raft from two galvanised iron water tanks had almost drained his brain, and he waited carefully before pushing on. As he neared the jetty he saw that the mooring lines had been slashed deliberately, the wooden box frame crushed by some heavy water-craft, probably the hydroplane, which Strangman had berthed in the central lagoon.

Wedging the raft between two of the floating drums, where it floated unobtrusively among the shifting debris, Kerans pulled himself up on to the balcony and stepped over the window-ledge into the hotel. Quickly he made his way up the staircase, following the trail of huge blurred footprints on the blue carpet mould which led down from the roof.

The penthouse had been wrecked. As he opened the outer wooden door into the suite a ragged glass panel of the interior air-seal fell to the floor at his feet. Someone had moved through the rooms in a berserk frenzy of violence, systematically smashing everything within sight. The Louis Quinze furniture had been hacked to pieces, dismembered legs and arms hurled through the internal glass walls. The carpeting over the floor lay in a tangle of long torn strips, even the cord underlay ripped apart so that the floor seals could be hacked and breached. Its legs lopped, the cabinet of the desk lay in two divided sections, the crocodile skin pared from its edges. Books were scattered underfoot, many of them slashed cleanly into two. A rain of blows had fallen upon the mantelpiece, huge gouges cut into its gilt lip, and enormous stars of frosted glass and silverscreen burst across the mirror like frozen explosions.

Stepping over the litter, Kerans ventured briefly on to the terrace, where the wire mesh of the mosquito screen had been ballooned outwards until it burst. The beach chairs where he had lain for so many months were chopped to matchwood.

As he expected, the decoy safe behind the desk had been sprung, its door open on the empty vault. Kerans went into the bedroom, a faint smile crossing his face when he realised that Strangman's house-breakers had failed to find the deep safe behind the bedroom mirror over the escritoire. The dented cylinder of the brass compass he had idly stolen from the base, still pointing to its talismanic south, lay on the floor below the small circular mirror, which it had shattered into a pattern like a magnified snow-flake. Kerans carefully rotated the rococo frame, released the hinge and drew it back to reveal the unbreached dial of the safe.

Darkness fell from the sky, throwing long shadows into the suite as Kerans' fingers raced through the tumblers. With a relieved intake of breath he pulled back the door, quickly slipped out the heavy Colt ·45 and its carton of slugs. He sat down on the wrecked bed and tore the seals off the carton, then loaded the chamber, weighing the massive black weapon in his hand. He emptied the carton and filled his pockets with the slugs, then tightened his belt and went back into the lounge.

As he surveyed the room, he realised that by a curious paradox he bore Strangman little malice for wrecking the suite. In a sense its destruction, and with it all his memories of the lagoon, merely underlined something he had been tacitly ignoring for some time, and which Strangman's arrival, and all it implied, should have made him accept—the need to abandon the lagoon and move southwards. His time there had outlived itself, and the air-sealed suite with its constant temperature and humidity, its supplies of fuel and food, were nothing more than an encapsulated form of his previous environment, to which he had clung like a reluctant embryo to its yoke sac. The shattering of this shell, like the piercing doubts about his true unconscious motives set off by his near drowning in the planetarium, was the necessary spur to action, to his emergence into the brighter day of the interior, archaeopsychic sun. Now he would have to go forward. Both the past, represented by Riggs, and the present contained within the demolished penthouse, no longer offered a viable existence. His commitment to the future, so far one of choice and plagued by so many doubts and hesitations, was now absolute.

In the darkness the sleek curved hull of the depot ship rose into the air like the velvet belly of a stranded whale. Kerans crouched down in the shadow of the stern paddle, his lean bronzed body merging him into the background. He hid in the narrow interval between two of the blades, each a riveted metal slab fifteen feet wide and four feet deep, peering through the coconut-sized links of the drive chain. It was shortly before midnight, and the last of the foraging parties was leaving the gangway, the sailors, bottle in one hand and machete in the other, lurching off across the square. The cobbles were littered with burst cushions and bongo drums, bones and burnt-out embers, all kicked about in a careless mêlée.

Kerans waited until the last of the group made their way off among the streets, then stood up and secured the Colt in his belt. Far away, on the opposite side of the lagoon, was Beatrice's apartment, its windows in darkness, the light on the pylon extinguished. Kerans had considered climbing the stairs to the top floor, but safely assumed that Beatrice would be aboard the depot ship, an unwilling house-guest of Strangman.

Overhead a figure appeared at the rail, then withdrew. Distantly a voice shouted something, another replied from the bridge. A hatchway from the galley opened and a pail-full of filthy slops were tossed down into the square. Already a substantial pool of abyssal fluid had gathered under the ship; soon it would fill the lagoon and the ship would float again away.

Ducking under the band of the drive chain, Kerans stepped up on to the lowest blade, quickly pulled himself hand over hand up this curved radial ladder. The paddle creaked slightly, rotating a few inches under his weight as the slack in the drive chain was taken in. At the top he transferred to the steel boom which carried the paddle axle. Steadying himself on the overhead guy-rope controlling the blade-scraper, he crawled slowly along the foot-wide boom, then stood up and climbed over the passenger rail into the small well of the flag-deck. A narrow companionway led up diagonally to the observation deck. Kerans scaled it soundlessly, pausing as he passed the two intervening decks in case any sailor with a hangover was moon-gazing at the rail.

Hiding in the lee of a white-painted gig berthed on the deck, Kerans moved forward, ducking from one ventilator to the next, reached a rusty winch which stood a few feet from the dining table where Strangman had entertained them. The table had been stripped, the divans and chesterfield drawn up in a row below the giant painting still propped against the funnels.

Voices sounded below again, and the gangway creaked as a last departure stepped down into the square. In the distance, over the roof-tops, a signal flare glowed briefly against the chimney stacks. As it faded Kerans stood up and walked past the painting towards the hatchway hidden behind it.

Suddenly he stopped, hand reaching for the butt of the Colt. Little more than fifteen feet away from him, on the berthing wing of the bridge, the red end of a cheroot glowed in the darkness, apparently detached from any corporeal form. Poised on the balls of his feet, and unable to either move forward or withdraw, Kerans searched the darkness around the glow, then picked out the white brim of the Admiral's peaked cap. A moment later, as he inhaled contentedly on the cheroot, the gleam of his eyes reflected the glowing tip.

While the men below crossed the square, the Admiral turned and surveyed the observation deck. Over the edge of the wooden rail Kerans could see the butt of a shot-gun cradled loosely in his elbow. The cheroot swivelled to one side of his mouth and a cone of white smoke dispersed in the air like silver dust. For a full two or three seconds he looked straight at Kerans, silhouetted in the darkness against the mass of figures on the canvas, but he gave no hint of recognition, apparently assuming that Kerans was part of the composition. Then he strolled slowly into the bridge-house.

Picking each footstep carefully, Kerans advanced to the edge of the painting, then ducked into the shadows behind it. A fan of light from the hatchway lay across the deck. Crouching down, the Colt steady in his hand, he slowly descended the steps on to the empty gaming deck, watching the doorways for any sign of movement, for a levelled gun barrel among the curtains. Strangman's suite was directly below the bridge, entered by a panel door in an alcove behind the bar.

He waited by the door until a metal tray slammed in the galley, then leaned on the handle and eased the door off its latch, stepped silently into the darkness. For a few seconds he paused inside the door, adjusting his eyes to the dim light cast into the ante-room through a bead curtain hidden behind a chart cabinet on his right. In the centre of the room was a large map table, roll-maps under the glass top. His bare feet sank into the soft carpeting, and he stepped past the cabinet and peered through the beads.

The room, some 30 feet long, was Strangman's principal saloon, an oak-lined chamber with leather couches facing each other down the side walls, a large antique globe on its bronze pedestal below the forward row of portholes. Three chandeliers hung from the ceiling, but only one was lit, over a high-backed Byzantine chair with stained-glass inlays at the far end of the room, shining on the jewels which spilled from the metal gun-boxes drawn up on a semicircle of low tables.

Head back against the chair, one hand touching the slender stem of a gold-lipped glass on a mahogany table at her elbow, was Beatrice Dahl. Her blue brocade dress was spread out like a peacock's tail, a few pearls and sapphires which had spilled from her left hand gleaming among the folds like electric eyes. Kerans hesitated, watching the door opposite which led into Strangman's cabin, then parted the curtain slightly so that the beads tinkled gently.

Beatrice ignored this, obviously too familiar with the sound of rustling glass. The chests at her feet were loaded with a mass of jewelled trash—diamanté anklets, gilt clasps, tiaras and chains of zircon, rhinestone necklaces and pendants, huge ear-rings of cultured pearl, overflowing from one chest to another and spilling on to the salvers placed on the floor like vessels to catch a quicksilver rainfall.

For a moment Kerans thought that Beatrice had been drugged—her expression was vacant and blank, like the mask of a wax dummy, her eyes on some distant focus. Then her hand moved, and she raised the wine glass perfunctorily to her lips.

"Beatrice!"

With a start she tipped the wine across her lap, looked up in surprise. Pushing back the beads, Kerans stepped quickly across the room, caught her elbow as she began to rise from the chair.

"Beatrice, wait! Don't move yet!" He tried the door behind the chair, found it locked. "Strangman and his men are looting the streets, I think there's only the Admiral up on the bridge."

Beatrice pressed her face to his shoulders, with her cool fingers traced the black bruises showing through his bronzed skin. "Robert, be careful! What happened to you? Strangman wouldn't let me watch!" Her relief and pleasure at seeing Kerans gave way to alarm. She glanced anxiously around the room. "Darling, leave me here and get away. I don't think Strangman will harm me."

Kerans shook his head, then helped her to her feet. He gazed at Beatrice's elegant profile, at her sleek carmine mouth and lacquered nails, almost bemused by the heady scent of perfume and the brocaded rustle of her gown. After the violence and filth of the past days he felt like one of the dust-begrimed discoverers of the tomb of Nefertiti stumbling upon her exquisite painted mask in the depths of the necropolis.

"Strangman's capable of anything, Beatrice. He's insane. They were playing a sort of mad game with me, very nearly killed me."

Beatrice gathered the train of her skirt, brushing away the jewels that clung to its fabric. Despite the lavish assortment before her, her wrists and breast were bare, one of her own small gold clasps in a contoured twist around her neck. "But Robert, even if we get out——"

"Quiet!" Kerans stopped a few feet from the curtain, watching the strands balloon faintly and then subside, trying to remember whether there was a porthole open in the ante-room. "I've built a small raft, it should carry us far enough. Later we'll rest and build a larger one."

He started to walk towards the curtain when two of the strands parted fractionally, something moved with snake-like speed and a whirling silver blade three feet long cleft the air and spun towards his head like an immense scythe. Wincing with pain, Kerans ducked and felt the blade skim past his right shoulder, tearing a shallow three-inch weal, then impale itself with a steely shudder in the oak panelling behind him. Voice frozen in her throat, Beatrice backed wild-eyed into one of the occasional tables, knocking a chest of jewels across the floor.

Before Kerans could reach her the curtain was thrashed back by an enormous arm and a huge hunch-backed figure filled the doorway, his one-eyed head lowered like a bull's below the transom. Sweat poured from his huge muscled chest, staining his green shorts. In his right hand was a twelve-inch barb of gleaming steel, about to thrust upwards at Kerans' stomach.

Side-stepping down the room, Kerans steadied the revolver in his hands, the huge Negro's single cyclopean eye following him. Then he stepped on the open teeth of a necklace clasp, involuntarily stumbled back against a sofa.

As he steadied himself against the wall Big Caesar launched himself through the air at Kerans, the knife driving through the air in a short arc like the tip of a propeller. Beatrice screamed, her voice abruptly drowned in the tremendous roar of the Colt. Jolted by the recoil, Kerans sat down in the sofa, watched the mulatto crash crookedly against the doorway, the knife spilling from his hand. A strangled bubbling grunt erupted from his throat, and with a cataclysmic wrench, which seemed to sum up all his pain and frustration, he tore at the bead curtain and ripped it from the transom. The bunching muscles of his torso contracted for the last time. Draped in the curtain, he fell forward on to the floor, his vast limbs like a bloated giant's, the thousands of beads spilling around him.

"Beatrice! Come on!" Kerans seized her arm, steered her past the prostrate body into the ante-room, his right hand and forearm numb from the jarring discharge of the Colt. They crossed the alcove, and raced past the deserted bar. Overhead a voice shouted from the bridge, and footsteps hurried across the deck to the rail.

Kerans stopped, looking down at the voluminous folds of Beatrice's gown, then abandoned his plan to retrace his entry over the stern paddle.

"We'll have to try the gangway." He pointed to the unguarded entrance by the starboard rail, the beckoning night-club cupids with flutes to their ruby lips dancing on either side of the steps. "It may look a little obvious, but it's just about the only way left now."

Half-way down, the gangway began to rock in its davits, and they heard the Admiral bark down at them from the bridge. A moment later the shot-gun roared out, the pellets slashing through the clapboard roof over their heads. Kerans ducked, at the mouth of the gangway craned up at the bridge, now directly overhead, saw the long barrel of the shot-gun sticking into the air as the Admiral manoeuvred about.

Kerans jumped down into the square, took Beatrice by

152

the waist and swung her down. Together they crouched under the hull of the depot ship, then darted across the square to the nearest street.

Half-way there Kerans looked over his shoulder as a group of Strangman's men appeared on the far side of the square. They shouted to and fro with the Admiral, then spotted Kerans and Beatrice a hundred yards away.

Kerans started to run on, the revolver still clasped in his hand, but Beatrice held him back.

"No, Robert! Look!"

In front of them, stretched arm to arm across the full width of the street, another group approached, a white-suited man at its centre. He strolled along, one thumb hooked casually into his belt, the other signalling his men on, his fingers almost touching the tip of the machete brandished by the man next to him.

Changing direction, Kerans pulled Beatrice diagonally across the square, but the first group had fanned out and cut them off. A star-shell went up from the deck of the ship and illuminated the square in its roseate light.

Beatrice stopped, out of breath, helplessly holding the broken heel of her gold slipper. She looked uncertainly at the men closing in on them. "Darling . . . Robert—what about the ship? Try to get back there yourself."

Kerans took her arm and they backed into the shadows below the forward paddle, hidden by the blades from the shotgun on the bridge. The exertion of climbing aboard the ship and then running about the square had exhausted Kerans, and his lungs pumped in painful spasms, so that he could barely steady the revolver.

"Kerans. . . ." Strangman's cool, ironic voice drifted across the square. He advanced at a relaxed amble, just within range of the Colt but well screened by the men on either side of him. All carried machetes and pangas, their faces amiable and unhurried.

"Finis, Kerans. . . Finis." Strangman stopped twenty feet from Kerans, his sardonic lips wreathed in a soft smile, surveying him with almost kindly pity. "Sorry, Kerans, but you're being a bit of a nuisance. Throw away the gun or we'll kill the Dahl girl, too." He waited for a few seconds. "I mean it."

Kerans found his voice. "Strangman——"

"Kerans, this is no time for a metaphysical discussion." A note of annoyance crept into his voice, as if he were dealing with a fractious child. "Believe me, no time for prayers, no time for anything. I told you to drop the gun. Then walk forward. My men think you abducted Miss Dahl; they won't touch her." He added, with a touch of menace: "Come on, Kerans. We don't want anything to happen to Beatrice, do we? Think what a beautiful mask her face will make." He tittered insanely. "Better than that old alligator you wore."

Phlegm choking his throat, Kerans swung around and handed the revolver to Beatrice, pressing her small hands around the butt. Before their eyes could meet he looked away, inhaling for the last time the musky perfume on her breasts, then began to walk out into the square as Strangman had ordered. The latter watched him with an evil smirk, then suddenly leapt forward with a snarl, whipping the others on.

As the long knives lanced through the air after him Kerans turned and raced around the paddle, trying to reach the area behind the ship. Then his feet slipped in one of the foetid pools, before he could catch himself he fell heavily. He scrambled to his knees, one arm raised helplessly to ward off the circle of raised machets, then felt something seize him from behind and roughly pull him backwards off balance.

Recovering his foothold on the damp cobbles, he heard Strangman shout in surprise. A group of brown-uniformed men, rifles at their hips, stepped rapidly from the shadows behind the depot ship where they had been hiding. At their head was the trim, brisk figure of Colonel Riggs. Two of the soldiers carried a light machine-gun, a third man two boxes of belt ammunition. They quickly set it up on its tripod ten feet in front of Kerans, levelled the perforated, air-cooled barrel at the confused mob backing away from them. The rest of the soldiers fanned out in a widening semicircle, prodding the slower of Strangman's men with their bayonets.

Most of the crew were shambling backwards in the general mêlée across the square, but a couple of them, still holding their pangas, attempted to break through the cordon. Instantly there was a short decisive volley of shots over their heads, and they dropped their knives and fell back mutely with the rest.

"Okay, Strangman. That will do very nicely." Riggs rapped his baton across the Admiral's chest and forced him back.

Completely disconcerted by all this, Strangman gaped blankly at the soldiers swarming past him. He searched the depot ship helplessly, as if expecting some large siege cannon to be wheeled forward and reverse the situation. Instead, however, two helmeted soldiers appeared on the bridge with a portable searchlight, swivelled its beam down into the square.

Kerans felt someone take his elbow. He looked round at the solicitous beak-like face of Sergeant Macready, a submachine-gun in the crook of his arm. At first he almost failed to identify Macready, only with an effort managed to place his aquiline features, like a face dimly remembered across the span of a lifetime.

"You all right, sir?" Macready asked softly. "Sorry to jerk you about like that. Looks as if you've been having a bit of a party here."

CHAPTER THIRTEEN

TOO SOON, TOO LATE

By EIGHT O'CLOCK the next morning Riggs had stabilised the situation and was able to see Kerans informally. His headquarters were in the testing station, with a commanding view over the streets below, and particularly of the paddle-ship in the square. Stripped of their weapons, Strangman and his crew sat around in the shade under the hull, supervised by the light machine-gun manned by Macready and two of his men.

Kerans and Beatrice had spent the night in the sick-bay aboard Riggs' patrol cruiser, a well-armed 30-ton PT boat which was now moored against the hydroplane in the central lagoon. The unit had arrived shortly after midnight, and a reconnaissance patrol reached the testing station on the perimeter of the drained lagoon at about the time Kerans entered Strangman's suite in the depot ship. Hearing the ensuing gunfire, they descended immediately into the square.

"I guessed Strangman was here," Riggs explained. "One of our aerial patrols reported seeing the hydroplane about a month ago, and I reckoned you might have a little trouble with him if you were still hanging on. The pretext of trying to reclaim the testing station was a fair one." He sat on the edge of the desk, watching the helicopter circle the open streets. "That should keep them quiet for a bit."

"Daley seems to have found his wings at last," Kerans commented.

"He's had a lot of practice." Riggs turned his intelligent eyes on Kerans, asked casually: "By the way, is Hardman here?"

"Hardman?" Kerans shook his head slowly. "No; I haven't seen him since the day he disappeared. He'll be a long way off by now, Colonel."

"You're probably right. I just thought he might be around." He flashed Kerans a sympathetic smile, evidently having forgiven him for scuttling the testing station, or sensible enough not to press the matter so soon after Kerans' ordeal. He pointed to the streets below glowering in the sunlight, the dry silt on the roof-tops and walls like caked dung. "Pretty grim down there. Damn' shame about old Bodkin. He really should have come north with us."

Kerans nodded, looking across the office at the machete scars sliced into the woodwork around the door, part of the damage gratuitously inflicted on the station after Bodkin's death. Most of the mess had been cleaned up, and his body, lying among the bloodstained programme charts in the laboratory below, flown out to the patrol cruiser. To his surprise, Kerans realised that callously he had already forgotten Bodkin and felt little more than a nominal pity for him. Riggs' mention of Hardman had reminded him of something far more urgent and important, the great sun still beating magnetically within his mind, and a vision of the endless sandbanks and blood-red swamps of the south passed before his eyes.

He went over to the window, picking a splinter from the sleeve of his fresh uniform jacket, and stared down at the men huddled under the depot ship. Strangman and the Admiral had gone forward towards the machine-gun, and were remonstrating with Macready, who was shaking his head impassively.

"Why don't you arrest Strangman?" he asked.

Riggs laughed shortly. "Because there's absolutely nothing I can hold him on. Legally, as he full well knows, he was absolutely entitled to defend himself against Bodkin, kill him if necessary." When Kerans looked round over his shoulder in surprise he continued: "Don't you remember the Reclaimed Lands Act and the Dykes Maintenance Regulations? They're still very much in force. I know Strangman's a nasty piece of work—with that white skin and his alligators—but strictly speaking he deserves a medal for pumping out the lagoon. If he complains, I'll have a job explaining that machine-gun down there. Believe me Robert, if I'd arrived five minutes later and found you chopped to bits Strangman could have claimed that you were an accomplice of Bodkin's and I'd have been able to do nothing. He's a clever fellow."

Tired out after only three hours' sleep, Kerans leaned against the window, smiling wanly to himself as he tried to resolve Riggs' tolerant attitude towards Strangman with his own experiences of the man. He was conscious that an even wider gulf now divided Riggs and himself. Although the Colonel was only a few feet away from him, emphasising his argument with brisk flourishes of the baton, he was unable to accept wholly the idea of Riggs' reality, almost as if his image were being projected into the testing station across enormous distances of time and space by some elaborate three-dimensional camera. It was Riggs, and not himself, who was the time-traveller. Kerans had noticed a similar lack of physical validity about the rest of the crew. Many of the original members had been replaced—all those, among them Wilson and Caldwell, who had begun to experience the deep dreams. For this reason, perhaps—and partly because of their pallid faces and weak eyes, in so marked contrast to Strangman's men, the present crew seemed flat and unreal, moving about their tasks like intelligent androids.

"What about the looting?" he asked.

Riggs shrugged. "Apart from a few trinkets filched from an old Woolworths, he's taken nothing that couldn't be put down to natural exuberance on the part of his men. As for all the statues and so on, he's doing a valuable job reclaiming works of art that were perforce abandoned. Though I'm not sure what his real motives are." He patted Kerans on the shoulder. "You'll have to forget about Strangman, Robert. The only reason he's sitting quiet now is that he knows he's got the law on his side. If he hadn't there'd be a battle royal going on." He broke off. "You look all in, Robert. Are you still getting these dreams?"

"Now and then." Kerans shuddered. "The last few days have been insane here. It's difficult to describe Strangman— he's like a white devil out of a voodoo cult. I can't accept the idea that he'll go scot free. When are you going to re-flood the lagoon?"

"Re-flood the——?" Riggs repeated, shaking his head in bewilderment. "Robert, you really are out of touch with reality. The sooner you get away from here the better. The last thing I intend to do is re-flood the lagoon. If anybody tries I'll personally blow his head off. Reclaiming land, particularly an urban area like this right in the centre of a former capital city, is a Class A1 priority. If Strangman is serious about pumping out the next two lagoons he'll not only get a free pardon, but a governor-generalship to boot."

He looked down through the window, as the metal rungs of the fire escape rang in the sunlight. "Here he comes now. I wonder what's on his evil little mind?"

Kerans went over to Riggs, averting his eyes from the maze of festering yellow roof-tops. "Colonel, you've got to flood it again, laws or no laws. Have you been down in those streets; they're obscene and hideous! It's a nightmare world that's dead and finished, Strangman's resurrecting a corpse! After two or three days here you'll——"

Riggs swung away from the desk, cutting Kerans off. An element of impatience crept into his voice. "I don't intend to stay here for three days," he snapped curtly. "Don't worry. I'm not suffering from any crazy obsessions about these lagoons, flooded or otherwise. We're leaving first thing tomorrow, all of us."

Puzzled, Kerans said: "But you can't leave, Colonel. Strangman will still be here."

"Of course he will! Do you think that paddle-boat has got wings? There's no reason for *him* to leave, if he thinks he can take the big heat waves coming, and the rain-storms. You never know. If he gets a few of these big buildings refrigerated he may be able to. In time, if he reclaims enough of the city, there might even be an attempt to reoccupy it. When we get back to Byrd I'll definitely put in a formal recommendation. However, at present there's nothing for me to stay for—I can't move the station now, but it's a fair loss. Anyway, you and the Dahl girl need a rest. *And* a brain-lift. Do you realise how lucky she is to be in one piece? Good God!" He nodded sharply at Kerans, standing up as a firm rap sounded on the door. "You should be grateful that I came here in time."

Kerans walked over to the side door into the galley, eager to avoid Strangman. He paused for a moment to look up at Riggs. "I don't know about that, Colonel. I'm afraid you came too late."

CHAPTER FOURTEEN

GRAND SLAM

CROUCHED DOWN IN a small office two floors above the
barrage, Kerans listened to the music playing amid the
lights on the top deck of the depot ship. Strangman's party
was still in full swing. Propelled by two junior members of
the crew, the big paddles rotated slowly, their blades dividing
the coloured spot lights and swinging them up into the sky.
Seen from above, the white awnings resembled the marquee
of a fairground, a brilliant focus of noise and festivity in the
darkened square.

As a concession to Strangman, Riggs had joined him at
this farewell party. A bargain had been struck between the
two leaders; earlier the machine-gun had been withdrawn
and the lower level placed out of bounds to the Colonel's
men, while Strangman agreed to remain within the perimeter
of the lagoon until Riggs had left. All day Strangman and
his pack had roved the streets, and the random sounds of
looting and firing echoed to and fro. Even now, as the last
guests, the Colonel and Beatrice Dahl, left the party and
climbed the fire escape to the testing station, fighting had
broken out on deck and bottles were being hurled down into
the square.

Kerans had put in a token appearance at the party,
keeping well away from Strangman, who made little attempt
to talk to him. At one point, between cabaret turns, he had
swept past Kerans, deliberately brushing his elbow, and
toasted him with his goblet.

"I hope you're not too bored, Doctor. You look tired. Ask
the Colonel to lend you his punka-wallah." He turned a
wicked smile on Riggs, who was sitting erectly on a tasselled
silk cushion with a circumspect expression on his face like a

district commissioner at a pasha's court. "The parties Dr. Kerans and I are used to are very different affairs, Colonel. They *really* go with a bang."

"So I believe, Strangman," Riggs replied mildly, but Kerans turned away, unable, like Beatrice, to mask his revulsion for Strangman. She was looking over her shoulder across the square, a small frown for a moment hiding the mood of torpor and self-immersion to which she was again returning.

Watching Strangman from the distance as he applauded the next cabaret turn, Kerans wondered whether in some way he had passed his peak, and was beginning to disintegrate. He now looked merely loathsome, like a decaying vampire glutted with evil and horror. The sometime charm had vanished, in its place a predatory gleam. As soon as he could, Kerans feigned a mild attack of malaria, and made his way out into the darkness and up the fire escape to the testing station.

Now determined on the only solution available, Kerans' mind felt clear and co-ordinated again, extending outwards beyond the perimeter of the lagoon.

Only fifty miles to the south, the rain-clouds were packed together in tight layers, blotting out the swamps and archipelagos of the horizon. Obscured by the events of the past week, the archaic sun in his mind beat again continuously with its immense power, its identity merging now with that of the real sun visible behind the rain-clouds. Relentless and magnetic, it called him southward, to the great heat and submerged lagoons of the Equator.

Assisted by Riggs, Beatrice climbed up on to the roof of the testing station, which also served as the helicopter landing stage. When Sergeant Daley started his engine and the rotors began to spin, Kerans quickly made his way down to the balcony two floors below. Separated by a hundred yards or so on either side, he was directly between the helicopter and the barrage, the continuous terrace of the building linking the three points.

Behind the building was an enormous bank of silt,

reaching upwards out of the surrounding swamp to the railings of the terrace, on to which spilled a luxurious outcrop of vegetation. Ducking below the broad fronds of the fern-trees, he raced along to the barrage, fitted between the end of the building and the shoulder of the adjacent office block. Apart from the exit creek on the far side of the lagoon where the pumping scows had been stationed, this was the only major entry point for the water that had passed into the lagoon. The original inlet, once twenty yards wide and deep, had shrunk to a narrow channel clogged with mud and fungi, its six-foot-wide mouth blocked by a rampart of heavy logs. Initially, once the rampart was removed, the rate of flow would be small, but as more and more of the silt was carried away the mouth would widen again.

From a small cache below a loose flagstone he withdrew two square black boxes, each containing six sticks of dynamite lashed together. He had spent all afternoon searching through the nearby buildings for them, confident that Bodkin had raided the armoury of the base at the same time that he had stolen the compass; sure enough, he finally found the trove in an empty lavatory cistern.

As the helicopter engine began to fire more loudly, the exhaust spitting brightly into the darkness, he lit the short 30-second fuse, straddled the rail and ran out towards the centre of the barrage.

There he bent down and suspended the boxes from a small peg he had driven into the outer row of logs earlier that evening. They hung safely out of view, about two feet from the water's edge.

"Dr. Kerans! Get away from there, sir!"

Kerans looked up to see Sergeant Macready at the further end of the barrage, standing at the rail of the next roof. He leaned forward, suddenly spotting the flickering end of the fuse, then rapidly unslung his Thompson gun.

Head down, Kerans raced back along the barrage, reached the terrace as Macready shouted again and then fired a short burst. The slugs tore at the railings, gouging out pieces of the cement, and Kerans fell as one of the cupro-nickel bullets struck his right leg just above the ankle. Pulling himself over the rail, he saw Macready shoulder the gun and jump down on to the barrage.

"Macready! Go back!" he shouted to the Sergeant, who was loping along the wooden planks. "It's going to blow!"

Backing away among the fronds, his voice lost in the roar of the helicopter as it carried out its take-off check, he helplessly watched Macready stop in the centre of the barrage and reach down to the boxes.

"Twenty-eight, twenty-nine . . ." Kerans concluded automatically to himself. Turning his back on the barrage, he limped away down the terrace, then threw himself on to the floor.

As the tremendous roar of the explosion lifted up into the dark sky, the immense fountain of erupting foam and silt briefly illuminated the terrace, outlining Kerans' spread-eagled form. From an initial crescendo, the noise seemed to mount in a continuous sustained rumble, the breaking thunder of the shock wave yielding to the low rush of the bursting cataract. Clods of silt and torn vegetation spattered on the tiles around Kerans, and he stumbled to his feet and reached the rail.

Widening as he watched, the water jetted down into the open streets below, carrying with it huge sections of the silt bank. There was a concerted rush to the deck of the depot ship, a dozen arms pointing up at the water pouring out of the breach. It swilled into the square, only a few feet deep, blotting out the fires and splashing against the hull of the ship, still rocking slightly from the impact of the explosion.

Then, abruptly, the lower section of the barrage fell forwards, a brace of a dozen twenty-foot logs going down together. The U-shaped saddle of silt behind collapsed in turn, exposing the full bore of the inlet creek, and what appeared to be a gigantic cube of water fifty feet high tipped into the street below like a flopping piece of jelly. With a dull rumbling roar of collapsing buildings, the sea poured in full flood.

"Kerans!"

He turned as a shot whipped overhead, saw Riggs running forward from the helicopter landing stage, pistol in hand. His engine stalled, Sergeant Daley was helping Beatrice out of the cabin.

The building was shaking under the impact of the torrent sweeping past its shoulder. Supporting his right leg with his hand, Kerans hobbled into the lee of the small tower which had held his previous observation window. From his trouser belt he pulled the ·45 Colt, held the butt in both hands and fired twice around the corner at the approaching hatless figure of Riggs. Both shots went wild, but Riggs stopped and backed off a few feet, taking cover behind a balustrade.

Feet moved quickly towards him and he looked around as Beatrice raced along the terrace. Reaching the corner as Riggs and Daley shouted after her, she sank down on her knees besides Kerans.

"Robert, you've got to leave! Now, before Riggs brings more of his men! He wants to kill you, I know."

Kerans nodded, getting painfully to his feet. "The Sergeant—I didn't realise he was patrolling. Tell Riggs I'm sorry——" He gestured helplessly, then took a last look at the lagoon. The black water surged across it through the buildings, level with the top line of their windows. Upended, its paddles stripped away, the depot ship drifted slowly towards the far shore, its hull sticking up into the air like the belly of an expiring whale. Spurts of steam and foam erupted from its exploding boilers, bursting out through the gashes in the hull as it was driven across the sharp reefs of the half-submerged cornices. Kerans watched it with a quiet contained pleasure, savouring the fresh tang that the water had brought again to the lagoon. Neither Strangman nor any members of his crew were visible, and the few fragments of splintered bridge and funnel swept away by the water were swallowed and regurgitated by the boiling under-currents.

"Robert! Hurry!" Beatrice pulled his arm, glancing back over her shoulder at the darting figures of Riggs and the pilot only fifty yards away. "Darling, where are you going. I'm sorry I can't be with you."

"South," Kerans said softly, listening to the roar of the deepening water. "Towards the sun. You'll be with me, Bea."

He embraced her, then tore himself from her arms and ran to the rear rail of the terrace, pushing back the heavy fern fronds. As he stepped down on to the silt bank Riggs and Sergeant Daley appeared around the corner and fired into the foliage, but Kerans ducked and ran away between the curving trunks, sinking up to his knees in the soft mud.

The edge of the swamp had receded slightly as the water poured away into the lagoon, and he painfully dragged the bulky catamaran, home-made from four fifty-gallon drums arranged in parallel pairs, through the thick rasp-weeds to the water. Riggs and the pilot emerged through the ferns as he pushed off.

While the outboard kicked into life he lay exhausted on the planking, the shots from Riggs' ·38 cutting through the small triangular sail. Slowly the interval of water widened to a hundred and then two hundred yards, and he reached the first of the small islands that grew out of the swamp on the roofs of isolated buildings. Hidden by them, he sat up and reefed the sail, then looked back for the last time at the perimeter of the lagoon.

Riggs and the pilot were no longer visible, but high up on the tower of the building he could see the lonely figure of Beatrice, waving slowly towards the swamp, changing tirelessly from one arm to the other, although she was unable to distinguish him among the islands. Far to her right, rising up above the encompassing silt banks, were the other familiar landmarks he knew so well, even the green roof of the Ritz, fading into the haze. At last all he could see were the isolated letters of the giant slogan Strangman's men had painted, looming out of the darkness over the flat water like a concluding epitaph: TIME ZONE.

The opposing flow of water slowed his progress, and fifteen minutes later, when the helicopter roared over, he had still not reached the edge of the swamp. Passing the top floor of a small building, he glided in through one of the windows, waited quietly as the aircraft roared up and down, machine-gunning the islands.

When it left he pushed on again, within an hour finally navigated the exit waters of the swamp and entered the broad inland sea that would lead him to the south. Large islands, several hundred yards in length, covered its surface, their vegetation crowding out into the water, their contours completely altered by the rising water in the short period that had elapsed since their search for Hardman. Shipping the outboard, he set the small sail, made a steady two or three miles an hour tacking across the light southerly breeze.

His leg had begun to stiffen below the knee, and he opened the small medical kit he had packed and washed the wound in a penicillin spray, then bandaged it tightly. Just before dawn, when the pain became unbearable, he took one of the morphine tablets and fell off into a loud, booming sleep, in which the great sun expanded until it filled the entire universe, the stars themselves jolted by each of its beats.

He woke at seven the next morning, lying back against the mast in bright sunlight, the medical kit open in his lap, the bows of the catamaran rammed lightly into a large fern-tree growing off the edge of a small island. A mile away, flying fifty feet above the water, the helicopter raced along, machine-gun fire flickering from its cabin at the islands below. Kerans shipped the mast and glided in under the tree, waiting until the helicopter left. Massaging his leg, but fearful of the morphine, he made a small meal of a bar of chocolate, the first of ten he had been able to collect. Luckily the petty officer in charge of stores aboard the patrol boat had been instructed to give Kerans free access to the medical supplies.

The aerial attacks were resumed at half-hour intervals, the aircraft once flying directly overhead. From his hiding-place in one of the islands Kerans clearly saw Riggs looking out from the hatchway, his small jaw jutting fiercely.

However, the machine-gun fire became more and more sporadic, and the flights were finally discontinued that afternoon.

By then, at five o'clock, Kerans was almost completely exhausted. The noon temperature of a hundred and fifty degrees had drained all energy from him, and he lay limply under the moistened sail, letting the hot water drip down on to his chest and face, praying for the cooler air of the evening. The surface of the water turned to fire, so that the craft seemed to be suspended on a cloud of drifting flame. Pursued by strange visions, he paddled feebly with one hand.

CHAPTER FIFTEEN

THE PARADISES OF THE SUN

THE NEXT DAY, by good luck, the storm-clouds moved overhead between himself and the sun, and the air grew markedly cooler, falling to ninety-five degrees at noon. The massive banks of black cumulus, only four or five hundred feet above, dimmed the air like a solar eclipse, and he revived sufficiently to start the outboard and raise his speed to ten miles an hour. Circling between the islands, he moved on southwards, following the sun that pounded in his mind. Later that evening, as the rain-storms lashed down, he felt well enough to stand up on one leg by the mast, letting the torrential bursts rain across his chest and strip away the ragged fabric of his jacket. When the first of the storm-belts moved off the visibility cleared, and he could see the southern edge of the sea, a line of tremendous silt banks over a hundred yards in height. In the spasmodic sunlight they glittered along the horizon like fields of gold, the tops of the jungle beyond rising above them.

Half a mile from the shore the reserve tank of the outboard ran dry. He unbolted the motor and threw it into the water, watched it sink through the brown surface in a faint wreath of bubbles. He furled the sail and paddled slowly against the head-breeze. By the time he reached the shore it was dusk, the shadows sweeping across the huge grey slopes. Limping through the shallows, he beached the craft, then sat down with his back against one of the drums. Staring out over the immense loneliness of this dead terminal beach, he soon fell into an exhausted sleep.

The next morning he dismantled the craft, ported the sections one by one up the enormous sludge-covered slopes, hoping for a southward extension of the waterway. Around him the great banks undulated for miles, the curving dunes dotted with cuttle-fish and nautiloids. The sea was no longer visible, and he was alone with these few lifeless objects, like the debris of a vanished continuum, one dune giving way to another as he dragged the heavy fifty-gallon drums from crest to crest. Overhead the sky was dull and cloudless, a bland impassive blue, more the interior ceiling of some deep irrevocable psychosis than the storm-filled celestial sphere he had known during the previous days. At times, after he had dropped one burden, he would totter down into the hollow of the wrong dune, find himself stumbling about the silent basins, their floors cracked into hexagonal plates, like a dreamer searching for an invisible door out of his nightmare.

Finally he abandoned the craft and trudged on ahead with a small parcel of supplies, looking back as the drums sank slowly below the surface. Carefully avoiding the quicksands between the dunes, he moved on towards the jungle in the distance, where the green spires of the great horsetails and fern-trees reached a hundred feet into the air.

He rested again below a tree on the edge of the forest, carefully cleaning his pistol. Ahead of him he could hear the bats screech and dive among the dark trunks in the endless twilight world of the forest floor, the iguanas snarl and lunge. His ankle had begun to swell painfully; the continual extension of the damaged muscle spread its original infection. Cutting a branch off one of the trees, he hobbled forward into the shadows.

168

By evening the rainfall started, slashing at the huge umbrellas a hundred feet above, the black light only broken when phosphorescent rivers of water broke and poured down on him. Frightened of resting for the night, he pressed on, shooting off the attacking iguanas, darting from the shelter of one massive tree-trunk to the next. Here and there he found a narrow breach in the canopy overhead, and a pale light would illuminate a small clearing where the ruined top floor of a sunken building loomed through the foliage, the rain beating across it. But the evidence of any man-made structures was increasingly scanty, the towns and cities of the south swallowed by the rising silt and vegetation.

For three days he pushed ahead sleeplessly through the forest, feeding on giant berries like clusters of apples, cutting a heavier branch as a crutch. Periodically, to his left, he glimpsed the silver back of a jungle river, its surface dancing in the rain-storms, but massive mangroves formed the banks and he was unable to reach it.

So his descent into the phantasmagoric forest continued, the rain sweeping relentlessly across his face and shoulders. Sometimes it would stop abruptly, and clouds of steam filled the intervals between the trees, hanging over the waterlogged floor like diaphanous fleeces, only dispersing when the downpour resumed.

It was during one of these intermissions that he climbed a steep rise in the centre of a broad clearing, hoping to escape the drenching mists, found himself in a narrow valley between wooded slopes. Crowded with vegetation, the hills rolled around the valley like the dunes he had crossed earlier, enclosing him in a green dripping world. Occasionally, as the mists swirled and lifted, he caught a glimpse of the jungle river between the peaks half a mile away. The wet sky was stained by the setting sun, the pale crimson mists tracing the hill crests in the distance. Pulling himself over the wet clay-like soil, he stumbled into what seemed to be the remains of a small temple. Tilting gate posts led towards a semicircle of shallow steps, where five ruined columns formed a ragged entrance. The roof had collapsed, and only a few feet of the side walls still stood. At the far end of the nave the battered altar looked out over an uninterrupted view of the valley, where the sun sank slowly from sight, its giant orange disc veiled by the mists.

Hoping to shelter there during the night, Kerans walked down the aisle, pausing listlessly as the rain renewed itself. Reaching the altar, he rested his arms on the chest-high marble table, and watched the contracting disc of the sun, its surface stirring rhythmically like the slag on a bowl of molten metal.

"Aaa-ah!" A faint almost inhuman cry sounded thinly into the wet air, like the groan of a stricken animal. Kerans looked around him quickly, wondering if an iguana had followed him into the ruin. But the jungle and the valley and the whole place of stones were silent and motionless, the rain streaming across the cracks in the collapsing walls.

"Aaa-ah!" This time the sound came from in front of him, somewhere towards the fading sun. The disc had pulsed again, apparently drawing forth this strangled response, half in protest, half in gratitude.

Wiping the moisture from his face, Kerans stepped cautiously around the altar, drew back with a start when he almost tripped over the ragged remains of a man sitting with his back to the altar, head propped against the stone. The sounds had obviously come from this emaciated figure, but it was so inert and blackened that Kerans assumed it must be dead.

The man's long legs, like two charred poles of wood, stuck out uselessly in front of him, sheathed in a collection of tattered black rags and bits of bark. His arms and sunken chest were similarly clothed, strung together with short lengths of creeper. A once luxuriant but now thinning black beard covered most of his face, and the rain poured across his hollowed but jutting jaw, which was raised to the fading light. Fitfully the sun shone on the exposed skin of his face and hands. One of the latter, a skeletal green claw, suddenly rose like a hand from a grave and pointed at the sun as if identifying it, then fell limply to the ground. As the disc pulsed again the face showed some slight reaction. The deep recesses around the mouth and nose, the hollowed cheeks that encroached so deeply over the broad jaw that they seemed to leave no space for the buccal cavity within, filled for a moment as if a single breath of life had passed momentarily through the body.

Unable to advance, Kerans watched the huge emaciated figure on the ground before him. The man was no more than a resurrected corpse, without food or equipment, propped against the altar like someone jerked from his grave and abandoned to await the Day of Judgement.

Then he realised why the man had failed to notice him. The dirt and raw sun-blistered skin around the deep eye sockets turned them into blackened funnels, at the base of which a dull festering gleam reflected faintly the distant sun. Both eyes were almost completely occluded by corneal cancers, and Kerans guessed that they would be able to see little more than the dying sun. As the disc fell away behind the jungle in front of them and the dusk swept like a pall through the grey rain, the man's head raised itself painfully, as if trying to retain the image that had burnt itself so devastatingly upon his retinas, then slumped to one side against his stone pillow. Flies began to swarm across the ground and buzzed over his streaming cheeks.

Kerans bent down to speak to the man, who seemed to sense his movement. Blindly, the hollowed eyes searched the dull nimbus beside him.

"Hey, fellow." His voice was a feeble rasp. "You there, soldier, come here! Where have you come from?" His left hand scuttled around the wet stony clay like a crab, as if looking for something. Then he turned back to the vanished sun, oblivious of the flies settling on his face and beard. "It's gone again! Aa-aah! It's moving away from me! Help me up, soldier, we'll follow it. Now, before it goes for ever."

He held his claw out to Kerans, like a dying beggar. Then his head slumped back again and the rain poured over his black skull.

Kerans knelt down. Despite the effects of the sun and rain, the remnants of the man's uniform trousers showed him to be an officer. His right hand, which had remained closed, now opened feebly. In his palm was a small silver cylinder with a circular dial, a pocket compass carried in aircrew rescue kits.

"Hey, soldier!" The man had revived abruptly, his eyeless head turning towards Kerans. "I order you, don't leave me! You can rest now, while I keep watch. Tomorrow we'll move on."

Kerans sat down beside him, undid his small parcel and began to wipe the rain and dead flies from the man's face. Taking the ravaged cheeks in his hands like a child's, he said carefully: "Hardman, this is Kerans—Doctor Kerans. I'll go with you, but try to rest." Hardman showed no response to the name, his brows creasing slightly in puzzlement.

While Hardman lay back against the altar, Kerans began to dig up some of the cracked flagstones from the aisle with his clasp-knife, carried the pieces back through the rain and built a crude stone shelter around the supine figure, covering the cracks with creeper torn from the walls. Although shielded from the rain, Hardman became slightly restless in the dark alcove, but soon fell into a shallow sleep, now and then breaking into stertorous breaths. Kerans went back through the darkness to the jungle edge, picked an armful of edible berries from the trees, then returned to the shelter and sat beside Hardman until the dawn broke over the hills behind them.

He stayed with Hardman for the next three days, feeding him with the berries and spraying his eyes with what was left of the penicillin. He strengthened the hut with more of the flagstones, and built a rough palliasse of leaves for them to sleep on. During the afternoon and evening Hardman would sit in the open doorway, watching the distant sun through the mists. In the intervals between the storms its rain-washed beams lit his green-tinged skin with a strange intense glow.

He failed to remember Kerans, and addressed him simply as 'Soldier', sometimes rousing himself from his torpor to issue a series of disconnected orders for the morrow. Increasingly, Kerans felt that Hardman's real personality was now submerged deep within his mind, and that his external behaviour and responses were merely pallid reflections of this, overlayed by his delirium and exposure symptoms. Kerans guessed that his sight had been lost about a month earlier, and that he had crawled instinctively to the higher ground supporting the ruin. From there he could best perceive the sun, the sole entity now strong enough to impinge its image upon his fading retinas.

On the second day Hardman began to eat voraciously, as if preparing himself for another advance through the jungle; by the end of the third day had consumed several bunches of the giant berries. The strength seemed to return suddenly to his great ragged frame, and during the afternoon he managed to support himself on his legs, leaning back against the doorway as the sun sank behind the wooded hills. Whether he now recognised Kerans the latter was unsure, but the monologue of orders and instructions ceased.

Kerans felt little surprise when he woke the next morning and found Hardman had gone. Rousing himself in the thin dawn light, Kerans limped down the valley towards the edge of the forest, where a small stream forked on its way towards the distant river. He looked up at the dark boughs of the fern-trees hanging in the silence. Feebly he shouted Hardman's name, listening to its muted echoes fall away among the sombre trunks, and then returned to the hut. He accepted Hardman's decision to move on without comment, assuming that he might or might not see the man again in the course of their common odyssey southwards. As long as his eyes were strong enough to sense the distant signals transmitted by the sun, and as long as the iguanas failed to scent him, Hardman would move forward, feeling his way through the forest hand over hand, head raised to the sunlight breaking among the branches.

Kerans waited a further two days at the hut, in case

Hardman chose to return, then set out himself. His medical supplies were now exhausted, and all he carried was a bag of berries and the Colt, containing two shells. His watch was still running, and he used it as a compass, also keeping a careful record of the passage of the days by notching his belt each morning.

Following the valley, he waded through the shallow stream, intending to reach the shores of the distant river. Intermittently heavy rain-storms beat the surface of the water, but these now seemed concentrated during a few hours in the afternoon and evening.

When the course of the river required him to move in a westerly direction for several miles to reach its banks, he gave up the attempt and pressed on southwards, leaving the deeper jungle of the hill region and entering a lighter forest, which in turn gave way to large tracts of swamp.

Skirting these, he abruptly stepped out on to the shores of an immense lagoon, over a mile in diameter, ringed by a beach of white sand, through which protruded the top floors of a few ruined apartment houses, like beach chalets seen at a distance. In one of these he rested for a day, trying to mend his ankle, which had become black and swollen. Looking out from the window at the disc of water, he watched the afternoon rain discharge itself into the surface with relentless fury; as the clouds moved away and the water smoothed itself into a glass sheet its colours seemed to recapitulate all the changes he had witnessed in his dreams.

That he had travelled over a hundred and fifty miles southward he could tell from the marked rise in temperature. Again the heat had become all-pervading, rising to a hundred and forty degrees, and he felt reluctant to leave the lagoon, with its empty beaches and quiet ring of jungle. For some reason he knew that Hardman would soon die, and that his own life might not long survive the massive unbroken jungles to the south.

Half asleep, he lay back thinking of the events of the past years that had culminated in their arrival at the central lagoons and launched him upon his neuronic odyssey, and of

Strangman and his insane alligators, and finally, with a deep pang of regret and affection, holding her memory clearly before his mind as long as he could, of Beatrice and her quickening smile.

At last he tied the crutch to his leg again, and with the butt of the empty ·45 scratched on the wall below the window, sure that no-one would ever read the message:

27th day. Have rested and am moving south. All is well.
Kerans.

So he left the lagoon and entered the jungle again, within a few days was completely lost, following the lagoons south-ward through the increasing rain and heat, attacked by alligators and giant bats, a second Adam searching for the forgotten paradises of the reborn sun.

FINE SCIENCE FICTION AND FANTASY TITLES AVAILABLE FROM CARROLL & GRAF

☐ Aldiss, Brian/NON-STOP	$3.95
☐ Amis, Kingsley/THE ALTERATION	$3.50
☐ Asimov, Isaac et al/THE MAMMOTH BOOK OF CLASSIC SCIENCE FICTION (1930s)	$8.95
☐ Asimov, Isaac et al/THE MAMMOTH BOOK OF GOLDEN AGE SCIENCE FICTION (1940s)	$8.95
☐ Ballard, J.G./THE DROWNED WORLD	$3.95
☐ Ballard, J.G./THE HIGH RISE	$3.50
☐ Ballard, J.G./HELLO AMERICA	$3.95
☐ Ballard, J.G./TERMINAL BEACH	$3.50
☐ Ballard, J.G./VERMILION SANDS	$3.95
☐ Burroughs, Edgar Rice/A PRINCESS OF MARS	$2.95
☐ Dick Philip K./DR. BLOODMONEY	$3.95
☐ Dick Philip K./CLANS OF THE ALPHANE MOON	$3.95
☐ Dick, Philip K./THE PENULTIMATE TRUTH	$3.95
☐ Dick, Philip K./TIME OUT OF JOINT	$3.95
☐ Disch, Thomas K./CAMP CONCENTRATION	$3.95
☐ Disch, Thomas K./ON WINGS OF SONG	$3.95
☐ Lovecraft, H. P. & Derleth, A./THE LURKER ON THE THRESHOLD	$3.50
☐ Malzberg, Barry/GALAXIES	$2.95
☐ Moorcock, Michael/BEHOLD THE MAN	$2.95
☐ Moorcock, Michael/FANTASY: THE 100 BEST BOOKS (Cloth)	$15.95
☐ Stableford, Brian/THE WALKING SHADOW	$3.95
☐ Stoker, Bram/THE JEWEL OF SEVEN STARS	$3.95
☐ Sturgeon, Theodore/VENUS PLUS X	$3.95
☐ Sturgeon, Theodore/THE GOLDEN HELIX	$3.95

Available from fine bookstores everywhere or use this coupon for ordering.

Carroll & Graf Publishers, Inc., 260 Fifth Avenue, N.Y., N.Y. 10001

Please send me the books I have checked above. I am enclosing
$_____ (please add $1.00 per title to cover postage and
handling.) Send check or money order—no cash or C.O.D.'s
please. N.Y. residents please add 8¼% sales tax.

Mr/Mrs/Ms _____

Address _____

City _____ State/Zip _____

Please allow four to six weeks for delivery.